MOTHER OF THE BRIDE

Kate Lawson was born on the edge of the Fens and is perfectly placed to write about the vagaries of life in East Anglia. In between raising a family, singing in a choir, walking the dog, working in the garden, taking endless photos and cooking, Kate is also a scriptwriter, originating and developing a soap opera for BBC radio, along with a pantomime for the town in which she lives. As Sue Welfare, Kate published six novels, two of which are currently under development for TV.

As the mother of four boys, Kate will never be the Mother of the Bride – but after writing this book, she is quite glad about that . . .

For more information on Kate go to www.katelawson.co.uk and visit www.BookArmy.co.uk for exclusive updates.

By the same author:

Mum's the Word
Lessons in Love
Keeping Mum

KATE LAWSON

Mother of the Bride

AVON

AVON

A division of HarperCollins*Publishers*
77–85 Fulham Palace Road,
London W6 8JB

www.harpercollins.co.uk

A Paperback Original 2010

1

First published in Great Britain by
HarperCollins*Publishers* 2009

Copyright © Kate Lawson 2010

Kate Lawson asserts the moral right to
be identified as the author of this work

A catalogue record for this book is
available from the British Library

ISBN-13: 978-1-84756-117-6

Set in Minion by Palimpsest Book Production Limited,
Grangemouth, Stirlingshire

Printed and bound in Great Britain by
Clays Ltd, St Ives plc

ACKNOWLEDGEMENTS

I'd like to offer a heartfelt thank you to the members of the clergy I spoke to about modern marriage, the possibilities, the services and the preparations. The generous gift of your time, your advice, your patience and good humour was much appreciated and any mistakes in interpreting the things you told me are entirely my own.

DEDICATION

Mother of the Bride is dedicated to Speedy and the Hellhound, to my lovely boys, their gorgeous women, and my brilliant friends, to Maggie Phillips, my good friend and agent, and all the great people who I sing with in Singers Inspired. You know who you are.

Chapter One

Lunchtime on the last Bank Holiday of the summer and Molly Foster was standing on the quay at Wells-next-the-Sea close to the radio car, where a man dressed as a bear was juggling rubber herrings. Alongside him stood an Elvis impersonator in a white jumpsuit and rhinestones, and beside him a woman called Linda, who knitted jumpers from the fur collected after grooming her three Newfoundlands – encounters that were all in the day's work for a presenter on a local radio station.

Molly had one side of her headphones pressed to her ear, keeping the other one off so that she could hear the activity on the quay. The last track had played out and the East Anglian Airwaves FM station jingle was coming to a close. Ready with the mike, all the while nodding and smiling inanely at her guests, holding eye contact so they didn't wander off, Molly was waiting for the moment when they went live to air.

'You okay? All ready?' she mouthed. Everyone nodded in unison, all except Elvis who curled his lip and said, 'A-huh-huh.'

'Here we go then,' she said, smile widening.

Phil, her broadcast assistant, should have been doing the sheepdogging but, thanks to some technical glitch, he was

1

hunched over in the back of the radio car – a converted people carrier with a retractable mast that the station used for outside broadcasts – fiddling with the control panel.

Molly hoped that what she could see billowing out from the open door was steam from Phil's coffee and not smoke.

Meanwhile through the headphones, Molly heard her producer, Stan, back at the studio, cue in her next caller. The music faded out at which point Molly said, 'Great track, that. Perfect for a sunny day by the seaside – speaking of which, we're here live on Bank Holiday Monday at beautiful Wells-next-the-Sea as part of our Great British Summer Days Out series. We've got some fantastic guests lined up for you in today's show. But first of all on line one we've got Maureen from Little Newton, who wants to talk about – what is it you're talking to us about today, Maureen?'

'Death,' said Maureen in a monotone. 'I want to talk about how it felt when my cat Smokey died.'

'Right,' said Molly, pulling faces at Phil, who had stopped fiddling and was now busy flirting with two teenage girls in bikinis.

'I'm sure that we all feel very sorry for your loss, Maureen. I know that my pets are very important to me but we were hoping that you were going to talk to us about your memories of the good old British seaside holiday – kiss me quick, fish and chips on the prom.' Molly jollied the unseen woman along.

'Smokey loved fish, particularly the heads,' said the unstoppable Maureen. 'We used to save them for him. Little tinker used to bury them down the back of the sofa if you didn't watch him. I had him cremated last March. Fourteen, he was. I've got the urn here with me. He loved the radio. Not you but that other chap, the one with the glasses, what's his name?'

'Right,' said Molly, waving now, desperately trying to drag Phil's attention away from the wriggling, jiggling, giggling girls and back to the job in hand.

From somewhere close by she could hear a mobile phone ringing with the distinctive Laurel and Hardy theme, downloaded by her live-in lover Nick as a joke. She felt a flush of heat; how the hell had she managed to leave *her phone* on? It was the ultimate no-no. On TV and on radio, before you go on air you always check your mobile is switched off and if you're not sure then you take the battery out, except of course hers was ringing and it seemed to be getting louder. It rang once, twice – after six rings it cut off and Molly turned her attention back to her caller.

'I've been having grief counselling,' Maureen was saying. 'And we've had a séance – he's still here, you know. Him and Timmy the rabbit . . .'

'Well, thank you for that, Maureen. And we're lucky enough to have Ken Barber with us here today,' said Molly, praying that someone back at the studio would have the good sense to pull the plug on Maureen.

To her right the bear man was mid-throw.

'Ken is currently working his way around the coastline of Great Britain, staging a one-man show to raise public awareness about the state of the British fishing industry. Now for the listeners at home, Ken, let's just describe what you're wearing, shall we?' At which point Ken growled at her.

Molly forced a laugh; bloody man. 'So, not very talkative, our Ken – maybe listeners would like to ring in and guess what Ken is dressed as . . .'

'Jess from Norwich is on line two,' said Stan in her ear.

'Let's go to our next caller, Jess from Norwich,' said Molly. 'Hello there, Jess. How's your Bank Holiday shaping up?'

'Mum?' said a familiar voice.

3

'Jess?' Molly could feel her colour rising.

'I couldn't get through on your mobile so I got the studio to put me through instead,' Jess gushed excitedly.

'Well, that's nice of them,' said Molly, with forced good humour. 'We're live this morning here on Radio EAA –' Molly swung round to Phil and made frantic throat slitting gestures so he would cut the live feed, but he was oblivious.

'I know,' said Jess.

'You know?'

'Of course I do,' Jess sounded drunk. 'Stan said this couldn't wait. Actually I told him *I* couldn't wait. I've got the most brilliant news, Mum – I wanted you to be the first to know. Max just asked me to marry him and I've said yes. I've said yes, Mum. *I'm going to get married!*' The last few words were a shriek of pure delight followed by giggling and then Molly heard Jessica say, 'Here, you talk to her – just say hello. Yes, she's on air, but it'll be fine, go on, yes, just say hello. She wants to talk to you . . .'

Which wasn't strictly true, mainly because Molly hadn't quite caught up yet. But there was nothing much she could do, short of pulling the lead out, and then Max came on the line and said in that deep, dark, self-assured voice of his, 'Hi there, Molly. Jess is insisting that we ring everyone. She wanted you to know straight away.' He paused. *'Mum.'*

Before Molly could say anything, back in the studio Stan put on a Robbie Williams number and while it was playing Jess came back on the line, all squeaky and excited and full of joy.

'Isn't it brilliant? I mean, I am just *so* excited. Max went down on one knee and everything and he'd already got the ring and it fitted. It's like this big flower and all these little coloured stones and it was just so romantic. God, there is so much to do; we were thinking Christmas? Sleigh bells,

4

reindeer – maybe we should fly everyone out to Lapland, what do you think? I'm going need your help to get this together because Max is really busy. I mean, what are the chances of there being any decent snow in England? And you know I've always loved snow, mind you maybe we could hire one of those machines. Is that a bit naff? Oh, isn't it exciting, Mum? If we had snow I could have one of those fur-trimmed hoods and a long cloak and the pageboys could wear tartan waistcoats. Maybe we could have it in Scotland. Oh my God, they could all wear kilts then – Max is shaking his head. What do you think? Aren't you going to say something?'

Molly opened her mouth to speak but there weren't any words in there.

'Mum? Are you still there?' asked Jess, sounding a little anxious, and then presumably to Max, said, 'I think she might be cracking up.'

Never a truer word was spoken, thought Molly. Finally she found her voice and said, 'Well, well done you – both of you – congratulations. Look, do you think I can ring you back later? We're right slap-bang in the middle of a show here . . .'

'I know. They're playing our song,' said Jess wistfully.

'Look, I've got to go, sweetie. We're interviewing some guy who is singlehandedly trying to save the British fishing industry. He uses comedy to make his message more interesting.'

'Uh-huh, the bad-tempered herring juggler in the bear suit,' said Jess.

'That'll be the one,' said Molly. 'How did you know?'

'Stan told me about him. You are pleased though, aren't you? You know, about me and Max?'

'Of course I am, I'm really pleased for both of you. Have you rung your dad yet?'

'No, he and Marnie are still away on a cruise at the moment. We've just emailed them. And then we're going to ring Max's parents. You don't sound very pleased,' said Jess.

'I'm working, sweetie.'

'I wanted you to know first.'

Robbie sang on in Molly's headphones.

'So you are pleased?'

'Of course I'm pleased. Just a bit shocked. You know me, it's not often that I'm speechless.' Molly forced a laugh, trying hard to recover her composure. 'It's a bit of a surprise, that's all. I mean, I hadn't realised that it was that serious.' Inwardly Molly groaned. 'Though I mean, *obviously it is,*' she stumbled on. 'Look, can I ring you back later?'

'Okay,' said Jess, giggling.

'Have you rung Jack yet?'

Jess snorted. 'Not yet, every time I ring my little brother's phone it goes to voicemail. I'm sure he's trying to avoid me.'

'I don't think it's you, Jess, I think it's Pippa.'

'No! Pippa? She's not still after him, is she? Are you serious? They split up months ago. She must be mad . . .'

'I think that is the general consensus. He thinks she's stalking him.'

'Really? God, shows how long it is since I've talked to him. Mind you, she *must* be desperate if she's stalking Jack. Anyway, I'll leave him a message.'

'I've got to go –'

'Talk to you later,' Jess said, and then the line went dead.

'You okay?' asked Stan through Molly's headphones.

'What do *you* think? What the hell are you playing at, putting Jess through live on air?'

'It was lovely. Really touching – and I thought you'd want to know.'

6

'I did, but not on air – it was nuts to put her through. What the hell are they going to say upstairs?'

'They'll love it,' said Stan. 'Trust me. The phone lines are jammed solid. See you at three.'

As soon as they finished broadcasting Molly unhooked the pocket battery pack for her radio mike and her headphones and handed them back to Phil. 'I just need to thank the guys who were on the show.'

'Sure thing – and congratulations, *Mum*,' Phil said, with a grin.

Molly turned to her guests and the impromptu audience that had gathered around the radio car. 'Thanks for coming along, you were brilliant. Great show, we've had lots of calls. Well done,' she said warmly, shaking hands and paws and smiling, signing autographs and handing out pens and balloons and various other station freebies to anyone who wanted them.

'Congratulations on the wedding,' said one woman brightly.

Molly smiled. 'Thank you.'

'Very exciting. Did you know anything about it?'

'No, not at all – bit of a surprise,' said Molly, scribbling her name on a glossy eight-by-ten.

'Oh, it'll be lovely,' said the woman. 'One minute you're taking them to nursery school, next thing you know they're getting married. My oldest daughter got married last year – I'm a granny now.'

Phil meanwhile was putting away the PA system, and retracting the giant aerial which very slowly slid down into the body of the car like a giant periscope all clad around with a curl of gold cable.

'Ah, show business,' he said, as Molly handed out an

autographed paper sunhat to a small child with a horribly runny nose and what looked like it might be impetigo.

'Thanks for coming,' said Molly, ignoring Phil. 'And I hope you have a lovely holiday.' The little boy skipped away to rejoin an exhausted-looking young woman in a sundress who, along with a bad case of sunburn, had a baby on one arm and was heavily pregnant. Molly caught herself staring; the young woman looked a lot like Jessica. Another five years or so and it could *be* Jessica. Looking away Molly dropped the give-aways back into a plastic stacker box.

'You are extremely cynical for one so young,' she replied, sliding the box into the back of the car.

Phil apparently took it as a compliment. 'Jess telling everyone she was getting married on air was a masterstroke. Did you know she was going to do it?'

'Of course I didn't know,' said Molly indignantly. 'It's incredibly unprofessional –'

'There's nothing people like better than a bit of romance. We could do a feature on the show, do a countdown to Jessica's big day. Have a competition – I can see the strapline on the website now, *"Be a bridesmaid at Jessie's Big Fat Norfolk Wedding"* You want me to bring it up at today's planning meeting?'

Molly fixed him with an icy stare. 'No, I do not, no, don't you dare bring it up at the planning meeting. Okay? No one's interested.'

'All those people coming up to get your autograph were interested.'

Molly said nothing.

'Oh come off it,' said Phil. 'Anyone who is anyone has got their wedding all over the glossies these days. Everyone's obsessed with it. Who's marrying who, what they're wearing, who's invited, who isn't, who's likely to have a fist fight break out over the canapés, are they going to fly out to Italy or up to – where's that castle in Scotland they all schlep off to?'

Molly held up her hands. 'Stop it, you're scaring me – you're a boy. Boys hate weddings.'

'It's not me, it's my girlfriend and all her mates. Our whole flat is stacked with celebrity magazines, who's got fat, who's far too thin, who'll never love again, who's had lipo. I can't help it. I never used to read that kind of crap, I was strictly an *Autocar* and *What Hi-fi* guy, but it's addictive. The weddings are a bit of light relief really.'

'Okay, okay, I'm getting the picture.'

'So how about talking to the management? Shoehorn Jess's big day into the show?'

'Have you got no shame?'

'Not much, why? You could probably wangle all kinds of freebies.'

'So when my daughter and future son-in-law kneel down at the altar rail instead of having price tags on the bottom of their shoes they'll have little stickers on there saying, "Sponsored by Linda's Luxury Buffet Services?"'

'Why not? The price weddings are these days. And you could invite all the famous people you know. Get the paparazzi there.'

'I don't know any famous people, Phil,' said Molly, heaving one of the PA speakers into the back of the car.

'Yes, you do. You've interviewed loads of celebrities.'

'Yes, but there is a big difference between interviewing them and inviting them to your daughter's wedding. Give me a hand with this, will you?'

'Says who?' persisted Phil. 'There was that bloke off "The Bill", oh and that girl who was on "Holby City". Some of the guys at Norwich City football club, Delia – oh, and that really famous artist bloke who got that big prize.'

Molly raised an eyebrow. 'Remind me not to hire you as Master of Ceremonies on the door announcing the arrivals. "Oh look, here's the woman who used to go to school with the one that's getting married."'

Instead of being offended, Phil grinned. 'Oh wow, does that mean you're going to invite me to the wedding?'

'Oh, for goodness' sake. Come on, let's get the rest of this stuff stowed.'

'A few celebs would really add a certain something to Jess's wedding.'

'That's right, Phil, a security nightmare and lots of photographers elbowing my family out of the way so they could get a good shot of some bird with a trout pout and a spray-on tan.'

'But you got on with them really well.'

'That's what I'm paid to do, Phil, I got on with that clown in a bear suit but it doesn't mean I'm going to invite him round for tea.'

'So where's Jess having her engagement party?'

Molly looked up from the box of electronic oddments she was currently packing away under a seat. 'What?'

'The engagement party. I mean, presumably she's having one, isn't she?'

Aware that she had her mouth open Molly closed it fast and said, 'Phil, I only just found out that they're getting married. I don't know what she's having yet, or come to that where or when.'

But Phil was on a roll. 'When my sister got married we had this big engagement party at the Norwich Arms – and my parents put an announcement in *The Times*. And then there was the stag night and hen night. We had a great time. My sister and my mum and all my sister's mates flew to New York, and the blokes all went to Amsterdam, and then my parents organised a do for the groom's family so we could all meet up and get acquainted before the big day.'

Molly decided that she had heard quite enough. 'Fish and chips?' she suggested, nodding towards the parade of shops that fronted the little harbour.

Phil grinned. 'Do you want me to go and get them in case someone nicks the van?'

Molly glanced at the EAA radio car. Painted in the station's livery, it was an unmistakable mix of orange, pink and lime green with 'EAA' emblazoned down one side and across the roof. At least if it was involved in a police chase it would give everyone a sporting chance of picking out the right vehicle.

'We'll eat in,' she said.

While Phil finished off the lock-down, Molly broke out the lipstick and dealt with the ravages of headphone hair.

'My sister used a wedding planner,' said Phil conversationally as they headed off across the car park and joined the queue outside French's chippie, where holiday-makers were gathered two abreast.

Molly wasn't really listening; her stomach was rumbling, she was tired and they still had to get back into Norwich to drop the radio car off before going on to a management meeting.

'They asked me to be an usher. We all had these cravats and cummerbunds that matched the bridesmaids' dresses.' He mimed.

Molly settled into line. 'The wedding planner, was it a person or a wall chart?'

'She was called Cheryl-Ann. She did all the arrangements at the hotel where my sister had her wedding. She was very keen on themes.'

'Who, your sister?'

'No, Cheryl-Ann. She had a whole book full. My sister brought it home for everyone to have a look through – pirates, princesses, wenches.' He grinned. 'And that was just for the civil partnerships. My sister picked this one Cheryl-Ann had done before called Spring something or other – there were a lot of daffodils involved and a lamb.'

Molly decided not to ask whether the lamb was gambolling up the aisle with a ribbon round its neck or on the buffet in slices.

Chapter Two

'Hello? Hello, Dad, can you hear me?'

In a cottage on the Somerset coast, Jess was curled up on an enormous floral sofa that dominated the tiny sitting room of the place Max had rented for their romantic break. Despite it being summer it was chilly and Max had lit the fire. Mobile phone pressed tight against her ear, Jess was straining to pick out her father's voice amongst a sea of static.

'Puss?' said a familiar voice. 'You there?'

'Dad? Dad? Is that you? How are you?'

'Fine. We got your email. Congratulations. Sorry if the line's a bit strange but I'm using some sort of internet phone thing that the chap here's rigged up for me. I just wanted to let you know that we're delighted. Aren't we, Marnie? Absolutely delighted – couldn't be more pleased for you. Presumably you've already told your mother?'

'Yes, I rang her a little while ago,' said Jess, enunciating every syllable in case he missed some important detail, her finger wedged in her other ear so that she could concentrate on his voice. Max was watching her from the armchair pulled up at the other side of the hearth.

Her father sounded as if he were a million miles away.

'How's the holiday going?' she asked.

'Fine. I've had Delhi belly and Marnie has come out in some sort of a rash – we're having a lovely time,' he said, without a hint of irony.

'So where are you?'

Jess heard him turn away from the phone and say, 'Where are we again?'

Her father, Jonathon, had an innate distrust of all things foreign and when Jess and Jack were small had refused to take them anywhere abroad for holidays and only begrudgingly travelled there for business – *there* being anywhere other than Britain.

After her parents had split up and Jonathon had married Marnie they had come to a compromise, based on the two of them taking frequent cruises, which Jess suspected was acceptable only because her father felt that cruising wasn't so much travelling as moving a little piece of England closer to all those countries Marnie was so keen for him to see.

'We're somewhere in . . .' He hesitated as if waiting for a prompt. 'Croatia.' He made it sound like the outer reaches of the Horsehead Nebula. 'We went to see some thing this morning and I think Marnie's planning to go and see more things tomorrow. But anyway, never mind me. You and Max – it is Max, isn't it? Well done, I'm really pleased. *We're* really pleased. Obviously we'll need to talk about the arrangements for the wedding and what your plans are when I get back. I want to see the cut of his jib and all that – make sure his intentions towards my little girl are honourable.'

Jess winced at her father's idea of a joke.

'So, have the pair of you set a date yet?'

'We were thinking maybe Christmas – well, December anyway.'

'Ah, right. December? So not that far away then. Have to

get your skates on with the planning. You say you've spoken to your mother?'

'Yes.'

'And what did she say?'

'Not much but I'm sure we can sort it out between us.' Jess put her hand over the receiver. 'Do you want to talk to him?' she mouthed to Max.

Max shook his head. Meanwhile her father was saying, 'I'm sure you're right, Puss, and your mother has always been good at that kind of thing. Okay, well, look, why don't the two of you come over as soon as we get back home? Not quite sure when that is – I'll ring you. Lost all track of time, you know how it is with holidays.'

Jess smiled as they said their goodbyes; what her dad meant was that he didn't know when they were due home because Marnie had made all the arrangements.

'Are you going to ring your mum and dad now?' she asked, waggling the phone in Max's direction after she had rung off.

He shook his head. 'No, I don't think so. I was thinking that maybe we should go back to bed. I could light the fire in the bedroom. What do you think?'

Jess smiled. You didn't need to be much of a mind-reader to work out what he meant. 'Or we could just huddle together for the warmth,' she said, all innocence.

'Sounds like a plan, be terrible to freeze to death in the middle of the summer, wouldn't it?' Max purred as he kissed her, which made her heart do that funny, fluttery, skip-a-beat, horny thing.

'Are you going to ring your mum and dad later?' asked Jess, as Max took her by the hand and led her up the steep, winding stairs.

'I was thinking that maybe we ought to go round and

15

tell them. They're a bit old-fashioned about that sort of thing.'

'Oh, okay,' said Jess as he started nibbling at her neck and unbuttoned her shirt. 'What sort of thing?' she started to ask, but the words got lost as he kissed her harder and pulled her down into a great billow of duvet, bolsters and pillows.

Chapter Three

'Flowers, food, frocks, cars, dresses – balloons, doves. My sister had doves.'

'Yes, all right, thank you,' said Molly to Phil, who was busy counting off what you needed for the perfect twenty-first-century wedding. 'Why don't you go and make us some tea?'

They were back in the offices of EAA FM and Molly, who was sitting at her desk waiting to go in to their regular strategy meeting with their manager, had been Googling weddings. The good news was that there were hundreds of thousands of websites, offering every kind of service and paraphernalia imaginable – dozens of books, CDs and DVDs and lord only knew what else online, as well as innumerable sources of advice to help her help Jess in the quest for the perfect occasion.

There were Wild West-themed weddings, weddings with Liberace lookalikes, weddings in caves by candlelight. Molly's main problem was, having spent most of her working life looking for weird and wonderful things to attract her listeners, she found it impossible not to be drawn towards the bizarre. What couple in their right mind wanted to be married underwater or, come to that, while bungee jumping? As she scrolled through the pages Molly hoped Jess had something a little less strenuous in mind.

Nina Holman, the station's senior office administrator, stood behind her, peering over Molly's shoulder.

'So if that's the good news, what's the bad news?' Nina asked conversationally.

Molly sighed. 'Well, according to this we should have started organising the wedding in June last year.'

Nina waved the words away. 'Oh, come on. How hard can it be? I mean, even Phil knows what you need. It'll be fine. Surely the bride and groom do most of it themselves these days, don't they? Oh look – great outfit. That's half your problems solved.' Nina pointed towards the screen. 'That bluey-green one on the end with the straw hat. Don't look so worried, let's face it, we fly this place by the seat of our pants all the time. Organising a wedding will be a doddle.'

Molly bypassed the frock commentary. 'Yes, but that's because we're dealing with the great British public – and I know they can be fickle and peculiar, but unlike Jess they're not likely to cry all over me and use emotional blackmail to get what they want.'

Nina took a sip of coffee. 'Oh, I dunno, there was that bloke in Great Yarmouth last summer . . .' She laughed. 'All right, all right, I hear what you're saying. And I'm here for you. If you need a hand or a shopping buddy or just a shoulder to cry on, count me in. I've always been a sucker for a big hat and matching shoes. I'm thinking maybe lavender and cream . . .'

'And I'm thinking it's going to take a lot more than a decent frock to pull this off. Look at this list.' Molly flicked back to a page she had previously bookmarked and then scrolled down, and down, and down.

'Bloody hell.' Nina leaned in closer to pick out some of the details. The list was so long it was almost a joke. After a couple of minutes speed-reading she pulled away.

18

'Are they serious? It says here,' she pointed indignantly at the screen, 'that traditionally the bride's family organise it and pay for it all and then when everybody else has finished necking your champagne, and you've Hoovered the confetti out of the Axminster, *you're* the one who sends slices of cake to the people who didn't make it. Did no one tell the guys who wrote this that they abolished slave labour a while back?'

'Apparently not. I was planning to print the list off and tick things off as we go.'

Nina gave her a long, hard look. 'I don't think we've got that much paper in the office, Molly. Or, come to that, that you have that much time. Surely you can't be expected to do it all, not these days. Have you considered suggesting that the pair of them elope?'

'It'll be fine. Knowing Jess, she'll want to do most of it herself.'

'You hope,' said Nina with a wry grin.

'We'll get it sorted out, I mean, how hard can it be?' said Molly with a confidence she didn't feel.

She flicked back to the Mother of the Bride outfitters' websites. One thing that was very noticeable was just how many sites offered *the perfect outfit* in larger sizes; presumably comfort-eating after all that planning, thought Molly miserably as she returned to the to-do list.

Top of the list was choosing where they would get married. Would they want a church, or a registry office, or one of the myriad venues where you could hold a civil service? Was Max religious? Was he Jewish, Greek Orthodox, Zoroastrian, maybe he was a Buddhist? Maybe they would want a humanist ceremony in a field or something involving a hand-fasting, organic rice cakes and biodegradable confetti?

She really needed to talk to Jess.

And then there was the matter of who should they invite,

and who was going to chauffeur the old aunties or ensure that Uncle Eric from Chester knew where the cheap hotels were? Looking down the who-does-what list Molly could hazard a guess.

Besides all of that, Phil was right, if you went for the full nine yards there was so much to arrange: the frocks and cars, and flowers, photographs and videos, and then the reception, the food, drink, cake. Just thinking about it made her feel slightly queasy.

News, like flu, spread fast through the office of EAA, so by mid-afternoon there didn't seem to be a soul in the building who didn't know Jessica was getting married.

Working on the radio station was like being part of a warm, if dysfunctional, family. Each presenter had a back-up team; sometimes there was a co-presenter and there was always a producer who worked with the presenter to create programme content. There was at least one broadcast assistant per team to act as gofer, chauffeur and general dogsbody. This made up the basic family unit, and then there were the cousins and second cousins; the editors, the weather men, news readers and sports reporters, two guys who worked on website content, people who answered the phones, PAs, cleaners and receptionists, security and all manner of techies as well. By the state of Molly's email inbox there didn't seem to be anyone on the station who hadn't heard the news.

'Could be worse,' said Stan, her producer, as handed her the notes for their up-and-coming meeting with their boss.

'You mean Jess could be making me a grandma instead?'

Stan held up his hands in protest. 'Seriously. All I'm saying is, "Wedding Countdown Special".' He handed her a clipboard. 'I've already heard it muted by the water cooler.'

'Over my dead body,' said Molly grimly.

Nina tapped the agenda. 'Item four, programming ideas

for the new season. It would be easy pickings, Molly. Just think about it,' she said with a grin.

'I have and it still sucks.'

'Conference room in ten minutes. And Rob's on his way down apparently,' said Stan, pointing to his watch. 'Oh, and here comes young Phil with the tea.'

At which point the phone on her desk rang. Molly picked up the receiver and tucked it under her chin, waiting until Stan and Nina moved away before she spoke and starting to flick through the MoB's outfit website.

'Hello, you're through to Molly Foster at EAA.' All she could hear was a peculiar distant clicking and crackling. At first Molly thought it might be an automated cold call until she realised she could hear someone breathing heavily on the other end of the line, and was about to slam the phone down when Jonathon said, 'Molly, is that you? You there?'

'Yes, how are y—' she began, but before she could get any further Jonathon snapped, 'Is Jessica pregnant?'

As was often the case when Molly spoke to her ex-husband, she instantly found every word he said infuriating.

'Does it matter if she is?' she demanded, while thinking how very like Jonathon not to have asked Jess himself.

'Well – well no, obviously, of course not. I mean I didn't say anything when she rang because I didn't want to upset her, she sounded so happy,' he blustered. 'But if she is I just didn't want her to think that she has *got* to get married to this Max just because she's – well, you know.'

'Pregnant? A fallen woman? Unclean? An awful lot has changed since the dark ages of our youth, Jonathon, people don't *have* to get married any more, in fact they don't seem to *have* to do anything they don't want to. Those days have long gone. Thank God.'

'I suppose we should just be relieved that given all that, he's still going to stand by her.'

Stand by her? Molly groaned inwardly; Jonathon Foster, closet Victorian.

Jonathon paused, obviously needing a moment or two to catch up. 'So are you saying that Puss isn't pregnant?'

'As far as I know, no, I'm sure she would have said something but I will ask.'

'In that case, what's the bloody hurry? I mean she barely knows the chap.'

'She's young . . .'

'Well, he isn't. What is he? Forty? What's the hurry? They barely know each other.'

Molly decided to ignore him and press on. 'She's in love and, let's face it, when you're that age you think waiting for anything is a silly idea.'

'Personally,' said Jonathon, using a tone that suggested Jessica's news was entirely Molly's fault, 'I don't understand what the rush is – I mean *we* weren't like that, were we?'

Molly laughed. 'Of course we were. I remember my mum and dad suggesting we waited another couple of years and saved up and you were absolutely furious.'

'Things were different then,' snapped Jonathon. 'We were more mature, more sensible. We took things seriously.'

'Did we? I seem to remember the real reason we wanted to get married was so that your mother would let us sleep together when we stayed at your parents' house – I don't think it had much to do with having noble plans for a shared life of poverty and pain and procreation.'

There was a pause and then Jonathon said, 'So, what do you think of him?'

'Max?'

'No, the Pope. Of course Max, who else is my only daughter planning to marry?'

'*Our* daughter,' Molly said tersely.

'Whatever. The thing is, *what is he like?*'

'You've met him, haven't you?'

Jonathon sniffed. 'Of course I've met him. Once or twice but only in the "Hello, pleased to meet you, so you're the bastard who is sleeping with my little girl" kind of way.'

Molly laughed; sometimes, Jonathon could also be delightfully self-aware.

'They dropped in on their way back from somewhere or other and then Jess brought him over to have Sunday lunch with us,' Jonathon continued. 'What does that tell you about anybody? He seemed nice enough, but who knows? He could be an axe-murdering psychopath for all I know. Something in banking, isn't he?'

'No, that was Glenn. The one before, the one who went off to America? San Francisco?'

'Ah.' There was another pause and then Jonathon asked, 'So what does Max do?'

'IT, project management, I think. I'm not sure what exactly.'

'Ummmm, not a banker then? I suppose we should be grateful really.'

'We have to trust Jess to make her own mind up, after all she knows him better than we do. These are her decisions to make. She's not a child any more.'

'So you say.'

'Jonathon, we'd already got her and Jack by the time I was her age.'

'Yes, but we were different,' said Jonathon. '*Things* were different.'

True, now it seemed that adolescence lasted until you were well into your thirties, thought Molly ruefully, whereas when she and Jonathon had been dating, it ended as soon as you left school. She felt younger now than she had in her twenties – probably looked younger too, she decided, catching sight of her reflection in the monitor.

'Right, well, I suppose we should get together and discuss the wedding, then. Money and the arrangements and things. I know that in the good old days the bride's father used to stump up for the whole shebang but as you said, times have changed.'

Molly groaned inwardly; the one time Jonathon took notice of something she'd said it was obviously going to rebound.

'Before all this kicked off I had been thinking of giving Jess something towards the deposit on a house or a flat,' Jonathon said.

'They still might prefer that . . .'

Molly looked back at the website she'd been browsing through. With the cost of a wedding today Jonathon wouldn't be far out. The price of a deposit on a first time home equalled just about what it would cost to throw a half-decent wedding. In fact the all-inclusive charge on a featured venue of the month cost more than Jonathan and Molly had paid for their first house.

'How about we talk everything over once Marnie and I get back?'

'Fine by me. So you'll ring Jess and make the arrangements?'

'Oh.' Jonathon sounded genuinely surprised. 'I was rather hoping you'd do that.'

'But if we're coming to yours . . .'

Jonathon gave a funny little throaty cough.

24

'You want everyone to come to mine?' said Molly. Mind-reading was right up there on the list of talents required to deal with Jonathon. She certainly didn't miss being married to him one little bit. 'Not your place?'

'I don't think that's a very good idea, do you? I don't want to upset Marnie,' he said.

'But it's all right to upset Nick?' asked Molly, her tone level.

'You know how things are, Molly –'

What Jonathon actually meant was he didn't live with Nick and therefore he didn't give a rat's arse about how upset Nick might or might not get, because Nick wasn't anything to do with Jonathon, and Marnie – five foot two, six stone wet, with a tongue that could strip paint, and a temper to match – most definitely was. Seeing the way Jonathon ran around trying to placate Marnie, Molly had come to the conclusion that sometimes it paid to be difficult.

'Besides,' he was saying, 'your place is so much easier to get to, and you've got more parking. Our place is a bit tucked up for all those cars.'

All those cars – two more at most. Molly wondered just how many reasons Jonathon would be able to come up with before she put him out of his misery. On screen she had found a really beautiful oyster-coloured suit with a hat – apparently a complete snip at nine hundred pounds.

'Fine,' she agreed.

'Fine?' said Jonathon.

'Look, I'm at work, Jonathon, I'll email you. Have a nice holiday.'

'See you when we get back, then.' Jonathon sounded crest-fallen at not having managed more sparring. 'So you're all right about everything?'

Molly looked heavenwards. What was that supposed to

mean? She decided not to ask him. 'I'll ring Jess when I get home and then we can arrange a time for you to pop over.'

'Oh,' said Jonathon.

'Oh? What do you mean, "Oh"?'

'Well, I'd rather assumed I'd be coming over for lunch. We've got a lot to talk about. And I *am* going to be coughing up the lion's share for the wedding.'

The sheer gall of the man took Molly's breath away. What she wanted to say was, '*In that case maybe you should invite Jess and Max over to your place instead and count me out. You could arrange it between yourselves – after all, it is your only daughter who is getting married.*'

But she knew from years of experience that the resulting hissy-fit wouldn't be worth it, so what she actually said was, 'I have to go, Jonathon. I'll let you know what Jess says.' And with that she hung up, which was perfect timing as she could see their boss, Rob Harwood, making his way into the conference room.

Picking up her notepad and clipboard Molly hurried over to catch him up. For all his apparent bonhomie and great show of just being another one of the station crew, one of the team, no one was under any illusions about who was top dog or what would happen if you ever made the mistake of treating Rob as just one of the boys.

In the conference room Stan was already sorting out a drink for Rob, Nina was there to ensure no one forgot budget or logistics, a girl from the front office was there to take notes while someone up from the sales department was there to talk about advertising.

Molly had already emailed her outline plan for next month's shows, although it was fairly academic; the framework for programme content in the broadest sense was more or less the same every year, give or take a public crusade or two.

In the summer they rolled out some kind of seaside special in August, finishing up on Bank Holiday Monday, before heading towards back-to-school and then autumn themes, beginning in September with harvest festivals and late-season breaks. October there were debates over Hallowe'en versus Bonfire Night, then there was Christmas and all that that entailed – the presents and pantomimes and cookery tips and how-tos. And then the New Year, with lots of phone-ins about presents you hated and resolutions made or broken, followed by the January blues and sales, segments on credit cards and canny ways with money, and the year rolled slowly into a new spring with lambs and farm visits and the first snowdrops, how this February was the wettest, driest, coldest, hottest or sunniest since records began, and before you knew it they were round to planning holidays on air, with a mix of local destinations and travel companies who had bought air time, and before you knew it, it was summer all over again.

Molly quite liked the slow seasonal rotation in programme planning; while some people saw it as dull, for her it had all the comfort of visiting old friends.

Rob looked up from his notes as Molly came into the conference room and smiled broadly. 'I hear congratulations are in order,' he said, as she pulled out a chair. 'Phone lines are still buzzing. Marvellous news, please pass my best wishes on to your daughter and the groom-to-be. Max, isn't it?'

Inwardly Molly groaned. Whoever was it said only bad news travels fast?

Chapter Four

'I know that I promised not to turn into Bridezilla,' said Jess. 'But there are things we ought to talk about, things I need to ask you, and want your opinion on. We haven't got that long to sort everything out – so what sort of wedding do you think we should have?' She paused. 'Max, you *are* listening, aren't you?'

The two of them were curled up under the duvet in bed in the little cottage with its view out over Watchet Harbour. Outside it was raining hard, but Jess couldn't have cared less about the weather. She had barely had time to catch her breath since Max had gone down on one knee and now the full weight of what he had asked her was beginning to sink in.

If Jess could have planned exactly how she wanted to be proposed to she would have been hard-pressed to top Max's efforts. It was breathtakingly romantic and so unexpected that, despite it being a horrible cliché, she had to keep from pinching herself to check that she wasn't dreaming.

At first Jess had thought Max was kneeling down to tie his shoelace and then just when she was going to ask him if he was all right he had caught hold of her hand. And even then Jess hadn't guessed, she just thought he might need a hand up because it was cold and they had walked for miles with her dog, Bassa. Then Max had said, 'Jess, I want to ask you something.'

And before she could think what it might be, Max had asked her to marry him.

Although replaying the scene in her head – and Jess had replayed it many times since Max had said it – Jess wasn't sure exactly whether Max had asked her so much as *told* her. She seemed to remember that what he had actually said was, 'Jess, I think that we should get married.' Because it didn't seem as if there had been any question that she could answer yes or no to. But it didn't matter, because it had all been so magical and so very special and incredibly romantic and then Max had said, 'I was thinking December – maybe Christmas, certainly before the New Year. What do you say?'

And although Jess hadn't said anything to Molly, it *had* been a surprise. In fact it was so unexpected that for a few moments Jess thought she must have misheard him.

All the time they'd been going out together Max had said things about how much he liked his own space, and how he wasn't really good with girlfriends, like they were some kind of pet, and how, although he really enjoyed being with her, he was a happy bachelor – which, although they seemed to get on fairly well and however smitten Jess was, hadn't given her much hope that the relationship was going anywhere.

And when on girly nights out Jess had expressed her concerns, her friends – who hadn't met Max yet because he was usually busy midweek – had said that maybe he was just playing with her, that whole *protesting too much so he wouldn't get hurt when she finished with him* kind of thing.

'He's got that little-boy-lost look. You can just tell he's been really hurt,' Jess had said to them. 'And he's gorgeous and is so mature – he makes me feel all fragile and feminine. And he is such a gentleman – a proper grown-up.'

One of other girls from her office had giggled. 'God, he sounds perfect, shame I was away when he came in. I'd hang on in there, sweetie.' And so Jess had.

Jess just hadn't thought Max was that serious, even if when they first started going out together he'd done things like whisk her away to Paris on Eurostar for the weekend, and when she had been feeling a bit down had a dozen red roses delivered to the design office where she worked. But then he'd come over all Mr Darcy and be preoccupied and prickly, which sometimes Jess saw as a challenge and other times was just bloody annoying. Then again no one was perfect and he always apologised. When he did and looked at her with those big brown eyes, she could feel herself melting.

Recently it had all slowed down a bit and they'd both been busy and tired and finding it hard to make time for each other. In fact until he'd gone down on one knee Jess had begun to wonder if maybe they had already peaked and whether there was any future in the relationship at all. Well, apparently there was. Jess grinned. Not just a future but a happy ever after.

She turned over and snuggled up against him. 'Are you awake?' she whispered.

They had been drinking champagne and talking and leaving garbled messages on answer machines the length and breath of the known world, and now more sober and very slightly hung over, it was all beginning to sink in.

Jess ran her fingers down his arm. She had always imagined eventually marrying someone like Max – the classic older man, someone urbane, mature, slightly distant, calm, generous, someone who would take care of her, look after her. Someone who was already established. If she had had a list Max would tick almost all the boxes. She suppressed another giggle.

31

Up until now she hadn't even been sure that Max loved her. *I mean how mad was that?* She knew that Max liked her but he had never mentioned the 'L' word, not at all, not once. Not ever. And now they were getting married. The grin was back. Married.

Mrs Jessica Peters – it had such a nice ring to it. *Mrs Jessica Peters* – she rolled the words around inside her head. *She was going to get married.* And it would be fine, just fine. After all Max was sensible and he was kind and exactly what she needed. Someone strong and understanding – an old-fashioned man, someone who had seen a bit of life, someone who knew what he was doing.

As she lay there Jess made an effort to quell any little flurries of doubt that surfaced. After all, everyone was nervous about getting married. It was only natural, marriage was a big thing and okay, maybe she had just got a little bit swept along by the moment, but who wouldn't?

Obviously Max hadn't got any doubts about it or he wouldn't have asked, or maybe he could see something in her that she couldn't? The idea made her smile. It was quite exciting to think that he could see her hidden depths.

Down on the beach, when Max had asked – or told – her, there had been this funny, awkward silence and then he'd said, 'So what do you say then?'

It was all Jess could do to stop herself from laughing because it sounded ridiculous that anyone wanted to marry her. Then, without really stopping to think about it, she'd said, 'Yes, please.' Which, on reflection, made it sound as if he had just offered her an ice cream or something.

In amongst all her thoughts and feelings there was a terrible sense of being overwhelmed by the sheer scale of the plans that needed making to make a wedding happen. They had sixteen weeks tops to get it all together; she'd worked it out in the back of her diary. The biggest thing Jess had organised up until now was a table for fifteen at the local curry house. At the same time she had a funny sense of joy and excitement and anticipation. There was part of her that was ready to settle down. 'There is so much to get organised, you will help, won't you?'

Max yawned and stretched. 'What did you say?'

'Plans – we've got to make plans. And lists. You will help, won't you?'

He blinked and then rubbed his eyes and reached out to brush the hair back off Jess's face. 'You worry too much,' he said.

'And I was thinking – does this mean I'm officially moving in?'

He grinned. 'Well, I certainly hope so.'

'I meant when we get back. After all it would make life a lot easier and my lease is up.'

'I'd kind of assumed we'd wait until after the wedding,' Max said after a few seconds. 'I know it's a pain in the arse but would you mind waiting? It's not long and I'd really like to get the house sorted out. Decorated.'

'We could do that together. I'm a dab hand with a paint roller. I wouldn't mind helping.'

'I know you wouldn't, eager beaver,' said Max. 'But I'm up to my eyes with work at the moment. I'd been thinking I'd get someone in to do it, and it'll be a lot easier if the house is empty. I need to clear my office out and move the servers first . . .' He paused. 'You don't mind, do you?'

'Well, no,' Jess said with a shrug, masking her disappointment. 'No, not at all, it's fine.'

He laughed and poked her. 'No, it's not. You're annoyed.'

'Well, I just thought . . .' she began, but he was ahead of her.

'It won't be for much longer. If I were you I'd enjoy it. In another few years you'll probably be sick of the sight of me.' Max smiled and then leaned in to kiss her. 'I know my place isn't all that huge but it'll do us to start off with and then maybe later we could buy somewhere bigger – you happy with that?'

He kissed her again, more tenderly this time, and as she pulled away, and not for the first time, Jess admired the view. There was no doubt about it: Max Peters was a catch.

They'd met when he'd been brought in to upgrade the computers where she worked. He wasn't the normal engineer but had been doing a favour for a friend and as he came in, their eyes met and Jess had had one of those totally heart-stopping moments of lust. He *was* gorgeous and knew it.

Debbie, who sat at the desk opposite, and was about to go on maternity leave, had purred and then whispered, 'Wipe the drool off your chin, sweetie.' And then five minutes later Max had walked over to her desk and before she knew what had hit her he had asked Jess out for dinner and she had said yes. Just like that.

'Way, way too smooth,' Debbie had said, swigging Gaviscon like it was vodka, not quite able to hide the appreciation in her voice as Max went off to sort out one of the other machines.

And now here she was six months later, getting married to him. Jess drank him in with her eyes; she liked those nicely defined muscles in Max's arms, those broad shoulders and the way his hair – thick and almost black, and shot through here and there with grey – curled into the nape of his strong muscular neck. He swam and worked out two or three times a week and there was something about those big brown eyes of his that suggested he had been hurt, but with a lot of love the right woman could heal him – and apparently it turned out she was that woman.

Jess grinned lazily. Maybe happy ever after wasn't just a fairy story after all.

By some stroke of genetic good fortune his skin turned the colour of golden syrup at the merest glimpse of sunshine, so that as she moved closer and slid into the crook of his arm, Jess was aware of how very pale and delicate and feminine she looked next to his strong, beautiful golden body. It gave her a little ripple of pleasure. No two ways about it, Max Peters made her mouth water and she was going to marry him and be Mrs Peters. As he pulled her closer all her doubts began to ebb away. She was going to marry Max Peters and live happily ever after and the very thought of it made her smile.

'So, about these plans and lists,' she murmured.

'Plans and lists?' he teased.

Jess nodded. 'Uh-huh. Lots of them.'

'That's what the bride's mother's for,' Max said, stretching again. 'Are you hungry?'

'I'm being serious,' Jess said.

'And so was I – I'm absolutely famished.'

'About the wedding.'

'Oh, don't look so worried; mothers, they love it, all that arranging, the frocks, the flowers, the caterers.'

'I'm not sure my mum's like that,' said Jess. 'She's really busy.'

Max laughed. 'They're all like that once you scratch the surface. You okay?'

Jess nodded. 'Yes, I'm fine. I'm tired, a bit hung over.' She looked at Max's face, trying to work out what he was thinking. 'You're frowning? You're not cross I asked you to help, are you? I am really excited.'

He smiled. 'I'm not cross, baby. I'm just not great at all that kind of thing. Actually, I'm rubbish, if you want the truth. And I'm incredibly busy at the moment.'

Jess wrinkled up her nose. 'What about when you got married first time around, didn't you help with the arrangements then?'

'That was a long while ago now,' Max said, pulling himself up onto one elbow. 'Lucy's mother organised it all. We got married in the chapel on their family estate. All I did was turn up. If I remember correctly she even sorted out the morning suits for me and the best man. Let's not talk about that. What do you fancy to eat? We could take a drive along the coast if you like or nip into town. Pick up something and cook it here.'

Jess made the effort to smile.

Lucy. The Honourable Lucy Troughton-Warbridge-Hays, Max's first wife, the woman who had left Max with that whipped-puppy look. The wife who he had married when they were both too young and who he had loved with all his heart. *The wife whose photograph still hung in his office even after all these years.*

When Jess had pointed it out Max had blushed furiously and taken it down. 'Sorry – you know I didn't even notice it was there,' he'd said, sliding it into a drawer. Lucy Troughton-Warbridge-Hays, the wife who had run off with his best friend and best man Stephen, who between them had broken his heart and ensured that Max Peters had been a career bachelor – up until now. Jess couldn't help wonder what it was that had changed his mind. Was it that finally at forty he thought it was time that he settled down? Time to put down roots and have a family? Did he see Jess as someone special, the kind of woman he could trust and wanted to spend the rest of his life with? Surely the answer had to be yes? The thought made her feel warm and fluttery inside.

Jess looked up into his big dark eyes. 'Do you love me, Max?'

He smiled and kissed the end of her nose. 'What do you think?'

'And you will help with the wedding, won't you?'

'Of course I will,' Max said, and rolled back the duvet. 'But I've already told you that I'm not great at that kind of stuff.' He sounded offhand and casual, but Jess needed him to be keen, eager, and enthusiastic – and told him so.

Max, feet on the floor now, sighed. 'I am, Jess, sweetheart, and I trust your judgement. Absolutely. After all, you've agreed to be my wife, haven't you? Just shows you've got great judgement and the most *fantastic* taste.'

Jess laughed and threw a pillow at him.

And then Max got out of bed and pulled on a robe. 'Besides,' he said, 'it's no big deal.'

Jess was about to protest when Max leaned over and held a finger to her lips and then, leaning closer still, kissed her briefly. 'Poor choice of words. What I meant was, it will all get sorted out. You have to understand I've got a lot on my plate at the moment, with the McKeeley project and Jacobson going live in the spring as well as all the usual crap. It's going to be a busy few months.'

Jess stared at him, wondering whether it was meant as a joke. 'Well, if you're that busy maybe we ought to wait – I mean, I don't mind waiting.'

'Well, I do,' said Max emphatically. 'In my line of work you can never guarantee what the schedule is going to be. We've just got to seize the moment.' Laughing, he made a tickling, nipping lunge at her which made Jess shriek and giggle, then stood over her, hands flat on the mattress, pinning her down. It was a dominant, manly, sexy gesture that made her skin tingle all over.

'If you wanted to seize the moment maybe we should just slip away – do something romantic, drive to Scotland, get married at Gretna. I'm sure Mum and Dad would under-stand,' said Jess. 'Just the two of us. Drag two people in off the street to be our witnesses.'

Max's expression softened into something that made Jess's heart melt. 'But I don't want us to slip away, Jess – I want everyone to see us. I want us to have the most wonderful, perfect day with all our family and friends. I want everyone to see how beautiful you are, to say, "Wow, don't they make the most stunning couple". I want it to be just perfect. And it will be.'

'Oh, Max.' Jess felt her eyes filling with tears.

'And I'm sure your mum wouldn't want us running off and getting hitched without any fuss,' Max said, pushing himself back upright. 'I'll let the dog out and then I thought as we were up we might as well drive out to Exmoor – take Bassa for a bit of a hike and then see if we can find a nice pub somewhere. Unless you want to cook?'

'It's still raining,' protested Jess.

Max laughed. 'You won't melt. Come on, the fresh air will do us both good. We ought to make the most of it while we're down here. I don't know when I'll be able to take any more time off before the wedding.'

Wordlessly Jess got out of bed and pulled on her jeans. Actually Max was probably right, the fresh air would help clear her head. When she checked her phone there was a message from Molly. She tried to ring back but Molly had her phone on voicemail.

'Hi, Mum. I've got loads to tell you and talk about, but the signal down here isn't great. How about we come round on Saturday and we can catch up then? Love you.' And then, still smiling, Jess hung up. She hurried downstairs, excite-ment drowning out the little niggling worries she had about Max.

Chapter Five

'Where's Max? Couldn't he make it?' asked Molly, looking out into the porch through the open kitchen door. She was just sliding a batch of homemade bread out of the oven. It smelt wonderful. It was first thing on Saturday morning and making bread was Molly's idea of relaxing after a long and busy week.

Jess, in a summer dress over leggings, bundled into the kitchen holding her coat above her head, dripping water all over the flagstone floor. Bassa, her supersized Jack Russell-mongrel-mix followed hard on her heels, tail wagging enthusiastically.

'No, he's had to work this weekend. We only got back late last night and he needed to get back on site. The company he's working for are putting in some kind of new system in their new offices and he's got to be there – that's why we grabbed a few days away, while we could. I can see that I'm going to be an IT widow. God, that bread smells wonderful, are we having it for lunch?'

Molly nodded. 'Uh-huh, and there's homemade hummus, some tomatoes out of the garden, some cheese and a ham Nick boiled last night. Okay?'

'Oh God, yes,' Jess purred as she dumped the coat over a chair and then let Molly fold her into her arms.

'Congratulations,' said Molly, voice crackling with un-expected emotion as she pulled back to look Jess up and down. 'I can't believe my baby is getting married. Seems only a few months ago we were at the zoo feeding the llamas.'

Jess grinned. 'It was only few months ago, Mum, remember? We went to do some sort of promo with the radio station?'

'You know what I mean.'

Jess nodded. 'It's so nice to be home,' she said in a little voice. 'This week has been completely and utterly crazy. And it was really hard to talk on the mobile – I didn't want to do all that "Can you hear me? You're cracking up" thing –'

'It's fine and you're here now, so I want to hear all about it.'

Behind them Bassa did a wet-dog shimmy and shake, covering everyone and everything with a fine spray of mongrel-scented water. Molly's dog, Milo, a huge English mastiff, lifted his head to check out the new arrivals from the comfort of his basket by the Aga and then celebrated the fact they weren't burglars by closing his eyes and letting out a loud snore. Bassa made a beeline for Milo's biscuits while Molly indicated they should sit.

'I'm so, so glad you're here. We've got pink champagne on standby in the fridge – I was hoping that Max would be here too so we could share it while we have a chat about what you want to do about the wedding.' Molly struggled to hold back the unexpected flurry of tears that threatened.

Jess grinned. 'Oh, come on, we don't have to wait for Max, do we? Do you want to open it or shall I?'

Molly rubbed away a stray tear. 'First thing you need to learn about men is that they need to feel useful to feel loved,' and with that she turned and shouted, 'Nick? Jess is here, darling. We need a real man to come and open the champagne.'

And from somewhere deep in the cottage they both heard Nick laugh. 'I'm on my way,' he called.

'The garden is looking wonderful,' said Max, taking a sip of tea.

'Yes it is, isn't it? We've done terribly well with the mixed borders this year. It's so nice to see you, Max,' said his mother. 'Seems like ages since you've been down. Such a shame Daddy is out at the moment. You really should have rung and let us know you were coming. He only arranged to go and play golf with Archie this morning...' Daphne Peters let the silence fall and waited, in the way that all mothers wait, because she knew damned well that Max hadn't driven nearly three hours out of his way just to admire the dahlias.

'Actually, Mummy, I came down to tell you that I've asked Jessica to marry me,' Max said, setting his cup and saucer carefully back down on the tea tray. 'And she's said yes.'

'Really,' said Daphne with a smile. 'Well, that's absolutely wonderful news, Max. Congratulations. And not before time. You know your father and I have been terribly worried about you. I'm so pleased. It'll be lovely for you to be settled at long last. And she seems like a charming young woman. We both said so when you came for lunch – Daddy was most impressed. It's just a shame you couldn't have come down to see us together really. Couldn't Jessica make it today?'

Max shook his head. 'She's working this weekend. And to be honest I thought it would be better if I told you myself. Obviously I'll bring Jess over as soon as possible but I wanted to tell you on my own, rather than spring it on you unprepared.'

He lingered over the word *unprepared*. Daphne nodded; there was bound to be more.

'We're planning to get married in December.'

They were sitting in the conservatory, with its chintz-covered

41

cane furniture and view of the carefully manicured lawns and lovingly tended gardens, where a mother duck was busy leading a waddle of tiny ducklings down towards the pond at the bottom.

Daphne topped up his cup. 'December? Gosh, well, in that case, we'll all have to get our skates on then, won't we? I'll ring Marjorie and see if she'll make the cake.' Max's mother paused and watched him thoughtfully. 'Rather a short engagement, darling. Anything else you'd care to share with me?'

Max looked bemused. 'I thought I *was* sharing?'

Daphne Peters laughed. 'I meant, should I ask Marjorie to make sure the top tier is a decent size? I'm a woman of the world, Max, these things happen.'

Max looked more puzzled. 'Mummy, what are you talking about?'

'For the christening, Max – it's traditional to keep the top tier for the christening.'

Max stared at her as if she were speaking in tongues. 'Right,' he said slowly.

'What I mean is, are you planning to make me a grandmother as well as a mother-in-law?'

'Ah, children,' he said with relief. 'I presume so, eventually, but not straight away. Will you tell Daddy about the wedding for me?'

Daphne sighed; men. 'Of course, darling. Presumably Jessica's parents will be in touch so we can talk about the arrangements? You have met her people?'

Max nodded. 'Yes, they're nice. Divorced. Her father is in business, although I think he's semi-retired now, remarried – and her mother is on the radio.'

Daphne's expression brightened. 'Really? Three or four?'

'Nothing quite so grand, I'm afraid, it's a local station. She's some kind of presenter.'

Daphne nodded again. 'Well, that all sounds very jolly. I don't mean to pry, Max, but this hasn't got anything to do with –' She stopped short. 'Well, you know.'

Max looked up from his cup and saucer and said obliquely, 'With what?'

Sometimes Max and his father took obtuse to a whole new dimension, thought Daphne.

Jess held out her hand and wiggled her fingers so that Molly could inspect her engagement ring. They were sitting at the kitchen table and Nick was busy filling champagne flutes for a toast.

'Oh, that's really –' Molly hesitated, cautiously feeling her way around for the right adjective. 'Quite striking really,' she managed after a few more seconds.

Jess looked down at it and then up at Molly and pulled a funny little face. 'I know what you mean. It isn't something I'd have chosen for myself, but it's growing on me.'

'Growing on you?' Molly looked her daughter in the eye. 'You haven't told Max you don't like the ring, have you?' Jessica didn't say a word, so tactfully Molly pressed on. 'Jewellery is a really hard thing to choose for someone, even if you know them well. Most couples go out and choose the ring together. It is such a special thing; it would be nice to have something that you really love, don't you think? I'm sure Max would understand. Men aren't always great at picking things, you know what they're like.'

'What are we like?' asked Nick, handing them their glasses. A corporate bunny all week, at weekends he dressed like a roadie for a rock band.

'I was saying picking jewellery for someone can be tricky even when you know them well,' said Molly.

Nick held out his hand and without a word Jess put her

43

hand in it. He leaned in closer and took a long, hard look at the ring. 'Umm,' he said.

'It looks like roadkill, doesn't it?' said Jess glumly. 'The more I look at it, the more I hate it. How can I tell Max that I hate his engagement ring?'

Nick sat down next to her and put his arm around her shoulders. 'The best way is to try not to hurt his feelings, so try something like, "You know, Max, your taste in totty is spot on, but to be perfectly frank your taste in jewellery is complete shite."'

At which point Jess laughed, which was a great relief because for a few seconds there Molly was convinced she was going to cry.

'No, what you need to say,' Nick continued, 'is that it's a very beautiful ring but not the kind of thing that you would usually wear, and that you want something you can wear every day, so when you look at it you think of him. After all you've got to wear it the rest of your life.'

Molly raised her eyebrows. 'I'm impressed. This from a man who gets palpitations at the mention of marriage.'

'Come on, I'm not the only one. Who was the woman who said she'd rather push needles in her eyes than get married again?'

'What I said was . . .' Molly looked at him and grinned. 'Did I really say that?'

Nick nodded. 'You most certainly did.'

'Well, maybe I was being a bit hasty. Anyway, don't go shifting the blame. You're a marriage cynic too,' said Molly.

'That doesn't mean that I'm not a romantic,' he said, sounding genuinely hurt. 'Remember that time I had three tons of well-rotted horse manure for the garden delivered on your birthday. We even gift-wrapped the tipper truck.'

Jess laughed. 'You're all heart.'

'Do you know where Max bought the ring?' Molly asked.

Jess picked up her rucksack and started to rootle around in it. 'I've got the box in here somewhere. Oh, here we are.' She pulled out a navy blue velvet drawstring bag, extravagantly lined in purple silk. Inside was a matching box with the initials LP intertwined discreetly on the lining of the lid. On the bottom of the box it said *LovesPleasures, Jewellers*, and a Cambridge phone number.

'I'd talk to Max and arrange to go back to the shop together and change it for something you both like.'

'I don't want to upset him,' said Jess, taking off the ring and slipping it back into the box.

Molly gave her a long, hard look. 'It's going to upset him a lot more if you don't wear it.'

'All right, all right,' said Jess grimly. 'I know what you're saying, and to be honest if I can't talk to him about this then we're on a hiding to nothing really, aren't we? Don't judge him by the ring. Max is an absolute gem – he'll understand, and you're right, what are the chances of picking the right ring for anyone first time?' Jess paused and smiled wistfully. 'It's a shame it's so awful because Max going out and choosing it for me is such a romantic thing to do.'

'I know,' said Molly, although she suspected that had Max really known Jess he would have guessed that something overblown and fiddly really wasn't going to work, whereas something stylish and simple and contemporary would have done.

Jess took a long pull on her champagne and then licked her lips. 'Oh, God, that's lovely. Can we have this for the wedding?'

'You're meant to wait for the toast,' said Molly, raising her glass. 'To Jess and Max.'

'Jess and Max,' they murmured as Jess took another slurp.

45

'Talking of Max, where is he?' asked Nick. 'Is he still outside? Is he on his way?'

'No, no, he's working this weekend and to be honest I'm not sure how good men are at this kind of thing.'

'What kind of thing?' asked Nick.

'Weddings,' said Jessica with a sly grin. 'You know, cakes and commitment, all that getting married stuff. I'm panicking and really banking on you guys to help me out with this.'

'Ouch,' said Nick, flinching as if she had punched him. 'You know I think you're absolutely right. I'll leave you to it, if you don't mind – weddings make me come over all faint.' And with that he headed off into the sitting room with the papers. As he got to the door he said, 'Has your mother mentioned the radio idea to you yet?'

'What radio idea?' said Jess.

'*So,*' said Molly, glaring at Nick as he grinned at her through the glass door to the kitchen. 'About the wedding . . .'

Chapter Six

'Mum, we are *not* turning my wedding into a radio feature, all right?'

'I know, I know,' said Molly, holding up her hands. 'And that's exactly what I told Rob.'

Jess shook her head. 'Max would be horrified. His family are – well, I've only met them a couple of times but they're . . .' Jess hesitated, trying to find the right words. 'They're really old-fashioned and a bit posh. His mother is in the WI, his father's retired and on the committee at the golf club. He was something big in the city.'

'I know, but Rob just thought it would be a great programming idea. He was suggesting that we do a weekly segment for my show. You and Max building up to the big day, going to see people – the florists, caterers, that sort of thing, you and me going to look at dresses – right up to the ceremony. It'd just be me and maybe a sound guy.'

'No,' said Jess incredulously.

But Molly pressed on. 'Okay. I have to say it wasn't my idea, but you can see where Rob's coming from?'

Jess sniffed. 'It's all a bit tacky.'

Molly nodded. 'Actually it could be a lot tacky but I did tell him that I'd ask you. What Raf said – he's the station's advertising whiz kid – was that you'd probably be able to negotiate a discount if you bought something from any of the suppliers we featured.' She paused. 'I'll take that as a no then, shall I?'

Jess groaned. 'You won't tell Dad about this, will you, please? You know what he's like when people start mentioning discounts. I don't want a bargain-basement wedding, Mum. We want something special and lovely.'

'I know, and so do I, but I had to ask,' said Molly. 'And I promise, not a word to your dad.' She mimed zipped lips. 'And I'll prime Nick not to say anything either. Anyway – let's get down to business, shall we?' She pulled out the great sheaf of papers that she'd printed off.

Jess's eyes widened as Molly spread them out on the kitchen table. 'Bloody hell, what's all that?'

'It's a list of things we need to do,' sighed Molly.

'Really? So what *do* we need to do?' asked Jessica.

'First two things, it says here,' Molly began, slipping on her glasses, 'you need to decide what kind of wedding you want and then pick two or three dates – to give yourself a bit of flexibility just in case the place you want isn't free. And after that there are the caterers, cakes, cars, flowers, photographers, maybe video, dresses, invitations, music. It'll be all fine though – once we've got the place booked.' When Molly looked across at Jess, her daughter was ashen. 'Are you all right?'

'I suppose so.' Jess nodded and then smiled. 'Yes, I'm really, really excited and also really, really nervous. Is that normal?'

Molly reached out and touched her hand. 'I think so. Me too. I've never organised a wedding before other than me and your dad's. We'll do it together and it will be just perfect, I promise. We need to talk to your dad about money and Nick and I will help too.' Molly paused. Max was the first of

Jess's boyfriends that Molly didn't feel she knew, and here he was taking her away. 'Have you talked to Max about what he'd like?'

'I have.' Jess rolled her eyes. 'And he told me he wasn't very good at that kind of thing.'

'I don't think any of them are but he's got to have some input. After all, it's his wedding day as well.'

'He said I could have what I like.'

Molly laughed. 'So we're saying what exactly? That we organise it all and he just shows up?'

'I think that probably just about sums it up,' Jess said and then waved the words away. 'Trouble is, Max is really busy at the moment and I think he just wants to get on with it. I thought what we could do is come up with two or three ideas and run them past him, and then let him help with the final decisions. Guided by me, obviously.' As she spoke Jess reached down into her bag and pulled out a pile of bridal magazines. 'I bought these. It's like a total bloody minefield. What man in their right mind wants to sit down and flick through these lot with someone saying, "Do you like this and what do you think about this?" every thirty seconds? No – I reckon we should whittle it down to the final few ideas and then I'm sure he'll be happy to look.'

Molly nodded. 'How about we work out how many people you want to invite and that will help you decide on a venue?'

'Okay. People and venue,' said Jess, opening up a pad and pulling out a pen.

'Church, registry office or some sort of wedding venue? A hotel or something?' said Molly.

'Max is divorced.'

'So?'

'So, how about we have some more champagne and start looking through all these?' said Jess, pushing the magazines

49

into the centre of the table to join her mother's pile of papers.

'And then there's the Internet,' said Molly.

'Okay,' said Jess. 'Who is going to say, "do you like this" and "what do you think about this?"'

'We'll take it in turns and if we get too overwhelmed Nick can give us a hand. Let me get my laptop. There's a note-book and some post-it notes,' Molly said, sliding them across the table. 'Presumably now you're getting married you've cancelled the house hunting?'

'What?'

'Presumably you'll be moving in with Max?'

Jess looked uncomfortable. 'Well, no, actually. We've talked about it but his house is full of stuff. It really needs clearing out and redecorating.'

'That's half the fun.'

'I know, but we're going to wait. I mean, obviously I'll move in after we're married, but I'm still looking for some-where at the moment.'

'If you want to move back here for a few weeks you know you're really welcome.'

'Thanks. One the girls in the office said I could have a room at her place too, so hopefully I'll find somewhere just for two or three months. Trouble is, I'm used to my own space.'

'Well the offer's open. I'll get the laptop.'

When Molly got back from her office Jess had refilled their glasses and had found some nachos in a cupboard. As Molly slipped back into her seat she noticed a little blue notebook on top of the pile of magazines and was about to pick it up when something about the expression on Jess's face stopped her.

'You want me to make notes in this?' Molly asked casually. And then she looked closer and realised that it was an old exercise book. Written on the front in a rounded childish script it said, *Jessica Alice Foster. Medthorpe High School. English Composition.*

'You've had that a long time,' said Molly.

'First year at High School. It's my wedding book,' Jess said in a funny, self-conscious little voice.

'Your wedding book?'

Jess nodded. 'The very same.'

'Can I look?' said Molly.

'You promise not to laugh?'

'At your wedding book? Of course I won't laugh.'

Jess picked it up and thumbed through it. Molly watched, catching a glimpse of the round, young handwriting as the pages flickered by and wondered wistfully where all those years in between had gone. 'It's not *just* my wedding book, obviously,' said Jess. 'We had to write about our hopes for our future, for homework. I really liked my teacher and once I got going it was hard to stop. I wrote about wanting to have a dog of my own and learning to scuba dive and getting this amazing job as a designer and flying all over the world, and having my hair dyed purple.'

'And getting married?'

'Yes, but not just that. Anyway, when it came to handing it in I didn't want anyone else to read it. I'd said too much – you know what I mean? There was too much of me showing in it. And I was afraid my teacher might read it out. So I wrote something else and handed that in instead.' Jess opened the book again, this time to the place where she'd left a slip of paper. 'Here,' she said, flattening the pages out with her hand, and sliding it across the table. 'My wedding, by Jessica Alice Foster.'

Molly leaned closer. On one page was a pencil drawing of a girl with plaits in a long cloak, holding hands with a tall, dark-haired man. It had all been very carefully coloured in. The happy couple stood under a stone arch festooned with creepers.

Touched, Molly looked up. 'Oh, Jess. It looks just like you. How come I've never seen this before?'

Jess laughed. 'It was way too secret and embarrassing. I've hidden it for years, in the bottom of the shoebox along with my plaits. Remember when I made you take me to have them cut off? I wanted to look grown-up and sophisticated, but you know, I never regretted anything so much in my life.' She ran a carefully manicured finger over the face of the girl. The little picture captured the naïve charm of an eleven-year-old with all of her life ahead of her. 'You think it looks like Max?' said Jess, peering at the man.

'A bit, although I'm not sure about the wooden leg and the patch.'

Jess laughed. 'I was going through a pirate phase. And no, before you ask, I wasn't planning to have a pirate-themed wedding.'

Molly grinned. 'Shame really. Nick would look great with a cutlass and a parrot. So what else does it say about your wedding?' She was anxious not to pry into the book that Jess had kept hidden for so long.

'Well, I want something romantic – I was thinking maybe medieval-looking – a romantic heroine, with a cloak rather than a train.'

'And a hood?' Molly pointed to the drawing.

Jess nodded. If there was anyone who could carry off the romantic heroine it was her; she was tiny with creamy white skin, huge blue eyes and a cascade of dark brown, wavy, shoulder-length hair shot through here and there with copper. She looked as if she had walked straight out of the pages of a Daphne du Maurier novel.

'I'm going to ring Helen.'

'Helen, you mean Helen you were at college with?'

Jess nodded. 'Uh-huh. She's based in London now but she's been working with a repertory company. Helen does all their costumes, and so I was going to ask her to be my bridesmaid and make our dresses. We can look around as well but she's really good and they'd be extra special if she makes them.'

'So maybe we should go with the pirate theme after all – you know, something a bit romantic hero for Max –'

'Frock coat and knee britches, like a highwayman. And me in a scarlet velvet cloak trimmed with white fur.'

They giggled, the champagne playing havoc as it bubbled through Molly's bloodstream. She glanced across at Jess and smiled; even as a little girl her daughter had always liked dressing up.

'Oh, talking about frock coats and highwaymen, I've found this fantastic place in Scotland,' Jess said, tapping out a web address on Molly's laptop. The image of a fairytale castle on the edge of a loch appeared through some computer-generated mist.

'Sleeps Fourteen,' said Molly, reading the blurb.

'Oh, bugger. Does it? Maybe we could find somewhere else for the rest of the guests,' said Jess, scanning down the rest of the screen.

'The way this reads it sounds as if it's way out in the back of beyond. I don't want to be a killjoy but how are people going to get there? I suppose you could just have close family and friends and then have a big party when we get home.

'No, Max wants everyone there.' Jess pulled a face and tapped in another address. 'I've found this fab place in Norway – you get to be taken to the chapel in a sleigh pulled by reindeer. I was thinking about the ice hotel but apparently it's below zero all the time in all the rooms. I mean how sexy are chilblains?'

By lunchtime, Molly and Jess had a mass of pages bookmarked on the computer and dozens of post-it notes stuck on magazines, and definite plans were emerging. Although it was fun looking at different styles, places and prices, Molly could see that she could very soon die of boredom, whereas Jess looked as if she could go on for ever.

Nick came through to help them sort out lunch. 'How's it coming along?'

'Good,' said Jess.

'We need to talk to Jonathon and Max,' said Molly, clearing away the champagne glasses.

'Even though I love him dearly, trying to plan all this I've come to the conclusion that I'm marrying a man I know nothing about,' Jess hiccupped. 'I don't even know what religion he is.'

'In that case he is most probably Church of England,' said Nick, sliding a plate piled high with buttered slices of freshly baked bread onto the table. 'Otherwise you'd probably have heard something about his Jewish roots, his Catholic guilt or his minority oppression. Here, you should eat some of this and soak up some of the alcohol.'

Jess nodded. 'I've only had a couple of glasses. Maybe I should ring him and ask him? After all, it is lunchtime. Surely even Max stops for lunch?'

'Maybe it's not a good time, not if he's at work,' said Molly.

'Oh no, he'll be fine, he won't mind,' said Jess, waving the words away. 'Besides, I want to tell him that I love him and I ought to let him know how we're getting on. And anyway he said it was all very casual today, all hands to the pumps,

54

installing this new system, everyone mucking in. I'm sure he won't mind. Really.' She pulled her mobile out of her bag.

While Molly set about helping with lunch Jess and Bassa went outside for a bit of privacy and a better signal.

'How's it going?' asked Nick, picking over the last of the nachos.

Molly groaned. 'It's fine. The trouble is in my head Jess is still three, running around in her wellies with a net curtain on her head, a sword in one hand and a water pistol in the other.'

'Feisty bride?' said Nick.

Molly laughed. 'You better believe it. Jonathon used to say we'd have to pay some man to take her off our hands.' Molly's gaze moved instinctively to the kitchen window to watch Jess walking across the grass.

'She'll be fine,' Nick said.

'She's still my baby,' said Molly, voice tight with tears. 'And why isn't Max here helping her? He should be here. We don't know anything about him.'

Nick slipped his arm around her. 'No, but we will. And Jess is sensible – we have to trust her.'

'That's what I said to Jonathon.'

'And?'

'I didn't believe it then either.'

Outside the rain had stopped, so Jess headed over to the swing that Nick had fixed up under one of the big apple trees at the bottom of the garden. Bassa bounced alongside her, tail wagging, glad to be out. As Jess walked the phone rang and rang, and she was about to ring off when someone picked up.

'Hi, honey,' said Jess. 'Not working too hard, are you?'

'Oh, hello,' said a very polite female voice. 'This is Max Peters' phone. I'm terribly sorry but he's not here at the moment. May I take a message?'

'Oh,' said Jess, totally wrong-footed and almost instantly sober. 'Oh, sorry – where is he?'

'He's left his phone on the table. I thought I'd better answer it.'

'Oh, right,' said Jess. 'Well, if he's busy could you give him a message for me? Can you tell him –'

But before she could finish the woman's voice warmed. 'Jessica, is that you?'

'Yes, yes it is,' she said, still not quite able to place the voice.

'Oh, I'm so glad you rang. Max told me you were terribly busy at work this weekend, which is such a shame. We would have loved to have seen you and congratulate you both on your wonderful news. We are so pleased. But I do appreciate things are a little busy at the moment. I just wanted to say that we couldn't be more delighted for you both, my dear. Congratulations.'

'Mrs Peters?' Jess began, the penny having dropped.

'Do call me Mummy, or is that too old-fashioned? I've never been terribly keen on Mum, or Mother come to that. Maybe you should just call me Daphne.' Max's mother laughed. 'Anyway I was telling Max that the two of you really must come down as soon as possible. I was wondering if you would like me to arrange the cake? We can obviously discuss the design but I have a very good friend. Marjorie. Cordon bleu – fabulous cook. She did the cake for – well, what I'm saying is, if you'd like me to arrange it then I'd be absolutely delighted to call her.'

Jess didn't know what to say, so she settled for, 'That sounds wonderful, and I'm sure we'll be down to see you soon.'

'Lovely. We were all just planning to go out for lunch at the Lion. Which reminds me, perhaps you and your parents might like to come down for lunch? Max said you were busy next weekend and I know Hampshire is a terribly long way from Norfolk, but it would be lovely if we could all get together – maybe the weekend after? Do let me know.' She laughed, the sound like the tinkling of cut glass. 'After all, there is so much to organise and we haven't got that much time. I'll tell Max that you rang, shall I?'

'Yes, please,' said Jess, totally dazed. 'That would be lovely.'

And then Daphne was gone and Jess found herself staring at the phone. It rang in her hand seconds later.

'Jess,' said Max.

'What is going on, Max? You told me you were working all this weekend.'

'I was, I am,' he blustered. 'Well, I am tomorrow.'

'That isn't what you said when you dropped me off at my place last night. You said you couldn't stay because you had to be up early to get some system in. And your mother said you'd told her that I was working.'

'Jess, I'm really sorry.' His voice was barely above a whisper. 'The thing is, I wanted to talk to my parents on my own. They're a bit old-fashioned when it comes to this sort of thing. I just wanted to break it to them gently, that's all.'

'You make getting married to me sound like bad news.'

'That isn't what I mean at all – but it was just something I needed to do. Please try and understand.' He paused, presumably waiting for a reply, but Jess couldn't find the right words. 'You're upset,' he said.

'Of course I'm upset! I've just spent most of the morning trying to organise a wedding without you, with no idea what

57

you like or what you want. I wanted to talk to you about it and you're over at your mother's.'

'I told you what I wanted, something special, I want everyone to see us – a wonderful, perfect day with all our family and friends. No sneaking off to some secret location.' He paused. 'Please don't be upset that I wanted to tell Mummy and Daddy my way. On my own.'

'I'm not upset that you wanted to tell them on your own, I'd have understood that. What I don't understand is why you didn't tell me the truth.'

'May we talk about this later? We're all about to go out to lunch.'

Jess wondered what she could possibly say.

'I'll call you later,' he continued. 'How are all the wedding plans coming along?'

'That was what I rang to –'

'Sorry, sweetie, I've really got to go. My father's in the car outside,' and with that Max hung up.

Speechless, Jess stood with the phone in her hand, furious with Max and feeling horribly hurt. What the hell was he playing at? The phone rang again and without looking at the caller ID Jess pressed receive. 'I really hope you've rung to say something nice,' she snapped. 'I've been here all morning going through these bloody wedding books on my –'

'Jess?'

Mouth open, Jessica was caught mid-sentence.

'It's me. Remember me? Jack. Your baby brother? I was just ringing up to say congratulations. Bad timing?' he joked.

'No, no, not at all – just a misunderstanding,' she hedged. 'So how are you?'

'I'm fine. More to the point, how are you?'

'Good, great,' Jess lied, nodding furiously despite the fact that he couldn't see her. 'Really well, just getting a bit stressed out by all the stuff we've got to do for the wedding.'

'It's months away yet.'

'Yep, but not enough months apparently. According to this list Mum downloaded off the Internet we should have started booking everything about ten years ago. And we want some really special –'

'That's what I was ringing up about. I was talking to my boss, Bert, yesterday and he wondered if you might like to have the wedding here.'

'At Vanguard Hall?'

'Uh-huh, I mean you can at least think about it.'

'Oh God, that would be perfect. It's lovely there.'

'I think you'd probably have to have the legal bit somewhere else but you could have the reception here if you wanted to. He suggested you come over and take a look round. He was thinking you might like to use the Tythe Barn – after all it's got loos and fire exits and all that stuff for when we open the gardens up in the summer. Do you know the room I mean?'

'The one they do tea and cakes in?'

'That's the one. Anyway, it's something to think about. Bert's been mulling over whether to go for the wedding trade. It's big business – and I know he won't be offended if you say no.'

'Oh no, God, it would be wonderful,' Jess murmured. 'Did he say what it would cost? Only I haven't spoken to Dad yet so I don't have a clue what we've got to spend.'

'It's on the house. Bert is keen on family. And besides, because he's toying with the idea of opening the hall up for weddings he wants to get a feel of what he's letting himself in for.'

'How many people do you think it would hold?'

'No idea – come and take a look around and see what you think. I'd imagine you could easily get a hundred people in the barn, say ten tables of ten. I'll ask him.' Jack paused. 'And well done you. Seems so grown-up. I hope you and Max are really happy.'

'Thanks, Jack.'

There was a warm silence and then Jack continued, 'I was going to ask, is he on some sort of medication? Only he must be mad taking you on, maybe I should warn him.'

Jess laughed; that was more like it. 'Cheeky bugger. How are you anyway?'

'Me, I'm fine – I can't talk for long, me and Ollie are supposed to be working, or at least I am.'

'Ollie?'

'Yeah, head gardener and chief slave driver. I've got to water the walled garden. How about you ring me later to sort out when you're coming over?'

'Ok, I'll talk to Mum.'

Jess didn't really have much chance to think about the revelation that Max was down in Hampshire until she came off the phone, and then it hit her.

'Bastard,' Jess hissed as she wandered back into the house. Why on earth had he lied to her?

Molly looked up from the piles of lists. 'Sorry?'

Jess waved the words away. 'Nothing,' she said.

Molly smiled back at her. 'So how was Max?'

'Absolutely fine, just off to lunch,' Jess said, trying to sound matter of fact. 'Now where were we?'

'Lunch,' said Molly, handing her a plate. 'And how's his work going?'

'Just fine,' lied Jess, sitting down at the kitchen table, not quite meeting Molly's eye. 'And it looks like we've got a cake and possibly a venue.'

60

'Great,' said Molly, peering at her. 'Are you all right?'

'I'm fine, just hungry,' Jess said. The last thing she wanted was to talk about Max, because she knew that it wouldn't take much to make her cry. What the hell was he thinking of? Old-fashioned or not, surely it wouldn't have hurt for them to have gone down to see his parents together.

Chapter Seven

The day just went on and on and so it was almost eight by the time Jess and Bassa finally left for the drive back to Swaffham.

Molly was exhausted. They had spent all day looking at wedding magazines and websites, and drawing up endless lists. They had eaten dinner in amongst a pile of wedding plans. Nick had been an absolute star; he'd fed them, oohed at all the pictures Jess had pushed under his nose, said all the right things in all the right places and was now busy packing the dishwasher.

Not for the first time Molly marvelled at her good fortune in finding a man like Nick after all these years, a man who loved her and her children – who repaid the compliment by loving him right back – and who loved her in ways so numerous and so palpable that she couldn't imagine what life had been like without him.

'Right,' said Nick, handing her a mug of tea and settling himself down alongside her. 'Hit me with it.'

'Well, Jess's idea is that we plan everything all in one big go, present it as a *fait accompli* to Jonathon and Max and then just get it all booked and organised, maybe with a couple of tweaks en route. Which sounds perfect in practice but in reality everything we looked at gave Jess something else to think about.'

'You want more champagne? I think there's another bottle in the fridge.'

Molly groaned. 'Give me a break.' She felt as if she had been mugged by a froth of organza and baby's breath. She pushed the pile of magazines and notes and torn-out pages to one side of the kitchen table and slumped forward, head on hands.

'Thank God she's gone.'

'You were brilliant.' Nick grinned. 'Don't flag now – I've got a night of wild passion planned. Blindfolds, baby oil, furry handcuffs.'

His grin held until Molly laughed.

Nick aped rejection. 'Don't tell me; what you really want is a hot bath, and an early night?'

'What would I do without you?' asked Molly.

Nick considered the possibility for a moment. 'Have all of the duvet yourself and get to watch what you want on the TV?'

Molly nodded. 'There is that. You know that the next few weeks are going to be total hell, don't you? And this is even before my nearest and dearest start moaning that they haven't got an invitation or it's too far away or on the wrong day.'

'You've done the guest list already?'

Molly pulled a sheet of paper out from the pile. 'More or less. Actually I don't think there is much we haven't taken a stab at.'

Nick moved behind her and rubbed her neck and shoulders, thumbs working into a great raft of knots and creaks, making Molly groan with a mixture of pain and relief.

'Any woman who can deal with a juggling bear can cope with organising a wedding.' He pulled Molly's notebook back across the table and scanned down the list. 'Registry office, followed by a humanist wedding at Vanguard Hall, wedding dress by Helen, invitations by Jess, Max's mum to organise the cake, a ceilidh, food, photos and bar TBA.' He paused. 'There, you see. Fantastic. You've already done most of it.'

Molly looked up at him, loving his naïve optimism. 'That's provisional. We've got about a million other things to organise.'

Nick bent down and kissed her tired, weary lips. 'TBA,' he said. 'Piece of cake.'

Which sparked something deep in Molly's fuddled brain. 'Oh God, yes, cake,' she said, grabbing a pen and pulling the notebook towards her. 'I've got to buy cake boxes to send to the people who can't come.'

Max arrived at Jess's cottage at around the same time as she did; the difference being that Max looked fresh as a daisy, was freshly shaved and was carrying a huge bunch of flowers and a helium balloon, whereas Jess had Bassa, a bag full of wedding magazines and the makings of a really good headache.

'I've come to say that I'm sorry,' he said, as she locked up her car and headed inside. 'I didn't mean to upset you today.'

Jess waved the words away and carried on walking. 'You didn't upset me, Max, you lied to me, there's a huge difference.'

She dipped into her pocket to retrieve her house keys, getting tangled up with her bag and Bassa's expanding lead as she did.

'Here, do you want me to take Bas and your bag?' he offered as she struggled to unlock the front door.

'No, you're fine. It'll take longer than doing it myself.'

He leaned in closer. 'I didn't think you'd understand.'

Jess sighed. 'You didn't give me the chance to understand.

And since when have I been the kind of person that flies off the handle?'

Max held the flowers out towards her. 'Pax?' he said. They were her favourites, sunflowers and the purplest of purple irises.

Jess smiled despite herself and shook her head. She had already got her hands well and truly full with the bag and the dog. 'Max, the flowers are lovely but for future reference, please just tell me the truth, even if it hurts, rather than any number of lies. If you had told me about going to see your mum and dad I would have been fine about it.'

They stood awkwardly in the hallway, Bassa eager to be in, Jess half in and half out of her door, Max still holding the flowers out in front of him like a shield.

'I'm sorry. I know it's ancient history but my ex, Lucy, was always jealous of how well I got on with my parents,' Max said. 'She was always telling me that I neglected her.'

'Well, I'm not Lucy,' said Jess. 'And I'm close to my parents too.'

'Is it all right if I come in?' he asked.

Jess hesitated, just long enough for him to look uncomfortable.

'I thought you were going to have an early night. Didn't you tell me that you'd got to be in to work by five today and tomorrow?' said Jess, in a low voice.

Max looked contrite. 'Just tomorrow. I'm sorry. I don't know what else to say. I don't have to stay if you don't want me to. I didn't mean to hurt you. Really – I'm crap at relationships.'

He looked so deflated that Jess stood to one side. 'Come on in. Just don't lie to me again. All right?'

He kissed her. 'Okay.' As he stepped past her Max switched on the lights and then bent down to unclip Bassa, who belted

66

off into the kitchen. 'He looks pleased to be home. How did it go with your mother?'

Jess lifted a hand to silence him. 'Wait, while we're on the subject of the truth, Max, I need to be honest with you too.' Now she had all his attention.

'What do you mean?' he asked, looking anxious.

Jess reached into her pocket and pulled out the little pouch with her engagement ring in it. 'I've been trying to think of ways to tell you without hurting your feelings.'

Max's face turned ashen. 'What?' he murmured and Jess realised with a start that he thought she was giving him back his ring, changing her mind. Her expression softened.

'Don't look so worried,' she said gently. 'I was only wondering if you would mind if we changed my engagement ring?'

Max sighed with what she guessed was relief. 'What, is it too big? I thought it fitted perfectly?'

'It does, but it's just that I'm not very keen on the design. It's quite big and cumbersome, and I'd really like to have a ring I want to wear all the time. It would be nice to have something that we'd chosen together. Don't you think?'

'Oh,' he said, sounding a bit put out. 'But I thought you really liked it.'

Jess wasn't quite sure what to say next; she had rather assumed that Max's reaction would be something along the lines of *okay, sure – let's go and change it*, not to have to justify why she didn't like it.

'It's not my kind of thing. The design I mean,' she said, feeling increasingly awkward. 'And it's a bit big for my hands, don't you think?' She spread her fingers to make the point. 'Especially once I've got a wedding ring on as well.'

'Well, if you don't like it, you should have said something when I gave it to you,' he said.

Jess tried out a smile and a different tactic. 'How would that have sounded? *Yes, of course I'll marry you, but I hate the ring?*'

He was about to say something but Jess decided that it might be better if she kept on talking. 'I was so excited and so blown away by how romantic and how lovely it all was,' she said gently, 'The whole thing on the beach was so perfect, that the ring was – was –' She felt around to find the right word without saying something that would make things any worse.

'Almost secondary?' suggested Max.

'Something like that,' said Jess. 'It was such an amazing moment that I wasn't really thinking about the ring at all, I was thinking about us – the future – all those things.'

'So what kind of ring would you prefer? I want you to have something you like, obviously.'

'Couldn't we go and choose it together?'

Max looked uncomfortable. 'Well, not really – I bought it from this little independent jewellery designer in Cambridge. Everything they make there is a one off. I'm not sure when they're open. How about if you tell me the kind of thing you'd like and I'll bring a selection of rings home and you can choose one?'

'Or maybe we could call them, arrange to take a trip over there.' Jess looked up at his face. 'Surely they won't let you just bring a tray of rings home?'

Max shifted his weight, looking ill at ease. 'I'm almost certain they won't mind. They know me there. I've bought quite a few things from them over the years, cufflinks and presents for friends and things for my mother. Christmases, birthdays. They're very good. And I want it to be something special, not just picked from hundreds of others, mass-produced, from any old jewellers.'

68

It struck Jess that Max didn't want her to know how much the ring cost; that had to be why he didn't want her to go and choose one for herself. The thought made her smile; he could so old-fashioned at times, bless him. Maybe this was the time to gratefully accept without pushing him any harder.

She took a deep breath. 'That's a lovely thought, Max, and I do appreciate it. If they'll do that, then of course. Okay – it'll be lovely.'

'So what sort of ring would you like?'

Jess held out her hands for him to look at. 'Something more delicate, not quite so chunky, maybe tiny diamonds or a solitaire. And maybe white gold? I've got quite small hands. What do you think?'

Max nodded. 'Yes, of course, yes, you're right.' And for the first time since she had seen him by the car he smiled. 'I promise I'll sort that on Monday. And I'm sorry.'

'For?'

'For lying to you, for not choosing the right ring and I can see exactly what you mean about it not being right for you.'

'You can?'

He nodded and then he kissed her gently. 'I'll put it right, I promise. Now I don't know about you but I'm famished. How about I order us a take-away while you tell me all about how it went with your mother today?'

Molly meanwhile had settled back into a bath with only her head above the water. Nick had put bubbles in it that he'd bought her last time he was in Paris and the water smelt of freesias and honeysuckle.

She had a glass of wine on the go and was listening to Nina Simone's voice rising up the stairs from the hi-fi in the sitting room below, the music as perfect and smooth as spun silk. 'If we ever get married I'd like to have this at our wedding,' Molly said.

'I thought you were bored with organising weddings,' said Nick from the other end of the bath. He'd got himself a margarita and a book propped up precariously on the soap rack.

'Yes, but ours would be different. I wouldn't have to worry about asking what anyone else wanted for a start.'

'Oh, that's nice,' he said, pretending to take the hump. 'So, I don't get an opinion?'

'You know what I mean – we could have just what we liked.' She paused. 'It seems so weird. My baby is getting married.'

'So you said. It could be worse,' Nick said. 'She could be making you a granny.'

Molly ignored him. 'And we don't really know anything about Max.'

'We don't have to.' Nick topped up the hot water.

'It doesn't seem fair that all those years have gone. One minute they're just babies and then they're at school and getting jobs and before you know it they're getting married,' said Molly, feeling the tears welling up. 'It's all gone too quickly. I've never organised anyone else's wedding before. Looking at all those lists today, what exactly does the mother of the bride do?'

'By the look on your face, mostly cry and panic.'

'I totally misread this thing with Max and Jess – I didn't think she was that serious about him.'

'You don't like him very much, do you?'

'I don't really know him,' said Molly with affected coolness.

'Molly?' Nick looked sceptical.

'Well, we've only seen him a couple of times, haven't we? He just doesn't seem Jess's type at all.'

'Maybe he's her grown-up choice – like there's a moment

you stop going for gooey puddings and take the cheese and biscuits or start thinking that broccoli and broad beans are really nice?'

Molly raised her eyebrows. 'So Max is Jess's pick from the adult menu?'

'Just a thought.'

Molly wasn't convinced. 'I suppose at least it means that Jessie is over Glenn.'

'The one who went off to America?'

'Broke her heart. I was really worried that after he went she might get back with Will – you remember the one who used to shred beer mats and tissues?'

'Or go to Goa with Beano?' said Nick.

'Oh God, I'd forgotten about that. Beano is lovely though. He always reminds me of a daddy-longlegs; he's so skinny and gangly.'

'And can drink, smoke and snort his way through life with an enthusiasm that startled even the most robust of us. So, when's Jess moving in with Max and do we need to hire a van?'

'Apparently not, they're waiting until after they're married to move in together.'

'A bit Victorian, isn't it?' said Nick.

'Max is having his place redecorated, but the lease is up on the cottage Jess's renting so she's got to find somewhere. Mr Petrovsky, her landlord, is really nice, but he needs her to move out so that he can move his daughter and her husband and their new baby in.' Molly sat up. 'You don't think that's why Jess is marrying Max, do you? To get a house?'

'Don't be silly; she's got loads of friends and places to stay if she needed to. She could move back here for a few weeks until she found somewhere if she wanted to.'

'I already told her that.' Molly settled back in the bath.

'*Married,*' she murmured after a few seconds. 'It sounds such a big thing for Jess to be doing.'

Nick peered at her. 'Before you say anything *we're not getting married,* all right? So don't ask.'

'Oh, spoilsport,' Molly teased. 'I was thinking we could maybe have a double wedding. Me and you, Jessica and Max.'

'I can't see Jess wearing that one, can you?'

Molly laughed. 'No, me neither, although all my friends think it's high time you made a respectable woman of me.'

'It'd take a lot more than getting married,' Nick said. 'And besides I like what we've got. If it ain't broke don't fix it, is what I say.'

'They want to buy hats.'

'Uh-huh, and now that Jess is getting married they'll have their chance.'

'You're all heart,' said Molly. She took another sip of wine and slipped back amongst the bubbles.

'So what are you thinking now?'

'Here's to marriage.'

Nick winced and topped up his glass. 'Here's to spending the rest of my life living in sin with you.'

Molly lifted her eyebrows. He grinned and so Molly relented. 'Okay, you win. I'll drink to that,' she conceded, lifting her glass. 'Although if we *are* ever going to get married can we do it before I look like ET in the wedding photos?'

It was Nick's turn to lift his eyebrows. He opened his mouth to speak but Molly cut him short. 'Don't you dare say it,' she said.

Nick, still grinning, sunk down beneath the water like a great hairy whale.

*　*　*

Meanwhile in the sitting room of Jess's cottage, Max was finishing off the last of the Singapore noodles and nodding as Jess came to the end of the edited highlights of eight solid hours of planning and a lifetime's worth of imagining what her wedding day might be like.

'So, what do you think?' she said breathlessly. 'Assuming we pass on the radio station's offer of following us around every step of the way, and my dad arm-wrestling everyone for discount.'

'What's Vanguard Hall like?'

Jess smiled. 'Absolutely lovely. Really quirky and magical. Me and mum have been there loads of times to look round the gardens. It would be perfect – you'll love it.'

Max tipped his head, suggesting to Jess that he wanted to hear more.

'It's near Holt and the estate is owned by a guy called Bert, who's part eco-warrior and part crusty old aristo. There's the farm, which is huge, and then the main house, which is this weird Gothic pile with all sorts of odds and ends tacked on, and they've got greenhouses, a fantastic walled garden – the farm is organic – and there's this amazing old Tythe Barn which Bert says we can have for the reception. They use it as a tearoom in the summer – it's got this spectacular beamed roof. The whole place is like something off a picture post-card. Jack's worked there as a gardener since he left horticultural college. He's got this tiny little cottage in the grounds that looks like something out of Hansel and Gretel.

And they've got the most fabulous gardens designed by Bertie's wife Freya, a bluebell wood, a lake and loads of deer and they've got sculptures in the woods that Freya and her friends made – they are amazing, magical. Bert opens it up to the public two or three weekends a year for charity. It will make the most perfect place for a winter wedding. Trust me, you'll love it. And we need to get moving. I've got a list.' Jess leaned over the side of the sofa and pulled out a notebook. 'We haven't got that long to sort it all out.'

Max pulled a face. 'I'm not really sure about all this dippy-hippy business.'

Jess stared at him and laughed. 'What *dippy-hippy* business?'

'Well, the whole Tythe Barn, bluebell wood, humanist wedding thing. I thought we'd just have a proper traditional church wedding.'

'Max, you're divorced and I'm an atheist.'

Max looked perplexed. 'And?'

'And so the best we could probably hope for is a church blessing and I'm not sure how likely that is when I tell the vicar I don't believe in God.'

'You could always lie.'

Jess stared at him, trying to work out whether or not he was joking.

'I mean, what would it matter?' Max continued. 'Surely not everyone who has a church wedding is a regular church-goer or a devout Christian? And in your case God can't write it all down in a big book and use it against you later, because you don't believe in him.'

'And you do?' snapped Jess.

'Well no, not really, I believe in something, but my parents –' he began.

'I am *not* lying on our wedding day. And at a humanist wedding we would still have vows and make promises and we can choose readings and music – it's just more personal. We help to write them.'

Max looked even more sceptical.

'All right, how about we just go for a straight registry office do?'

Max shook his head. 'I don't think so, do you? And I also think we ought to think very carefully before we decide against the idea of getting the radio station involved.'

Jess laughed. 'Tell me you're joking. You *are* joking, aren't you?'

'I'm just saying maybe we ought to look into it. And it would be fun, don't you think? It could work in our favour.'

Jess waited to hear just how Max thought that might work out.

'Maybe you should talk to your mum about it,' he said, scraping the final nest of noodles into his mouth. 'The same with the chance of discount. It wouldn't hurt to ask, would it?'

Jess shook her head. 'What about your parents? I thought they were raving traditionalists – wouldn't they hate all that kind of thing?'

Max looked hurt. 'Just because they're old-fashioned doesn't mean they're not broad-minded.'

Jess sighed. 'They'll need to be if they're working with Mum's lot.'

Chapter Eight

The following weekend Jonathon was sitting at Molly's dining table, having eaten a huge Sunday lunch, waxing lyrical about the virtues of media sponsorship and the free market economy.

'I think that making a radio feature about the wedding would be a splendid idea,' Jonathon said to Max, while topping up his wine. 'And why not see what we can sort out discount-wise?' Turning to Molly, he added, 'And of course it would be nice to have it recorded for posterity, as well. Obviously. What sort of thing has your marketing department got in mind?'

Molly took a deep breath but Max was ahead of her.

'I agree with Jonathon,' he said. 'It would be wonderful to have it recorded for posterity.'

The day was not going well. It had started going down-hill at around half past eleven – half an hour earlier than planned – when Molly had looked out of the kitchen window and seen her ex-husband parking his Mercedes across the drive. Wiping her hands on a tea towel she had hurried outside.

'Jonathon, do you mind not parking there? Jess and Max haven't arrived yet. Could you bring it in? You're blocking the whole driveway.'

The window of the brand-new Mercedes glided silently downwards and framed her ex-husband in the driver's seat. He was balder and fatter and ruddier-faced than the last time she had seen him, and was wearing a paisley cravat with a cream linen jacket and a horrible pale lilac shirt. No doubt a Marnie makeover.

Jonathon said, 'It'll be fine here. They can park on the verge. It's too tucked up round the back. I'll scrape the paintwork on all those bloody bushes.'

Molly was about to protest when she noticed that Marnie was in the passenger seat and there was someone else sitting in the back. Nick meanwhile had come out to watch Jonathon's manoeuvres. Currently Jonathon was making a great job of ruining their grass as he shunted the car backwards and forwards until he was satisfied with his positioning. When he climbed out the drive was completely blocked.

'I see Jonathon's arrived,' Nick said somewhat unnecessarily. 'Any particular reason why he wants to blockade us in?'

'Probably so we can't make a run for it,' said Molly grimly, turning back towards the house. 'He's brought reinforcements.'

'Not the missus, we *are* honoured,' said Nick.

Molly flicked him with the tea towel.

Marnie, size six, spray-tanned and dressed as if she was out for a day at Ascot, waited for Jonathon to help her out of the car. She was wearing a black and white sleeveless silk dress, with a little jacket thrown over her shoulders, along with high-heeled strappy white mules and a matching clutch bag. All her jewellery – earrings, bracelet, necklace, everything – matched.

There was nothing remotely cuddly or welcoming about

78

the second Mrs Foster. Marnie looked for all the world as if she had been made by stretching chamois leather over a wire coathanger. Assisted by Jonathon, she picked her way across the gravel as if she were tiptoeing through a lake of raw sewage.

'Marnie, how nice. We weren't expecting you,' said Molly, painting on a polite smile.

Marnie smiled back, or at least she bared her perfectly capped teeth. 'Molly,' she purred, looking her up and down. 'I told Jonathon that he really ought to ring but he didn't think you'd mind my coming, you know what he's like. The more the merrier, he said.'

Molly watched Marnie's immobile, wrinkle-free face. There was nothing even remotely merry about Marnie.

'Jonathon thought it might be useful if I came along to help out, give you all a hand. We don't want any disasters on JJ's special day, now do we?' she said.

No one amongst their immediate family or friends had ever called Jessica 'JJ'. It was Marnie's attempt to show Molly that she had some sort of special relationship with her daughter. And all the while Molly kept on smiling, making every effort to hide just how much Marnie irritated her.

'Oh, by the way, this is Noonoo Jacobson,' Marnie continued as a woman the size of a bull eased herself carefully out of the back of the car. 'Noonoo was the wedding co-ordinator for my daughter Mimi's wedding.'

'Do any of these people have proper names?' said Nick sotto voce as Noonoo, who was carrying a large portfolio, made her way across the mangled verge on tiny, tiny feet.

As she reached them Noonoo swung the strap of her chic black carrying case up over her shoulder, and extending both tiny hands in presidential fashion gave Molly the limpest, warmest, most moist handshake she had encountered since she had interviewed Boris the gay tag-team wrestler back in '89.

'I'm delighted to meet you, most people just call me Noo,' she simpered, from a Cupid's-bow mouth balanced above a stack of chins. 'I'm absolutely sure that together we can make JJ and Max's *the* most perfect wedding experience. I've heard so much about you and JJ, oh and you must be Nick,' she said, little moist hands moving on to clasp him to her bosom.

'Actually,' said Molly, 'Jess and I have already sorted a lot of it out –'

But no one was listening.

Nick smiled and wriggled free. 'If you'll excuse me I need to get back inside. I'm in charge of the food,' and then to Molly, he added, 'I'd better go and put some more potatoes in.'

'Marnie has become a real friend,' said Noonoo to no one in particular.

'Looks more like her lunch,' said Nick under his breath, as Molly guided everyone through into the kitchen. It was quite crowded, and despite Molly's best efforts, no one seemed to want to go through into the sitting room or the dining room; instead they grouped round the kitchen table and generally got in the way.

Gamely Molly started on a round of social chitchat and offering people drinks. Nick was about to start peeling more potatoes when Noonoo announced that she and Marnie were both on a diet – remarkably the same one, so that there was no need to go to the trouble of preparing extra food. The diet involved eating only orange foods on Sunday, and some kind of strange combination of colours and supplements the rest of the week. Victoria Beckham was very keen on it apparently, and Noonoo had been taught the principles by a Taoist convert called Alan.

Not thoroughly enough, thought Molly darkly, as Noonoo squeezed past her.

Both women had brought along little pots of parboiled carrot sticks and steamed pepper to nibble on and, as Nick observed as he disappeared off to set the dining-room table, presumably Noonoo could top up in the week by snacking on her clients.

Jonathon had brought a couple of bottles of champagne, which he wanted someone to put in the fridge. Noo wanted to explain why they could drink it, despite it not being orange, Marnie wanted to nose around Molly's house so she could sneer and Molly was getting hotter and more stressed.

Jess and Max showed up just before twelve. Jess arrived first, carrying two bottles of wine and a big dish of home-made tiramisu.

'Some idiot has parked right across the drive,' she said crossly, as she slid dessert onto the kitchen table. 'We couldn't get in. Max has had to park up the road.'

'Jessica, Puss,' said Jonathon, coming over to greet her before Molly could explain. 'Did you see the new car?'

'I could hardly miss it,' grumbled Jess. 'We nearly ran into it. Why did you leave it there?'

Jonathon hugged her. 'And where is this man of yours?'

'Halfway up to the bypass. Why don't you buy a car you can park?'

Marnie laughed, air-kissing for England. 'JJ darling, how lovely to see you. You know how your father loves his cars.'

Jess shook her head in frustration, while Marnie set about introducing Noonoo. Jess gave Molly a wild panicky look as Marnie started to explain who Noo was.

'I'm not sure that we'd thought about having a –' she began, but Marnie wasn't planning to be thwarted.

'Noo is an absolute angel, sweetie. And having a planner

takes all the aggravation out of the arrangements and obviously nothing's settled yet, so why don't you just hear what she's got to say and then you can make your mind up?'

'Actually, Mum and I –' But any protest was whisked away by the arrival of Max with Bassa on his leash. Bas was wildly excited to see everyone and started to yip and bark and wag.

Molly was putting the tiramisu in the fridge when Marnie started whining. 'Oh darling,' she complained stepping back, holding a hand to her face. 'You know that I'm allergic to dogs.'

'I'm sorry,' said Jess, catching hold of the lead and reeling Bassa in. 'Sorry, sorry – we didn't know you were going to be here.'

Jess glanced across at Molly, who held up a hand. 'We'll put him in the conservatory with Milo; I'm sure he won't mind sharing his bed and biscuits.'

'Oh, do you have a dog too?' asked Noonoo, staring down at Bassa as if there was a fair chance that he might explode. Bassa had his own reply in mind. Giving Molly a knowing look he wandered across the kitchen, cocked his leg, and peed all over Noo's precious portfolio. It took a split second for everyone to register what he'd done.

Noonoo shrieked, 'Oh, my God, oh, my God! It's hand-tooled leather!' while Molly leapt in with kitchen roll, struggling with an altogether inappropriate fit of giggles, as she started to mop up the spreading puddle; good old Bassa, she couldn't have put it better herself.

Picking up the portfolio Jess started machine-gunning apologies, while Max scooped up Bassa and bundled him through into the conservatory. In amongst it all Nick appeared with a tray of glasses. 'Anyone like a sherry?'

*   *   *

Once calm had been restored and they had all eaten, Noo got to her feet and started to unpack her portfolio, arranging things on an easel, which Jonathon had brought in from the car. It wasn't exactly how Molly had expected lunch to end, nor come to that how she had expected her discussions with Jonathon about Jessica's wedding to go, but the way the day was shaping up Molly decided it was pointless fighting it.

'Where's the ring?' asked Marnie conversationally, as Noo finished her arranging. 'Or isn't a ring what you do these days? I know fashions change – although personally I've never thought that diamonds date.' She laughed.

Molly looked up, wondering what Jess would say. Jess smiled coyly. 'Well, we've chosen it. It was wonderful – the jeweller let Max bring a tray of rings home so we could choose it together – but I haven't got it at the moment. It was a bit big so Max took it back to have it altered.'

'I'm going to pick it up when it's been resized,' explained Max.

Molly smiled. 'What's it like?' she asked encouragingly.

Max glanced at Jessica, who beamed. 'It's absolutely perfect. It's white gold with this lovely twist in the metal, a bit like a wave, and in the curve of the twist there is a solitaire diamond. It's lovely and I'm so pleased with it.' And as she spoke Jessica's gaze met Max's, who reddened furiously and caught hold of her hand.

'It's perfect, just like Jess,' he said.

Molly felt herself smiling.

'We wanted something that Jess loved and would wear every single day – something really special.'

Jess's smile held. 'And it is,' she murmured. 'It's beautiful.'

Molly felt the tears welling up and for a moment she glanced across at Jonathon, whose eyes were glittering. Maybe he wasn't that bad after all. Even if they didn't love each other anymore they both loved their precious girl. Eyes twinkling, Max pressed Jess's fingers to his lips. Molly had never seen Jess look so happy.

'Sounds like the perfect time for a toast, I reckon,' said Jonathon, sniffing away the emotion. 'I think we should open the champagne.'

Nick obliged by bringing in the glasses and handing the bottle over to Jonathon so that he could pop the cork.

Once everyone had settled down Noonoo stood up, taking a second or two to compose herself and wait for hush before she opened up a flip chart. On the first page in a fancy font it said, 'Welcome to your Perfect Wedding'.

A look went round the table between Molly, Nick and Jess.

'My name is Noo Jacobson, and I'm a wedding planner and civil partnership co-ordinator,' said Noo, as if no one could have guessed.

For one glorious moment Molly thought Noo was going to add, 'And I'm an alcoholic,' which, while it wasn't particularly funny in itself, struck her as hilarious. Across the table she caught Jess's eye – apparently a bizarre sense of humour was some sort of genetic failing because she too was rolling her eyes and trying to suppress a giggle.

Molly bit her lip; obviously Noo was going to give them the whole show whether they wanted it or not.

'I successfully completed my training four years ago after a successful career in retail management – I have a wealth of experience and a solid track record in co-ordinating weddings alongside many other private and personal family events. Some time ago I realised I had a natural gift for creating the perfect wedding scenario for my clients and have specialised ever since.'

Molly felt her heart sink. This was a carefully rehearsed

presentation more suited to an audience of fifty rather than the six of them gathered around Molly's dining table. Alongside Jonathon, Marnie was saying, 'I really wish that I'd known about Noo when we organised our wedding.'

Jonathon smiled wryly at no one in particular. 'Me too, it would have saved me hours of listening to you agonising over every last detail and spending God knows how much on dresses and all the accessories, shoes, bags, hats – I mean how many outfits did you end up buying in the end? Five, six?'

Marnie shushed him furiously, while Noo continued, 'I can provide my clients with almost any service, anything they require, both in the UK and abroad, including up-to-date advice on local customs, residency rules, legalities and visa requirements. So far I've arranged weddings in the Canaries, the Caribbean, Cyprus, the Maldives and Wales. My clients and I go on a voyage of discovery together, almost a spiritual quest to achieve their perfect day – and we often end up as friends, in fact one couple actually invited me to join them on their honeymoon.'

Molly closed her eyes; it was an image too far.

'Anyway I'm here today to introduce you all to Joyful Heart Weddings,' she said, hands together in front of her as if she was about to give a sermon. 'We offer a wide range of traditional and concept weddings to a very discerning clientele. Marnie was kind enough to suggest that I come and talk to you about our service today.' She nodded at Marnie, who smiled graciously.

'First of all the obvious advantages to a busy working woman and her family, where everyone has numerous commitments with little time to spare, is that I can take all the hard work out of the wedding event for you. I have access to a wide database of suppliers, services and ideas. We can search out all those special little touches you'd like for your perfect day and present them to you in a complete managed package for one inclusive price with no hidden extras. We can stage-manage the entire event for you as well, offering peace of mind with our fully bonded all-inclusive insurance. And should you require it, besides the venue, the catering and all that wedding arrangements entail, we can even arrange that special honeymoon if you would like us to.'

Noonoo, mid-flow, flipped the page on the chart to a picture of a traditional wedding, the bride and groom standing in front of a church with their family. Molly heard Jess groan.

'Can we just stop a minute here please?' said Molly, jumping into a split second's silence between the words. 'I mean, I appreciate that this all looks very impressive and I hate to rain on your parade, but Jess and I have already spent hours planning the wedding.'

'Yes, we're more or less there,' said Jess.

There was a little pause, during which Marnie looked daggers at Molly. Jonathon said, 'Molly, I know you mean well but Marnie went to an awful lot of trouble to arrange for Noo to come over today and I think we should at least look at what she has to offer. Marnie said the service Noo provided was very good – you have to admit Mimi's wedding was wonderful.'

Marnie was nodding.

Yes, who could forget the unfortunate Mimi stuffed, corseted and magic-knickered into a shiny satin dress that showed every crease, wrinkle and roll of what lay beneath, a dress that would have looked fabulous on Marnie but was terrifying on someone shaped like an American refrigerator.

Mimi, who apparently suffered with her glands, had had her lank, greasy hair scraped up under a tiara the size of the Taj Mahal and clutched a bouquet shaped like a swan, a nod apparently to the ugly duckling made good. Everything had been swan-shaped, now Molly came to think about it.

The church had had so many flowers in it that guests could barely breathe for pollen and perfume, and the bridal couple and their twelve bridesmaids – having been driven to the church in a fleet of vintage Rollers – had been whisked away to their honeymoon in a hot-air balloon, from which Mimi had thrown her bouquet, nearly blinding the video cameraman when it hit him square in the lens.

Molly had a photograph of the happy couple grinning at the camera, Mimi arm-in-arm with a short, skinny, ginger boy with bad skin, buck teeth and a bulbous nose. They lived in Wales now; apparently he was something big in animal feed and a real catch. Molly remembered thinking if she'd caught him, she'd have thrown him back.

She would have felt sorry for Mimi, if Mimi hadn't been a spiteful, selfish, peevish creature, who had tortured Jess from the moment they'd met.

'What do you say, Max?' asked Jonathon, the sound of his voice breaking into Molly's thoughts. 'Noo sound like a good idea to you?'

'It's fine by me,' Max said. 'I've already told Jess that she can have anything she wants. After all, it's her big day and she already said that she and Molly are very busy. And I'm up to my eyes.' He turned to Jess, who was staring at him open-mouthed. 'Well, you said you needed help,' he pointed out. 'And now you've got it.'

Noo took that as a cue and launched straight back into the script. 'While our main business is in the traditional market, we've done a lot more themed weddings in the last few years and have several more in the pipeline. A theme helps set the tone and establishes a style for the whole event, as well as making your wedding stand out from the crowd. It's also more fun for your guests.' Noo flicked over another page. 'The discerning couple are becoming more and more adventurous. This summer we did our first Guys and Dolls wedding, followed by Gangsters and Molls.'

Molly stared at a wedding party all dressed up in mobster gear, the guests arranged around a 1930s V8 Ford complete with running boards. The bride and groom looked like extras from 'Bugsy Malone'.

'And we've just done our first Glenn Miller wedding.' Noo flipped the page again to show the grainy interior of an aircraft hangar hung with bunting and banners. The buffet table, set with sausage rolls and jugs of squash, looked like it was laid out for VE Day. 'These days your wedding celebrations can be almost anything you can imagine. Next year we've got a Teddy Bears' Picnic wedding and a Moulin Rouge civil partnership – you should see the outfits.'

While Max, Jonathon and Marnie appeared to be totally enraptured by Noo's presentation, Molly, Nick, and Jess stared at each other in a mix of disbelief and horror.

There were railway weddings, pantomime weddings, colour-themed weddings, football team weddings, weddings for the over 50s and finally what Noo referred to in hushed tones as *the traditional family package* which seemed to involve smiling plump girls marrying jolly bald men dressed in grey morning suits.

'So you can arrange for us to have a church wedding?' said Max enthusiastically.

Noonoo, tiny hands still clasped, nodded. 'Certainly, if that is what you want. I mean if you're prepared to pay we can do more or less anything.'

'See,' said Max triumphantly.

'Well, there we are then, seems to me that we've got the perfect solution,' said Jonathon, topping up his champagne. 'Takes all the sweat out of it. Nonoo can arrange the wedding and all the details,' Jonathon turned to his daughter. 'I was thinking around a hundred guests. I appreciate I'm going to have to take the lion's share of this – Now about the radio station, Molly, what do you think they can offer us?'

'Us?' Molly stared at him. 'Jonathon, we are arranging our daughter's wedding, not negotiating a contract for an engineering company.'

He looked puzzled.

And then Jess said, 'Dad, please don't think I'm being ungrateful but I really don't want a themed wedding. I spoke to Jack last week and Bertie, who owns Vanguard Hall has offered to let us use it for the recepion, and my friend Helen is going to make my dress. And then the guys in the design studio where I work said they'd print all the stationery as a wedding present –'

Marnie looked totally aghast and to be fair Max didn't look much better.

'Jess,' said Max.' You heard your father. And you saw how lovely all those weddings that Noo's arranged are. I thought we'd agreed that we want the whole thing to be really special, didn't we?'

'Of course I want it to be special,' snapped Jess, 'but I'm not getting married in a church and I don't want to end up at some bloody hotel dressed up as Vera Lynn while someone from EAA records the whole thing for bloody posterity with commercial breaks to sell double glazing.'

'You're getting overwrought,' said Marnie. 'It's understandable, we've all been there, darling. There is a lot of pressure when you're getting married.'

Jess looked around in frustration. 'I'm not overwrought – I'm just telling you what's going to happen.'

'It all sounds very cut-price to me,' snipped Marnie. 'You'll be asking me to help out with the sandwiches next. And if it's going to be on the radio, we don't want to let the side down, do we?'

And then Max said, 'Jess, my parents are very traditional. If we don't have a church service then they won't think it's a proper wedding. And I suppose I was thinking traditional too – white lace, doves, orange blossom and morning suits. A real wedding.'

'It's a shame you didn't say all this before when I asked you what kind of wedding you wanted,' growled Jess.

'I just want a proper wedding. I thought you understood that.'

'With me dressed up as a meringue?' said Jess grimly.

Max smiled. 'No, you just being as beautiful as you always are.'

'Ahhh,' Noo sighed. 'Isn't that lovely.'

Molly suppressed the desire to lean across the table and punch her.

'So a classic white wedding it is then,' Noo continued. 'I have to say that in my opinion, it does take some beating.'

Marnie clapped her hands together in what Molly took to be pure delight. 'Well, that's that sorted out. Oh, I'm so glad that we came over. This is going to be such fun, JJ. Noo and I found the most wonderful dress for Mimi from this lovely shop in Norwich – they've got a branch in Bond Street and they are just *so* good.'

Noo was nodding. 'We found that it's easiest if we book an evening in the shop. Wasn't the lady who owns it a sweetheart, Marnie? She couldn't have been kinder. And they provide canapés and champagne. It was a completely lovely experience, wasn't it?'

Jess looked at Molly, her expression not unlike the time she had had to have a broken arm set under local anaesthetic.

'And given the timescale we really must sort out a venue as our top priority.' Noo pulled out a diary. 'I'll run through a few local possibilities with you this afternoon if you like, but we actually need to arrange those visits ASAP. Time is of the essence here. Marnie has been wonderful arranging today,' Noo added conspiratorially.

'Obviously I was only too happy to help,' Marnie simpered. 'I think we all appreciate that you're busy, Molly, and what with Jess working full-time too, and we *did* do Mimi's wedding last year. Now, about a date.' She pulled a Palm Pilot out of her clutch bag.

'I was thinking the first weekend in December,' said Max, 'so we don't clash with people's Christmas plans.' At which point Marnie started poking the screen of her handheld with a little stylus.

Jess hadn't moved. Molly felt her hackles rising; she had never felt so marginalised in all her life.

'Morning or afternoon?' said Noo, glancing down at her calendar.

Jess meanwhile looked as if she was drowning, while across the table Jonathon was busy helping himself to Nick's best port.

'Wait, can we just stop and take this more slowly?' said Molly. 'I feel we're being railroaded here.'

Marnie gave her a murderous look. 'Railroaded? I really don't think you understand, Molly. We have to get moving – it's touch and go now whether we'll be able to get a decent venue.'

'I'm not sure if you missed this but we've already got a venue,' Molly said slowly, in case Marnie missed it again. 'Jack's boss has said we can use Vanguard Hall.'

'And it's perfect,' said Jess.

'I understand exactly what you're saying but we should still look at some others.' Noo smiled at Max and Jonathon. 'I think we should keep our options open, don't you?'

Jess got up, wearing a fixed smile. 'If you'll excuse me, I think I'm going to go and let Bassa out,' she said, easing her way around the table.

'Jess?' said Molly. 'Are you all right?'

Jess looked back over her shoulder. 'I need to clear my head. Too much champagne,' she said in a way that made Molly more anxious rather than less. 'I won't be long.'

'Right,' said Noo. 'Well, in that case, maybe we should talk about venues? And shall I leave it to you to contact the church or would you prefer me to do it?'

'Whoa there,' said Molly, holding up her hands as if she was trying to hold up a freight train. 'Surely the whole point of this is that we do it together?'

She glanced anxiously at Jess, who was heading outside.

Jonathon, Max, Noonoo and Marnie all turned to look at Molly. 'I don't understand,' said Marnie. 'I thought we were all singing off the same hymn sheet here.'

'Ah yes, now that's something else we need to talk about,' said Noo, grabbing a pencil. 'Which hymns do you want?'

Molly got up to go out after Jess but Max caught her arm. 'It's all right,' he said gently. 'I'll go.'

Molly was about to protest and then realised with a horrible sinking feeling that this was how it was going to be from now on. Max and Jess, Jess and Max. Max was going to be her husband and he would be looking after Jess from now on. And despite the fact that Jess was all grown-up and that over the years Molly had watched boyfriends come and go, watched Jess's heart being broken, watched her break hearts of her own, watched the chasing and the dating, the making-up and the tears, and shared the confidences and laughter, cursed the phone calls, worried when she had stayed out late, all those things they had shared, Molly realised that this was some kind of end; her heart ached. The shock of it must have registered on her face because Max said, 'Unless of course you want to go?'

Molly shook her head. 'No, you're fine,' she said with forced lightness. 'You go.' And with that, she sat down like someone had knocked all the wind out of her.

Jess meanwhile made her way across the garden towards the orchard, arms wrapped tight around her waist, torn between feeling furious and weepy and silly. Bassa was only too happy to come along for the emotional rollercoaster ride, running backwards and forwards across the lawn, weeing and sniffing, while Milo, Molly's mastiff, ambled alongside her, keeping watch.

Surely when you got married it was meant to be the bride's day – *her* day, *her* wedding. The trouble was if she said it out loud, just how childish and spoilt did it sound? Obviously the whole thing was bigger than just her – *obviously*, but surely her opinion was meant to be important? Actually, wasn't she supposed to have the casting vote?

Jess sniffed away a furious tear. Trust Marnie to muscle in on the act. And who the hell was bloody Noonoo? She picked a windfall apple up from the grass and threw it at one of the fruit trees, where it exploded in a satisfying blood-bath of pip and pulp and peel. Jess was so angry and so upset that she didn't hear Max making his way across the grass behind her.

'You okay?' he asked, making her jump with surprise.

'No,' she said, struggling not to burst into tears.

He looked more concerned. 'What's the matter? You do look a bit pale. Are you all right?'

Sometimes men can be so slow on the uptake, Jess thought. 'No, I'm not all right.'

He peered at her. 'Too much champagne?'

'No, not too much champagne. I'm furious. This is crazy. Me and mum have already sorted all this out,' she growled. 'Vanguard Hall is beautiful and I really want Helen to make my dress and who the fuck is Noonoo? And whoever thought that naming someone after a comfort blanket was a great idea?' She threw another apple as hard as she could across the garden and then looked up at Max. He had a great big grin on his face. She realised how stupid it all sounded and despite how put-upon she felt, Jess laughed. Max laughed too and pulled her in tight against him and then she started to cry.

'It's not funny,' she sniffled between tears. 'I'm just so annoyed with Marnie and Noo and my dad. I want this to be *our* wedding, not another set of pictures Noo can paste into her Weddings Done and Dusted scrapbook.'

He nodded and, pulling out a handkerchief, wiped away her tears. 'Your dad is only trying to help and I'd imagine he's been well and truly strong-armed by Marnie. He probably feels he can't say no. And even though she is a pain in the arse, having someone like Noo around to do all the legwork will take the weight off you and your mum. And those weddings she showed us are amazing.'

Jess back-handed away tears. 'I'm just feeling like everyone else is taking it away from us, from me –'

'Well, don't. This is our big day and it's going to be perfect. Trust me.'

Jess smiled, feeling the tension ease. What was all the fuss about? Max was right, she needed to get a grip.

'There is one thing I do want to talk about, though,' he said. 'A church wedding is really important to me.' Max paused as if waiting to gauge her reaction. 'And to my family. Like I said, my mother and father are very traditional. They're both Christian. They go to church on and off all year, not every week but almost. It was how we were brought up, my sister and I – Sunday school, singing in the choir, confirmation, the whole nine yards. I know you're not keen –'

'It's not about being keen, Max, it's that the words don't mean anything to me. I want to make promises to you that are real, Max. Promises I can keep, that are ours. And –' Jess looked up into his face and saw all sorts of emotions in his eyes and stopped. 'This whole church thing really is important to you, isn't it?'

He nodded. 'Yes, yes it is.'

Jess took a breath, eyes still on his face. She had heard all sorts of horror stories about spoilt brides, girls screaming and squealing over wedding plans, about families falling out and never speaking again, but she had never thought it actually happened, and if it did, it most certainly would not happen to her. But standing there in the garden, with Noo waiting inside with her bloody flip chart and Marnie planning jolly shopping trips to buy the dress, Max out here trying to persuade her to do something she really, truly didn't want to do, Jess could see it all: one minute you're engaged and the next you're Bridezilla. And they were only at the very start of planning. God alone knows what it was going to be like by December.

'Because you're divorced we would probably still have to have a registry office wedding beforehand,' she said. 'And then a church blessing.'

Max nodded. 'I know.'

'We could write our own vows for the registry office. I want to say something meaningful.'

Max pulled a face. 'I think that we should get the legal part over as quickly as we can and concentrate on the church ceremony. Make that the real focus. It worked for Charles and Camilla –'

Jess stared at him. 'They're older than my mum and dad,' she said.

'Well, you you know what I mean.'

Jess guessed that she was being expected to make a decision. Seconds ticked by. Wasn't it a relatively small sacrifice in the great scheme of things to agree? After all did it matter that much exactly *how* they got married? Surely the important thing was that they *were* getting married, making a commitment to spend the rest of their lives together. Were the mechanics of how that commitment was made that important? A single day, a few hours in amongst a lifetime of being together? Jess took a deep breath. Sometimes you had to be big about things. Magnanimous.

'All right,' she said very slowly. 'If it is that important to you. Then okay – but I'm not lying to anyone,' Jess added with as much good grace as she could muster, and Max beamed.

'Thank you,' he said and kissed her hard. 'Now about the reception –'

Jess held up her hands. 'Whoa there, cowboy. One bridge at a time. I really want us to go and look at Vanguard Hall.'

Max looked as if he was going to say something and then, apparently thinking better of it, said, 'Okay, I'll tell you what. Why don't we see what Noo's got in mind and go and see those as well. After all we know we've got the hall if we want it as a fallback.'

That wasn't how Jess saw the offer of Vanguard Hall at all but didn't say so. 'I've just said yes to the church thing. Can't I at least choose where we have the reception?'

Max laughed. 'Don't look so stressed. This isn't a competition, sweetie. I wasn't saying we *couldn't* have the reception there. I was just saying it would be silly not to go and look at a few other places as well. Just because it's free doesn't make it good.'

While Max and Jess were outside talking in the garden, Molly cleared away the rest of the things from the dining table and made more coffee, which gave her the chance to look out of the window to see if she could see Jess. Just as she was carrying the tray of coffee back into the dining room, Jess and Max walked in behind her.

Molly looked anxiously at Jess as she took a mug from the tray. To her surprise Jess smiled. 'It's all right. Max and I had a bit of a talk in the garden and the whole church thing is really important to him and his family. So, a church wedding if we can have one and if not –'

Max smiled as their gaze met. 'Then we'll be having a straightforward registry office wedding and then a church blessing afterwards. Make that the focus.' He looked at Jess and smiled. 'Which will be just perfect.'

Noo clapped her hands together in a show of delight. 'Oh gosh, that's fabulous, a proper white wedding – oh, that's wonderful. I'm a great advocate of tradition.'

Molly stared at her in amazement. Noo took going with the flow to a whole new level.

'Have you decided on which church you'd like?' said Noo, pulling out her notebook. 'I don't know if you're aware that you can have a wedding in more or less any church now as long as you've got some kind of connection to it – I've got the details here. Actually we might be able to get someone to perform the whole wedding ceremony. Being a divorcé doesn't necessarily mean you can't get married in a church, it varies from case to case and vicar to vicar.'

Jess glanced up at Max. He smiled. 'I think that, Jess, you should really choose the church.'

For a few seconds Jess look completely lost. 'I thought from the way you were talking you'd got somewhere in mind.'

He laughed. 'The only church I know well is in the village where my parents live and it's a bit of a trek from here. But if –'

Before he could suggest that they all decamped down to Hampshire, Molly said quickly, 'There's one in the next village, Crowbridge – it's where my parents were married and your aunt Carol got married there too. Do you remember when you were a bridesmaid, Jess? There's a lovely little hotel and pub right opposite. They had Carol's reception there.'

'Where's that?' said Noo, pen poised.

'St Mary's, Crowbridge, it's the next village to Denham. It's only about a mile away from here, and it's a lovely little church,' said Molly and then, thinking on her feet, added, 'Or maybe we could ask Bert if we could use the church on the estate at Vanguard Hall? It would make sense to have the wedding and reception close to each other.'

Max gave her a long, cool look, which stopped Molly in her tracks.

'Actually while we were in the garden Jess and I talked about that and we thought that we ought to take a look around at a few other places before we said yes to – what did you say his name was again?'

'Bert,' Molly said, trying to keep her tone light and even.

Max laughed. 'Great name. Presumably he is one of the famous West Norfolk Berts?' he said sarcastically.

Molly felt her hackles rising, but it was gentle, laid-back Nick who said, 'I wouldn't be so quick to dismiss it if I were you. The old boy is lovely as well as being loaded – his real name is Lord Bertram Vanguard Rees Stokes.'

For an instant, Molly saw that Nick had piqued Max's interest and it made her prickle with annoyance.

'Oh, really?' Max said. 'In that case we'll definitely go and have a look. The way Jess described it I was thinking it was some sort of derelict barn in a farmyard.' He tried to make it sound like a joke and certainly Noo and Marnie laughed, but Molly couldn't bring herself to join in. Even though she tried to give him the benefit of the doubt it was obvious that Max was a complete snob, and she really disliked him for it.

'Right,' said Noo, when the laughter faded. 'I've got some lists here of the things we need to sort out.' She pulled half a dozen leather-bound folders out of her bag.

'What we need to do now is synchronise our diaries,' Noo said, glancing at her watch, with all the concentration of someone about to storm a beach.

Molly glanced around the table wondering how the hell Sunday lunch had turned into a military manoeuvre.

Chapter Nine

When everyone had finally left Molly looked at her diary. Assuming they could book everything for the first Saturday in December they had twelve weeks left. Twelve weeks. She could almost hear the clock ticking.

Once she got home and while Max was in the shower, Jess rang her dad. 'Dad, about Noo and Marnie and all the wedding,' she began.

'Puss,' said Jonathon, cutting her short. 'You must know that Marnie is only trying to give you a hand and she is terribly good at organising things. You know how she likes to help.'

'Take over, you mean.'

He laughed. 'Come on, don't be so snippy, you know that isn't going to happen, not with you and your mother around. And besides everyone agreed there was a lot to do, so why not spread the load? The last wedding your mum helped arrange was ours – and I'm certain things have moved on a bit since then. Times change. Marnie's always telling me that. And she's done two weddings in the last few years.' His tone softened. 'You know I just want everyone to be happy – and she's very fond of you, you know that. And this Noo woman seems very competent.'

'But –'

'But nothing, Puss,' Jonathon said in the same gentle voice. 'It'll be all right, I promise. You can have exactly what you want – and if Marnie wants to take on a big slice of the arrangements then to be honest I'd let her. Better one volunteer than ten pressed men . . .'

Jessie laughed; it was an expression straight out of her childhood.

'That's better, Puss. You know what Marnie's like, she'll move mountains to make sure it all goes like clockwork. Just talk to her. I'm sure it will be fine.' Jonathon paused. 'And I want you to know how much I love you. I can't believe my little baby girl is all grown-up and getting married.'

Jess could hear the emotion in his voice. 'Oh, Dad,' she whispered.

'Go on, I'll talk to you next week,' said Jonathon, brightening. 'Before you have me make a fool of myself.'

'So where are we with our wedding special?' Rob asked as he made his way past Molly's desk. She looked up. At least he had the good grace not to ask her first thing. She had emailed him on Sunday evening to let him know that, to her surprise, it was a goer.

'We're making progress,' she said. Although she didn't say so Molly was looking forward to spending more time with Jess, even if it did mean seeing more of Marnie.

'Good, good, only I'm upstairs later on. I'd like to give them an update if I can.' He nodded towards the lift.

Molly, Phil and Stan had been sitting around her desk, checking through the running order for the day's show, and hadn't actually expected to see hide nor hair of Rob until later in the week. Certainly they weren't thinking updates on something that hadn't been decided until the night before.

102

Their main focus was the show that was about to go on air, the one with a vicar desperate for the return of the old-fashioned harvest festival, the twin sisters – both ex-page three girls – opening a restaurant serving the best of local seasonal Norfolk food in a converted barn just outside Old Hunstanton, and after the twelve o'clock news a plan to discuss the contents of a perfect packed lunch, a slot sponsored and catered by a local delicatessen.

Rob waited for a response.

'Well,' said Molly, lying through her eye teeth, 'we're tracking down a florist –'

'And a nursery that grows specialist flowers for bouquets,' said Stan. 'Oh, and then there's cakes.'

Phil, presumably anxious to look good in front of the boss, picked up his notepad and flicked through what Molly guessed could only be blank pages. 'And we're waiting to hear back from a wedding photographer about getting the best out of your photos and we're going to a dress shop to talk to the owner about choosing the right dress,' he impressed.

Molly smiled; it was an impressive effort under pressure.

'So, you taking your girlfriend?' asked Rob conversationally.

'No, I'm keeping the whole thing very quiet,' said Phil sheepishly.

'Then we were thinking a make-up artist and hairdresser who will do a run-through of tips and advice for the bride-to-be,' said Molly, on a roll now.

'So far sounds good. And presumably we'll be following the happy couple on all these jaunts – you know, keep it tight, keep it *personal*,' Rob said to Molly.

Molly nodded. 'We're also thinking music, church music, venues, vicars. Maybe something on all the superstitions, something old, something new. There's plenty to go on.'

Rob nodded. 'Okay, good, good, good. We'll be wanting some web content for this as well. And we need to organise a *Meet the Happy Couple* session. Any thoughts about what order we're airing these in? Personally I would have thought choosing the dress would be the biggy? Do we keep that as the climax? Maybe we could do a couple of slots on that. One on the advice and then the second one with Jess going in and choosing the frock. Obviously you record them at the same time, but you get my drift? We need to think "story" with this – build up the anticipation.' And then Rob smiled, that big, rakish, wolfy smile of his. 'Good work,' he said. 'Good work.' And with that he headed off towards the lift.

Molly had been so certain after talking to Jess that Max would say no to the whole idea that she hadn't bothered formulating a plan. So when Max kept saying they should go for it, she had really been thrown.

'I think recording it for posterity will make the whole day extra special,' Max had said, as Noo packed away her box of tricks.

Molly didn't like to tell Max that Rob would have auctioned his own granny live on air if he thought it would help increase the station's ratings. Instead she had nodded and smiled and gone to make more coffee. Noo was keen too, presumably because she could see that it would give her a lot of free publicity.

During the meeting Molly's mobile, set to vibrate, had been buzzing away like an angry listener. As soon as Rob was out of earshot Molly flicked the phone open. There was a message from Jess asking her to call ASAP.

'Hi, hon,' said Molly when Jess picked up. 'How're you doing?'

Jess laughed. 'Don't ask. I'm working through a list a mile long. Noo's filled up my inbox with junk mail, and the postman arrived this morning weighed down with enough brochures and catalogues to deforest half Scandinavia. I've rung the vicar and arranged for me and Max to go over to the rectory on Friday evening.'

'All sounds like it's going well.'

Jess laughed. 'I wish. Thanks for lunch. It was great to see you and Nick. What I rang for was that Noo wants to know when we can go and see the venues. I've already told her that I want you there, and Max. So, how are you fixed for tomorrow night?'

'Tomorrow?' Molly flicked through the diary on her desk. 'I'm free – where are we going?'

'Well, the Crowbridge Arms is too small, so we're going to the Juniper Inn near Dereham and then somewhere called Vince's Park which is near King's Lynn. I'll email you the directions. Then Halley Hall near Swaffham on Thursday – apparently they've all still got rooms available for the first weekend in December. But we'll need to be quick, apparently.'

'But they're miles away.'

'I know but Noo said we could lay on a coach,' said Jess grimly.

'I suppose that's a good idea. Okay, look, email the directions and I'll see you tomorrow. I need to let Rob know so we can sort out someone to come with us.'

'I can't believe Max said yes to the wedding being recorded,' said Jess.

Molly was about to speak but Jess cut her off. 'And don't tell me it's going to be fun. Remember I've grown up with all this bollocks. Max doesn't have any idea what he's letting himself in for.'

'What I was going to say was we'll keep the recording as low-key and unobtrusive as possible –'

Jess laughed. 'Yeah, right – with one of the crew dressed in a Metallica teeshirt stopping everything and saying, "Do ya mind just doing that bit again, Vicar, because there was a plane flying over and can you stop that baby crying, Missus – okay, in your own time, from the top."

Mind you,' Jess continued, 'I suppose if it all goes belly-up Max's got no but himself to blame – oh, and Max's parents have asked if we'd all like to go down there for lunch on Sunday. They want to meet you – well, *us* really.'

Molly smiled. 'I'm glad we're still us.'

Jess laughed. 'We'll always be us, Mum. And there's one other thing.' She said it in the way only children can, part emotional blackmail, part vulnerable and needy.

'I feel a favour coming on,' said Molly wryly.

Jess giggled. 'I just wondered – and you can say no, obviously – if you're going anywhere near Cambridge any time this week?'

'You mean between trips to Swaffham and where were all the other places? Why?'

'Well, Max and I are up to our eyes at the moment. I've got loads on at work, and I'm doing a lot of extra hours so I can blag some time off to do wedding stuff and I was really hoping Max was going to pick up my engagement ring from the jeweller's before we go down to Hampshire on Sunday. I'd really like to show his mum and dad, but he's just rung to say he can't get away – and that I'll have to wait until he can find time to go.'

'And so what are we saying here?' asked Molly. Across the office Stan was tapping his watch. They needed to get into the studio. Through the heavy plate glass of the reception area Molly could see the vicar had arrived, along with the top-heavy twin restaurateurs.

'He's working late all this week – he's had to wangle time

106

off to go and see these venues and the vicar on Friday night as it is. So I told him that I'd ask you and he said it would be great if you could go and if not he'll go next week. I wouldn't ask but –'

'But I'm the only one mug enough to do it?'

'I didn't say that, Mum. But you're finished by lunchtime if you're not on an OB.'

'I don't *finish* then, Jess, I'm off air then. Radio programmes don't plan themselves, you know. Cambridge is an hour and a half's drive away from Norwich and then another hour home if I'm lucky. I can't do it today . . .'

There was a little pause at the far end of the line. Molly teased a pen out of the pot on her desk. 'All right then. Go on, tell me where I've got to go. I need to be in the studio in two minutes. How about if I picked it up Wednesday?'

Jess let out a sigh of relief. 'That would be brilliant. You're a star, Mum, I owe you.'

'You certainly do. Now, have you got an address?'

On Wednesday, by the time Molly had said goodbye to her studio guests, made a few phone calls and sorted out some pressing paperwork, it was mid-afternoon. So it was nearly five by the time she arrived in Cambridge, and despite that, it was still busy – very busy.

It was the tail end of summer and the whole of the city centre seemed to be jam-packed full of foreign exchange students, tourists, coachloads of day-trippers, people clustered around tour guides and every street was alive with visitors. Trying to find somewhere to park was close to impossible. On the third time around the block Molly found a space on Castle Hill, and then hurried back down into town.

Magdalene Street led down to a narrow bridge over the Cam and was lined with tiny independent and fascinating shops, stylish boutiques, a leather shop, a place that did hats to die for – and others that sold wonderful food and classic patisserie. It was tempting to linger; maybe this was the place to buy an outfit for Jess's wedding? Maybe the place but certainly not the time. Molly glanced down at the directions Jess had given her, and as she read her shorthand heard her daughter's voice in her head.

'Over the bridge, turn right into St John's St, keep on for a little way – it will be on your left, apparently you can't miss it.'

Molly glanced at her watch, wondering what time LovesPleasures closed and whether she was going to make it, and then spotted it around the next corner. Tucked between a boutique and a bookshop was a narrow-fronted shop with dark blue paintwork and a cheery little cream-and-navy striped awning that made it look like a sweet shop. An old-fashioned bell rang as Molly opened the door.

Inside the place was very still and quiet, and had a grown-up hippy chic vibe. The beautifully lit glass cabinets were dressed with leaves and barleycorns. From a large central urn a great twist of ivy grew up and had been trained across the beams and down around the counter. The jewellery was arranged into collections; this one an homage to the Tiffany lamp, this to the sea, with individual pieces made in the shape of cockleshells and tiny, tiny starfish. Molly's eyes moved slowly over the various cabinets, drinking in the details. The jewellery, if not always to her taste, was certainly eye-catching.

'Hi, anything I can help you with?' said a voice from behind the counter.

Molly turned round. Framed in a doorway, which appeared to lead through to a workshop, was a tall, whip-thin woman dressed in a sleeveless vest and faded jeans. She had broad shoulders and long strawberry-blonde hair, which she tucked behind her ears as she spoke.

'Hello,' said Molly. 'I've come to pick up a ring. You're resizing it – making it smaller, I think. It's for my daughter.'

'Certainly, what was the name?' the woman asked, opening up a little card index on the counter top. She had a warm, well-educated voice and a face wrinkled with sun and laughter.

'Jessica Foster?'

The woman nodded, and started to flick through the cards before disappearing back into the workshop, while Molly continued to work her way along the jewellery displays. There was a lot to look at. In one cabinet was a selection of amber beads, some set in strings, other single pieces on chains or made up in silver mountings. They looked as inviting and mouth-watering as boiled sweets. In another were pearls set out on olive-green silk, while alongside them on a swathe of cream silk were elegant white-gold designs, understated and contemporary.

'I'm terribly sorry,' said the woman. 'But I don't seem to be able to find it. I don't usually work in the shop, our usual girl is off sick today. Are you certain that your daughter bought it here?'

Molly nodded. 'Positive. As far as I know it was made here. Did you make all these?' She indicated the cases.

The woman's eyes brightened. 'A lot of it. But we have other guest designers. There are three of us.' She paused, looking slightly self-conscious. 'I'm afraid it's bit of a passion.'

Molly smiled. 'Nothing wrong with passion.'

'Your daughter's ring –'

'I think it was probably one of these pieces, or something like it,' said Molly pointing to the case of white-gold work. 'An engagement ring. She said it was like a wave with a solitaire.' And then Molly had a revelation. 'Actually, I've probably given you the wrong name. I think her fiancé brought it in, so it's probably under his name. Max Peters?'

A flicker of recognition passed across the woman's face and she smiled. 'Ah, right. Let me look,' she said, but even as she was going back into the workshop something about the way she moved suggested that she knew exactly the ring Molly meant.

'Here we are. I think this is it. Max Peters.' The woman made a show of reading the label on the little white packet and then slid the contents out and opened up the navy ring box. Inside was the most perfect, most elegantly understated white-gold ring with a delicate rolling wave, in the peak of which was cradled a small single diamond. 'It's one of mine. It's called *Morning Star*.'

Molly beamed. 'Oh, I am sure that is it. It's perfect. I can see why Jess chose it.' She opened her bag and took out her wallet but the woman shook her head.

'It's fine. There's no charge.' She paused. 'I hope that your daughter is very happy,' she said, and as she spoke the woman took out a little velvet bag and dropped the ring box into it. 'There we are. Any problems, please don't hesitate to come back.'

Molly looked up and for the briefest of moments thought that the jeweller was going to say something else but she didn't. Instead she smiled. Molly thanked her and headed off back towards the car.

She called Jess on her mobile on the walk back to the car. 'Got it,' she said.

She could hear the delight in Jess's voice. 'Thank you. Did you have a look at it?'

'It is gorgeous.'

'I know,' Jess giggled. 'You were so right about me saying something to Max.'

Chapter Ten

'And through here we have the Anderton Suite . . .' It was Thursday evening, and their guide on the wedding venue tour, a perfectly manicured, coiffured and charming woman called Julia, opened the impressive double doors of the former stately home with a well-practised flourish. At the threshold she paused for a moment or two to allow them to take in the view and make the right noises. Beyond the doors was a large, long, sparsely furnished rectangular hall, with claret deep-pile rugs rolled out over a dark wooden floor the colour of burnt toffee. Dominating the centre of the room was a huge circular table dressed with linen and satin swags, topped by an enormous flower arrangement. To their right were floor-to-ceiling windows that ran the length of the wall; dressed in convoluted tasselled and pleated gold-and-claret silk, they had to be twenty feet tall at least. Hanging from the ceiling were three ornate chandeliers, their crystal drops glinting and shimmering in the late afternoon sunlight. There were portraits set into ornate panels hanging on the other long wall and a huge gilt-edged mirror above the fireplace. The room was like something from the set of Cinderella.

Molly smiled and held up a hand before Julia could say anything else. 'That was lovely,' she said, switching off the digital recorder. 'Now if we could just go inside and then we'll carry on with the rest of the interview. It's the most superb room, Julia.'

This was the final venue they were being taken to by Noo. Apparently, in the world according to Noo, the first one, Vince's Park, lent itself superbly to Jess's romantic vision of the perfect traditional wedding, which was a bit worrying.

Once upon a time Vince's Park must have been a nice, large family hotel but now apparently weddings were their main trade and somewhere down the line they had embraced pink as their new religion. The main function room looked like a cross between Jordan's boudoir and something out of a Disney movie, although the passion for pink started as soon as you reached the main doors, which were hung with matching pink bridal wreaths.

Once inside there were acres of pink carpet, pink ceilings, pink-and-gold chairs, pink tablecloths, pink powder rooms and big pink bows on anything that didn't move – and not a subdued baby pink but something closer to bubblegum.

While Noo had gushed and told them how hard the owners had worked on the ambience, Molly and Jess had stared in disbelief, rapidly coming to the conclusion you could have too much of a good thing – and a bad thing too, come to that. It would have been like getting married inside a kidney.

The décor at the Jupiter Inn was better, being elegant and understated, but who wanted a hotel wedding co-ordinator who teetered in late on white stilettos, reeking of cigarettes and answering every question with, 'Oh, I dunno actually, I'll have to talk to someone about that,' in a high-pitched estuary English whine? Apparently she and Noo had trained at the same wedding academy.

So Halley Hall, set in its own grounds in the heart of the Norfolk countryside, had been a breath of fresh air. Outside the Anderton Suite Molly switched on her recorder; Julia smiled nervously.

Molly smiled. 'You're doing brilliantly. It's coming over really well.'

Julia smiled back and then nibbled nervously at her bottom lip. 'I'm finding this all quite nerve-racking really. It's quite good fun, but I'm just so used to just *doing* it and not thinking – you know what I mean.'

Molly nodded. 'You're fine, you're a natural. Now what we'll do is go inside and you can tell me all about the room.'

'And what would you like me to do?' asked Marnie, who was standing in a huddle behind Julia with Max, Jess and Noo.

If only I could tell you, thought Molly. 'If you could just come in behind Julia, that would be great. Probably best if you don't talk but feel free to look around, and then I'll bring you in as we need to. Okay? So, here we go. Julia, would you like to tell us where we are now?' Molly asked in her carefully honed encouraging voice.

'We're in the Anderton Suite. This is our most prestigious wedding venue and largest set of rooms here at Halley Hall.' Julia turned slightly, pointing back the way they had just come. 'We have the dedicated foyer and entrance through there, which makes this particular suite of rooms nice and private for our wedding party as they arrive. Several of our previous brides have said that it feels almost like it's *their* country house for the day.' She laughed nervously and nodded toward the microphone. 'I thought you'd have a lot of people with you to record all this.'

Molly nodded. 'It's less intrusive this way, more intimate,' she said, not mentioning that Rob wouldn't pay the over-time for anyone else. 'So tell me about the Anderton Suite? What's so special about it?'

113

'It's the perfect room for larger weddings or parties. We're licensed to conduct civil ceremonies here. And then after the ceremony we ask the wedding party and their guests to go back out into the lobby area for photos and champagne, while the staff re-sets the main room with tables for the wedding breakfast. We can cater for up to one hundred and fifty guests, seated, or two hundred for drinks and canapés. As you can see it is a really beautiful room with some of the original painted plasterwork and three full-sized crystal chandeliers.'

Molly gave her the thumbs up. Julia bit her lip again. 'Was that all right?'

'Brilliant,' Molly said, without stopping the recording. 'Would you like to tell us a bit more about Halley Hall? Working here you see it every day but our listeners have no idea what a little gem it is.'

Max looked pained. 'Excuse me, can we stop recording now? I appreciate we signed up for this but surely you've got enough material,' he said grimly.

Molly pasted on a smile. 'I'm afraid this is what it takes,' she said and turned her attention back to Julia, who was now a little ruffled.

'Am I boring? We could always cut it short.'

'No, not at all,' said Molly warmly. 'It sounds absolutely great.'

Julia took a breath. 'Right, this particular room has the most fantastic views out over our Italian gardens and on nice days these French windows can be opened up and your guests have full use of the terrace. We find that a lot of couples like to use this area for their photographs, although I should point out that confetti is banned . . .'

Molly glanced at Max, whose expression was a blank mask.

'That's great. I think we've probably got enough on that.

And don't worry about any little mistakes, we'll edit those out. It will be fabulous.'

'Gosh, I'm shaking,' said Julia, who had hair so straight and unmoving it looked as if it might have your eye out if you got close enough. 'Would you let me know when it's going to be on? You know, the bit with me in it?'

Molly nodded. 'I'll make sure someone rings you. Now, If we could just do a little bit with the food then I think that's about it.'

'Wonderful, if you'd like to follow me,' said Julia, dropping back into her spiel. 'Through to your left is a little sitting room which comes as part of the suite. It's ideal for the bride and groom to catch their breath and get changed before going away, or maybe take a little break from proceedings. We'll take a look through there in a moment. It's a super room, very comfortable, complete with an *en-suite* shower room and complimentary refreshments. Obviously we can accommodate any of your guests who wish to stay overnight, either before or after your special day, in the main hotel, and we have a choice of three beautifully appointed bridal suites available should the bride and groom wish to spend their wedding night here.'

Max smiled at Jess. 'Wonderful, isn't it?' he said. 'I'm very impressed.'

Jess glanced at Molly who, now that she had stopped recording, was busy flicking though the glossy brochure they had been given at the start of the tour. Her mother had an expression that she had perfected over the years for interviewing people. It gave her face a kind of positive, encouraging neutrality that betrayed nothing of what she was actually thinking or feeling. She was wearing it now.

When Molly wasn't interviewing, Noo, Marnie and Max

had been getting along with Julia, their designated wedding co-ordinator, as if they were all part of some secret wedding arrangers' society. However while Marnie and Noo made noises of approval and commented on the colour, the various rooms ('*here at Halley Hall we can offer you three totally different wedding venues under one roof*') the decor, the convenience of the parking and the fabulous views, both Molly and Jess held back. To some extent it was because Molly was working but Jess knew her mum well enough to guess that it was more than that.

They had seen all three wedding suites: the tiny Vladimir Suite – a picture in blue, gold and white 'ideal for the smaller, more intimate wedding party, with maximum seating for twenty-five', via the Gold Drawing Room, 'with its charming original wood panelling, gold ornamented ceilings and exquisite blue carpets and drapes,' through to the final suite of rooms where they found themselves now.

And Jess had hated them all. She looked up at the chandeliers feeling distinctly underdressed, despite wearing her new best linen trousers and the designer sweater Molly and Nick had given her for her birthday. Max squeezed her hand and winked. It did nothing to reassure her.

The room was stunning with its high ceilings and huge windows, but despite the moulded, gilded plasterwork, the tasselled drapes and exquisite floral displays on the tables, it had more than a slight whiff of school dining hall about it, and whichever way Jess looked at it, it wasn't her.

It wasn't that the chandeliers weren't wonderful or the fireplaces grand. It wasn't that Julia wasn't lovely. It wasn't that the gardens didn't look fabulous or the marble spiral staircase ('*the perfect backdrop for your wedding photos*') wasn't like something out of a romantic novel. It was that it didn't feel like anywhere Jess *wanted* to get married.

This was hopefully the last of the venues they had been forced to see during the past week and if she was being honest Jess hadn't liked any of them – the bottom line was they just weren't her.

Jess didn't like pink or the slick presentations or the shows of opulence. She wanted to celebrate her wedding at Vanguard Hall with Max and her family and his and all their friends, with Bassa the dog in a bow tie and Nick and her father getting drunk together. Looking up at the ornate ceiling, Jess decided that whatever Marnie had planned, she was going to take Max out on a trip to Vanguard Hall as soon as possible, so he could see for himself that it would be the most perfect place for their wedding.

'If you'd like to follow me through into the sitting room,' said Julia pleasantly, guiding them through a doorway into a much smaller oak-panelled room with a view out over a large formal pond and gravelled garden.

The cheery, sunlit room was full of brightly coloured, overstuffed chairs and large sofas with a long coffee table set between them. There were brochures on the coffee table. Along one wall was a sideboard with flowers and a tray with glasses, napkins and side plates on it.

'Chef has arranged for a selection of sample dishes from our wedding menu to be brought through for you, so you can have a little taster. I'm certain it'll help with your menu choices,' Julia simpered, looking from face to face. 'We've also got a selection of juices, fine wines and champagnes. Oh, and I haven't mentioned music yet, have I? Besides having a first-class sound system in all the wedding suites we've got a super string quartet that we use – it's just so lovely when your guests arrive – and the acoustics in the reception room are almost perfect.' Julia turned to Marnie. 'And so tasteful.'

Over the course of the week Jess had reconciled herself

to the fact that even though the venues really liked the idea of being on the radio with Molly, one look at Marnie, in her dinky little shoes and expensive designer dress, and all the people at all the venues had realised they were also talking serious money here. Today Marnie was a picture in shades of turquoise, while Noo was wearing yellow and black, which made her look like a plump, cheery bee.

'Sounds wonderful,' said Max.

'Oh, what a lovely idea,' gushed Noo. 'That is such a nice touch, don't you think, Marnie? Very sophisticated.'

'And then of course we can organise a disco afterwards or a band if you prefer. Something for every taste. We can also arrange your photographer and we have our own on-site florist.'

Jess glanced at Molly and rolled her eyes. Molly was keeping her work face on.

'We can pop all that in with your quote options. Anyway, I'll just go and let Chef know that we're ready,' purred Julia, and then looking directly at Molly, continued, 'Are you planning to record us eating?'

Molly smiled. 'I'm rather hoping you're going to describe the dishes for us, as well as what they taste like – or maybe your chef might like to do it? We could always come to the kitchen, maybe see how the food is made, if it makes it easier for you. People really enjoy that kind of thing.'

'I'll go and see what he says,' said Julia.

As she left, Molly flicked on the recorder to pick up a bit of ambience. 'Well, I think this is just fantastic,' said Max, lingering over the word *well*, as Julia glided off into the depths of the hotel. He wandered over to the windows. 'Wonderful setting. Just look at the gardens.'

Marnie had settled herself down on a sofa. 'I agree. And

it's easy for people to find. Everything is right here. Lovely facilities. And the rooms are simply gorgeous. I'm sure your father would love it, JJ.' She opened up the brochure she had been carrying around and thumbed through the pages. 'I mean, just look at what they've got here – excellent restaurant, the spa, the pool, the grounds – it's perfect. Obviously we'll have to have this suite. It would be ideal. We said a hundred guests, didn't we?'

Noo already had her notepad out. 'A hundred, that's right; this would be so nice.'

'I hate it,' whispered Jess under her breath. Molly raised an eyebrow, wondering if she ought to switch the recorder off. Jess made the effort to paint on a smile, while Molly kept her expression in neutral.

'We've still got Vanguard Hall to go and see,' Jess said aloud.

They all turned to look at her.

'Well, of course we have, darling,' said Max. 'But I think it would have to go a long way to beat this place, don't you? It's ideal. Everything's here, and it's so convenient. If we had the reception at this other place we'd have to book everything separately.'

Marnie nodded. 'Exactly. This way we'll just hire a coach for the guests so that they can come straight from the church to the reception rather than having to drive. What do you think, JJ?'

'That you need to see Vanguard Hall. This place just isn't me at all.'

Marnie's smile tightened. 'Darling, if it's about the cost you really don't have to worry. I've already spoken to your father and he understands perfectly. And he wants you to have the best. We don't want to be silly with money but we really don't have to scrimp either.'

'My dad's money,' Jess snapped.

Marnie's expression hardened, but before she could say anything Molly leapt in with, 'Surely the most important thing is —'

'Is that it's Jess's day,' said Max. 'Yes, I'm sure we're all agreed on that, aren't we?'

Marnie nodded, her smile so brittle it looked as if she had early-onset rigor mortis. 'It goes without saying. But what I mean was, if you're worried about the budget —'

'I'm not worried at all,' said Molly pleasantly. 'The point I was going to make was that this is *Jess's* wedding.'

'Well, of course it is,' purred Marnie. 'Obviously. But even so, perhaps we ought to make a provisional booking, just in case.'

At which point the door opened and a waiter and waitress came in pushing a trolley, closely followed by Julia.

'Righty-oh, here we are. Well, first of all,' said Julia, making a show of composing herself, 'we'd like to show you a selection of canapés and while we're trying those I've brought along some sample menus that we suggest for the reception, although they're not written in stone. And then we can have a little taster of some of Halley Hall's signature dishes.' She glanced at Molly. 'Chef will be along in a couple of minutes to talk us through them — he's delighted to be asked to talk on air.'

And then, while the canapés were handed around everyone smiled and waited for the great man to arrive.

'That bloody sodding woman is driving me totally and utterly nuts,' snapped Jessica, throwing her handbag into the back seat of Molly's car and slamming the door shut as she climbed in alongside Molly. Then she held up her hands. 'Actually no, that's not true. They are *all* driving me totally and utterly nuts. Noo is like some kind of hired echo. "Ooh, that's so nice, ooh yes, Marnie, I think you're so right," Jess whined in a cruel impression of the wedding planner. 'She's not an asset, she's a Greek chorus. Tell me one thing, *one thing*, that she's come up with without Marnie coming up with it first. "Oh, a string quartet is so tasteful." I don't understand why she's been hired. Those other places she took us to were awful. And she must be costing Dad a fortune. And what does she do, for God's sake? And exactly whose wedding is this?'

Jess didn't mention Max, and so Molly decided not to bring him up. They were in the car park outside Halley Hall and had just waved Marnie and Noo off in Marnie's nice shiny new Alfa that Jonathon had bought her for her birthday, and Max in his low-slung TT.

Jess slumped down in the seat. 'This is crazy. I'm a grown-up. I don't have to put up with this crap, the world according to Marnie. I don't want a Marnie wedding, I don't live in a Marnie universe. But then again I don't want to upset Dad either, he's been so sweet about everything and I know he'd be really hurt if I tell Marnie what I think about her and her perfect sodding wedding. She is sucking the life out of me. All I really want is –'

'Your wedding at Vanguard Hall. I know. What about Max?'

'He's impressed obviously, you know what men are like.' Jess rolled her eyes. 'I've come to the conclusion he's easily led.' She paused. 'It'll be fine. I just need to take him out to the hall so he can have a look round. Once he's seen it he'll understand why I want to get married there. I mean, who wouldn't?'

Molly decided to bite her tongue. 'Buckle up, we'll go and have a cup of tea back at the house. Nick is cooking a paella with Nigella's cheesecake for dessert.'

121

Jess sighed. 'Comfort food. Oh Mum, you're such a genius – that's exactly what I need.' And then she started rootling around in the glove compartment. 'Have you got any sweets in here?'

'There might be some mints, but you've just eaten a plateful of canapés and all those little parcels with – what exactly *was* that green stuff?'

'God knows.' Jess pulled a face. 'Wouldn't keep a sparrow alive. What I was thinking was that, as it's going to be a winter wedding, we could have something seasonal, like big bowls of chunky homemade soup and fresh-baked crusty bread, or maybe sausage and mash or a hog roast. And then the ceilidh.'

'Sounds great,' Molly said, wondering what Max's parents would make of eating their wedding feast out of a burger bun.

Jess sighed. 'I keep telling Marnie but she just smiles and nods. When I came up with the sausage-and-mash idea she said, "JJ, we're talking about an important social event here, darling, not a bonfire party." Bloody woman, what she doesn't seem to understand is that it's *my* important social event. She's trying to get this wedding in the county magazine. You know her daughter Mimi was in there – three-page spread. Full colour. She's just trying to make it two years running.'

'She's very fond of you,' said Molly, manoeuvring the car along the broad tree-lined estate road. One thing Julia was right about – Halley Hall was the most perfect setting.

'*Mum.*' Jess sounded outraged. 'Why can't you just bitch about her? She's my wicked stepmother – aren't you meant to hate her? She's muscling in on my wedding and she's ended up with Dad and all his money.'

Molly raised an eyebrow. 'I think they're perfect for each other.'

Jess snorted. 'You are way too soft.'

Molly had made a point of never running down Jonathon or any of his weird and wonderful women in front of the children. After a few false starts, including Debbie the Double D Dancer and Kelly-Marie, a girl who was only two or three years older than Jess, Molly had been delighted when Jonathon had settled for Marnie. He would have made a sad and very lonely old bachelor. And while the money had been nice, there were some things in life worth far more – and life *without* Jonathon was one of them.

Jessica screwed up her nose, for a moment looking for all the world like the grumpy twelve-year-old Molly remembered, the one who couldn't find her sports kit and didn't want to do double games anyway. 'It would make it so much easier if we all hated each other.'

Molly laughed. 'Come on, cheer up. We've done what Marnie suggested and looked around and as far as I'm concerned that's the end of it. If you're absolutely certain that Vanguard Hall is the sort of wedding you want then we'll just book it all. We've still got our list. Dad will understand.'

'You think? I'm worried that it'll hurt his feelings if I say I don't want what Marnie wants.'

Molly nodded. 'He'll be fine about it. He knows exactly what Marnie's like. I mean, who'd have thought he'd end up going on cruises and eating foreign food?'

Jess sat back. 'The other night I dreamt that on my wedding day Marnie just sent a car for me. Everything else was organised. I just had to turn up and Noo was there to zip me into my frock.'

'And what was it like?' asked Molly with a grin, as they pulled out onto the main road.

'I don't know. I woke up in a cold sweat. You know, I'm

going to be a nervous wreck by the time we get to the wedding.'

'Tell you what, how about we go and see Vanguard Hall on Saturday and then have a family conference. What does Max say about all this?'

Jessica laughed. 'Typical man. He thinks that having Marnie and Noo doing all the donkey work is a great idea. Which reminds me, Marnie is still trying to sort out an appointment with this woman they went to for Mimi's dress. You will come with me, won't you? Only I can see myself being stuffed into some hideous meringue nest and everyone purring about how lovely I look and before you know it they'll have it boxed up and this place booked and I'll be getting into the car that Marnie sends for me.' Jess paused, turning to try and catch Molly's gaze. 'I was hoping it was just going to be you and me doing this.'

Molly glanced across at her. 'Me too. Don't worry, we'll wrestle it back. I promise.'

'God, I hope so.'

Molly laughed. 'At least thanks to Marnie you know what you *don't* want. And by the time we've finished we'll have recorded enough material to run the wedding special of the century.'

Jess pulled a face. 'I suppose there is that.'

'And Max's parents this Sunday?'

Jess nodded. 'We haven't got to record that as well, have we?' she said, only half-joking.

Chapter Eleven

Jess wasn't the only one having bad dreams.

'Molly, stop it,' said a man in a really nice suit. He sounded quite anxious, but then again, she *was* desperately trying to fight him off. The man had a firm hold of her arm and was trying to stop Molly from pushing Marnie face-first down into the giant chocolate fountain that was standing in the foyer of Halley Hall.

Molly was attempting to drown Marnie in front of a queue of bemused wedding guests, who were all clutching fondue forks and plates of strawberries and marshmallows. People in good clothes with big hats were getting splashed with warm Belgian chocolate. Fortunately, other than a few minor royals and a man from the local Co-op, they all seemed to be total strangers.

It occurred to Molly as she pushed Marnie down for the third time that maybe she resented the woman's interference with the wedding a lot more than she was letting on. The man, who seemed very familiar, was still holding onto her arm, only now he was joined by Noo and Julia, and they were nowhere near as gentle.

'Stop, stop,' said Julia, shaking her hard. 'You can't do this, you can't drown Marnie, she's the mother of the bride.'

'No, she's not,' roared Molly furiously. 'I'm the mother of the bride. I am –'

'I know you are,' said the man. 'Now are you going to wake up? You're frightening the dog.'

Molly's eyes snapped open and she could see Nick peering down at her in the lamplight. They were in the sitting room and Milo was looking at her nervously from behind the arm of a chair. She was on the sofa and Nick had presumably been watching TV.

'I must have fallen asleep,' she said, somewhat unnecessarily, straightening her clothes. 'I never fall asleep on the sofa.'

'Well, you did tonight. Overtired, I reckon, like a toddler after a long day out – fractious and overwrought,' said Nick.

'Where's Jess?' said Molly, looking around the room.

'She left about half an hour ago. She said she'd ring you tomorrow after she and Max have been to see the vicar. She didn't want to wake you, so I thought I'd leave you until I went up to bed and then –'

'I was having a nightmare.'

'I know,' he said ruefully, rubbing his arm. 'You tried to punch me.'

'Only because you were trying to stop me drowning Marnie.'

Nick raised an eyebrow but had the good grace not to comment.

'You should have woken me to say goodbye to Jess,' said Molly, yawning and stretching. 'She hated Halley Hall.'

'By the sound of it she wasn't keen on any of them. Anyway, she was fine when she left. When she'd finished talking to Max on the phone you'd got to the snoring and drooling stage – seemed a shame to disturb you. We took some great photos, though. Jess was saying that maybe we should have them made into Christmas cards.'

Molly punched him again and he grinned. 'Tea,' he said.

Max slipped into the driver's seat and sat with his hands on the steering wheel while Jess got in beside him. It was Friday evening at around eight thirty and they had just been for their first meeting with the vicar.

'Marriage lessons?' said Max, not turning the ignition key.

'You heard the lady, that's what she said,' said Jess, dropping her bag into the footwell and stopping for a second to admire the way her engagement ring glittered in the light. 'Actually I'm really glad we went. I feel a lot better about the whole thing now. I thought Shona was really nice. And you heard what she said, it's part of her pastoral duty to talk to couples about what marriage means.'

'I *know* what marriage means,' Max said. 'I just can't believe that anyone in this day and age expects that we're going to turn up for marriage lessons. And going to church every week to hear the bloody banns read – doesn't she realise we've got lives? I'm working all hours that God sends at the moment. You'll have to go.' If he saw any irony in what he was saying, Max hid it well.

'Oh, come on, lighten up. I'm not going on my own, Max. *You're* the one who wants a church wedding,' said Jess. 'And you heard what she said, not all vicars are prepared to marry couples when one of them has been divorced –'

He sniffed. 'Oh yes, and there's all that too. You'd think we were still living in the bloody dark ages. I'm not wildly keen on all this in-depth discussion about why my previous marriage failed. Raking it up after all these years – I'd sooner forget all about it, thank you very much.'

'She did say that we could have a blessing instead if we

127

wanted to.' Jess pulled the little booklet that the vicar had given her out of her bag. 'A Service of Prayer and Dedication after a Civil Marriage.'

'You mean like a consolation prize? It's bloody ridiculous.' And then he paused. 'I'm sure we didn't go through all this rigmarole last time. And I don't want to go over why it went wrong.'

Jess didn't want to argue, not after nearly a week apart with only snatched phone calls and meeting at wedding venues. Leaning in close she stroked his arm. 'Stop being such a grump. If things hadn't gone wrong first time around then we wouldn't be here now, would we?'

'I suppose not.' Max sighed, and very slowly seemed to let the tension ease out of his body, then turned and cuddled her up close to him. 'Sorry, sweetie – ignore me. I've had a bloody awful week trying to fit in all these extra commitments around work. I don't mean to snap at you. This job is taking up every waking hour and –' He stopped. 'Actually you don't need to hear about this, and I certainly don't want to talk about it any more.' He slipped his arm from around her shoulders and ran his fingers back through his hair. 'When I'm like this I'm impossible.'

Jess laughed. 'You're not wrong there, but we can work round it. I'm famished. What time did you book the table for?'

'Ah,' Max said and made a funny clicking sound with his tongue and teeth, a sound that suggested that she had caught him out.

'What?' Jess stared at him. 'Oh, don't tell me you've forgotten. We're supposed to be going out for a curry tonight. Wedding lesson, followed by Tiger beer, tikka masala and sag aloo. Okay, don't worry. How about we go to the pub instead?' She pointed across the road.

'Crowbridge Arms, fine ales and foods,' she read from the sign above the door.

'I meant to tell you on the way here. I'm really pushed for time. I was thinking of just grabbing a take-away and then getting back to the grindstone.'

'Oh, okay.' Jess leaned over to the back seat and pulled her mobile phone out of her jacket pocket. 'I'll ring the order through, shall I? What do you fancy?'

Max turned the key in the ignition and the Range Rover he used for work rumbled into life. 'Actually I need to get home, I'm on call till six tomorrow morning and meantime I'm got shedloads of work to do.'

Jess stared at him. 'So what does that mean? We eat fast and you bugger off and leave me with the washing up?'

He stroked the hair back off her face and then casually flicked his wrist over to check his watch. 'Would you mind if I just dropped you off at your place tonight, only I'm going to be no company at all. My head's full of all the stuff I need to do. I need to be getting back.'

'Okay, so you mean *you're* going to grab a take-away at home and eat it on your own?' said Jess miserably. 'This is ridiculous. I was hoping we could talk about tonight and the vicar and the wedding and all the things I need your opinion on – going to see Vanguard Hall for a start. I've hardly seen anything of you this week –'

'Come on, Jess.' His tone was teasing now. 'Soon you'll be seeing me all the time. And then you'll probably look back on these as the halcyon days when I wasn't always under your feet.' He grinned. 'I've already said I trust you and your good taste. You have what you want.'

'*I want to see you.*'

Max's smile held. 'I know and I want to see you too but not tonight. We'll be married soon and then you'll see more than enough of me, probably be sick of the sight of me inside six months. Anyway we can talk about all the wedding stuff on the drive down to Hampshire on Sunday.'

'What about tomorrow? I thought you were coming to look round Vanguard Hall with me and Mum?'

'I thought you'd settled on Halley Hall.'

Jess stared at him. 'You are joking, aren't you?'

'I'm sorry, sweetie, I can't come tomorrow. I thought you'd already sorted it all out.'

'When were you planning to spring this one on me? This is getting to be beyond a joke, Max. I need help with all this.'

'You've got your mum and Marnie and Noo – how many other opinions do you want?'

She glared at him. 'Just one more. Yours. I don't understand what's going on with you, Max.'

'What do you mean? Nothing's *going on.*'

'Do you want to get married to me?'

He looked bemused. 'What on earth is that supposed to mean? Of course I do. I've been to the venues, been to see the Vicar of Dibley in there –'

'Just asking me isn't enough.'

He paused. 'I don't know what you mean.'

'There are so many other things that need sorting out.'

'We've already had this conversation, honey – everything will be fine. It'll all get done.'

Jess stared at him. 'No thanks to you.'

He looked hurt. 'Oh, come on. That's hardly fair. I'm really busy at the moment. I'm working.'

'And so am I, but I'm still managing to fit it all in.'

She waited for him to say that somehow his work was different, for him to make her even angrier, but he simply shrugged and said, 'You're right. Tell you what, how about we grab supper together and then I go home? Your place, you order. My treat.'

Jess didn't say a word.

'Come on then, tell me how the wedding plans are going?' he said as they pulled away from the rectory.

Jess sighed, resisting the temptation to punch him.

When Max had gone home Jess sat on the sofa for a long time stroking Bassa. This wasn't exactly how she had planned to spend the run-up to their wedding. With a sigh Jess picked up the empty take-away cartons and took them through to the kitchen. She was about to switch off the light when she noticed something written on the blackboard by the fridge. The words made her heart leap.

It said: 'I know I'm crap at all this, Jessie, but I do love you.'

Jess smiled. There were bound to be a few teething problems and Max was right, they'd got the rest of their lives together. Her smile widened out into a grin; she knew that she loved Max and Max loved her. He really, really did.

Chapter Twelve

First thing Saturday morning, Molly and Jess were on their way to see Jack and his boss, Bertie. Vanguard Hall was situated in the centre of a triangle between Fakenham and Holt and Wells-next-the-Sea, in one of the prettiest parts of North Norfolk, just a few miles inland from the coast.

It was the most perfect day to go exploring the estate. The old hall sat amongst its early autumn splendour like a contented ginger tomcat curled up in the long grass. As they drove in through the main gates Molly slowed down so that she and Jess could take in the views out over the parkland. They had visited Jack enough times to know that it was worth looking at.

Down past the lodge cottage the gravel drive curled through the woodland to give tantalising glimpses of the handsome old house beyond. Here one wing was framed by a stand of limes and a rolling stretch of park, then, as the roadway turned another corner, horse chestnuts created the frame with a great rippling lake as the middle ground. There was a boathouse next to a jetty where a tired blue-and-white rowing boat floated sleepily at its moorings. With the last of the early autumn morning mist lingering between the trees, every view was a watercolour.

Turning another corner the whole front of the main house

was finally revealed against a great backdrop of trees, and it was here that Molly turned off the main driveway and down into the woods. Jack's cottage was on one of the little service roads away from the main house, close to the walled kitchen garden. It was like something out of a fairy tale, with its red-tiled roof and dormer windows tucked up under the low eaves which swept down to just above head height, so it almost looked like the cottage was wearing a hat. There was a stack of logs heaped up to one side of the door and on the other side were several pairs of work boots, sheltered by a deep porch.

As Molly and Jess pulled up alongside Jack's truck he wandered out, hands stuck in pockets, his tanned face split by a broad smile. Jack was tall, with unruly curly dark hair bleached at the tips by the summer sun. With those broad shoulders, and a faded checked shirt tucked casually into battered moleskin trousers, he looked like a model from a lifestyle magazine. The first thing that Molly thought as she saw him was how much living and working at Vanguard Hall suited him. He looked happy and relaxed and totally at ease with life, and who could ask for more?

Jess had sprung out of the car almost before Molly had stopped the engine. 'Jack,' she giggled as she bounded across the grass to meet him. Jack stood a head and broad shoulders above his sister; she hugged him tight, head pressed against his chest.

'Wow, just look at you,' she exclaimed, as Molly climbed out of the car. 'I always forget how very Lady Chatterley's Lover it is out here.'

'He was a gamekeeper. I'm a gardener.'

'I don't think it matters. You should let me fix you up with one of my friends. Out here all on your own in this lovely cottage, it doesn't seem right at all.'

Jack laughed. 'Uh-huh, so what you're suggesting is I can't find my own women?'

'Well, not sane ones; is what's-her-name still on your case?'

Before Jack could answer a tall, slim, dark-haired young woman, dressed in cropped jeans, flat sandals and a white shirt, wandered out of the cottage wiping her hands on a tea towel. She looked Spanish or maybe Mexican and had eyes so dark that it was impossible to tell where the iris began.

Jack turned to make the introductions. 'Jess, Mum – this is Krista,' he said, reddening slightly. 'She's working here at the moment.'

The girl smiled and held out her hand in welcome. 'I've heard a lot about you both. I'm a horticultural student, I'm on placement here,' she said in lightly accented English. Before Jess or Molly could say anything other than the briefest of hellos a tall, slightly older man stepped out from inside, and slipped on his boots. 'Hi,' he said, flashing a broad smile as he fixed the laces.

He was a few years older than Jack, with blond hair and big, capable hands, although what struck Molly first was how bright his cobalt blue eyes looked in his deeply tanned face.

'And this is Oliver Felgate, head gardener, and chief slave driver,' said Jack. 'Who is now leaving,' he added pointedly.

'Sorry, are we disturbing you?' said Molly, looking from face to face.

'No, not at all, we've just been going over next week's schedule,' said Oliver, catching hold of Molly's hand and shaking it firmly. 'And as Jack was expecting you this morning we thought we'd come over and do it here. Make him make the coffee for once.' He smiled at Molly. 'We've met before.'

Molly nodded. 'Yes, we have. During the open garden weeks – and at the Christmas party.'

Oliver was nodding now and smiling some more. 'Of course. That's right. How are you?' And after they had exchanged pleasantries he turned his attention to Jess. 'I hear congratulations are in order. He's a lucky man, whoever he is.' He glanced back at Jack. 'Just thank your lucky stars you don't look anything like your brother.'

Jess blushed furiously, which made Krista laugh and put a protective arm around her. 'Don't take any notice; he's cruel to us all. And your brother is not that bad for an Englishman. You're going to get married here at the hall?'

'That's what we're hoping,' said Molly as Jess nodded.

'I can't think of anywhere nicer,' said Krista, handing Jack the tea towel.

'I'm afraid we've got to be getting back,' said Oliver. 'Nice to meet you again. By the sounds of it we'll be seeing you again soon.' And then turning to Jack, he said, 'Don't forget to close up the greenhouses.'

Jack nodded. 'I won't,' and then lifted a hand in farewell as Oliver and Krista headed across the grass to another flat-bed pick-up tucked away in the shade.

'Come on in,' said Jack, waving them inside. 'Bert will be back later; he's had to go to a meeting in Norwich this morning – he should be back before two. So he's asked me to give you the grand tour and then we'll have some lunch. And Freya's around somewhere if you need to ask any questions. She said she'd come over and have a word with you as well. Is that all right?'

What a crazy question. On a fabulous day like today with the sun already high in the sky, Molly couldn't think of anywhere else she would rather be. From the expression on Jess's face they were sharing the same thought.

'It's such a shame Max couldn't come,' Jess said. 'I really wanted him to see it too.'

'He can always come over another day. Let's go inside and have some tea,' said Jack. 'And then I'll take you over to the barn and show you around. I think Krista's already put the kettle on.'

The inside of the cottage was cosy but untidy. There was one largish room with a big bay window that was about the same width as the room overlooking the front and then at the back of the cottage was a tiny kitchen. Designed for a single gardener, it was the most perfect bachelor pad.

In the bay window was a huge sofa draped with a blanket and to one side of the fire a large armchair with a tabby cat curled up amongst the cushions. Opposite the fireplace stood a small table and two chairs. The table top was already covered in mugs and cups arranged around a tin of biscuits, an open bag of sugar with a spoon stuffed in the top, and a carton of milk.

Molly laughed as she started to gather the detritus together. 'Very classy.'

'I was planning to clear up when Ollie and Krista showed up.' Jack grinned. 'Oh, come on, Mum, it's a still life.'

Molly picked up one of the mugs and peered into the top of it. 'Some of it is not so still.'

'Don't worry. It won't take long to rinse three up.'

'Some of these are going to need a lot more than a rinse,' said Jess, grimacing, as she helped Molly clear the chaos through into the kitchen.

While Jess washed up, Molly tidied. 'He needs a woman,' said Jess conversationally as her mother dropped a great stack of take-away cartons into a rubbish bag she found under the sink.

'And soon,' said Molly.

'I am here, you know. I thought you'd come round to talk about Jess getting married,' Jack said.

'We have but we'd like to ensure we all live long enough for her to make it down the aisle,' said Molly, scraping something unrecognisable into the bin. 'Have you got any bleach?'

Jack shook his head. 'It's not environmentally friendly. Anyway, about the wedding. Bertie thought the Tythe Barn would be the ideal place – it's got plenty of parking and loos and all that stuff. And there's room enough for a marquee out the front if you wanted one.'

'And it's beautiful,' added Molly.

'There is that,' said Jess, handing Jack the tea towel. 'And the kettle's boiled.'

'I can take a hint. Oh, and the other thing – are you still looking for a place to live or are you shacking up with the marvellous Max till W-day?'

'Why?'

'Well, you remember Heaven's Gate?' he said, sliding the first of the freshly dried cups onto the counter top.

'The little cottage by the estate church?'

'Uh-huh, one-up, one-down and a bathroom? I know it's not exactly a palace but Bertie told me to tell you that it's empty if you're interested.'

Jess stared at him. 'Are you serious?'

'Uh-huh. I mentioned that you were looking for somewhere short-term and he said if you wanted it you could have it – it's empty at the moment, so you could move in straight away. I mean it'll only be until you get married so it's not like he'd be tying it up for a long-term let or anything.'

'Do you know much he wants for it?'

'He said three hundred pounds a month – and you'd have to pay your own council tax and bills.'

Jess gaped. 'That's crazy – that's half what I'm paying at the moment.'

Jack grinned. 'Well, in that case you'd better snap it up

before someone else does and then you'll have plenty of money over to buy me a beer. Or maybe you could pay me back in cleaning and ironing.' He glanced around the kitchen.

Molly and Jess both looked at him.

'So I'll take it that that's a no then?' he said mockmiserably, then continued, 'anyway, I've got the keys to the barn and the cottage – which do you want to look at first?'

Molly looked across at Jess; she was positively beaming with delight. 'The cottage,' she said.

By the time they drove back to Molly's house to pick up Jess's car and rescue Nick from Bassa, Jess was positively bubbling with excitement. Spending Saturday with Jack and her mum had been lovely. The barn was perfect. Freya knew a great ceilidh band, the local pub ran a really good outside bar and Jack knew someone who could do them a hog roast. It felt like they'd more or less got the whole thing nailed.

'God, it's so perfect,' Jess said, voice full of glee. 'Isn't it?' She was sitting in the passenger seat, eating mints, talking nineteen to the dozen, flicking through the images on her digital camera of the photographs they'd taken at Vanguard Hall.

'God, I can't wait to show these to Max. The cottage is lovely – and the barn is gorgeous, all those fabulous beams. I was thinking we could have big swags of holly and ivy and red ribbon, really festive. Did I tell you Helen is coming down next week? She's got some sketches for me to look at. Maybe I should bring her over to show her the cottage – and what about the church? I mean, isn't that just stunning? It's so sweet and everyone can walk down through the estate to the reception.' Jess shimmied her shoulders in delight. 'God, I can't believe it. I'm going to ring the vicar tonight to see if she'll come over and conduct the service.'

Molly smiled. 'We need to talk to Marnie and Noo.'

Jess paused for a few seconds and then said, 'Mum, this is *my* wedding and this is what I want.' She sounded very, very sure of herself for the first time in days, and Molly was delighted.

'And what about the cottage? I'm really envious.'

Jess giggled. 'I've got to be out of my place by the end of the month so it couldn't have been more perfect, although I'm probably going to have to put some of my stuff into storage.'

'You can store it at ours if you like,' offered Molly. 'It's not for very long. What about work?'

'Well, it's only a couple more miles and come December I'm going to be living in Norwich with Max anyway. I can't think of a nicer place to spend my last few months as a spinster, can you?'

Molly smiled. At least that was something sorted out, and Jess was right, Vanguard Hall was perfect, although Molly couldn't help wondering as they drove away how Max and Marnie would take the news.

'So how did it go?' Max sounded tired and distracted.

'It was great. I really wish you'd been there,' said Jess, curling up on the sofa, phone tucked under one ear. 'I've just emailed you the photos.'

'I'm sorry I wasn't there. I'm not doing this very well at the moment, am I?'

'Not really.' Jess paused. 'I got the message on the blackboard.'

He laughed. 'I don't know how you put up with me.'

'Me neither. How's work?'

'Tedious – we'll probably be out of here by midnight.'

'I was thinking maybe I could drive over,' said Jess.

'Sweetie, it's a lovely idea and don't think I'm not grateful, but there's not a lot of point really. I won't be home till one, probably later, and I'll be seeing you tomorrow.'

'Right,' said Jess with a sigh. 'Oh, by the way, Jack's boss offered to let me rent one of the cottages on the estate for a couple of months. It's empty now – so I've been thinking maybe I could move in there next weekend. A lot of the stuff here came with the house so I'll just take the basics and get Mum to store the rest for me. The cottage is really tiny . . .'

There was a pause and then Max said, 'I thought Mr Petrovsky said you could stay there until you found somewhere else?'

'Well, he did and now I have. Mum said I could move in with them if I wanted to, but this is such a cool place. And if I move into the cottage at the Hall I haven't got to commit to a six-month let.'

Jess paused for a few seconds, wondering if Max might jump in and say it was silly to pack everything up twice and offer to let her move in with him, but sounding uncomfortable, he said, 'All seems a bit rushed to me. Won't he let you hang on for a little longer? It's only a few more weeks, really.'

'Last time we spoke he said he'd really like me out by the end of this month and this way I can be – just. I've just rung Helen and she said she'll give me a hand.'

'Ah,' Max said. 'Right. She's coming down next week, isn't she?' The way he said it suggested he clearly had no idea when Helen was coming.

Jess laughed. 'Don't tell me you'd forgotten. We're all supposed to be going out for supper.'

And then he paused again before saying, 'You do understand that I really need to get the house sorted out before you move in, don't you? I know we didn't really have much chance to discuss it, but I do need to get it straight, cleared out, decorated, move all the computers out.'

141

'No problem,' said Jess. 'I mean it's not ideal but I can live with it.'

'Right. And you're okay about tomorrow?'

'Going to see your parents? Of course. What time are you picking me up?'

'About nine?'

'Okay, I've given Mum and Nick the directions and I thought I'd print off some of the pictures of the Tythe Barn, and the little church and the rest of the estate to bring with me. Oh, and don't forget next week, Helen, supper or something.'

'Okay – tell me and I'll be there.'

'I was going to ask her to be my bridesmaid,' Jess said. 'You don't mind, do you?'

'No, not at all.'

'Good.'

'So in that case I'd better make an effort, hadn't I?' Max said.

Jess laughed. 'Promise?'

'I'll certainly try.'

Chapter Thirteen

'Do come in,' said Max's father, holding the front door open for Molly and Nick. 'Come through, come through.' He waved them into the hallway and the cool, inviting shadows of the house beyond.

It was Sunday morning, just before twelve.

The journey down from Norfolk had been lovely. Nick had done the driving and Molly had spent the trip watching the countryside unfurl like a bright sunlit banner while listening to 'The Archers' on Radio 4 and eating sweets. Short of being in bed with a mug of tea and the papers Molly couldn't think of many better ways to spend a Sunday morning.

The sun was shining, the autumn light buttery-warm and the village where Max's parents lived as pretty as a postcard.

The Laburnums was on the edge of the village and sat in a semicircle of weed-free pea gravel. It was an elegant 1930s property, half-timbered and rendered white, built in a style that whispered stability and old-fashioned family values.

They had barely cut the engine before Harry Peters, Max's father, had appeared at the doorway, all smiles and welcoming waves. Dressed in a well-cut sports jacket, a crisply ironed open-necked shirt, brown brogues and cavalry twills which Molly suspected were his concessions to casual, Max's father was exactly as she had imagined he would be. Handsome, very upright and nicely turned out in a rather conservative, understated way, he had the bearing of a man who had served in the RAF.

By contrast, Nick was wearing a very nice jacket over a Pink Floyd teeshirt and jeans, with proper shoes rather than trainers – which Molly knew from experience was his concession to weekend smart.

'You must be Jessica's mother,' Harry was saying.

'Please call me Molly,' said Molly, extending a hand. 'And this is my partner, Nick Richardson.'

Max's father nodded. 'Nick, Harry Peters, delighted to meet you. So how was the drive down? Find us all right, did you? A10, M11, M25, A3?'

Molly smiled as Nick and Max's father shook hands and dropped into the mysterious language of motorways that lets the most disparate of men bond.

'Not bad at all,' said Nick. 'Actually it was quite a good run. The M25 was clear as a bell.'

'Really?' said Harry, nodding. 'That was a piece of luck – a couple of weeks ago . . .'

Molly zoned out once they moved on to the junction numbers and tales of congestion past.

'Come on through and meet Daphne,' said Harry eventually. 'We thought we'd have drinks outside on the terrace while the weather holds. The happy couple aren't here yet but I'm sure they won't be long now,' Harry continued, all smiles and bonhomie. 'I've booked us a table at the Lion – just a few minutes' drive down the road, super food. We eat there quite a lot. Wonderful chef. They do some of the best roast beef I've ever had although don't –'

'Don't tell Daphne I said so,' said Max's mother, standing in the hallway at the bottom of the stairs. Tall and stockily

144

built, Daphne Peters was dressed in a pleated navy skirt, floral cotton blouse, pastel-blue cardigan and sensible shoes, her short grey hair tucked neatly away behind her ears. Great bones and bright dark eyes redeemed her from looking frumpy, and made her handsome instead. Daphne Peters struck Molly as capable and totally unflappable; the kind of mother Molly wished she had had, and sometimes wished she'd been. Daphne had the wholesome, unadorned beauty that the middle classes excel in, and she appeared genuinely pleased to see Molly.

The round of introductions made, Daphne said, 'We're so very glad you could make it. And we're delighted Max has finally found himself such a lovely girl.'

'At long last,' snorted Harry. 'He's brought her down to see us a couple of times. Charming girl – absolutely charming.'

Ignoring him, Daphne continued, 'Jessica is a real credit to you – such a pleasant young woman. We couldn't be more pleased. I'm eager to hear all the wedding plans. Do come on through, I thought that we'd have sherry in the conservatory while we wait for the others.'

'We've got a table booked for one o'clock,' said Harry, taking Molly by the elbow. 'Have you been to Hampshire before?'

Sherry schooners, along with a decanter and little bowls of biscuits and nuts were already arranged on a silver tray on a rattan side table just inside the conservatory. At the far end of the plant-filled sunlit room French windows opened up onto a small paved area set with seats and a swing.

'Well, well, well,' said Harry, smiling. 'Isn't this nice.'

Molly smiled. 'Thank you for inviting us. It's great to meet you both and under such wonderful circumstances. And what a view.' She looked out. 'You have a superb garden.'

'My passion,' said Daphne, following her gaze.

'Mine too.'

Daphne's smile broadened and Molly sensed any momentary shyness ebbing.

'You're a gardener?' asked Daphne.

Nick groaned. 'Oh no, not another one – I can't get Molly in once she's started, unless it's to get me out there to give her a hand with something or move something or dig something up.'

Harry nodded knowingly and pulled out a pipe which he packed with tobacco. 'Same here, no peace for the wicked. We've got this chap who comes in and helps twice a week but he never seems to be here when madam wants something done.'

Daphne rolled her eyes. 'Don't exaggerate. Two tubs of petunias – anyone would think I'd asked you to help re-site the Hanging Gardens of Babylon. I'm sure the reason Harry spends so much time at the golf club is just in case he's called on to move a bag of compost. We could take a little walk round later if you'd like to, once everyone's arrived.'

As she spoke Harry tipped the decanter in Molly's direction. Molly nodded. 'Thank you.' Under normal circumstances she would have run a mile from sherry but today felt like a sherry day, a sensible-older-generation-all-meeting-up-and-being-sociable day. Harry poured out half a glass of something that looked like stale urine and handed it to Molly. 'There y'go, my dear. Do help yourself to nibbles. Driving?' he continued conversationally to Nick.

''Fraid so,' said Nick.

'Ah, the short straw,' said Harry sympathetically. 'In that case would you like some orange juice or something?'

'Be lovely,' said Nick.

'Max tells us you're on the radio, that must be exciting,' said Daphne as Harry went off into the kitchen.

Adeptly they launched into the conversations that oil the wheels between strangers. Nick and Harry soon discovered they shared a passion for F1 racing, Daphne and Molly had the garden and family and Radio 4 and within minutes they were chatting away, if not quite relaxed then very close to it, and Molly found herself telling Daphne all about the Tythe Barn.

'It sounds absolutely lovely,' said Daphne, topping up the sherry glasses.

Molly, mouth full of homemade cheese biscuits, made an effort to nod. 'Oh it is, and the gardens are gorgeous. I think it's a real privilege to be able to use it. It's on the estate where my son Jack works.'

'Oh yes, of course,' said Daphne, eyes brightening with genuine interest. 'Jess was telling us about it last time she was here.'

The conversation bubbled on easily through barns and walled gardens and pruning roses, past fading wisteria and slugs, while on the other side of the table the men talked fast cars and journeys and jobs.

It felt easy and the slight tension Molly had been feeling about meeting Max's family was rapidly dissipating. The paved terrace was warm in the midday sun, with cool patches of dappled shade cast by nearby trees so that they could sit and take in the view without baking or being dazzled. Daphne was just telling Molly about the local horticultural club, of which she was chairwoman, when they heard a car crackling in over the gravel at the front of the house.

Harry set his glass down and got to his feet. 'If you'll excuse me,' he said. 'Sounds like more arrivals.'

'I'm really looking forward to hearing all about the

wedding plans but thought that perhaps we should wait until everyone is here,' Daphne said brightly. 'I mentioned to Jessica the other day that I have a friend who makes wedding cakes. I've got her card here for you both. They are quite superb – and obviously if we can help in any way, we'll be only too happy to.'

'Thank you, that's wonderful,' said Molly, as Daphne got to her feet and headed inside after Harry.

Nick looked up from his orange juice. 'All right?'

Molly nodded. 'Fine, how about you?'

He grinned. 'Good. Harry raced at Le Mans – one of the twenty-four hour races back in the Sixties.'

'Is that good?'

'Good? It's bloody excellent.'

A few seconds later they heard the voices of people arriving from inside the house. Molly looked up expecting to see Jess and Max, but instead Marnie teetered towards her in impossibly high-heeled red sandals, followed close behind by Jonathon.

Bare-legged and unnaturally orange, Marnie was immaculately made up and dressed in a black sundress so tight that she looked as if she had been sewn into it. She made a great show of air-kissing Daphne and Harry, who looked a little stunned by their new arrivals. She wasn't alone. Molly had no idea that they had been invited.

Jonathon smiled a greeting and raised a hand. He was carrying a large black leather portfolio and was wearing a straw fedora and a mauve cravat in a way that telegraphed Marnie's influence. He took the hat off when he saw Molly staring at him with raised eyebrows.

'Hi,' said Marnie with a rictal grin. 'Hope we're not late, are we?'

'Not at all, not at all. Looks like everyone turned up at

the same time,' said Harry cheerily, as Max and Jess followed in close behind them and said their hellos. 'Mind you, at least we're all here now. If you'd like to sort out the chairs, Max, would you? While I sort out the drinks. Molly, another sherry for you? Everyone all right for nibbles?'

'My God, the trouble we've had getting here,' said Marnie, before anyone else had a chance to speak. She dropped her handbag onto one of the cane chairs. 'I kept *telling* Jonathon that the sat-nav was wrong – but would he listen? We had to ask a man out walking his dog in the end. We were meant to be here half an hour ago. We went down the same road three if not four times, didn't we, Jonathon?' And then, apparently all in the same breath, she caught hold of Daphne's hand and said, 'So pleased to meet you. You must be Daphne. JJ has told me *so* much about you. And you must be Harry.' She swooped on him like a hawk onto a rabbit, taking hold of both hands as she pulled him close. 'I can see where Max gets his good looks,' she purred. Poor Harry Peters practically flinched as she kissed him again. 'I'm so glad to finally be here. It's been a nightmare. And I think I'm getting a headache.'

A step or two behind her were Max and Jess. Jess lifted a hand in greeting and rolled her eyes heavenwards, while Marnie made a great show of slumping onto the swing chair, slipping off her sandals and pulling her perfectly pedicured feet up alongside her.

'But at least we're here now. Isn't this lovely?' Marnie said with a sigh, looking around her as if they had just landed in some tropical idyll. 'I'm JJ's wicked stepmother, Marnie,' she explained, with an expression that promised swift retribution to anyone who decided that was anything other than a joke. 'We've both been dying to meet you, haven't we, Jonathon?'

149

'What?' said Jonathon and then blustered, 'Oh yes, yes of course. Very keen to meet you both. Delighted – where shall I put this?' He held up the portfolio.

'Oh, for goodness' sake, Jonathon, stand it on the floor,' snapped Marnie. Turning to Daphne, she said, '*Such* a catch, your gorgeous boy,' glancing up as she spoke at Max, who coloured furiously.

Daphne had the good grace to smile politely. 'How nice to meet you.'

'Well,' said Marnie as she slipped off her jacket. 'What a super house – and this is Jonathon, my husband, JJ's father.' She waved a tiny hand in his direction.

Molly, who had made a sterling effort not to let the surprise register on her face, smiled as Marnie m'wwaa'd air kisses in her direction. 'Molly, darling, what a lovely surprise. How super to see you.' She nodded towards Jonathon, still struggling with the portfolio. 'I've brought Noo's notes down with me for us all to have a look at later.'

'Lovely,' said Molly grimly. 'I don't know whether you've spoken to Jess yet, but we had the most brilliant day yesterday at Vanguard Hall.'

'It was amazing, I've brought some photos,' said Jess with a grin. 'And I found a cottage. How good is that?'

'Really?' said Marnie. 'How nice.' But even as she was speaking her eyes and her attention were moving away from Molly and Jess towards Harry, the perfect host, who was busy handing out sherry and nibbles.

'Gosh,' she said, peering at the bowl he was bearing. 'Are those cashews? Do you mind if I have one or two, only we didn't get a chance to stop on the way down because of the sat-nav. I'm not sure if Molly mentioned it, but I'm on a special diet,' she went on, making a great show of taking the tiniest handful and then breaking each nut in half.

Max meanwhile started making polite conversation about the traffic and the long drive down with Nick and Jonathon, and so it wasn't until they were getting ready to go to the pub that Molly had any time to catch up with Jess.

'I didn't know that Marnie and your father were coming too,' Molly said in an undertone as they made their way out towards the cars.

Jess looked sheepish and then sighed. 'No, me neither, well at least not until this morning. First thing I knew was when Dad rang up to check on the directions and get the postcode so he could punch it into the sat-nav. I'd expected them to come down and meet Max's parents at some point but not today,' she said as they headed across the gravel. 'I thought it was just going to be us. It would have been a lot simpler.'

'So Max invited them?' Molly asked.

'You'd think so, wouldn't you? I can't remember him saying anything about it. But this week has been totally mad, what with all the wedding stuff, and work and going to see the vicar. Max said he'd spoken to his mum, and rang Dad and Marnie up earlier in the week and that he'd told me – but I can't remember it.' Jess made an attempt to paste on a smile and then she stopped and waved the words away. 'Don't mind me. I'm knackered and he's been working all week. We've barely spoken and when we have he's been tired and I've been grumpy and he's totally caught up in this new contract. Mind you, once we're married we'll have all the time in the world to talk – apparently.' She grinned. 'Anyway, what Max said was that it would be better for us all to meet up at once; you know, get it all over and done with.'

Molly nodded, although Max had managed to make it sound like some kind of mass dental appointment, which, from the look of pain on Jonathon's face, probably wasn't that far off the mark. 'He's probably right,' she said. 'Do you two want to come down to the pub in our car?'

Jess shook her head. 'No, Max is keen on us going on our own so we can leave when we want.'

Molly laughed. 'Sounds ominous. Are you thinking of making a run for it?'

'Who knows,' said Jess. 'See you down there.'

'Everyone like to follow us?' said Harry, holding up a hand. 'We're going to turn right and then just follow the road down into the next village. It's only a couple of miles or so. Okay?'

No one else suggested car-pooling, so everyone headed off in convoy towards the Lion.

'This should be interesting,' said Nick, as he and Molly got into the car.

'I wasn't expecting Jonathon and Marnie to be here.'

He grinned. 'From the look of Marnie I don't think she realised that we were going to be here either.'

Molly pulled a face. 'It'll be fine. After all, we've all got to get together sooner or later to sort out the details. And Max's parents are lovely.'

Nick raised his eyebrows. 'Shame Jess can't say the same about hers.'

'What do you mean? I'm perfectly presentable.'

He shook his head with amusement. 'You should have seen your expression when Marnie walked in.'

Molly closed the car door.

Max's father had booked a table in a quiet alcove away from the rest of the diners in the pub, which meant that they could talk and easily hear each other above the background hubbub.

The Lion was a classic English rural pub with low beams,

inglenook fireplaces and an embarrassment of horse brasses. There seemed to be a lot of to-ing and fro-ing about who sat where, mostly instigated by Marnie, but in the end Harry headed up one end of the table, Jonathon the other, with Daphne to Harry's right and Marnie to Jonathon's right. Max and Jess sat along one side and Molly and Nick on the other. While everyone ordered, Harry gracefully deferred to Jonathon and Marnie when it came to choosing wine, and when Jonathon insisted they should have a couple of bottles of champagne there wasn't a single voice raised in dissent.

'Well,' said Jonathon, getting to his feet, glass in hand. 'I just wanted to say how very nice it is to meet you all. I'm absolutely delighted that my lovely daughter has managed to bag herself such a fine chap and I'm sure you're equally pleased Max here has hooked up with such a charming young woman. I know from Marnie that she and Molly and Jess have all been frantically busy and that the wedding plans are all well underway, and so I think we should have a little pre-wedding toast to the happy couple. And may this be the first of many happy family get-togethers.'

Toasting was getting to be a bit of a habit, thought Molly as she lifted her glass.

'Well said,' said Marnie.

Harry beamed.

Daphne smiled indulgently at her son, glasses were raised to Jess and Max, and as Molly glanced around the table she caught the look of love and warmth that passed between Jess and Jonathon, and felt a rush of pure joy. It felt like the most special perfect moment.

After the toast conversation naturally turned to the wedding plans.

'So how far have you got with all the arrangements?' Daphne began. 'I know we're a bit of a way away but if there is anything we can do, anything at all? You're happy for us to arrange for the cake, Jess? We can talk about what you want and my friend has a website. And I was thinking perhaps we could do some of the flowers?'

'Yes,' said Harry. 'And I know traditionally the bride's father picks up the tab, but well, what I'm trying to say is that you and I should have a little chat after lunch, Jonathon.'

Jonathon smiled. 'That's very kind of you. I know that Marnie and Molly and Jess have been traipsing the length and breadth of Norfolk to try and find a decent venue and sort everything out.'

'And at such short notice,' Marnie chipped in. Molly noticed that as she spoke Marnie beamed at Max, who smiled right back. 'Actually we can't complain, we've been terribly fortunate. My daughter, Mimi, got married last year and we used the most fantastic wedding planner then. She is terribly good and so we thought, well, if it worked once, why reinvent the wheel?' Marnie smiled. 'We've all been doing a lot of homework and footwork and been to see some super places. But now that the big decisions have been made we can let Noo, that's the planner, do all the rest of the donkey work – so nice to just have the job of choosing, isn't it?' She smiled at Jess, whose expression was a little bemused.

Daphne smiled encouragingly. 'As I said, if we can help,' she said, and then turned to Jessica. 'The big question is, have you found the dress yet?'

Jess smiled, eyes sparkling. 'No, but Mum and Marnie and I are going to go and look at some next week to get some ideas and I've got this friend, Helen, who is a designer, who is going to make –'

'Helen works in theatre, darling, not haute couture,' said Marnie with a sniffy little wrinkle of her nose. 'When we were shopping for my daughter last year we found this super

154

little shop in Norwich. We thought we'd make a start there – they have such lovely dresses.'

Jess continued, talking over Marnie. 'Helen won an award at college for her costume design. And it's a winter wedding so I'm hoping that between us we'll be able to come up with something exquisite. She's coming down next week –'

On the far side of the dining table Marnie pulled a little *what-can-you-do* face.

'It all sounds very exciting I have to say,' said Daphne.

'Oh, which reminds me,' said Jess, glancing at Max for moral support. 'We've been working on the guest list, so if you'd like to give us a list of people that you'd like to invite –'

Daphne nodded. 'Of course, although I'm sure Max can sort that out.' Just as Max looked about to protest, the waitress arrived to serve the first of the starters, while at the head of the table a second waitress was handing out bread.

'So Molly tells me you've decided where you're going to have the wedding,' said Daphne, as the girl slid a little dish of pâté and French toast in front of her. 'And Max was telling us you've already chosen the church.'

Jess, who until now had looked quite subdued, beamed. 'I'm dying for Max to see it. The Tythe Barn is absolutely perfect.' She grinned. 'I'm so excited. I've been telling him about it on the way down. The estate where we're going to have the wedding reception has got this fantastic little Gothic chapel. I'm going to speak to the vicar to see if she'll consider marrying us there.' As if suddenly aware that she was babbling, Jess blushed furiously and said, 'And obviously we'll send you a list of B&Bs and hotels as soon as we can. There are a few places nearby and being early in December I don't think it's going to be that much of a problem.' She glanced across the table and said warmly, 'I'm sure Marnie's wedding planner will be able to help sort it all out for us. This place is –'

But before she could launch into a description of Vanguard Hall, Marnie jumped in and said, 'Probably absolutely charming. We've been to see some wonderful places over the last week, but I think we were all agreed that one stood head and shoulders above the others.'

Jess stared at her.

Marnie turned her attention to Daphne. 'It's perfect. They've got the most gorgeous wedding suite available for the date we want. Talk about a stroke of luck. Big country house, super grounds, lovely guest rooms, really good restaurant. And obviously the church is already booked so that's that all sorted out. Everything else is relatively simple, especially with Noo, our planner, on board.'

A peculiar little hush descended on the table. Molly saw Jess's stunned expression, while Marnie, oblivious, poured herself another glass of champagne.

'Sorted out?' Molly said cautiously.

Marnie smiled and took a sip from her glass. 'Yes, church wedding at St Mary's followed by the wedding reception at Halley Hall, first weekend in December. You have to admit we've been really lucky to get the date we wanted. And I've got Noo sorting out coach hire – I was wondering if they have a choir at the church?'

Jess was ashen. 'You are joking, aren't you? You haven't booked Halley Hall, have you?' she said. 'We only saw it on Thursday.'

Marnie stared at her. 'Someone needed to make a decision, sweetie.'

'That would be me and Max,' said Jess. 'Please tell me that you haven't booked it.'

Marnie narrowed her eyes. 'Sorry?' She did an odd little false laugh. 'Did we miss something here? Of course I've booked it, JJ – we were really lucky that it was still available.

156

And we all loved it, didn't we? They have lots of enquiries – wedding parties are their main business.'

Everyone was silent.

'Well, you're just going to have to unbook it,' said Jess in what Molly thought was a remarkably calm voice given the circumstances. 'You'll have to ring them up and tell them that we've changed our minds. Or get your precious Noo to do it.'

'It's not as easy as that,' said Marnie, shifting uncomfortably. 'Perhaps we ought to talk about this later? Now is hardly the time.' She pressed a napkin to her lips and smiled at Daphne and Harry, before trying out the same expression on Molly and Nick. It cut no ice.

The atmosphere around the table had gone from convivial to tight as cheese-wire in under thirty seconds.

'You knew that we were going to see Vanguard Hall before anything was decided,' said Jess. 'You knew that's where I wanted to get married. Mum and I went yesterday to make sure I wasn't taking everyone on a wild goose chase. They've got a fabulous little church on the estate that Bertie said we could use. It's exquisite, like something out of a fairy story, and the Tythe Barn is stunning.'

Marnie laughed, apparently trying to break the tension. 'Darling, I know you said that we should go and take a look, but who wants to be sweeping out some old barn before we can use it, not to mention shooing piglets out of the church.' She laughed again, trying desperately to make eye contact, trying to make everyone join her in her little joke. 'We talked about this, JJ. Everything is on the spot at Halley Hall. Daphne and Harry can stay there. There are some lovely rooms in the main hotel and some super self-contained accommodation in the stable annexe if anyone wanted it – it is perfect.'

She turned to Harry and Daphne, looking for support.

'We had to strike while the iron was hot. You have to understand Julia, their wedding co-ordinator, said she could only hold the date for a day or two, and two other couples had already expressed an interest.' Marnie's expression was that of a drowning woman, clinging tight to a sinking ship. Finally, desperately, she said, 'I did talk to Max about this . . .'

Jess swung round to stare at him. 'You knew about this?' she gasped.

Max looked anxiously from face to face. 'Well yes, when Marnie rang up and we talked about it – we'd all seen it and everyone loved it and then she said she really thought we needed to make a decision, and I know how much stress you've been under trying to sort it all out, so I gave her the go ahead –'

'And you listened to me rabbiting on about Vanguard Hall all the way down here and you didn't *say* anything?' Jess swung back to look at Marnie. 'Why on earth did you ring Max, why didn't you ring me? Or Mum?'

From the expression on Marnie's face there was no straight answer to that question – although Molly guessed it was because as far as Marnie was concerned there were only two ways to do things in life, Marnie's way or the wrong way.

'I was worried about all this old hall nonsense. We all want your wedding to be memorable for all the right reasons, especially if it's on the radio. And I thought that you liked Halley Hall. We thought this was one less thing for you to worry about – one less thing on the to-do list,' simpered Marnie.

'I still don't understand why you didn't ring either of us,' said Molly, pressing Marnie for an answer. 'Surely we can cancel.' She looked at Jonathon, trying to keep the tone even and reasonable. Jonathon as usual wasn't saying a word but was fiddling with a slice of bread. Max looked uncomfortable, Nick looked as surprised as everyone else and Harry and Daphne just looked horribly embarrassed.

Marnie squared her narrow shoulders, not that it did very much to disguise her discomfort. 'I don't see what all the fuss is about. Halley Hall is perfect.'

There was silence.

'The thing is,' she continued, when it was obvious that nobody was going to say anything, 'as there isn't that much time between now and the wedding, Halley Hall asked for quite a substantial deposit and when I was speaking to Julia, she said that if we paid fifty per cent up front then she would arrange for us to have precedence with hotel bookings, free upgrades and spa vouchers for any of the wedding party staying there, as well as insurance – and a really good discount on wines and champagne.'

Jess was looking daggers at Marnie.

'It was a really good deal. So no, I'm afraid that we can't cancel without your father losing a lot of money,' said Marnie. 'I mean, we all said how lovely it was. It's perfect. I can't see what's not to like.'

'Yes, but the thing is,' said Molly, 'Jess didn't like it. She hated it.'

Marnie stared at them both. 'She should have said something.'

'*I did say something*,' growled Jess. 'I told you I wanted everyone to go and look at Vanguard Hall, I told you what kind of wedding I wanted. I told you exactly what I had in mind and you ignored me. Totally.' Her voice was slowly getting higher and louder. 'You didn't like what I wanted, because you think you know best, but you don't.' Jess was getting more and more hysterical with every word.

Marnie looked around. 'Darling, please. I really think you should keep your voice down, people are looking.'

'I don't care who's looking,' snapped Jess. 'How could you do this, Marnie? How could you? Dad, you said it would be all right – you promised me she wouldn't take over and she has. This is supposed to be my special day and you've totally and utterly ruined it.'

'I'm sure we can find a way to sort this out. We need to talk to the hotel – exactly how much are we talking about here?' Nick asked quietly.

Marnie's lips snapped tight as a submarine door.

'Ten thousand pounds,' said Jonathon calmly, through a bite of buttered roll. 'Give or take. It wasn't exactly that, but we thought it would be easier if we rounded it up. You know, make the thing easy to work with – and Marnie negotiated a very good deal. I saw the figures and I thought, if that's what my Puss wants, well that's what she shall have.' As he finished Jonathon beamed at Jess, who promptly threw down her napkin, burst into tears and stormed out of the restaurant.

'So, how's your meal?' said the waitress, sliding another basket of bread rolls onto the table.

Chapter Fourteen

Molly was the first one out in the car park, a millisecond ahead of Max. They looked right and left. Jess wasn't anywhere in sight.

'Which way do you think she went?' asked Molly.

'Well, the beer garden's packed, so probably that way,' he said, pointing towards the village. They headed out into the narrow street, Molly getting increasingly anxious. It was two or three minutes before they found Jess. She had taken herself off a little way down the road and was standing on a stone footbridge crossing a stream. She had her back towards them and appeared to be watching the water below.

Max took a step towards her and then glanced nervously at Molly. 'Do you want me to talk to her?'

Molly stared at him. It struck her as very odd thing to ask. 'What are you going to say?'

He sighed and stuffed his hands in his trouser pockets. 'Good point. I'm not sure, really. Probably just how sorry I am. I want you to know that I didn't actually mean to give Marnie the go-ahead to book the wrong venue. You don't think that Jess will think I did it on purpose, do you?'

'I don't know what Jess thinks, Max.'

He's saving his own skin, thought Molly, grimly.

As the two of them hurried over to where Jess was

standing, she heard their footsteps and turned around, great big tears rolling down her face. Eyes puffy, red-faced, she wiped them away, taking most of what was left of her make-up with them.

'Go back to the pub, please,' she said, her voice tight and crackling with emotion. 'I just want to be on my own for a little while. I'll be fine – really – just go in and start your lunch. I need a minute or two to get myself together. Please.'

'I'm so sorry,' said Max, holding back as if she might be an unexploded landmine.

Molly glanced at him and then at Jess. Why the hell didn't he just cuddle her? 'I don't like the idea of you being out here on your own. Is there anything I can do?' she asked. 'Anything?' As their eyes met, Jess's bottom lip began to tremble again.

'I'll be fine, Mum. Just fine. I mean no one's going to die just because Marnie booked the wrong wedding venue, are they?' Her voice broke in another flood of tears.

'Oh baby,' Max said, shifting his weight hesitantly. 'I'm so sorry –'

Jess looked up at him. 'It's really not your fault. Marnie should have rung me or Mum, not you.' She scrubbed her eyes again. 'What on earth must your mum and dad be thinking, they'll think you're marrying a nutter. Go back inside. I won't be long. I promise.'

Molly caught the look that passed between them. Jess was self-conscious, while Max looked embarrassed and uncom-fortable.

'We can't just leave you out here,' said Molly, pulling a tissue out of her bag. 'Is there anything you want?'

Jess rubbed her face with her sleeve. 'Well, if you really wanted to help, you could go back in there and strangle Marnie,' she said, managing a funny crooked smile and a choking laugh. 'How could she do that? How could she?' Her voice cracked. 'God, I am so angry with her. I can't tell you. I didn't want her involved at all, just you and me, but I didn't want to upset Dad, and I thought this way we would keep the peace.' She sniffed. 'I've been standing here thinking this is crazy. Most girls would give their right arm to be married at somewhere like Halley Hall. I feel like Paris Hilton throwing a hissy-fit – but it was really important to me that this was about Max and me and our friends and family, not some bloody stagey-showy place. And all that money . . .'

She looked stricken, and then Max put his arms around Jess, who curled up against him and sobbed, and Molly, refusing to be shut out, stepped closer and said, 'Come on, let's go back inside. Let's go to the loo and wash your face.'

'Good idea,' said Max, keeping his arm around Jess's shoulders. 'Come on.'

'I don't think I can go back in,' said Jess miserably, but Max wasn't taking no for an answer. They made slow progress along the street till they got to the Lion, where Max let go of her.

'Go and talk to your mum and dad,' Molly said to Max as she took Jess's hand. 'We'll be fine.'

Max nodded and headed back to the dining room, looking relieved.

In the ladies' loo, Jess washed her face and did the best to repair the damage wrought by way too much crying. She brushed her hair, tidied her clothes and generally made a show of pulling herself together, before sitting down on one of the little plump overstuffed chairs by the sink. All the while Molly stood behind her, keeping guard, feeling as upset and furious as her daughter, and angry with herself for not being able to protect Jess from Marnie.

'How can I possibly go back in there and eat lunch now?

They'll think that I'm such an idiot.' Jess's voice wobbled again. 'Max's parents are really nice but they're so sensible and old-school. They probably think that Max is marrying a complete and utter lunatic.'

'I'm sure they don't think that at all.' Molly paused. 'You sort your make-up out. Let me go and have a word with them. I'm sure they'll understand. Take as long as you like.'

Walking out of the loo, Molly wasn't altogether sure what she was going to say or come to that what she was going to find when she got back to the table. As it was, Daphne was the first one who spotted her and, while putting on a good show of British stiff upper lip, nevertheless looked horribly uncomfortable when their gaze met. Marnie meanwhile was talking to Max and Harry as if nothing had happened, while at the head of the table Jonathon looked on, his face totally impassive.

'Ah, there you are,' said Marnie, as Molly pulled out her chair. 'We wondered where you'd got to.'

Nick glanced up, expression concerned and anxious. 'How's Jess?'

'Yes, how is Jess? Is she coming back? Only, I'm famished!' said Marnie. 'We've asked them to hold the main course till she gets back.'

The insensitivity of the woman was breathtaking. Molly turned her attention to Jonathon who met her eye with an expression of empathy. 'She's really upset and concerned about what you might think.'

Jonathon nodded and dropped his napkin onto the table. 'Fair enough, I can understand that. I think it might be better if Marnie and I left. I'll settle up – maybe you and I can talk about this later, Molly?'

Molly nodded. 'I think that's a good idea. Thank you.'

Marnie swung round indignantly. 'What? But we can't go,

we haven't finished lunch yet. Look, surely, Molly, you can understand that I did what I thought was best under the circumstances. I'm sure Jess will be able to see that.'

'I'll ring them on Monday to see if we can do anything about the booking,' Jonathon said, getting to his feet. He leaned across the table and caught hold of Harry's hand, pumping it firmly. 'Very nice to have met you.'

'Ah – you too,' said Harry. 'If there's anything we can do.'

Jonathon nodded and said his goodbyes to Daphne while Marnie stared indignantly at Molly. 'I really think I ought to go and have a word with JJ – I can't see what all the fuss is about. I mean this is *absolutely* ridiculous. We've come all this way. We're supposed to be celebrating. She can't skulk in the toilet for the whole of the afternoon. What on earth will Daphne and Harry think?' Marnie stepped a little closer and in a stage whisper said, 'Are you sure she isn't pregnant – or bulimic?'

Molly, resisting the temptation to punch her, caught hold of Marnie's arm and said, 'I think Jonathon is right. I think if would be much easier if you left now.'

Marnie was indignant. 'Obviously we're all sorry that JJ is upset but we couldn't have her having her wedding in some barnyard. Surely you have to see that I'm right about this?'

Molly leaned in closer still. 'Marnie, you're missing the point here. This is *their* wedding, not yours, not mine. Jess has tried very hard to be polite and not offend you because she doesn't want to upset you or her father, but to be perfectly honest after what you've just done today and seeing how hurt she is, I don't care who I upset. You've so overstepped the mark – if you've got any sense at all you'll bugger off out now before I forget that I'm supposed to be being civilised about this.'

Marnie's colour deepened to something close to scarlet. She opened her mouth and for one glorious moment Molly thought that was she going to say something else but instead she had the good sense to pick up her handbag and, letting out a theatrical sigh, allowed Jonathon take her arm and head outside.

Across the table Molly noticed Daphne sigh with relief.

A few minutes later Jess reappeared from the ladies' loo, looking puffy-eyed, uncomfortable and embarrassed. Max got to his feet and went to bring her over.

'You want a drink?' he said gently, taking hold of her arm. 'You okay?'

'I'll be fine, thank you.' She smiled at him. 'And I'm so sorry –' she began, bottom lip starting to tremble, but Daphne held up a hand.

'Don't apologise, my dear. It's perfectly understandable. Now –' She raised the hand higher to catch the attention of one of the waitresses. 'Let's have some lunch, shall we? I don't know about you but I'm ravenous.'

Nick caught Molly's eye and in the facial shorthand that develops between couples asked if she was all right. Molly smiled ruefully, grateful for the feel of his hand on hers under the table.

Jess slipped into the seat alongside Max and took a long pull on her wine. 'I needed that,' she said with a long, breathy sigh.

Remarkably the rest of lunch went quite smoothly. Daphne determinedly grabbed the reins and chatted about the weather, the garden and how she felt sure that Jess's choice of dress would be just perfect. She asked all sorts of questions about Helen's design career and the cottage Jess had found and discussed what sort of flowers they might have for the wedding.

Daphne, evidently calm in a crisis and stoic under fire, pressed on – if not exactly ignoring the elephant in the room, then throwing a large plaid conversational rug over it and carrying on with classic British sang-froid. Following her lead Molly launched into the fray, as did Nick, and between them they just about salvaged lunch, helped by the fact that the food was fabulous.

It was around three when they all finally headed back to The Laburnums for a cup of tea and a round of farewells before driving back to Norfolk. Jess did a good job of keeping it together and, although subdued, at least she didn't cry, not quite – but there were several times during the course of the meal that Molly caught her eye and could see her daughter struggling to hold back the tears.

Max and Jess, blaming pressure of work and things to do, didn't linger. 'How the hell are we going to sort this one out?' said Molly, standing in the driveway waving them off.

Nick sighed thoughtfully. 'Let's see what the hotel has to say – don't worry, I'm sure there is a way we can fix this.'

'You promise?' said Molly.

He grinned and slipped his arm around her waist. 'No, but I'll certainly do my best.'

'More tea?' asked Daphne.

Molly nodded. 'Would be wonderful.'

'Would you still like to take a little stroll around the garden or have you got to make tracks too?' Daphne said, as they headed back towards the house.

Molly glanced at Nick, who said, 'Entirely up to you. I'm fine, Harry was planning to show me his collection of Fangio photos and memorabilia.'

Molly pulled a face. 'Is that good?'

Nick grinned. 'Oh yes, Juan Manuel Fangio. Formula One racing driver – came from Argentina, born around 1911.

167

He dominated the first decade of motor racing. A lot of people still consider him to be the greatest driver of all time.'

'Right.' Molly laughed. 'Anything else I should know?'

Nick smiled. 'Apparently Harry's been collecting Fangio memorabilia all his life.'

Daphne lifted an eyebrow. 'Along with golf equipment, fly-fishing rods and malt whisky.'

Molly saw Nick's eyes brighten. 'In that case you two can be as long as you like,' he said with a wry grin.

Outside the afternoon heat had settled down to a gentle simmer and it was nice to be out in the air after the hubbub of the pub. The two women strolled down towards the stream in companionable silence. The air was heavy with the scent of honeysuckle and from close by came the sounds of someone cutting the grass. Molly took a deep breath, enjoying the scent of a great scramble of roses covering one of the fences; time, she suspected, to deal with the omnipresent elephant.

'I'm really sorry about the way lunch turned out. I wanted to thank you for handling Jess so gently. I had no idea that Marnie was going to be here, let alone drop a bombshell. Nick and I had really been looking forward to meeting you both.'

'Likewise.' Daphne smiled ruefully. 'Hardly your fault, though. Max had told us about Marnie but . . .' She paused, her expression suggesting she was carefully measuring what she said next. 'I felt so sorry for Jessica. It was a terribly insensitive thing to do. Let's hope there is some way to put it right. Do you think you'll be able to cancel the booking?'

'I don't know. I'm going to talk to Jonathon about it. I'm sure we can do something.'

Daphne nodded. 'Poor Jess. It was so much simpler when we were young. The local church and the church hall, a few sandwiches and a band. It was hardly rocket science. Harry didn't even have to decide what to wear – he just turned up in his uniform.' She smiled, her expression full of memories of her own wedding day. 'We were terribly hard up in those days. I remember my mother and I altering my older sister's dress. Me standing on a chair while she pinned me into it. I think I had a new veil and definitely shoes, but there certainly wasn't anything like the fuss they make these days. My mother's next-door neighbour ran up my bridesmaids' dresses on an old Singer sewing machine. Lovely they were, in a kind of lemon-yellow silky material. I remember we had to make them calf-length because she ran out of material.'

Molly smiled. 'We were about the same; although I did have a new dress, we borrowed a veil and my auntie baked the cake –'

Daphne laughed. 'Those were the days.'

Half an hour later the two of them wandered back into the kitchen. 'It's been so lovely to meet you, but I really do think we should be making a move,' said Molly. 'It's a long drive home.'

Daphne nodded. 'Of course. Would you like that cup of tea before you go? I can almost guarantee that Harry is only halfway through the great Fangio tour.'

Molly hesitated for a split second and then nodded. 'That would be nice – would it be okay for me to use your loo?'

Daphne plugged in the kettle. 'Certainly, I'd use the one upstairs if I were you. Harry smokes his pipe in the one in the hall, and no matter how much I complain about it he refuses to give the damned thing up. It's up the stairs, straight down to end of the corridor, last door on the right.'

Molly went upstairs, taking her time. It had been quite a day. She felt tired and was getting a killer headache; the wine she'd had at lunchtime certainly wasn't helping.

The first floor of The Laburnums continued the rest of the house's theme of magnolia walls, with broad expanses of heavily patterned floral carpet and matching lampshades. Here and there were large pieces of furniture – an ottoman used as a window seat, topped with chintz cushions that matched the curtains of the window overlooking the drive, a tallboy with a top covered in a collection of china trinkets, and family photographs in silver frames. Open doors gave glimpses into over-furnished bedrooms with padded eiderdowns and fringed rugs, the whole house giving an impression of solidity and stable, old-fashioned family life.

Molly found the bathroom and before going back downstairs washed her face and hands and dragged a comb through her hair. She glanced in the mirror above the sink and was surprised by how well she looked.

God, what a day. It was nice to have a minute or two alone to gather her thoughts and compose herself.

From downstairs Molly could hear the sound of male voices and good-humoured laughter. Obviously Harry and Nick had bonded in unexpected ways. Mentally she ran through a checklist of things to do when they got back. If they were lucky a phone call would be all it would take to sort things out and maybe the Marnie episode, when they looked back, would be the best thing any of them could have hoped for, if it got her out of their hair.

Molly went out onto the landing. In the hallway below Harry was telling Nick a story about some dinner he and Daphne had been to, and as he was talking Molly's attention drifted to the collection of photos on the tallboy. There were pictures of babies and weddings, children with a dog; there was Harry in his RAF uniform, pipe in hand, looking dapper and very 'Dambusters' with children either side of him that presumably were Max and his sister. There were school photos and holiday snaps, and beside them were more recent pictures of Daphne and Harry all dressed up at a wedding, Daphne in a sensible navy suit. Alongside that one was another picture of a family group gathered around the bride and groom. Molly moved in more closely and realised with a start that she was looking at Max's first wedding. Without thinking she picked up the photograph.

It was a striking image. Max was beaming delightedly at his new bride. His hair was longer and his face thinner; he was gangly with the unguarded expression of youth, all wrapped up in a slightly ill-fitting morning suit. His eyes were bright with emotion – he looked completely besotted – and for a moment Molly felt unexpectedly sad for him. All that promise, all that hope, all gone.

Molly's attention moved on to the bride, who, rather than looking at her groom, was staring confidently out at the camera, head tipped provocatively to one side, eyes alight with mischief. Her hair was styled back off her face in a classic chignon, decorated with a little tiara. She was wearing an explosion of white frothy lace and carrying a great water-fall of roses – but that wasn't what stopped the breath in Molly's throat.

Molly recognised the bride. For a few seconds she hesitated, looking more closely at those neat, well-made features. Surely she had to be mistaken? Molly took the photo over to the landing window to get a better look. Sure enough, she knew without a shadow of a doubt that she had seen the face in the photograph before. Worse still, she knew exactly *where*.

Those bright eyes, that confident manner. Max's first wife was the jeweller Molly had met in Cambridge. This was the woman who had served her in LovesPleasures, the one who had been so kind and so curious. This was the woman who had designed and made Jess's engagement ring.

As she mulled over the thoughts, Molly stood staring at the photograph and she didn't hear Daphne coming up the heavily carpeted stairs. She jumped when the other woman said, 'Oh, hello. I came up to get some more tea towels. Are you all right there?'

Molly nodded. 'Sorry, you must think I'm awfully nosy. I was just looking at this.' She held out the picture to Daphne, who coloured slightly.

'Oh, gosh,' said Daphne. 'I'm so sorry. I suppose I should really have packed all those away. I never thought – and it's such a lovely picture. I hope you're not offended?'

Molly shook her head. 'Not at all. They made a lovely couple.'

Daphne sighed. 'I know. It was a long time ago now but it broke Max's heart when Lucy left him. I did wonder at one point if he would recover.'

Molly paused, waiting for Daphne to carry on.

'I've always felt that they were both far too immature to marry. But you can't tell them that, can you? And Lucy – she was lovely girl but a bit of a handful, if you know what I mean, although as far as Max was concerned I'm sure that that was a lot of the appeal. You know what boys are like, the girl who won't be tamed, all that sort of thing, and young men love a challenge. Anyway, they hadn't been married very long when she ran off with his best friend, actually his best man. It was all very messy. When Max came home one afternoon she told him she had something to tell him.' Daphne paused, taking a long breath. 'Poor Max thought she was going to tell him she was pregnant.'

'Oh,' said Molly softly, hearing the pain in Daphne's voice even after all the time that had passed.

Daphne waved the memory away. 'All very unfortunate. Although I'm certain that Max has told Jess all about it.'

Molly nodded. 'I'm sure he has. What happened to her?'

'To Lucy? As soon as it all came out, they moved away, which I have to say was a huge relief for everyone. I couldn't bear to see her in the village. I'm not sure where they went to be honest, somewhere in Cambridge I think. Lucy designs jewellery. They opened up a shop between them. Terribly charming girl but . . .' Daphne paused and smiled, her expression held firmly in neutral. 'Well, who knows what goes on behind closed doors. All I know is that it's taken Max an awfully long time to get over it and that's why we were so pleased that he's met Jess. I'm sure she'll make him very happy. She always seems so level-headed and delightful. Poor girl, today must have been awful for her. I do hope you can cancel the booking for this wedding reception.'

As Daphne was speaking Molly was still busy turning the name over in her head. *Lucy Peters; LP – the same initials as LovesPleasures.* Surely it was impossible that Max *didn't* know that Lucy ran LovesPleasures, which led Molly to the inescapable conclusion that Max had deliberately chosen to have Jess's engagement ring designed and made by his ex-wife.

Daphne smiled. 'We haven't seen Lucy for years.'

Molly looked up and wondered if Max could say the same.

Chapter Fifteen

The drive home was long, uncomfortable and prickly, and Jess could barely bring herself to speak, she was so upset and angry. What should have been the most perfect day had turned into a complete disaster. She watched the countryside rolling past, while alongside Max kept his eyes firmly on the road. It couldn't have been that easy for him either, Jess thought; she knew how important it was for him that lunch with his parents went well, and it had hardly done that.

They were halfway home and every time Jess thought about Marnie and lunch and the wedding she got a great big, red-hot, indignant pain in her chest that made her want to cry, followed almost immediately by a sense of humiliation and embarrassment.

Sitting in silence, Jess could feel her emotions swing between feeling totally justified in her indignation and wondering if Max and his family and *her* family thought that she was behaving like a spoilt child, stamping her feet and being all precious and princessy. After all, who wouldn't want to be married at Halley Hall?

Max hadn't said a lot either but, knowing Max, that was because a) he didn't know what to say, or maybe b) he was waiting for Jess to speak first so that he could take the lead from her, or alternatively c) because he had got compartmentalising things down to a fine art and he was thinking of something else entirely, probably related to work. He was quite likely working on machine codes or deciding where to put his new printer.

Because Max was a lot older than she was, there was a part of Jess that hoped that he would come over all paternal and alpha male and tell her not to worry her pretty little head about the reception, that he would sort it all out. She glanced across at him. So far – nothing.

Eventually, when they were caught up in a long queue of traffic, Max turned to her and said, 'So, how're you doing?' As words of comfort and support they left something to be desired but Jess was relieved that at least he was talking to her – she was tired of the silence.

'Okay.'

He nodded. 'I looked at the website.'

'Sorry?'

'I looked at the website for the venue after we went there. You know, the hall, the one we went to look round, the one that Marnie booked.'

'You did?' Jess hadn't meant to sound quite so surprised but so far Max hadn't been particularly hands-on with any of the wedding plans.

He nodded. 'And I know that you're going to hate me for saying this, Jess, but I think that it's perfect.'

'Perfect?' she murmured. 'Halley Hall?'

Max nodded. 'I was really impressed when we went there. I know that it might not be exactly what you had in mind but it's fabulous. The ideal place for a fairytale wedding for my fairytale princess.'

Jess stared at him to see if there was a hint of sarcasm but saw none. 'You're serious?' she asked.

'Absolutely. It's going to be stunning in December. Did

you look at the photos they'd got online in the gallery? They arranged them by seasons, and the suite Marnie booked had this huge Christmas tree in the foyer and lights and all the trimmings. It looked wonderful – apparently they do a Victorian-themed decor in there in the winter, roast chestnuts, hot toddies – and the idea that the guests can stay there too makes it even better and so much easier. The hotel run some sort of pick-up service from the station if there is a party booking in.'

Jess felt a funny, uneasy sensation in her chest. Max had obviously been through the website with a fine toothcomb. 'You liked it?'

'I'm sorry, but I really did,' he said gently. 'I had no idea that you hated it. I would never have said yes to Marnie if I'd known. To be honest I thought it was superb, just the kind of thing I'd expect from you – tasteful, elegant. Something special. I can easily see a lot of my family wanting to make a weekend of it.' He paused, glancing across to catch her eye. 'I just wanted to tell you,' he said in the same quiet voice. 'And also to say that I'm happy to go with whatever you decide. It must have been horrible for you today and I'm really sorry.' Then he smiled and Jess nodded. Ahead of them the queue of traffic had started to move and Max's concentration went back to the road.

'And I'm sure this other place is just as lovely,' he said. 'Like I said, you've got great taste.'

This time Jess didn't nod. Vanguard Hall was lovely but in completely different ways. Ways that were important to Jess but not necessarily to other people: it was in the middle of nowhere, there were a few hotels locally but none within walking distance and certainly none of them a patch on Halley Hall. The nearest one had a pool table but no pool and the local village a Spar shop but no spa.

What Vanguard Hall had were stunning views and fabulous gardens with secret dells and a Tythe Barn oozing history and character and rural charm, but there were only three loos and they'd need to get caterers in and an outside bar, and possibly heaters, and get someone to shoo the bats out. The barn was lovely because it was also basically untouched and by untouched it meant that here and there the plaster was crumbling and ivy crept in through the windows of the area Bertie said the caterers could use as a prep room. While it might just about scrape by health and safety regulations on fire exits and disabled access, it didn't have wall-to-wall carpets and chandeliers or themed anything – and for Jess that was the charm. Vanguard Hall was lovely in impractical, romantic ways, ways that she could see crusty old relatives and family flying in from New York might not fully appreciate.

'So are you saying you would prefer it if we had the reception in Halley Hall?'

Max's eyes were still firmly fixed on the road. 'No, I'm not saying that. I'm just saying it is fabulous and it's a great venue but I'm really happy to go along with whatever you want.'

'Right,' said Jess, haltingly.

'So shall we got to my place or yours?' He grinned. 'I can't tell you how long this week has felt or how much I've missed you.'

Damn, thought Jess slinking down in the seat. 'About Halley Hall –'

In Nick and Molly's car they were also talking about the wedding – more specifically, the bridegroom, his ex-wife and the ring.

'So do you think Jess knows about the ring?' asked Nick.

Molly shook her head. 'I have no idea. But I would've thought if she did she would have said, *oh, and Max's ex-wife designed the ring*, wouldn't you?'

'Maybe she thought you would think that was weird,' said Nick, pulling in behind a people carrier full of what appeared to be Buddhist monks.

Molly shook her head. 'I doubt it. Remember, Jess grew up with a mother who once interviewed both ends of a pantomime horse *in situ* and went on the photo-shoot with a six foot seven bodybuilder who water-skied across the Channel dressed as Minnie Mouse. Jess knows the odd designer ex-wife wouldn't have fazed me one little bit.'

'Maybe she didn't think it was important enough to mention.'

'That doesn't work for me either. It would have been a lot harder for her to say she hated the first ring if she'd known Lucy designed it. She would have said, *I can't really say I hate it, because Max's ex-wife Lucy designed it. He'll think it's because of her*, or something.'

Nick laughed. 'Okay, Foster of the Yard. You know, you're wasted on local radio, you should be interviewing suspects and cracking cases. So you're saying Jess doesn't know?'

'It's the only thing that fits,' said Molly.

Nick sighed. 'Turning out to be a weird day one way and another, isn't it? Only thing though, surely Max would have known Jess would meet Lucy when she went to pick up her ring?'

'Not necessarily. Lucy said she didn't normally work in the shop. I'm assuming Max didn't think they'd meet. And anyway, Jess told him I was going. So even if Lucy had been there I don't suppose Max expected me to put two and two together and come up with his ex-wife.'

'So, what kind of man has his girlfriend's engagement ring designed by his ex-wife?' asked Nick.

'I don't know. Maybe Lucy was the easy option when it came to choosing jewellery? Or perhaps he thought Jess wouldn't mind?'

'Or more likely, that he thought she wouldn't find out,' said Nick. 'It has to be deliberate, every town and city has at least one jewellers', you don't just happen across your ex-wife's shop by accident. I think Max wants to let his ex know that he's getting married.' Nick glanced across at Molly. 'So . . .' he said slowly.

Molly sighed. 'So, am I going to say something to Jess or am I going to keep these lips zipped?' Molly mimed it as she said it.

Nick nodded. 'You took the words right out of my mouth.'

Molly groaned as she slid down into the passenger seat. 'There was nothing about this in the mother of the bride's handbook.'

Chapter Sixteen

'And how was your weekend?' asked Stan as Molly ambled into the office first thing on Monday morning. He was sitting at one of computers in their section of the open-plan offices of EAA, and when Molly peered over his shoulder she could see he was already working on the running order for the show.

She put her bag on the floor and pulled out her chair, clicking the mouse on her desk so that the twin of the screen Stan was working on came up on her own machine. 'Chequered probably best describes it. How about yours?'

Around them, unnoticed, was the detritus of life on a radio station. Besides the normal workaday stuff of offices, to one side of Stan's desk stood a life-sized cut-out of Obi-Wan Kenobi, currently wearing a yellow sunhat and shades. Behind Molly, in the walkway, heaped up on a plastic palm tree, was a pile of teeshirts from a recent holiday competition, while hanging above Stan's desk was an orang-utan, one hand wrapped around a ceiling brace, a microphone cradled in the other.

'Me and Enrico went on a tango weekend. Fantastic,' Stan added with a little tangoesque flourish of his hands. 'Two whole days of torrid Latin passion.'

Molly raised her eyebrows. 'Really. You want me to bring

that up at the next planning meeting? Tango with Stan might just be the perfect post-Christmas pick-me-up, programming-wise. All those people with a few extra pounds to lose. I can really see it hitting a nerve with them upstairs.'

Stan's expression suggested that he wasn't keen but Molly pressed on. 'Don't pull that face. I bet you look a real cutey in a pair of patent leather dancing pumps – and don't forget I owe you one,' she said, glancing down at her screen.

'What do you mean?' And then he cottoned on. 'Oh come on, it wasn't just me. Phil thought a wedding special was a good idea too. Wedding countdown has got to be a winner. We've had so many phone calls since Jess rang you, and we've got some really good stuff going up on the website. Here, have a listen of this. I've uploaded the first of the wedding-special trails.' He handed Molly a set of headphones. 'I reckon they're bloody good.'

Molly slipped on the headphones. There was a nice flurry of introductory noises, a church organ and sounds of a subdued but expectant congregation.

'Getting married is one of the most wonderful and exciting journeys we make in our lives,' Molly heard herself say, voice-over style, above the opening bars of the wedding march. 'Over the next few weeks we're going to be looking at just how exciting and how wonderful. Join me, Molly Foster, here on East Anglian Airwaves next week as we follow my daughter Jess and her fiancé Max on their journey of a lifetime.'

Stan grinned. 'Sounds great, doesn't it? I've got a couple more here.' He ran the cursor down over more titles. 'Chink of glasses, reception sounds. Light but informative, a little bit cheesy. Who wouldn't want to tune in?'

Molly hesitated for a few seconds but decided on balance not to answer that. She glanced at her watch, wondering whether there was time to speak to Jonathon before getting down to work. She couldn't help wondering if he had already rung Halley Hall.

When she and Nick had arrived home from Hampshire yesterday evening she'd tried to ring Jonathon and Marnie at least a dozen times, but infuriatingly first of all no one answered and then the line was constantly engaged.

Molly wasn't sure whether this meant Marnie had taken the house phone off the hook or that Jonathon had been wrestling with the powers that be at Halley Hall despite it being a Sunday. What she wanted to know was if he had rung Jess, whether he had talked to Max, if he had spoken to anyone at Halley Hall and what the hell they were going to do if they wouldn't let him have the money back? To make things worse Jonathon's mobile appeared to be turned off as well.

Molly had tried to ring Jess but her phone had been engaged too and her mobile was going straight to voicemail, although in Jess's case Molly suspected she was trying to avoid being browbeaten into anything else by Marnie. So Molly left a message and waited to be called back. When that didn't happen, she rang again, and again, and maybe again – she wasn't sure because she'd lost count after the first five calls.

It occurred to Molly that maybe she couldn't get through because Jess was talking to Jonathon, or that she had rung the hotel rather than trust it to Marnie or maybe she was talking to Max or maybe it was because Jess had decided she didn't want to talk to anyone ever again.

To try and get over the sense of growing frustration Molly had taken the dog for a long walk, but it didn't help, and – having taken her mobile to ring people while she was out – came back feeling even more frustrated and cranky than when she left.

Finally at around midnight Molly had given up. Jonathon and Jess would no doubt eventually ring her, so she settled on it being a fault on the line, or at least that was what she convinced herself after two glasses of Baileys, which Nick insisted she needed.

So, with the sounds of Stan's trail still fresh in her mind, Molly wasn't altogether surprised to find an email from Jess in her inbox. It was the contents that stunned her. It read:

```
Hi, Mum. It was brilliant to see
you and Nick yesterday.
I know you'll think I'm barking mad
but Max and I have been talking
about Halley Hall and I think it
might be okay after all. And before
you ask, no, I haven't been
abducted by aliens or brainwashed
by Marnie and Noo, but once we'd
talked it through I can see that
it'll probably be more practical
for everyone and people staying
and things - anyway I've rung Dad
to let him know it's okay, and
rung Bertie to say although we
loved Vanguard Hall we decided we
need somewhere with accommodation
- although I would still like to
punch Marnie for booking it
without talking to me first.
Love, x

PS. I've decided to move my stuff
into Heaven's Gate over next
weekend. I don't suppose there's
any chance of you and Nick giving
```

me a bit of a hand next Saturday,
is there? Jack's going to help and
Helen will be there, but Max, who
I'd got down as the extra muscle,
has got to jet-set off to some
meeting in New York mid-week and
won't be back till Saturday and
the last thing I want is someone
with jet lag manhandling all my
precious things. Love again,
me x

Molly stared at the email and re-read it twice more just to make she had understood it properly and then picked up the phone to ring Jess. Then she thought better of it and hung up. She'd ring later, when she'd finished sorting out the day's work and there was more time to concentrate on saying the right things. Meanwhile she typed:

Hi, Honey.
Of course we'll give you a hand –
and you know the offer to stay
with us is still open if you want
to. We've got plenty of room.
And yep, even though it was a bit
of a surprise I'm really happy to
help you have whatever kind of
wedding you want, you know that.
If you want Halley Hall that's
great but DON'T be pushed into it
because you think there's no
choice. If you don't want to have
it there then I'm sure we can

185

```
work something out - but if you
do then let's order lots of those
little parcel things with green
stuff in them.
Love you lots,
Mother of the Bride. X
```

Molly hoped that it struck the right note. As she pressed send, Phil appeared in her sightline; he was carrying a clipboard and looked as if he had the weight of the world on his shoulders.

'Morning,' she said. 'And how was *your* weekend?'

Slipping into the seat alongside her and waking up his computer, he said, 'My girlfriend, Michelle, found all the notes we'd made. You know; venue, vicar, vintage champagne, *honeymoon*.'

Molly waited.

'I told her it was for work but she wasn't having any of it, and then she found a pile of brochures I'd taken home to look for story ideas and *wham*... Switched on my phone this morning and I've got fifty text messages telling me I'm a sly old dog and saying things like *well done, mate* – and then her mum rang me on the way in to work to ask if we'd set a date.' His eyes narrowed. 'This is all your fault, you know.'

Molly laughed. 'No, I think you'll find that this is karma, Phil. Remember, you were the one who said a wedding would make a great story, you're the one who wanted to raffle off being a bridesmaid. Have you never heard of the karmic boomerang?'

Phil sniffed. 'No, but I have just had a text from my sister wanting to know if she can be matron of honour and a really snotty one from my mum asking me why she is the last to know.'

Stan looked up from his computer. 'I said it was a good idea too, what the hell is going to happen to me?'

They both looked at him. 'Civil partnership, Stan,' said Molly, with a straight face.

Phil, hunched over his keyboard, nodded. 'Uh-huh, I'm sending Enrico a website link even as we speak, www.gorgeousgayweddings.com.'

At which point the phone rang. It was one of the receptionists. 'Hi, Molly, I've got Jasper Wynn-Jones on the line for you.'

Molly raised an eyebrow. 'Jasper Wynn-Jones, anyone?'

Phil nodded. 'Oh yes, he's the poisonous spider man. You remember that guy from the wildlife place said he'd get someone to talk about spiders that are coming in, in imported fruit?'

Molly nodded, vaguely remembering the conversation. 'He's in today?' she said hesitantly, looking back at the running order. 'Give me a clue.'

Phil pointed to the screen. 'Healthy eating; choose your lunch with care.'

'What?'

'I came in early to avoid the sudden of rush of marriage congratulations. The woman we'd got booked to come in to talk about new, healthier school meals cancelled; I was thinking laterally.'

'And?'

'Booked the spider man.'

Molly said into the phone, 'Mr Wynn-Jones, how very nice of you to ring back. May I call you Jasper?'

'Certainly can. I was wondering what time you wanted me and my little chaps to be in?'

'I'm not sure if Phil told you, but we're running a campaign to encourage and support healthy eating,' said Molly

187

cautiously. 'As we've got the lunchtime slot we're hoping to catch people before they go out and get something.'

'Good idea.'

'We're helping people choose the healthy option, avoiding dangerous foods, red meat, transfats, things with lots of salt or sugar or bananas full of funnel webs –'

'Actually they're huntsman,' said Jasper.

'Sorry.'

'Along with a few black widows and tube webs of course.'

'Right,' said Molly.

'They're fascinating creatures.'

'I'm sure they are. Shall we say, eleven?' replied Molly.

'Lovely. See you then, then.'

Molly hung up and glared at Phil. 'What other little surprises have you got lined up for me?'

He managed to pull an I-have-no-idea-what-you-mean face and then pulled up a page on his screen. 'Jasper's got his own website,' he said.

By half past three Molly had finished the show and was working her way through the programme's to-do list, although she hadn't quite got over Jasper's spider collection that he had brought into the studio. Besides spider man, they'd had two organic farmers, a vegetarian restaurateur and a woman who made her own fruit juice on the show, and the phones had rung, and people had already been hitting the website and links to the web ads so everyone was happy.

The phone rang on the desk but, for once, Stan got there before Molly did. He nodded and listened and then passed her the handset. 'For you – some woman about wedding dresses? What day have we got the recording in the diary for?'

But it was too late, the call was through. 'Hello,' Molly said. 'You're through to Molly Foster, how can I help you?'

'Morwenna Hatch here. I'm just giving you a quick ring to confirm the details for tomorrow evening. I believe I spoke to your planner a couple of weeks ago?' The woman had a voice so improbably high that presumably when she got excited only dogs could hear her.

'Do you mean Phil, or maybe you talked to Stan?'

'Actually I spoke to a woman – your wedding planner? She's been to us before. Charming woman.'

Molly took a deep breath and, with a skill honed over years, made it sound as if she knew exactly what Ms Hatch was talking about. 'Ah. Do you mean Noo?'

'Yes, Noo, that's it. Rather unusual name. Anyway, tomorrow evening? I'm just checking to make sure you're absolutely *au fait* with all the details. We do have clients who get into all sorts of muddles, wrong time, wrong day – we like to make sure,' she purred.

'Right,' said Molly. 'In that case maybe we should just run through the details again – better safe than sorry.' Marnie had mentioned making an appointment to see dresses but Molly couldn't remember exactly when or where. Presumably Marnie had intended to firm up the arrangements over their ill-fated Sunday lunch.

'Excellent,' said Morwenna. 'I've booked you in for seven thirty – that's Mrs Molly Foster and Ms Jessica Foster, Noo Jacobson, and Mrs Marnie Foster, formal wedding, mother of the bride and bride, stepmother of the bride and planner?'

Sounded like hell on wheels. Molly glanced at her desk diary; there was no seven thirty pm. In fact, no anything – just a blessedly big gap, a home early, catch-up-on-the-ironing-while-listening-to-the-radio gap.

On the phone Morwenna was still talking. 'And am I right in thinking that we're billing Mr Jonathon Foster? Of course the fee is credited against the gown and any accessories you choose.'

'We have to pay to look at your dresses?' said Molly, not quite able to keep the incredulity out of her voice.

Ms Hatch laughed. 'Sorry, perhaps Noo didn't explain? I assumed you understood. We've been doing it for a couple of years now. We find it stops time wasters and lets us turn choosing your wedding dress into something to remember. We provide light refreshments – champagne and canapés – and a photographer, then, while you relax, two of our lovely models will show you a selection of the gowns we have available this season.

If Jessica wants to, she can try on any of the gowns, and then once we've taken the order we make arrangements for her to come in for a first fitting. We've found it takes the pain out of choosing the dress. Of course we have a full range of accessories in stock – plus a really super selection of bridesmaids' dresses.'

'Right,' said Molly cautiously. 'Well, that all sounds wonderful.'
And expensive.

'So we can confirm, seven thirty tomorrow?'

'Actually, Morwenna, before we do that I just need to have a quick word with my daughter, just to make sure.'

'Well, of course,' said Morwenna, although she did sound a little stiffer. 'Could I ask you to confirm by five thirty; we have to book our girls by six this evening.'

'Certainly, if you could let me have your number.'

Morwenna rattled it off.

'And the name and address,' asked Molly cheerily, hoping Morwenna wouldn't realise that she had no real idea of who she was speaking to or where Morwenna's shop was.

'Gownena,' said Morwenna, slightly surprised. 'I spoke to your planner. Noo?'

'Can you spell that?' asked Molly.

As soon as Morwenna hung up Molly rang Jess's mobile. It went straight to voicemail, which wasn't that surprising given that Jess was meant to be at work. 'No, I don't want to leave a message,' Molly growled to Jess's recorded invitation. 'I want you to answer your phone.'

As time was pressing she rang Jess's office. When the receptionist put her through Jess was on the defensive before Molly had a chance to say so much as hello.

'If this is about the Halley Hall thing, Mum, I don't want to talk about it now. I'm up to my eyes at the moment. I'll ring you as soon as I get home. Promise. And I don't want you to worry about me. I'm fine – okay?' she said, all in one breath.

'Whoa there,' said Molly, worried that Jess was going to hang up. 'I was worried about you but that wasn't why I rang. Do you know anything about Gownena?'

There was a pause at the far end of the line. 'Is this a quiz?'

'No. Apparently it's the dress shop that Marnie's daughter Mimi bought her dress from and she's booked us all in to go and see some sort of bridal presentation tomorrow night at seven thirty. If you don't want to go that's fine by me but the woman needs to know by five thirty.'

'Shit, I'd forgotten all about it,' Jess said. 'To be honest I don't want to go anywhere with Marnie. And whoever sold Mimi that dress needs shooting. She looked like a packet of badly packed chipolatas. *And* Helen's arriving tonight.'

'Well, that's all right. How about I tell Marnie she can't come and Helen comes along with us instead? It might be fun – give you some ideas.' Although Molly didn't say so, she really wanted the chance to see Jess. She added, 'They're laying on champagne and canapés.'

Jess sighed, her reply heavy with sarcasm. 'Oh well, in that case we have to go. It's getting to be a way of life, all this champagne lark.'

'If you want to go I could drive you home afterwards and run you to work on Wednesday morning – that way you could enjoy some of it. Apparently the bill is going straight to your father.'

'We've got to *pay* to look at wedding dresses?'

'That's just what I said. Looks like it's deductible from anything we buy. There might be something – shoes, veil, maybe a tiara?'

There was another pause and then Jess said, 'And you're certain you can put Marnie off?'

'I'll ring now. We could grab a bite to eat before we go if you like. My treat.'

'Sounds good.'

'Brilliant. Do you mind if I record it?'

'Okay. I mean, it's not like I'm actually going to pick my dress from there, so yeah – why not.'

'Okay. If you want to come to the radio station we'll go from there.'

'Fine.'

'About Halley Hall,' Molly began, but Jess had already hung up.

Chapter Seventeen

'Wow, oh, my God, just look at you,' whooped Helen, dropping her bag in the tiny hallway of Jess's cottage and throwing her arms round her. 'Whooooo hhhhhhhooooooo – so this is what a blushing bride-to-be looks like, is it?' she squealed, hugging Jess tight against her. 'My God, you're all skin and bone. You haven't been dieting, have you?'

Bassa rushed around their legs in circles of pure excitement until Helen let Jess go, hunkered down and scratched him behind the ears.

Jess laughed. 'Come on in.'

Helen looked around. 'Oh God, it's lovely in here. It seems a real shame you have to move.'

'I know, but there wouldn't be enough room here for me and Max even if I could stay – he's got so much stuff.'

Helen grinned. 'Oh and what, you haven't?'

The little two-up, two-down was filled with a quirky, colourful collection of pictures, throws, and all manner of *objets d'art* that had just about turned the corner from student clutter into Bohemian chic. Jess was the palest thing in the place; wearing a long, baggy teeshirt over faded blue leggings, she had bare feet and her hair was scraped back off her face, and she wasn't wearing a scrap of make-up.

'How was the drive?'

'Horrible. God, I'm dying to get these shoes off and have a cup of tea. I didn't disturb anything, did I? Is he here somewhere?' Helen asked slyly, eyeing Jess up and down.

'I wish. I've just got out of the shower. Anyway, you're early,' said Jess, tucking away a stray strand of hair back over her ears. 'And I'm running late – I'm trying to cram in some overtime to cover the time off I need to organise the wedding. Come on through. I'll get the kettle on.'

Helen scooped Bassa up into her arms, who repaid the compliment by trying to lick her face. 'You took so long to come to the door I thought I'd caught the pair of you in bed. So, where is the groom, then? Upstairs, getting his clothes on?'

'Max?'

Helen laughed. 'Of course, Max – who else are you engaged to?'

'He's not here at the moment. He's working late tonight.'

'Bugger, I was hoping to give him the once-over,' said Helen, following her through to the kitchen. 'I'm dying to meet him. What's he like?'

Jess shifted her weight. 'He's hard to describe. He's nice – dark hair, brown eyes, older, got his own house, works in IT. Can be a bit reserved until you know him.'

Helen waited. 'And?'

'And I'm sure you'll see him while you're here.'

'And that's it?' Helen glanced at her. 'You don't sound very certain.'

'Oh, don't mind me. I'm having pre-marital mood swings. I've seen less of Max since we got engaged than when we were just dating. It's one of those things; he keeps saying I'll probably look back on this as being bliss once we are married.'

'Not taking you for granted, is he?' said Helen in a joky, concerned best-friend voice.

Jess sighed. 'No, it's work. He's up to his eyes at the moment.'

'So, you're marrying a rich workaholic? Sounds good to me. Let me look at the ring.'

Jess held her hand out towards Helen and wriggled her fingers.

Helen grinned. 'That is *lovely* – come here, let me have a closer look.'

Jess held it up, practically under her friend's nose, and then finally slipped it off and handed it to her. 'Max chose it. He knows this really good jeweller in Cambridge who designs and makes all his own stuff,' she explained, watching Helen's face.

'Okay, so he's just gone up in my estimation.' Helen turned the ring towards the light and smiled. 'It's gorgeous and so are you.' Helen's eyes were prickling with tears. 'God,' she said, sniffing them away. 'It's lovely. And I'm so envious. I don't think I'm ever going to find anyone mad enough to marry me.'

'Don't be silly,' said Jess, taking the ring back and slipping it on her finger. 'There's someone for everyone and don't worry, we'll try and sort you out with someone really fit at the wedding.'

'I'm going to hold you to that,' said Helen. 'I've brought loads of sketches for you to look at and some fabric samples and lace and stuff – oh, and some fantastic buttons.'

Jess grinned. 'I can't wait. You're sure you're going to be all right here on your own all day while I'm at work?'

Helen laughed. 'Yes. I'm a big girl now, don't look so worried. I've been looking forward to seeing you for ages. The last few months have been crazy. It'll be great. I can lie in bed till lunchtime without a shred of guilt, take the dog out, go and visit my mum, read, watch daytime TV – you have got *no idea* how much I'm looking forward to it.'

'And help me pack?' Jess asked, hesitantly.

'And help you pack. It won't take long with two of us. Have you got plenty of boxes?'

Jess nodded. 'I brought a load home from work.' Then she said, 'Actually there is something else I wanted to ask you. I was going to wait till later but –'

'Oh, God, it's not something awful, is it?' asked Helen anxiously. 'You don't want me to wallpaper anything, do you? Oh, or kill anything – or skin it?'

Jess laughed. 'No, of course I don't. It's nothing bad at all. Well, at least I don't think so.'

'All right then. Go on then, spit it out,' said Helen, still sounding slightly apprehensive.

'I was wondering if you'd like to be my bridesmaid,' asked Jess, all smiles.

It took a few seconds for the words to register and then Helen whooped and jumped into the air. 'Really? You're serious? Oh wow – of course. I'd love to. Oh God, oh, that would be brilliant. I've never been a bridesmaid before. Oh wow – that's fantastic.'

Jess laughed. 'I'll take that as a yes then, shall I? And at least this way you'll know you're not going to be stuffed into some shiny pink monstrosity with frilly arms.'

Helen pulled a face. 'You've been looking at my sketches, haven't you?' she said, and then grinned and hugged Jess again. 'Oh wow, I'm really excited now. God, I can't wait to show you my ideas. I've been working on something really stylish but so sexy, sort of fantasy medieval, a bit fairytale – and now I can make myself one too.'

'Well, don't. I don't want you upstaging me. You look really good at the moment,' said Jess. 'Life in London obviously suits you.'

'I love it. And the job is mad but fabulous – I've met some

great people. Although it's not the same as being somewhere I know well with people who know me.' Helen paused. 'You'll still come up and stay, won't you? Now I've got the flat. I know getting married changes things but we won't lose touch, will we?'

Jess stared at her. 'Don't be daft, I'm getting married – I'm not emigrating. We're friends, Helen. We'll always be friends. Come on upstairs and let me show you your room –'

'I've got a room?'

'Well, you have at the moment. And a bed.'

'I've got a bed?'

'Uh-uh, unless of course you'd prefer to put a sleeping bag in the bath just for old times' sake?'

'No, I'll give that a miss, thanks.' Helen picked up her bag. 'I want to talk to you about this getting married thing.'

Jess laughed. '*This getting married thing?* It's not like no one's ever done it before.'

'I know, but when there was a chance you were going to marry Glenn that was fine. What I'm saying is it felt right and we all knew him, and I liked him, so that was all right. But what if I don't like Max? What if he doesn't like me? I mean, God, that would be awful.'

'What's not to like about you?' Jess said quickly.

'What I'm saying is, what if he doesn't like your friends?'

Jess stared at her for a split second and then said, 'Close your eyes.' She pushed open the door to the spare room. 'What was the spare room like last time you were here?'

Helen, with her eyes closed, said, 'Bare plaster, a pile of boxes and a nasty yellow carpet – oh, and a mystery stain on the ceiling.'

'Open them.'

Helen looked around. The tiny room was painted the palest

197

olive green, the windows dressed with cream London blinds that softened the late afternoon sun to a warm glow. On the bed was a heavy woven cream throw embroidered with scarlet tulips and Jess had echoed the red and greens of the throw with matching cushions arranged over the pillows.

The little room's mismatch of furniture had been pulled together by painting it all with a cream wash. On top of the tallboy was a dark green glass vase filled to overcrowding with scarlet tulips. Alongside it were two neatly folded dark green towels.

'Taarraahhh,' said Jess with a grin. 'What do you think?'

Helen smiled. 'Bloody hell, it looks like something out of *Homes and Gardens*, this is lovely. Nice – really nice, and I love tulips. The light is superb in here.'

'I know, I use it as a studio when there's no one staying.'

'Shame you've got to go.'

'I know, but just wait until you see my new place. Right. I thought we could have a take-away for supper. Chinese, Indian, pizza, Thai?'

Helen nodded. 'I don't mind. I'm absolutely famished.'

'Me too.' Jess paused by the door. 'I just wanted to say it's great to have you here. I've missed you and I'd forgotten just how much – you know.' Her voice faded away.

Helen smiled, her eyes welling up with tears. 'That we are the dynamic duo? Double trouble? How could you possibly forget that? I'm hurt,' she teased.

Jess managed a funny, crooked smile. 'Do you want that cup of tea or would you rather have a glass of wine?'

'Tea. And then wine,' said Helen, following her back out into the hallway. 'What's the new place like?'

'Heaven's Gate? God, you're going to love it. It's out of this world. I just wish I could have more time there really. It's on the estate where Jack works.'

'Your good-looking baby brother?'

'Uh-huh. The whole place is amazing, like something out of Hansel and Gretel. These little windows and a tile roof, dormers. Ivy, old trees, red bricks. It's lovely and it's empty, and I'll be in there next weekend.'

'Sounds like a plan.'

Helen followed Jess and Bassa down into the kitchen.

'I told Mum you were staying and she suggested we went over there one night too, she'd love to see you. Then she rang today to say that I'm supposed to be looking at wedding dresses tomorrow night.'

'But I thought I was doing the dress –' Helen began.

Jess held up a hand to silence her. '*You are* – I love your stuff and I trust you not to make me look like a meringue. It's just that my stepmother booked this wedding woman and they're driving me mad. I'll tell you all about it while I'm making tea.'

'So why are we going?'

'To the dress shop? They give you free food and booze.'

'Case closed,' said Helen with a grin.

'And Mum thought we might get some ideas; we're going to meet up beforehand and grab something to eat. Her treat.'

'Gets better. How about The Waffle House?'

'God, I haven't been there for ages. Can you make a wedding dress with an elasticated waist?'

'Certainly can, although I was thinking more corsets – they're just as good, you just unlace them a bit.' Helen sat down at the tiny kitchen table and pulled a sketchbook out of her handbag. 'You want to look now?'

Jess plugged in the kettle. 'God, yes, but let's eat first. Mum is dying to look at what you've done.'

'How is she?'

'Fine, stressed over the wedding but then again, me too

199

– I think it probably goes with the territory. You wouldn't believe the stunt my stepmother pulled,' said Jess, taking a pile of take-away menus down off the shelf. 'You want to decide what you want to eat and I'll ring it through?'

Two hours, a curry and a bottle of wine later, they were sitting out on the tiny patio behind the cottage at a table lit by candles and fairy lights.

Since Jess had last seen her Helen had done something to her hair that made her look all sleek and finished and very grown-up. Helen was small, no more than five foot two but a pocket Venus, all curves, dark blonde hair and brown flashing eyes.

'Great hair,' said Jess.

'The guy in the flat below me does it.'

Jess grinned. 'Really? New romantic interest or gay?'

Helen sighed. 'First one and then the other. I should have known someone that buff was bound to be bent as a box of frogs, but Gray's lovely – he trained at one of the big salons and now he works for himself.' Helen patted her hair and then looked more closely at Jess. 'I'm worried that you've lost weight. I don't think I've ever seen you so skinny – you're not on some sort of stupid get-slim-quick-so-I-can-get-into-a-size-six-for-my-wedding-day starvation diet, are you?'

Jess shook her head. 'No, I think it's pre-match nerves. Doesn't matter what I eat.' She nodded towards her empty plate. 'The weight keeps falling off.'

Helen pulled a face. 'Well, we can't have that. All my designs are working on the sexy, romantic, wenchy, get-'em-out-for-the-boys look.'

Jess glanced down at her chest and then laughed. 'I suppose we could always use socks. You're sure you can cope with helping me to move? I can understand if you want to chicken out.'

'Wouldn't miss it. How many times have we shifted each other's stuff? Seems silly to move again though. I don't understand why you don't just move in with lover boy.'

'You'll understand when you see the cottage I'm renting.'

'But why not move in with Max?'

'It's – it's –' Jess stopped, aware that Helen was staring at her. 'It's complicated.'

'What is?'

'Well, Max's house is lovely, walking distance into the city centre, but it is very *his* at the moment, if you know what I mean. He's already said maybe we could buy somewhere bigger between us later.'

'Uh-huh, so you're not moving in together at the moment *because* –'

'It's not all that big.'

'Right, and that's a problem because –'

'Because the whole house is full of computers. And when I say full I mean *full*.'

'Okay, so he just needs to move them out,' said Helen, mopping up the very last of her rogan josh with a fold of naan bread. 'It's not exactly rocket science, is it?' She was frowning.

'He is going to move them. He's been looking for an office to rent and then once that's sorted out and all the computers have been moved, the house will need decorating and then there'll be plenty of room for me and Bassa and all our stuff.'

Helen's expression didn't change. 'So why isn't he rushing to do that, so that you can move in now? I mean, think what you'd save in rent alone.'

'Because, like I said, he is up to his eyes in work, which

is brilliant – we could really do with the money – but it's not giving him much time to do anything else.'

Helen raised her eyebrows. 'Doesn't sound that complicated to me.'

Jess sighed. 'Well, that's Max. He's –'

'Complicated?' suggested Helen, slipping the naan into her mouth.

Jess, not quite meeting her eye, nodded. 'You could say that. I just didn't feel I could ask him.'

Helen stared at her. 'You're getting married to him – you should be able to talk about anything.'

'I know but it's –'

'Don't tell me. I can guess. Anyway, do you want to look at my ideas for the wedding dress of the century or not?'

Jess grinned. 'God, I thought you were never going to ask . . .'

Chapter Eighteen

Morwenna Hatch stood to one side of a heavily curtained doorway, all smiles, her hands clasped across her chest like an opera singer waiting for her audience to settle. Molly, Helen and Jess – shown to their seats by a skinny girl with greasy hair, presumably a minion of the formidable Ms Hatch – were now ensconced on a large sofa which stood on one side of Gownena's large upstairs room.

While the rest of the room was painted magnolia, the seating was covered in the deepest peach velvet, the same colour as the carpet that ran from the matching curtains to a circular area at the far end of the room, which was flanked by several large freestanding mirrors. The walls were hung with large, soft-focus photographs of various brides in full wedding paraphernalia.

Here and there were plinths topped with peach silk roses, various tiaras, shoes and veils and on the opposite side to where they were sitting was an ornate cream-and-gold pelmeted recess in which hung a row of what Molly assumed must be wedding dresses, each carefully swathed in a floor-length white muslin bag. They looked like sides of beef.

Standing to one side of the mirrors and the plush peach carpet was Gerald Hatch, currently fiddling with his tripod.

'This is my husband Gerald, who will be capturing your

evening for posterity,' Morwenna had said as they walked through the shop door, somewhat unnecessarily as Gerald was already backing up ahead of them, taking photographs. 'We've found that our brides like to have a record of their evening with us and of course it helps when you come to selecting your gown.'

Gerald had a moustache and was dressed in ginger cords, a checked shirt and sleeveless v-neck sweater. He also had a handshake like a limp haddock and a roving eye that made Molly wonder if Morwenna hadn't employed him in the shop simply to make sure she knew where he was at night. As he leered at them the girl scuttled around handing out little notebooks and gold pencils topped with peach tassels.

'Do you think there's going to be a test at the end?' whispered Helen.

Jess swallowed the giggle, while Molly made an effort to behave like a grown-up. It had been a good evening so far. They had had an early supper at the Waffle House for old times' sake and then walked down to Gownena's where Gerald had been waiting patiently for them outside on the pavement.

It was so nice to spend time with Jess having fun, thought Molly, as they settled down to enjoy the show.

Morwenna beamed at Molly. 'I'm so pleased that you could make it, given your busy schedule. We often hear you on the radio.'

Molly smiled. 'Thanks. And you're happy for me to record you?'

Morwenna nodded. 'Oh yes, we're delighted, aren't we, Gerald?'

From behind the camera Gerald smiled wolfishly.

'Whenever you're ready,' said Molly.

'Right,' Morwenna said. 'Well, ladies, we're absolutely

delighted to welcome you to Gownena's this evening. We have a really super selection of gowns and accessories to show you, including several key pieces from our new Ice and Fire winter collection. I understand that Marnie and Noo can't be with us this evening, which is a real pity, but I've promised to send them a copy of the CD with all the photos, along with a complimentary half bottle of champagne.'

For the briefest of moments Molly and Jess's eyes met and a great wave of relief passed over Jess's face. 'Was Marnie all right about it?' Jess began.

Molly nodded. 'I told her I thought we could manage on our own.' She turned towards Morwenna.

'Right, now, wedding dresses,' she continued, holding the mike closer to Morwenna. 'Maybe we could start again?'

Jess grinned and, catching hold of Molly's hand, whispered, 'Thank you, Mum.'

After the fracas on Sunday, Molly had decided they didn't need any more surprises and had rung Jonathon as soon as she got in from work the previous afternoon.

Given how elusive he had been on Sunday, Molly was relieved when he picked up on the second ring. 'Molly,' he said, all bright, breezy and businesslike, before she had had time to say anything. 'Glad you rang. Did you hear from Jess? It's all sorted out. Bit of a relief to be honest. She seemed terribly upset on Sunday.'

Molly sighed. Jonathon hated fuss. 'You should keep Marnie on a tighter leash.'

He was quiet for a few seconds and then said, 'Jess said that on reflection this place Marnie booked would be ideal.'

'And we both know that if Marnie hadn't booked it then Jess wouldn't have touched Halley Hall with a barge pole.'

There was another silence at the far end of the line, one

into which, for once, Molly felt no compulsion to jump. Finally Jonathon said sheepishly, 'You're probably right, but all's well that ends well.'

'Not exactly,' said Molly. 'Jess and I are going to look at wedding dresses tomorrow evening.'

'Righty-oh,' said Jonathon cautiously. 'That will be nice.'

'And apparently Marnie and Noo were thinking of coming along as well.'

'Were they?' Jonathon said, still choosing his words as if he was picking his way between unexploded bombs.

'Might I suggest that you thank Marnie for booking it and tell her that her presence is not required.' Molly paused. 'Is that clear?'

'Ah,' said Jonathon. Molly could hear him fumbling with something. 'Hang on a minute. Actually she did mention it. It's in the diary. I think she was rather hoping to make a bit of an evening of it. Given that all that nonsense with the venue is sorted out now. Here we are. She and Noo were planning to bring Mimi along and then take everyone out to supper afterwards. She's booked a table at some Japanese place, got very good reviews.'

'Mimi?'

'Marnie's daughter.'

'I know who Mimi is, Jonathon. What I don't know is why Marnie would want to bring Mimi along to look at wedding dresses for Jess?'

'Well, Mimi is home for a few days and they've always got along well, those two, haven't they? Jess and Mimi. And we, actually Marnie, thought that Mimi would be the perfect matron of honour for Jess. I don't know what they do exactly but Marnie said that Jess will need someone to help her out, carrying flowers and things.' He attempted a laugh. 'I'm not good with all this wedding stuff but anyway I heard them

206

talking on the phone. I assumed from what Marnie was saying that Jess had probably already asked her.'

'Right,' said Molly, trying very hard to stay calm. 'And is Marnie there now?'

'Actually she's out at her Pilates class. Would you like me to get her to ring you when she gets in?'

Molly had paused for a second or two, weighing up the pros and cons and in the end said, 'No, that's fine, Jonathon. Would you just tell her that we don't want her or Mimi or Noo there tomorrow evening. All right?'

Jonathon paused. 'Are you sure you wouldn't rather tell her yourself?' he asked, just before Molly hung up.

'So,' said Morwenna, her voice bringing Molly firmly back to the present. 'This evening you'll be enjoying a selection of this year's most exquisite wedding gowns for the winter bride.'

Then Morwenna nodded and someone somewhere turned on a CD of something romantic and vaguely classical. The heavy curtain lifted aside and out sashayed the first model, wearing a soft satin white off-the-shoulder bridal number with a fluffy trim.

'This is Angelique,' squeaked Morwenna, glancing down at the notes she was holding. 'This stunning dress from our own designers is available in white, oyster and champagne with the option of a matching floor-length feather-trimmed cloak. The embroidery on the centre panel is all hand-applied.'

Whatever that might mean, thought Molly grimly, as the model, a Katie Price lookalike who wouldn't have known what demure meant if came up and stole her handbag, turned towards them to show off the hand-applied embroidery. She was chewing gum.

'The natural feather trim is all hand-sewn,' continued Morwenna, as the girl paused at the far end of the catwalk, caught for an instant in perpetual reflection by the half-circle of mirrors.

'Beats stapling it, I suppose,' murmured Helen under cover of a cough, which helped no one focus on Angelique's performance. Angelique meanwhile did another turn. She really had the middle-distance unfocused model stare sorted, although Molly did wonder whether it might be that she usually wore glasses.

Behind her Morwenna's commentary went on. 'Matching shoes and the faux-pearl, crystal and feather-trimmed tiara are both available in store. We also offer the option of a matching veil in a wide of variety of lengths from shoulder-length, single-tier right through to double tier, cathedral-length with the option of scattered accents.' Morwenna smiled.

Molly wished she had done a little more research. *Scattered accents?*

'Angelique is followed by Beverly Ann, who is wearing one of this season's favourites from the Ellenora-Eve Fantastique collection,' said Morwenna, as the curtain swished back again and the second model sidled out onto the catwalk. What Beverly Ann lacked in looks she more than made up for in fake tan and buck teeth. Unlike Angelique, she did at least make eye contact and genuinely looked as if she was enjoying dressing up.

'Along with a complete range of wedding lingerie, hosiery and . . .' Morwenna was still talking and carried on talking as they went on through fake fur, shot silk, heavy brocade, white, gold, silver, champagne, oyster and ivory, right on past red dresses and bridesmaid dresses until Molly felt as if she was drowning under a sea of organza, orange blossom and over-the-top adjectives, while at the far end of the carpet catwalk Gerald kept on snapping and smiling, capturing their reactions, the frocks and Molly's growing unease, for posterity.

'And that,' Morwenna said, with a smug flourish after what seemed like an eternity, 'brings us to the end of our presentation for this evening.' She paused for dramatic effect. Jess, Molly and Helen felt obligated to clap.

Morwenna smiled warmly. 'Well thank you, how kind. Now I'm sure we could all do with a little more champagne and then perhaps you'd like to try some of the dresses yourself?'

On cue, the minion who had served them when they arrived scuttled out from a side door clutching the bottle and topped up their glasses. Morwenna brought over a tray of canapés and slid them onto a side table.

'Do help yourself. Gerald will be only too happy to take photos of you in any of the gowns. Would you like to try a corset while you're here?'

Before Jess could answer Molly caught sight of the expectant expression on Gerald's face. 'I think we'll give that a miss, thank you,' she said briskly.

Chapter Nineteen

Max heard his mobile ringing but ignored it, and he ignored the text that came in after that letting him know that there was a missed call. He was more focused on the state of his office than in being at all sociable. The whole house was in total disarray and it made him feel uneasy. Max folded the lid down on the box he had just finished packing, taped it shut and then sat back on his heels to take stock.

Despite his best efforts all around him was a terrible discord of cables and machines and monitors, and even though he knew where everything was and what everything was for, and that once it was moved and reassembled it would all be all right, the chaos made him feel dizzy and slightly nauseous.

Max had spent most of the evening carrying down piles of flattened cardboard cartons and packaging from the loft, one set for each machine. Before starting to pack the machines up, he had arranged all the boxes in a neat stack on the floor, along with a new reel of tape in a dispenser, and a roll of labels. Working steadily Max methodically packed one machine at a time, and so now standing by the door – after half an evening's work – was a row of boxes all ready for the off.

Not that it gave him much joy. The long tables where

his computers and monitors had sat hours earlier were haunted by narrow dusty footprints – a negative of what he had so recently removed. The room was always reasonably clean but it was impossible to get rid of all the dust. He stared at the empty tables while Possum, his sleek chocolate-brown Burmese cat, did a pushy, slightly agitated figure-of-eight between his legs, looking up at Max as he did so, mewling softly as if he was as disconcerted by the disarray as Max.

On the wall above where his desk had stood until recently there had been a photo of his ex-wife Lucy. He had taken it down twice now and then re-hung it. He wasn't sure what to do with it. It was currently in the bedroom but he could hardly leave it there.

Max bent down and scooped the cat up in his arms, a reflex action that didn't engage his conscious mind.

He had already cleared the smaller bedroom across the landing – an oversized single – where his server farm had been working away contentedly in racks lining three of the four walls since he moved in. He had already relocated those machines to a commercial server operation that promised all manner of security and backups and twenty-four-hour-a-day access, but still he missed the quiet hum of their industry.

At night the last thing Max had done for years before going to bed was to open the door to the little room and look at the tiny glowing lights on each machine, which let him know the room was alive and busy and earning him money. In the darkness they looked like a row of tiny eyes staring at him in the gloom. Now all that was left were dust bunnies around the skirting board and deep depressions in the carpet where the heavy storage racks had stood.

Until he had taken the shelving down Max had quite

forgotten that the room had once been a nursery. Around the pale blue walls was a frieze at waist height decorated with ducks and rabbits and clowns. There were other clues too, marks on the wall where someone older had been measured, and marks that he read as the rub of a cot or perhaps a little bed.

The room he was working in now seemed to be getting larger with every passing hour. Earlier he had taken down one of the desks and dismantled one of the stacks of metal shelving, and – coming back in after another trip to the loft – he was taken by surprise by the new space, although the missing furniture left its ghosts too against the pale sunshine-yellow walls.

When he'd first bought the house, this room had been described as *the master bedroom with en suite*, but as soon as the estate agent had pushed open the door Max knew it would make the most perfect office. It was large, with a chimney breast on one wall, still with its original fireplace and tiles. On the adjacent wall, tall, narrow windows set into a bay overlooked the street and the river beyond. It was a good room to work in, to sit at his desk, to watch the trees change with the seasons, to stare out at the Wensum as it wandered past, grey-green, dark blue or muddy brown depending on the season and the weather. The deposit for the house had come from his divorce settlement.

Working all alone, Max was mourning the room's passing. Each box felt like another hour spent beside the bedside of a dying friend watching them slowly fade away. Packing up his office and moving out was the end of an era.

As Max considered his change of circumstance, Possum curled up in his arms and purred as he idly stroked the cat's fine wedge-shaped skull. Max had always enjoyed the fact that the majority of his commutes involved a short schlep across the landing. Working late, getting in early had never been a problem – but come December all that would change. Jess would move in and he would move out into his rented office and join the rest of the drones making their way to work in the morning.

The mobile phone rang again but Max didn't pick it up. It was his personal phone and he didn't want to be disturbed, not this evening, not when he was in mourning for all the things he was about to lose.

'Oh, this is so annoying. I know he's home,' said Jess, fingers working furiously over the buttons on her phone. '*Come on, come on, pick up, I know you're there,*' she murmured to herself, and then added to Helen and Molly, 'Max said he'd be at home tonight and he knew we were going to be in town. I told him we might drop by.'

'You know what men are like, he's probably nipped out for a pie and a pint,' said Helen, pulling on her jacket.

Jess glanced across at her mother, who was busy locking up the car.

'Or maybe he's hiding,' Molly said wryly. 'I know Nick would be. What man in his right mind wants to play host to three women after they've spent an evening looking at wedding dresses? He's probably creeping out of the back door even as we speak.'

Jess shook her head. 'He's not like that.'

'I bet he is,' said Helen. 'Mind you, I'm glad we went. It gave me a few ideas and I *loved* those tiaras. And, Molly, you were just so good at getting out of there without buying anything. That woman was a total nightmare.'

'Never mind her, what about *him*?' said Jess, rolling her eyes. 'Did you see his face when she started on about us trying on those corsets? God, he'd probably have been in the cubicle snapping away while she laced me into one. Next thing, we need to start looking for your outfit, Mum.'

'Oh, can I come?' asked Helen. 'We need to find you a really spectacular hat.'

Still chatting they made their way around the corner, across the road and up the steps to Max's house. It had a great view out over the river. It was a handsome terraced house with bay windows, set back a little way from the road.

'Oh wow, this is nice,' cried Helen, glancing up at the frontage.

Jess beamed. 'Great for the city.'

'The road's busy. Is Bassa going to be able to cope?' asked Molly, glancing at the stream of traffic heading out of the city.

'With city living? I'm sure he'll be fine. There's a little garden at the back and there are quite a few places to walk him around here – and he'll adapt, he's that kind of dog,' Jess said, while trying to find the keys in her bag. 'I was thinking maybe we could all go for a drink. It's such a fine evening – there is a lovely place a bit further along the river. They do really good food.'

'Don't tell me you're still hungry,' Helen said. 'I couldn't eat another thing.'

'I didn't mean right now.'

'Oh right – you mean when I come and stay. It'll be handy once you're living here. Nice view. Are you taking bookings for visitors yet?'

Jess, finally producing her keys, grinned. 'Let me get moved in first.'

They were at the front door now. There was a porchway set back into the house, with an original black-and-white tiled floor, and stained-glass panels in rich ruby red, set into the door itself.

215

'That would be the perfect colour for my bridesmaid's dress,' said Helen, tapping the pane.

Jess laughed. 'Do I detect a subtle change in priorities here?' she said, as she slipped her key into the lock.

'Might do,' joked Helen.

As she spoke Jess turned the key but the door didn't open. 'Bugger. It's locked. Well, at least we know Max is in –'

'Maybe he's having a nap,' said Molly. 'After all, you did say he's been working all hours that God sends.'

Jess rang the bell. 'No, Max is not really the napping kind. He's probably working.'

She pushed the button again and somewhere deep inside the house Molly could hear the distant ding-dong of the door chimes, and then Jess pushed it again.

A few seconds later there was the sound of an upstairs window sliding open. 'Who is it?' snapped Max. Jess stepped back out into the tiny front garden, followed by Helen and Molly.

'Hi, it's me,' Jess said, waving up at the window. 'I did try to ring you but you didn't pick up.'

Molly watched as Max rearranged his annoyed features into something more sociable. 'So you did,' he said with a lopsided grin. 'Sorry, I couldn't get to the phone in time. Hang on, I'll be down in just a second.'

'If we're disturbing him we could always go and have that drink on our own,' whispered Helen, taking the words right out of Molly's mouth.

'Don't be silly,' said Jess briskly. 'It's fine, we just surprised him, and I really want you to meet Max – I've told him all about you, and Mum's never seen the house.'

Molly could hear the sounds of Max making his way down-stairs, his footfalls on every tread, his feet padding across the hall floor, the sounds of the locks turning. Far from feeling pleased Molly felt as if they were about to be shown into the headmaster's study. When Max opened the door he was all smiles.

'Hello,' he said, a little too brightly, his smile looking a little too brittle. 'Come on in. Sorry, I thought you might be –'

But Molly never heard who Max thought they might be as Jess hurried through the introductions.

'Max, this is my oldest and best friend Helen,' said Jess as they squeezed into the hallway.

'Less of the old,' said Helen.

'Pleased to meet you,' he said, and then to Jess, 'How did it go? Come in, come in – I'll get the kettle on or would you prefer a glass of wine?' Max saved a genuine smile for Jess, and putting his arm around her shoulders, pulled her close and kissed her gently. 'Good to see you, you look gorgeous.'

Jess glowed under his approval and then, reaching up, ran a finger over his unshaven cheek. 'Not letting yourself go now you're getting married, are you?' she said, with a sly grin.

Max was dressed in faded cargo pants and a long-sleeved teeshirt, sleeves pulled up to his elbows, thick dark hair swept back off his well-made face, and Molly could easily see why Jess was attracted to him, loved him even. But although he was smiling and welcoming there was still something rather cool about Max that Molly found unsettling.

Max meanwhile caught hold of Helen and pumped her hand. 'Lovely to meet you, Jess has talked about you a lot. I've got some white wine open in the fridge, come through. And Molly –' He kissed her on each cheek. 'How lovely to see you again.'

As she followed them towards the kitchen Molly wondered if she might warm to Max as she got to know him better.

217

Maybe that was it; she didn't know him well enough, or perhaps unexpectedly she was falling into the classic parent trap of thinking that no one was good enough for her little girl. Maybe she was going to be the mother-in-law from hell. Molly paused, re-running that thought. Surely that wasn't true, it couldn't be true – she had loved Glenn, and even though he was quite obviously trouble with a capital T, like everyone else, Molly had adored Beano, but Max was different. Somehow he didn't quite fit. Trying to make sure that none of this showed on her face, Molly followed everyone inside, reminding herself what she'd said to Jonathon; Jess was a big girl now – they should trust her judgement.

The large hallway was gloomy and felt cluttered and mannish; piles of shoes were tucked under an antique hall-stand that held all manner of coats and jackets and hats and a pair of skis. The walls were papered with scarred Anaglypta and painted in dark, unfashionable colours that showed their vintage. Once it had undoubtedly been very tasteful, but now it just looked shabby.

There were no pictures or flowers or any sense that a woman had been anywhere near the place in years, if ever, but the hall floor still had its black-and-white tiles, picture rail and ornate skirting boards. With a little love and work it could be stunning. As if reading her thought Max said wryly, 'Jess has got plans for the hall.'

Jess looked back over her shoulder, face split into a grin. 'Make that the whole house,' she said. 'I'm planning the makeover of all makeovers. Oh, are those boxes for me?' She pointed out a stack of carefully flattened cartons leaning up against the wall.

'No,' he said quickly. 'No, I'm afraid they're mine. For office equipment.'

'Oh, okay, I thought maybe you'd been saving them.'

'I have,' he said.

'Yes, but not for me, for my move at the weekend is what I meant,' Jess said, still smiling.

Max looked bemused but fortunately as Jess spoke a sleek feline oozed its way down the stairs and when it saw them, paused and narrowed its bright blue eyes.

'Possum,' said Max by way of an introduction, rather than calling the cat. The cat had hunkered down, frozen now, crouched halfway up the stairs, watching the new arrivals with deepest suspicion.

'How's he going to cope with Bassa?' asked Molly conversationally, as the cat began to swish its long, snaky tail from side to side, not taking his eyes off them for a second.

'He'll be fine. Every time they've met so far,' said Jess, climbing the stairs to retrieve the cat, 'Possum's won on points. Bassa just wants to be friendly, Possum just wants to win. Don't you, Poss?' She was having none of the cat's superiority and bending down scooped him up into her arms. The cat managed to look outraged for the briefest of instants and then gave in – seconds later he was purring like a train.

'You really are a complete tart, aren't you?' she murmured, stroking his head and back. The cat, eyes closed in bliss, responded with a long, languid purr.

'So how did it go?' asked Max.

'How long have you got?' said Jess, heading back down stairs. 'Lots of wedding dresses, three glasses of cheap champagne and one very dodgy guy with a camera. They're going to send us the photos.'

As Jess spoke they all followed Max through into the kitchen, which was as dated as the rest of the house and, although clean, was scattered with the detritus of single living.

Possum dropped silently out of Jess's arms and headed

for the back door where a tray, neatly arranged with cat food, biscuits and a tiny porcelain bowl of water, stood. At least the cat was well catered for.

'See anything you like?' Max asked, taking glasses out of the dishwasher; Molly suspected he was talking about their shopping trip rather than anything in the kitchen.

'No,' said Jess. 'And I've already told you, Helen's doing my dress. She's done some fantastic sketches, although unfortunately you can't look at them. Bad luck for you to see the bride before the big day.'

'Tea, wine?' asked Max as if he hadn't heard her.

'I could murder a cup of tea,' said Jess, easing off her shoes with her toes. 'Pull up a chair,' she said brightly to Molly and Helen. By the kitchen door no one moved. 'Unless of course you'd prefer to go through to the sitting room and admire our mustard velour corner unit.'

Max mimed a wince. 'Don't be cruel. It's retro. Another five years and people will be begging us for it.'

Jess snorted. 'You wish – come on, us girls'll go through, it's probably tidier in there anyway.' She got up and then said to Max, 'Do you want me to give you a hand?'

Despite the attempt at banter Molly didn't feel at all comfortable and so far Helen had barely said a word, which wasn't like her at all. Molly had the impression that they had disturbed Max while he was doing something terribly important, certainly more important than making small talk about frocks, and furniture.

'Would you like us to go?' asked Molly, finding herself quite unable not to, as Max busied himself with the wine and tracking down a tray. 'It feels like you're busy and we're interrupting you.'

Jess stared at her. 'Mum,' she protested, but instead of

leaping into the breach Max hesitated, quite obviously torn between the truth and good manners.

'No, no you're fine,' he blustered after far too many seconds. 'I was just upstairs clearing out my office out and – well, I was – I . . .' He stopped. 'Actually you're right. I'm up to my ears up there and I am really, really busy at the moment, but not too busy to make you a cup of tea or pour you a glass of wine.' He smiled ruefully. 'Actually I could do with a bit of a break. You go through and I'll bring it in. Wine all right for everyone?'

If nothing else he was honest, thought Molly.

Helen nodded without conviction. Jess guided them into the sitting room where they perched miserably on the ugliest corner suite Molly had seen in a long time while Jess headed back into the kitchen.

'Won't be a minute,' she said, closing the door behind her.

'Can we go now?' hissed Helen.

Molly shook her head. 'Apparently not.'

There was an uneasy silence and then Helen said in a tiny voice, 'Max isn't anything like I imagined he'd be.'

'I know what you mean,' Molly said, barely trusting herself to speak.

'Max –' Jess began indignantly as she headed into the kitchen.

But Max was ahead of her this time. 'No, your mum's right. I don't mean to be rude but there's so much I need to do at the moment, Jess. I'm trying to work, I'm trying to pack, I'm on call tonight, I've got the New York trip tomorrow and I really need to get everything cleared out before the wedding.'

'And I suppose I haven't got anything to do other than stay home and paint my nails? I'm working too, Max, and planning the wedding, and moving house,' snapped Jess crossly. 'And I can still find the time for you and my family and my friends. I was hoping that we could all go out for a drink and you could meet Helen properly, and I know Mum would like to look around the house and I wanted to tell you all about Cruella De Vil at the frock shop and her weird husband.'

She stared at him.

Max shifted his weight, looking tense and not quite meeting her eye. 'Jess, I'm sorry, I wouldn't be any company tonight, sweetie – mentally I'd be back here packing boxes,' he said, glancing round the kitchen. 'There's a lot to do.'

Jess glared at him. 'Oh right,' she snapped. 'A lot to do. I'm moving out this Saturday – and where are you? Bloody New York. I've just signed an agreement to move into a cottage when I could be moving in here. And *now* you start clearing stuff out of this place. This is nuts. Why couldn't you have done it before, Max? I would have been happy to have given you a hand. As it is, I've barely seen you all week and I just want you to come and spend an hour with me and Mum and Helen – she's my best friend. I want you to meet her and you want to stay here and pack. I told you we would come round.' She slipped her shoes back on. 'I did tell you –'

'Don't,' said Max, but Jess was already collecting her things together.

'It's all right, we're going,' said Jess. 'I know when I'm not welcome.'

'Jess – please wait.'

She spun round. 'Why? So that you can tell me that I'm being unreasonable and emotional? Well, Max, it's been a long day, I can do without the lecture.'

Max stopped and grinned, holding his hands up in

surrender. 'Actually I was going to say that you're right and that I'm behaving like a complete arse, and then I was going to wonder out loud how the hell you put up with me.'

Jess scowled at him. 'You keep saying that, but just saying it isn't enough,' she said.

'I'm really sorry. I was so caught up in what I was doing,' he continued. 'I'm rude and I'm anti-social and I'm really glad you came round.' Max stopped and looked at her. 'Really I am. How am I doing so far?'

Jess waited, face impassive, letting him stew until she couldn't bear it any longer. 'Not bad,' she conceded eventually, 'but you've got a long way to go to convince Mum and Helen. They're through there looking like they're waiting for a root canal.'

Chapter Twenty

'Jess, we're never going to get all that lot into the van,' protested Jack, staring at the enormous pile of boxes currently stacked in the sitting room and hallway of Jess's Swaffham cottage. 'I hired a Transit van, not a bloody articulated lorry.'

'Oh, don't be such a baby. I thought we could make two trips,' said Jess, struggling into the hall with yet another box. 'I'm going to put some of the stuff in my car.'

'You're going to need to buy a bigger car,' her brother said, looking round the tiny sitting room. 'Did you really get all this lot in here?'

'No,' said Jess, voice heavy with sarcasm. 'I thought I'd borrow some extra stuff to move just to annoy you.'

'I suppose we ought to make a start,' said Jack without much enthusiasm. He picked up a box. Helen meanwhile was making her way down the stairs carrying a pile of curtains.

'Right, that's the spare room all done and dusted – literally,' she said, briskly. 'I've left the cleaning stuff upstairs for when we've finished in the other bedroom and the bathroom.' She grinned as she spotted Jack framed in the doorway. 'Yo, handsome,' she purred. Jack grinned from ear to ear as she continued, 'My, my, look at you, all grown-up. I wondered when the beefcake was going to show up.'

He posed, still wearing a grin, while Helen shamelessly eyed him up. Jack was wearing an oversized teeshirt and shorts, along with battered Cat boots and thick socks scrunched down into the tops. It might not be a look that worked on everyone but Jack was six feet tall, tanned and muscular, his dark hair bleached at the tips by summer sunshine; he looked good enough to eat.

Jess, struggling with another box, raised an eyebrow. 'Do you mind? That's my baby brother you're ogling.'

'Oh, come off it, Jess,' said Helen. 'There's no harm in window-shopping – and there have got to be some perks to the job. I've been working my butt off all morning.' And then turning her attention back to Jack, she said, 'Talking of which, did anyone ever tell you that you've the most gorgeous bum?'

Jack laughed. 'Might have,' he said with a flirtatious wink. 'Now – how about we get on with moving all these boxes,' he continued, in a voice that was now 98.4% pure testosterone.

'Oh, please,' said Jess, looking heavenwards.

'I thought you'd have the van loaded by now?' said another male voice from behind him.

'Who's that?' asked Jess, peering past her brother and out into the street.

'The extra brawn you ordered,' said Jack, stepping aside to reveal his boss, Oliver.

Between the pair of them Jack and Oliver filled the hallway. Oliver, also in shorts and teeshirt and equally as hunky as Jack, smiled a hello, and held up a flat tin. 'Hi, I thought you could probably do with an extra pair of hands. And I brought cake. I'm hoping you haven't packed the kettle yet?'

'I wouldn't dare,' said Jess. 'I didn't realise you'd be coming over to help.'

'I thought Jack mentioned it, unless you don't need me, is that it?'

'God, no, a spare pair of hands would be really welcome,' said Helen from the stairs.

'I didn't realise just how much stuff I'd got,' Jess said apologetically. 'Let me introduce you. Helen, this is Jack's boss, Oliver. He's head gardener at Vanguard Hall.'

Helen grinned. 'Pleased to meet you,' she said. 'I'm Helen, cleaner and general dogsbody. Did you say that was cake?'

'Uh-huh, Krista baked it fresh this morning. I think it's cherry or maybe lemon. I forgot to ask.'

'Krista?' said Helen. 'Your wife?'

'No, a student who is working with us, Jess met her when she came over,' said Jack helpfully, prising the lid off the tin. 'She likes to bake. Says it helps her relax.'

'Nothing wrong with that. Give me that tin here, Jack,' said Helen, grin widening as she extended a hand. 'I'll go through and stick the kettle on.' She glanced at Jess. 'The day I'm dressed to clean house and the men of my dreams show up. *With cake.*'

'My best friend Helen, the lech,' said Jess, as Jack handed over the cake tin and Oliver picked his way carefully between the piles of crates, books and furniture.

'You're hoping to get all this lot into Heaven's Gate?' asked Oliver, looking around.

'No, Mum is storing a lot of it for me. I'm not going to be there for that long. So I thought I'd just take the basics.'

She paused, as Oliver looked at a box marked *red wine, white wine.* His gaze moved on from one large box to another. 'Right, so which is what exactly?'

'The only ones I'm taking are those with *HG Cottage* written on them,' explained Jess, pointing to a big red label.

'And I've put the room on it as well. See: *HG Cottage, wine, kitchen.*'

'Uh-huh,' said Oliver. 'And what about all the rest of it?'

'It says *Mum's*,' said Jess, feeling more and more self-conscious as he started working his way around her possessions. 'And the labels on those boxes are blue.'

'And is it in all in separate piles or is it mixed in together?'

Helen leaned through the kitchen door. 'Is this a private quiz or can anyone join in?'

'How's the tea coming along?'

'Fine. Kettle's on, cake's out – it's cherry.'

'Okay,' said Oliver. 'We should make a start. I've brought the flat-bed truck over from the estate so we could take another load on that.'

Jess nodded. 'Sounds great.'

'We really ought to move that first.' He pointed to Jess's red-leather sofa.

'Actually, that's going to my mum's. I don't think it'll fit into the new place. I was just going to take the armchairs and the little cane sofa from the conservatory.'

'Right-oh,' said Oliver, apparently unfazed as his gaze moved slowly round the room. 'Well, we need to get the sofa shifted eventually so how about we move it out of the way behind the door for the time being. We'll take all the stuff that's going to Heaven's Gate, and then come back and take all the things going to your Mum's. Does that sound about right?'

Jess nodded, suddenly relieved that Oliver was there, even more relieved that he was taking charge of the barely controlled chaos. 'Sounds like a plan.'

'Good. Come on, Jack, let's get this show on the road.'

Jack groaned. 'I was hoping for a cup of tea first.'

Oliver grinned. 'You just can't get the staff.'

'Oh yes, you can,' said Helen, coming in right on cue, bearing a tray with a teapot, mugs and a carton of milk, alongside the cake that had been neatly turned out onto the tin lid. 'If you know where to look.'

When the four of them finally made a start on the little house, it began to empty very quickly.

'God, the man is a complete slave driver,' moaned Helen as she traipsed out to the van with yet another box. As she passed Jess, who was carrying a standard lamp, she whispered, 'Is he taken?'

'What?'

'Taken?'

'Who?' asked Jess.

'Oliver of course,' Helen said.

'How on earth would I know?' said Jess, flustered.

'You are so slow. I'd have made a point of knowing. He's gorgeous. So who is this Krista person?'

Jess pulled a face and was about to say something when Jack passed them carrying a bedside cabinet. 'Krista's on placement with us working in the gardens at the hall,' he said, presumably catching some part of the conversation, although Jess wasn't sure exactly which part. 'She's a student. Brilliant at propagating –'

'Really, and how long is she there for?' said Helen, all ears.

'A year.'

Helen pulled an *oh bugger* face at Jess.

'She's not there all the time, she's at college; she does two days a week and the odd weekend,' Jack continued as he slid the cabinet into the lorry.

'Who's this? Krista?' asked Oliver, on his way back inside the house.

'Yeah – I was just saying she does odd weekends.'

Ollie laughed. 'Yeah, very odd some of them.'

Jess caught the most fleeting of glances between the two of them and then both men laughed.

What on earth was that supposed to mean?

'So, are you going out with Krista?' Helen asked Oliver. But before he could answer Molly and Nick pulled up behind the removal van.

'I still can't believe Max let her do this on her own,' said Molly grimly, as Nick turned off the engine.

'Sometimes these things can't be helped, and it's not like she's really on her own.'

'He wasn't to know that.'

'Come on, I know you don't like him but play nicely – looks like we've got help anyway. Who is that?'

'Jack's boss.'

Jess smiled as they clambered out of the car; the back seats were already folded down and ready for the off.

'Sorry we're late – I took Bassa and Milo for a walk before we came over so they wouldn't wee on anything while we're out. And before you ask, yes, Bassa's okay – ruling the roost. I thought we could bring him over once you've got everything straight at the cottage and if you want me to keep him for the weekend till you're settled in, that's fine.' Slowing down, Molly took a look around at the van – now almost packed – and Jess's car, also almost full up. 'God, you've been busy.'

'And we've had cake,' said Helen, from inside the back of the truck.

'Molly said you needed more manpower,' said Nick to Jess. 'Looks like we arrived too late.'

Jess smiled. 'It's never too late. The big van's full of stuff to go over to the new place. And we've left all the stuff that

Mum said we could store at yours in the cottage. Oliver suggested we move that out when we get back. Another ten minutes or so and I think we'll be ready to head over to Vanguard Hall.'

'We timed it just right then,' said Nick wryly. 'All the hard work's done.'

'You wish,' groaned Jess. 'There are a few more boxes to put on the lorry and then if you wouldn't mind driving over to the new place and helping unload that would be brilliant. To be honest I'm just about knackered, what with work and worry and weddings – my wedding stuff has got a box all of its own on the back seat of my car.'

'Truck is more or less full too,' said Oliver, nodding his hellos to Molly and Nick. 'I thought I'd head over to the Hall.'

'If you men are all buggering off we're not staying behind here to clean house, are we, Molly?' said Helen, hands on hips. 'If I scrub any more spots out of any more carpets I'm going to go mad.'

Jess laughed. 'I wasn't going to ask you to,' she said, waiting until the men had moved out of earshot and lowering her voice. 'I was going to suggest I drove Mum over to the new cottage in my car and you went in the truck with Oliver or in the van with Jack. Take your pick.'

Molly raised her eyebrows. 'Do I detect some match-making?'

Helen, eyes alight with mischief, said, 'Oh yeah, right – me in my painting jeans and an old shirt. I look like I'm out on the pull.'

'You never know,' said Jess, 'maybe the bag-lady look will be hot next season, and besides the pair of them like practical women. So – which one is it? Oliver or Jack?'

Helen tapped one finger thoughtfully on her chin and

231

looked skywards, as if deciding over dessert. 'So hard to choose,' she said with a grin.

'I really don't think I should be privy to this conversation,' said Molly, moving away. 'And I don't want to put you off, Helen, but I know all about Jack's sock drawer and the state of his bedroom.'

Chapter Twenty-One

While the last of the boxes were being sorted out, Jess unlocked her car.

'I'm going over to Halley Hall during the week to talk to their florist about colour schemes,' she said, handing Molly a box of groceries to put in the boot. 'And Helen brought me some fabric samples down. I was thinking maybe we could wrap a strip around each layer of the wedding cake in the same fabric – or maybe do bows or butterflies or make something like that out of it, so it all ties in. Oh, and Max and I are going to church tomorrow. Did I tell you we've got to have marriage lessons?'

Molly lifted her eyebrows.

Jess laughed. 'They're called something else but that's what it amounts to. I was wondering if you and Nick'd like to come?'

'To marriage lessons?' said Molly. 'I don't think so. I can just see Nick's face if I tell him we're off to marriage lessons. He'd probably run away screaming.'

Jess shook her head in mock-exasperation. 'I meant come to church with us. Actually I'm sure Nick's expression couldn't be any worse than Max's. When we got out of the vicarage he kept saying, "It wasn't like this when I married Lucy."'

Molly smiled, wondering if now was the moment to bring up the matter of the engagement ring.

Lucy Peters stirred a drift of powered chocolate into the froth of her cappuccino and then spooned it into her mouth, one spoonful at a time. She and Max had first discovered cappuccino together in a little café in Rome, back in the days when it was served only at breakfast, with an Italian version of warm, buttery croissants. Max remembered how it had felt sitting outside at a table on the pavement with her, on their honeymoon, watching the world go by. How excited he had been and proud and how very much in love. It seemed a very long time ago.

And here she was now, sitting in the café overlooking the Cam, eyes not on him but on the tourists below them who were being propelled through the grey-brown water in punts crewed by handsome, suntanned boys. She smiled as she watched them, tucking her hair back behind her ears, and although she wasn't twenty-three any more Lucy was still beautiful, almost more beautiful if that were possible. Watching her scoop the last of the foam from the cup his heart ached for all the might-have-beens and the chances lost.

'So,' Max said. 'How's it all going?'

Lucy looked up at him. 'Sorry? How's what all going?'

Max made the effort to sound casual. 'Everything. Life – sorting out the wedding.'

She laughed. 'Oh, that. I haven't really given it much thought, to be perfectly honest. It's really just a formality, sorts out all the legalities in case anything happens to one of us. Bit tedious, but we thought we might as well get it over and done with – none of us is getting any younger.'

'So you're all sorted then?' he said, with feigned casualness.

'Uh-huh. Registry office and then we're going to the coast with the kids to walk the dogs and have supper at this little fish restaurant. Just me and Stephen and a few friends. They normally close over the Christmas break but they're going to open up just for us. It's super, you really should go some time – oh, do you remember the Ballantines? It's theirs. They bought it about five years ago –'

'Howard and Gill?'

Lucy nodded.

'I didn't realise they'd moved this way. How are they?'

Lucy glanced down at her watch. 'They're just fine. Look, actually, Max, it's really nice to see you, but I promised I'd only be half an hour – one of the girls is off sick and my break is up, I'm afraid.'

'Oh, come on, surely you don't have to go back yet.' He smiled. 'You're the boss –'

'Unfortunately it doesn't work that way. Now is there something you wanted or is this purely a social visit?'

'No, no,' he blustered. 'I just wanted to – well –' He picked up his briefcase and, setting it on the table between them, pulled out an envelope. 'Here,' he said. 'I wanted to give you this personally.'

Lucy looked at the good-quality blank envelope. 'It's not a summons, is it?' she laughed, turning it over in her long, elegant fingers.

'No, no, not a summons. Although actually I suppose it is really. It's an invitation – to the wedding.' Max reddened, tongue-tied and struggling to find the right words. 'To our wedding. Jess and I –'

Lucy smiled but he suspected it was only politeness. 'Lovely. So she said yes, then?'

'Yes, you altered the ring,' Max said, realising too late that she probably meant it as a joke.

235

'So, no going back now?' she said.

'No. You will come, won't you?'

Lucy looked up at him and for the first time since she had walked in he had the sense that finally she was completely focused on him. 'Max, it's terribly sweet of you, but I don't think it would be a very good idea, do you?'

Max paused, wondering if Lucy truly expected him to answer that. Of course he thought it was a good idea – otherwise why would he have driven back from Heathrow via Cambridge, why had he invited her for coffee, why had he given her an invitation?

Very carefully, Lucy put the envelope on the table and he knew that she planned to push it back towards him, so he said, 'Please, Lucy, I would really like you to be there. Jess too. It would really help to lay a lot of old ghosts for everyone if you and Stephen came. Please.'

She stared at him. 'Jess knows that you've invited me?'

He nodded with confidence to hide the deceit. 'Actually,' he said, 'it was her idea.'

Lucy raised her eyebrows. 'Really?'

Max silently cursed himself for embellishing the lie but who would ever know? It was hardly likely that Lucy was going to go up to Jess at the wedding and demand to know if it was true or not. Even if, with her impeccable manners, Lucy went to thank Jess for the invitation, he doubted either of them would make a scene. And he wanted her there.

Cautiously Lucy slipped out the invitation, which was printed on heavy watermarked paper rather than card, and was folded very precisely in half.

'Unusual design,' Lucy said, without looking up. 'More personal.'

Max was relieved that she wasn't looking at him. 'That's exactly what Jess and I thought. We wanted to get a few special invitations out early so that people could put the date in their diaries. You know what printers can be like, so we did a few ourselves.'

'This is for both of us?' Lucy looked up at him now, expression quizzical, holding the sheet of paper out towards him. 'You're inviting Stephen as well?'

Max nodded and then laughed. 'Well, of course he's invited. You're a couple, aren't you? How many years is it now? Couldn't really invite one of you without the other now, could we?'

Lucy smiled and dropped the envelope and invitation into her bag. 'In that case, thank you – I'm not sure that he'll want to come, but we'll let you know. The thing is I really have got to get back to work now.'

Lucy stood up and started to collect her things together, her phone and bag and a long silky scarf that she wound around her neck, lifting her long hair out over it with the backs of her hands and fingers with a flicking motion that was seared on Max's memory from all the mornings they had woken up together. He used to watch her dressing, blown away by the fact that they were together and hardly daring to believe his luck, terrified that it was all an illusion, a dream that could be taken away on a whim – and of course it had been.

Watching her now, so familiar and yet so foreign, Max wanted to ask Lucy why she had left him; not the hot, angry, immediate reasons from all those years ago but the reason that had hardened up and grown out of that – the real reason that she had decided that what they had wasn't worth sticking with. Instead he said, 'So you'll come then?'

Lucy smiled. 'I really do have to be going,' she said and, leaning forward, she brushed her lips against his cheek. 'Thank you for the coffee. It was lovely to see you again.'

* * *

Back at Jess's cottage they were finally ready to leave.

Oliver, walking out of the cottage laden down with what surely had to be the last of the boxes said, 'Everyone set?'

'More or less,' said Helen and then added, 'Looks like I'm with you.'

'Righty-oh,' said Oliver. 'In that case I'll stow this lot in the back of the truck and then we can get going. I don't think we can get anything else on there if we tried.'

'I'll just go and grab my bag,' said Helen, taking time out to do a great big pantomime wink to Jess and Molly before she headed back inside. 'Won't be a minute –'

Jess glanced across at Molly, who raised her eyebrows in a question.

'Don't worry, I'm sure Oliver will be just fine,' said Jess. 'He's a big boy.' Five minutes later they were all locked up and off.

There was a moment when they first arrived in the hire van, cars and Oliver's truck, when everyone just stood outside the little cottage, so aptly named Heaven's Gate, and took in the view.

The tiny cottage, all wrapped around by swags of heavy white roses, was caught in a shaft of late-afternoon sunshine that was on the very cusp of autumn, the mellow golden light reflecting off the panes in the bow window, and streaming down, dappled and glittering, between the surrounding trees so it looked for all the world as if the cottage was caught in some kind of benign celestial spotlight.

'*Oh, my God,*' exclaimed Helen, who was standing alongside the truck with Oliver. 'Isn't that just the most beautiful place you've ever seen? I am so envious, Jess – no, not envious, *furious.* It is perfect. What a gem. If I lived here I don't think I'd ever want to leave.'

Jess smiled. 'You can always see if Oliver's boss will rent it to you when I move out.' Pulling the keys out of her pocket she made her way in through the picket fence and up the path to unlock the front door.

Helen followed hot on her heels, desperate for the grand tour.

The big metal key was like something out of a Dickensian melodrama and for a second or two Jess struggled with the lock until Oliver came to her rescue.

'Here, let me,' he said gently, his hand over hers. 'There's a bit of a knack, pull it towards you first –' The key turned and then with one light push the door swung noiselessly open. 'There we go, easy when you know how.'

Jess nodded. 'Thanks.'

He grinned. 'My pleasure.'

'Shame Max isn't here to carry you over the threshold. Maybe you should ask Oliver to do it instead?' Helen suggested, elbowing her way between them. If Jess blushed they both made a point of not noticing.

Inside the cottage was flooded with sunlight; dust motes hung and spun in the shafts of light. There was a small lobby area just inside the front door with hooks for coats, and then the stairs rose up to a galleried landing. To the left of the front door was one large L-shaped room with a double aspect, which served as sitting room and kitchen.

The floor in the sitting-room part was oak boards, stained and varnished and aged down to a deep golden brown. There were beams and creamy white walls and broad, broad sills running round inside the great bow window that dominated the front of the cottage. Around the corner, in the shorter leg of the L, was the kitchen, this with flagstone floors and handsome custom-made units that made the most of the tiny space. Windows ran along most of the back wall, giving a view out over the estate church, the churchyard and the woods beyond. At one end, a glazed door opened out onto a paved area set with tubs and a bench. Outside the garden was full of old-fashioned cottage flowers, and climbing jasmine and honeysuckle, their scents vying with the roses for domination.

Upstairs, off the stairwell, was one large, open double bedroom, beyond that a tiny box room and beyond that, tucked under the eaves, a bathroom, with a claw-footed bath claiming the centre of the room, and a view out over rolling fields and woodland.

Helen, busy exploring every nook and cranny, was practically purring with delight.

Just as they started to unload the van someone's mobile started to ring. There was some general patting down and then Jess grabbed her bag. 'It's okay, it's mine.'

'You're lucky, you can't usually get a signal out here,' said Oliver conversationally as she scrambled through the contents, trying to find it.

'It's Max,' Jess said as she glanced at the caller display, and there was a moment – the briefest of moments – when it felt as if he was intruding.

'Hi, how was the flight?' she said brightly, and moved away chasing privacy and better reception.

A couple of hours later, Molly, deep in thought, was busy putting the finishing touches to the bedroom, fluffing up a sea of white pillows and pulling the duvet straight. Even if everywhere else was chaotic, at least Jess would have somewhere comfortable to sleep. It looked beautiful, with the brass bed in the centre of the room and an old wooden blanket box, strewn with cushions, tucked up under the dormer window.

Stretching, Molly stood up and looked out into the lush green garden and landscape of the estate beyond. The trees and fields were tinged red-gold by the evening light as the sun set behind the church.

'Penny for them?'

Startled that she hadn't heard him, Molly swung round to see Nick in the stairwell, carrying a wicker linen hamper. 'I thought this would look nice up here.'

'You made me jump. I thought you and Jack were still over in Swaffham clearing out the old place?'

'We were, we have and the spare room at our place now looks like a well-stocked bazaar. I have got *no idea* how Jess managed to cram all that stuff into that little cottage.' Nick grinned. 'Oh, and I thought Bassa might like to see his new home and Milo wasn't going to be left behind so I brought them over with me. Jess is just taking them for a quick walk round the park.' He glanced over his shoulder as if he might be overheard. 'So Max didn't show up, then?'

Molly sighed. 'No, Jess said when he rang he was just on his way home from the airport. And that he was dead on his feet.'

They both looked at each other and then Nick opened his mouth to speak, but Molly was already way ahead of him. 'I know what you're going to say,' she said, holding up her hand. 'I've been thinking about it all afternoon. If it was you, and I was moving, there is no way you wouldn't be over here to give me a hand, even if you were totally knackered and the best you could do was pitch up late and bring me a chip supper.'

'And –' Nick began, but Molly was on a roll.

'And I can't believe Max didn't just sort his house out and let Jess move in there with him. They're getting married, for God's sake – and yes, it's lovely here, but this is totally ridiculous. They could have sorted out his place together, that's what couples do . . .' She paused and waved an arm around to encompass the room. 'We're going to have to move all this stuff out again in December. What are we going to do, Nick?'

'Make sure we book the van? It'll probably be busy around Christmas.'

Molly raised her eyebrows.

'I know.' Nick sat down on the bed. 'We've already had this conversation, but she's a big girl now.'

'A big girl who is making a big mistake. If she was my friend and not my daughter I'd be asking her what the hell she thought was doing and whether Max really is the right choice. I'm pussy-footing around it because –'

'Because?'

'Because I love her, Nick, and I don't want to hurt her and I don't want her to hate me . . .'

'Oh, baby,' Nick said gently, putting his arms around her. 'Maybe Max *is* the one, we don't know. It's not our call to make. I mean, when you meet the right one you just know, you feel that click of recognition, maybe that's what happened.'

'With Max?'

'We don't know. It's not up to us.'

Molly looked up at him. 'Is that what happened to you?'

He grinned. 'You know it is. We're right – we clicked – we knew. Maybe they did too.'

'Do you really believe that?'

He hesitated long enough for that to be an answer in itself.

Molly shook her head. 'I've got to say something. Trouble is I'm worried that if I tell her what I really think, she'll never speak to me again. And if I don't say something I'll never forgive myself if he hurts her.'

'You're being melodramatic.'

'No, I'm not. The more I think about it the worse it gets. His ex-wife designed Jess's engagement ring. How bizarre is that? And Jess should be all excited and happy and –'

'Stressed?'

'Yes, but in a nice way. But she isn't.'

'She seems just fine now,' said Nick, looking out of the window.

Molly's gaze followed his to the other window. Jess was outside on the grass, hands in her pockets, head thrown back, laughing at Oliver and Helen and Jack who were playing with two Jack Russells. Everyone was smiling and talking and despite it having been a long day, quite obviously at ease and having fun.

A few seconds later and Jack was inside and calling up the stairs. 'Mum, Nick – are you up there? Oliver wants to know if we'd all like to go over to his place for a barbecue? Apparently Krista's sorted it all out while we were moving Jess. Oh, and Jess said do you know where we put the wine?'

'Wine should be in the rack in the kitchen,' said Nick, glancing across at Molly. 'And we'd love to come, wouldn't we, Molly? We're more or less finished up here.'

Molly nodded. 'Down in a second.' She reached across and flicked on the bedside lamp. The room looked as inviting as anything she had ever seen. 'This is such a perfect place.'

'Uh-huh,' said Nick. 'So are you going to say something to Jess?'

Molly sighed. 'Probably, but not today . . .'

Jack was waiting for them at the bottom of the stairs, cradling two bottles of red. He nodded towards the counter top as they got downstairs. 'You want to take the white, Nick, while I lock up? Oh, and Mum, you'll need to grab a torch. There's a wind-up one in the cupboard by the front door. I thought we'd walk over to Ollie's through the copse – it's not far and beats driving all the way round – but by the time we come back it'll be pitch black. There's not a street light for miles.'

Chapter Twenty-Two

Max took another quick look at the map and then glanced back at the narrow single-track road up ahead of him like a silver ribbon in the moonlight, beneath a dense tunnel of overhanging trees. According to Jess, Vanguard Hall was supposed to be up here somewhere on the left – not that there was a signpost anywhere in sight.

He'd been driving for miles and was more or less convinced that he had to have taken a wrong turning off the main road – a main road that was now miles behind him. Parked up in a passing place, Max looked at Jess's directions.

'In through the main gates, follow main gravelled drive for about a mile, take first turning on left, then left again at cross-roads and straight on to the bottom of the lane. Cottage backs onto churchyard.'

If he could ever find the place. How hard could it be?

Max felt bad, guilty. Getting lost seemed like a just punishment for not being there to help Jess move. He hadn't meant to upset her, and he could see why Jess might be a bit put out with him for not being there for her, and then ringing to say that he was too tired after the flight to come over and see her. But it wasn't as if she was on her own. She had her mum and Nick and friends and family there to help. Okay, so maybe that wasn't what she wanted but sometimes we don't always get what we want in life. And going to New York had been important. It was for his career, their future – surely Jess ought to be able to see that, although obviously he hadn't mentioned the side trip to see Lucy in Cambridge on the way home.

Max pulled out his phone. There was no signal to speak of but he tried to ring Jess anyway. 'The number you have just rung is temporarily unavailable,' said a tinny female recording. 'If you would like to leave a message or . . .'

The night was horribly dark in the oppressive way that it can only be in the country. Max felt the hair on the back of his neck prickle and rise. Instinctively he tapped the door lock with his elbow and the central locking clunked reassuringly as it secured all the doors. Ahead of him a fox, as insolent and cocky as any hoodie, padded through the twin beams of his headlights. As it crossed the road it gave him a cursory glance before vanishing into the bushes on the far verge. It took Max a moment or two to realise the peculiar thumping sound he could hear was his heart beating furiously in his chest.

Pulling himself together he took another look at the map. This was crazy. Maybe he should just go home, if only he could find somewhere to turn around. Thank God they weren't having the wedding there. Christ, they'd probably have to send out search parties for half the guests.

Tired and frustrated, Max made the decision to turn back. After all, Jess was upset with him already, it wasn't going to get any worse. Although to be fair she hadn't said she was mad at him, he could just hear something in her voice. Max found women hard to read, but even he could tell Jess was hurt. He had never been any good at the whole emotional minefield of relationships; wasn't that why Lucy had left him?

Jess had said that of course she understood that he had to go to New York, and of course she understood he was really tired, but that she missed him and really wanted him there with her.

And then she'd said, 'It's fine. Just don't forget we told Shona we'd go to church tomorrow. Ten thirty.'

Max didn't tell her he had forgotten. Or that he couldn't remember who Shona was.

'And then we could come back here for lunch –'

'Okay, how about I bring champagne?' he'd said, all bright and chipper. 'To christen the new house?'

'Sounds lovely,' and she had sounded altogether happier and Max was pleased. 'Oh, and then don't forget on Monday we've got the radio interview.'

'Interview?'

'You're the one who said you wanted the wedding to be on the radio.'

'With your mum?'

'Well yes, it is her show.'

'Right, of course,' he'd agreed, as if he had known all along. And then Max said, 'I'm sorry I can't come over tonight but I am absolutely shattered.'

'It's all right,' Jess said. 'It's been a really long day here too and I'm all in. See you tomorrow.'

There hadn't really been any rancour in her voice, just a resigned, shit-happens kind of tone, which made him feel worse than if she had shouted at him.

On the back seat of the car was a peace offering: Belgian chocolates, a bouquet of the finest supermarket flowers he could find and a bottle of champagne. It would keep till the morning.

Having made up his mind to go home, Max drove off, looking for a place to turn around. Another half a mile down the road and he came across what looked like a farm gateway, tucked back in amongst a great stand of trees.

As he swung the car around Max realised that he'd finally found what he had been looking for – the entrance to Vanguard Hall with its handsome broad brick pillars and wrought-iron gates with some sort of crest set into the metalwork. With a great sense of relief and impending redemption Max sailed in through the gates. A few more minutes and his conscience would be wiped blissfully clean.

'That smells so good, and I'm absolutely starving,' said Jack. 'How long before it's ready?'

Oliver shrugged. 'Five minutes, ten at the outside. Pass me my wine, will you?'

Quite a lot of wine and a considerable amount of beer had flowed at Oliver's cottage since they'd arrived. Jack, Jess, Molly, Nick and Krista were sitting around a large table on the terrace waiting for Oliver to finish the food on the barbecue. It smelt wonderful. Krista had been really busy while they were out moving house.

Molly was two glasses into a bottle of Merlot.

'So how far have you got with the wedding plans? Have you got your dress yet?' purred Krista to Jess in her sexy foreign voice.

'We're more or less there. Helen's doing the dress for me,' Jess said, turning to her best friend. 'She's brilliant.'

'Really?' said Krista, and turned her attention to Helen, who giggled and then hiccupped. Maybe a couple of glasses of wine on empty stomachs hadn't been such a good idea. 'How wonderful – it's so exciting. So what is it like?'

'It's a secret. My lips are sealed,' Helen said, miming a lip-zipping gesture before dipping a nacho into a big bowl of salsa. 'If I told you I'd have to kill you afterwards.'

Krista laughed and topped up their glasses.

'I was thinking,' said Jess to Jack. 'How would you and Oliver like to be ushers?'

'In through the main gates, follow main gravelled drive for about a mile, take first turning on left, left again at crossroads and straight on to the bottom of the lane. Cottage backs onto churchyard.' On the other side of the parkland Max was reciting the instructions to himself as he crept along the long driveway down towards Vanguard Hall. He felt like he was driving in a Hammer horror movie. This was just the kind of place where people broke down on a dark and stormy night.

There were deer everywhere, bloody great things with saucer-sized eyes that reflected his headlights. The first one he came across made Max jump so hard he nearly drove into a tree, and then there were peacocks, whose cries carried for miles and sounded unearthly in the gloom, and owls that hooted and swooped down low along the road like wraiths on the hunt for lost souls.

Max had managed to miss the turning on the left first time around and he had ended up in the drive of the main house, which was in total darkness and silhouetted like an abandoned battleship against the night sky. Caught in the headlights the windows looked like sightless eyes. A swift three-point turn had disturbed another group of peacocks roosting in the trees, making them scream like banshees. Surely it couldn't be much further?

Meanwhile Jack was busy making everyone laugh as he mimed carrying out yet another great pile of possessions from Jess's old cottage, and complaining about all the wedding talk. So far Jess, Helen and Krista had worked their way through hair, dresses, bridesmaids, jewellery, and wedding music.

'We just need to sort out the flowers.'

'Maybe I could help you with that,' said Krista. 'I don't know if Jack told you but I originally trained as a florist.'

On the other side of the table Molly, basking in the light and warmth from the brazier Oliver had lit, listened, enjoying the conversation and the banter. It was good too see Jess back on form and so obviously having a good time.

'Oh, come on, can't we talk about something else?' complained Jack, looking horribly pained. 'How about dentistry, oh, or maybe income tax?'

Krista scowled at him. 'It's interesting.'

'No, it's not,' teased Jack.

Oliver was busy dishing out the food, while Molly and Nick carried on listening to the hubbub of conversation and watching the stars wink into view one by one. Without street-lights or traffic the daylight had quickly softened into shades of darkest blue and a rich Persian purple. Night had crept up on them, pinching out the last of the daylight and there was a slight nip in the air, letting them know the year had well and truly turned and was heading home towards autumn and winter.

'Would you like to come over for lunch tomorrow?' said Jess to Molly. 'I thought I'd cook as a bit of a thank you. Helen's got to go back first thing. I'm dropping her off in town so she can pick up her car and then Max and I will be going to church.'

'You could come over to have lunch with us if you like,' said Nick. 'Save you cooking. And it's only just up the road from St Mary's.'

Jess smiled. 'Thanks for the offer but Max is meeting me at the church and I really want him to come over and see the cottage. First meal here and all that – go on, please say you'll come. I was thinking while we're together we could all blitz the guest list, make sure I haven't missed off anyone important. I'm hoping to get the invitations sent out in a couple of weeks.'

It was Nick who replied. 'You sure you want us here? Don't you and Max want a bit of time to yourselves? There's still lots to do at the cottage. And – well, you know,' he said with a grin, raising his eyebrows suggestively.

Jess laughed. 'Don't you worry about us. We'll have plenty of time to ourselves when you've left. And anyway I'm just planning to stick a chicken in the oven, do a few potatoes and veggies and a packet of Aunt Bessie's Yorkshires. We're not talking strenuous here and presumably you won't be staying all afternoon.'

'In that case, sounds lovely,' said Nick. 'We'll be there.'

'What about church?' Jess said. 'I did mention it to Mum earlier – Shona, the vicar, asked if we'd go.'

Molly raised her eyebrows.

Jess smiled. 'Oh, come on, Mum, it would be lovely to have you there. It's meant to be a family thing.'

Nick nodded. 'I think she's right, Molly.'

Molly stared at him. 'Really?'

'Moral support.'

'And it'll be good for your soul,' said Jess.

Krista meanwhile was bringing out dishes of salad and baked potatoes. Jess and Nick were waiting for an answer. 'Oh, all right.' Molly gave in, and then to Krista said, 'Do you want a hand with that?'

Krista waved the words away. 'No, it's fine, you've been working all day.'

As she filled their plates, somewhere off in the distance they heard the sound of an engine.

'Is that a car?' wondered Jack.

Oliver, tongs in hand, glanced up. 'It's probably Kit, the gamekeeper. Bertie and the family are away in London this weekend. So I said I'd close the gates today but I was thinking of going later when we've finished up here. Didn't want anyone getting locked in.'

'I could go and do it if you like,' said Jack, leaning in to pinch a sausage from the plate. 'God, those are hot.' He puffed and blew.

'Serves you right,' said Jess, before anyone else could.

'So you want me to go and do the gates?'

'No, I'll do it once your mum and Nick have gone. What about you, Helen?'

'I'm staying. Sleeping on madam's floor tonight,' said Helen wryly, glancing affectionately at Jess. 'A friend in need is a friend indeed.' She laughed. 'Although given the amount of work I've done you'd think that she would at least give me the bed.'

'You could stay here,' said Krista. 'Oliver, you've got a spare bed, haven't you?'

'Really?' Helen purred.

The next junction Max came to wasn't really a crossroads, more of a ragged meeting of lanes. Max had had just about enough. The TT was covered in mud. He was being harassed by the wildlife. He had crashed down into potholes, his temper was frayed and he was tired, the jet lag was catching up with him. This part of the journey, the one that should have had him home and dry in a few minutes, seemed to have taken for ever and *straight on to the bottom* was proving anything but.

Finally, in the distance Max could pick out the lights of a cottage between the trees. As he turned the corner he could see a hire van and Jess's car and Nick's estate parked out front so he knew that he had the right place at last. He hadn't expected them all to still be there but it was too late to worry about that now. Max pulled up in front of the cottage, checked his hair in the rear-view mirror, popped a Polo into his mouth, wishing now that instead of going into Tesco's on the way over he'd bought Jess some perfume from the trip or something silly with 'I Love New York' stamped on it – she would have liked that – but at least he had brought her something. Max climbed out of the car.

He hoped that she would be pleased he had made the effort to drive over. Hopefully her parents wouldn't stay long once he arrived. Just a hello and how are you, and then off.

As he crossed the rough grass a security light flashed on, catching Max in a jaundiced yellow beam and revealing Heaven's Gate. Jess was right, it was absolutely lovely, like something from the lid of a shortbread tin – such a shame it was so far from anywhere else.

As he locked the car Max was surprised by just how quiet it was. He waited for a couple of seconds, listening. Bassa didn't bark. Jess didn't come out to greet him. He was surprised that they hadn't heard the car. There were lights on in the cottage but the curtains were drawn closed.

He picked his way across the grass and knocked on the front door. There was not a sound from inside, so he knocked again, harder this time. He checked his watch. It wasn't late. Maybe they had the TV on or music or were talking. The seconds ticked by and turned into a minute and then another.

'Jess,' he called, but his voice sounded horribly loud and he felt very alone.

With the champagne tucked under one arm, Max set off around to the back of the cottage to see if there was another door and realised, as he opened the gate, that the garden backed onto a graveyard. Seeing the neat rows of gravestones all lined up under the moonlight gave Max a real shudder of horror. Mist was starting to gather in the dips and hollows and in the long grass. He felt his pulse quicken.

To one side of the path was a large mausoleum with a life-sized angel crouched on top of it, the shadows making its eye sockets appear empty and sinister. Max swallowed hard, taking deep breaths to try and quell his growing sense of panic. It was fine, for God's sake, he was a grown man – and then an owl hooted somewhere close by and it was all Max could do not to turn and run. Was Jess mad? This wasn't heaven's gate, it was the gravedigger's cottage. Who in their right mind would want to live here? Then Max heard something large and lumbering moving in the bushes. That was the final straw. With a girly squeal Max was up on his toes and away. He ran out through the gate, jumped into his car and roared up the lane as if the devil himself was after him. It wasn't until he got to the crossroads that he slowed down and realised that he'd left his peace offering somewhere behind him and was still holding his breath. Without looking back he slammed the car into gear and drove away, a cold trickle of sweat running down the back of his neck.

Over at Oliver's cottage, despite everyone being totally exhausted, they were having a great time. Krista was busy sliding great wedges of some kind of flan topped with filo pastry onto their plates – as if they could eat anything else. Oliver was opening more wine.

Molly had never been to a barbecue like it. There were all kinds of salads and homemade bread, all beautifully put together in the apparently effortless way that only comes

254

from being a good cook. As Krista reached her with dessert Molly held up a hand to decline, but too late.

'One little piece won't hurt you,' Krista said, not prepared to take no for an answer.

Around the table everyone was beginning to flag, the food, the wine and the long day having just about finished them off, although Krista was still keen to talk about the wedding.

'It's such a shame you're not having it here, Jess. We could have all pitched in to help,' she said, slipping onto the bench alongside Helen.

'That would have been lovely,' said Jess. 'But Max and I decided it would be more practical for everyone if we had it at the other place. People can stay and – and . . .' Her voice trailed off. 'Well, you know . . .' She glanced at Molly and then looked away. Molly guessed it was in case she revealed just how disappointed she was. 'Actually I'd have loved to have got married here. It's perfect,' she said after a few seconds. 'But we're not . . .'

For a moment they were all quiet. All Molly could hear was the sounds of the leaves on the edge of the night breeze and the muffled call of a fox from somewhere in the distant woodland. Oliver threw another piece of wood onto the brazier, sending sparks bright as fireworks into the velvety blue darkness. There was no other light for miles.

Jack held a bottle out towards her. 'One for the road, Mum?'

Molly laughed and then nodded. 'Why not, Nick's driving.'

Nick, deep in conversation with Oliver, looked up at the sound of his name and smiled at her, his eyes alight with love and joy and the contentment that comes from being certain that you are loved. It made Molly's heart ache. Around them the dogs dozed and played in and out of the shadows. It was the most perfect evening.

Chapter Twenty-Three

'I can't remember the last time I went to church,' whispered Molly, toes wriggling around in court shoes that probably hadn't seen the light of day since around the same time. She'd forgotten just how cold and uncomfortable churches could be and wished that instead of wearing a smart summer dress and matching jacket, she'd had the good sense to wear an overcoat and Ugg boots. The cold seeped up through the flagstone floors like rising damp.

Mentally Molly was working through a to-do list. She needed to contact the vicar to get permission to record the wedding and then, even though Jess and Max weren't having their cake made locally, she needed to track down someone who made wedding cakes to interview, and chase up the flower nursery and the importer who brought things over from Holland. Then there were wedding cars. Had Jess sorted the cars out?

'Are we there yet?' whined Nick, in an undertone.

'Behave yourselves,' hissed Jess, who was sitting at the other end of the pew, although to be fair she was smiling. 'It'll be lovely.'

Molly tried hard to stop planning and concentrate on being in church with her only daughter who, it had to be said, looked radiant.

The pew ends were decked with swags of carrots and onions, the steps up to the screen and pulpit were stacked with small wicker baskets full of tins and oranges and cakes and whatever else it was that passed for harvest these days. It looked like a Gothic supermarket. The front two rows on either side of the aisle were reserved for cubs and beavers and brownies, scouts and guides, who they had passed congregating outside on the gravel on their way in. If the noise coming from the back of the church was any measure then at least the service was going to be lively.

Sitting halfway back by a pillar and a pile of pumpkins Jess, Molly and Nick were waiting for Max to arrive and for the service to begin. Molly looked around. The church was quite small and lovely and very welcoming inside, and looked oddly Mediterranean with its white walls and plain pitched wooden ceiling. It had been like this for as long as Molly could remember.

She had gone to carol services at St Mary's as a child and been to weddings and funerals and baptisms over the years. As an adult she hadn't bothered with God very much and he never rang, so they had pretty much agreed to leave each other alone.

There were lots of people in the church, which rather surprised her, although she suspected most were parents and grandparents of the children waiting outside.

In the pew in front of them an elderly woman in a heavy tweed coat that smelt slightly of mothballs and Youth Dew carefully slipped slivers of paper into her hymn book to mark the pages, reminding Molly of every church service she had ever been to.

'Maybe we should have waited outside in the sunshine,' said Nick in a whisper. 'I can't feel my feet.'

Jess looked at her watch as the children began to

process in led by Shona, the vicar, various helpers, and the choir.

'Max ought to be here by now,' Jess said, glancing round. 'I told him it would be starting at ten thirty.'

Each group of children was led by one carrying a token basket of produce which they very solemnly set down in amongst the others. Shona, now standing on the chancel steps in front of the screen, smiled and welcomed everyone.

'It's so nice to see you all here today,' she said, as the children settled into the rows and quietened. Her smiling, benign gaze moved slowly along the rows, catching Molly's eye. 'I know that not everyone here has been to church before or maybe hasn't been in a long time but I want you to know that that doesn't matter; what matters is that you're here now – and that you're very welcome.'

Which was the very moment when Max arrived, flustered and flapping and a long way from quiet. Molly winced as she heard him hurrying down the aisle, shoes tapping over the flagstones.

As he slipped into the pew alongside Jess, he said, 'Sorry, sorry – God, I couldn't find anywhere to park. I didn't know there were going to be children here. So where are we?' By some trick of the acoustics, it sounded as if he had shouted it. Shona waited and once Max had stopped talking began again.

Molly kept her head down and started looking for hymn numbers.

The service was quite short, with lots of rousing hymns and brisk, cheery readings, with several of the children taking part. Molly smiled as proud parents looked on. It took her back years. Alongside her, Nick smiled too, as a tiny girl with ginger hair and a crop of freckles lisped her way through a piece about Godth gwacious bounty.

It was altogether charming, as was Shona, who managed to be both warm and dignified. After a few rousing verses of 'Come, ye thankful people, come', it was time for a quick blessing and away.

Outside in the sunshine Molly joined the line to shake the vicar's hand, behind Jess and Max, and alongside Nick, while around them the children were giggling and running about, delighted to be outside after the confines of the church.

Max had barely spoken to Jess or Molly or Nick since they got outside, while Jess on the other hand appeared to be overcompensating for Max's sullenness by being unnaturally buoyant and bubbly.

Shona smiled at they reached her. 'Nice to see you both. Enjoy the service?' she asked.

'Oh, it was lovely,' said Jess, beaming. 'Wasn't it, Max?' He didn't speak, instead he just stood there with a fixed expression, so Jess turned and continued, 'This is my mum, Molly, and her partner, Nick. They came to give us some moral support.'

Molly took Shona's hand and smiled; they were around the same age. Shona had the look of a woman who could deal with whatever life threw at her while handing out sensible advice and comfort. Her handshake was friendly and firm and Molly immediately warmed to her.

'Delighted you could make it,' Shona said, and then they did the things about the weather and the attendance and the wedding and after a minute or two Shona moved on to the people behind them.

'She seems really nice,' said Molly. 'Have you got her number? We need to talk to her about recording the service.'

Jess nodded while Max began walking off down the hill. Jess was obviously distracted too now. 'I'd better go and see Max,' she said.

Molly glanced at Nick, who said nothing. 'We'll see you in a little while,' Molly called after her. 'I'm just going to nip home and change. Is there anything you want us to bring for lunch?'

Jess shook her head. 'No, no, I've got everything – thanks,' and she was gone after Max.

'Max? Max, wait for me. Are you okay?' cried Jess, hurrying down the driveway.

'I'm fine. I'm just parked awkwardly,' Max said, still heading away from her towards the road.

Jess stopped hurrying. 'Max, for God's sake, will you stop?' she snapped and finally something in her tone of voice made him swing round. 'What's the matter? You pitch up late, you barely speak to me or Mum and Nick, you haven't asked me how I am, how the move went, you haven't kissed me, or hugged me, or anything.'

He sighed and ran his hands back through his hair. 'Sorry, sorry, sorry. It's all been a bit of a flap this morning. I hadn't expected it to take so long to get over here or for there to be a church full of children.'

Jess stared at him. 'I did tell you it was Harvest Festival.'

'Did you? Well, it hadn't occurred to me it would be so full. I thought the whole thing was going to be a bit more low key.'

Jess laughed. 'Low key? What's that supposed to mean?'

'You know, not many people. It was much more formal when I was a child. They all looked at me –'

'They all looked at you because you came in late and blundered down the aisle making a noise.'

'I did not blunder,' he protested indignantly and then he smiled and his expression softened. 'Okay, so maybe I blundered a bit. Sorry, it's been a busy week.'

Jess raised her eyebrows. 'You don't say.'

And then Max leaned closer and sighed. 'I'm a bit pre-occupied at the moment, work is a nightmare and I've been clearing the house and I was bit surprised – It's not that I've got anything against women vicars personally, but it hadn't occurred to me that she would be taking the service.'

Jess laughed incredulously. 'What? What did you think she was when we went to see her, the real vicar's PA?' But Max hadn't finished and quite obviously wasn't listening.

'I rang my parents to let them know that we'd cleared up the situation with the venue for the wedding reception. I think they're both relieved that that's all sorted itself out. And Mum's emailed me a list of family and friends.' He pulled a folded sheet of paper out of his jacket pocket and handed it to her. 'I've added a few names.'

'Great,' Jess said.

'Just one thing,' said Max. 'I think this morning sort of brought it home to me.' He hesitated. 'My parents aren't going be at all happy with the idea of us being married by a female vicar.'

'What?' Jess stared at him but he didn't budge. 'Oh, for God's sake. You *are* joking, aren't you?'

'They're traditionalist, Jess – but I'm sure it'll be fine. We'll just ask someone else to do it. I'm sure Shona will under-stand.'

'No,' said Jess firmly.

'I'm sure they must have come across this sort of thing before.'

'I'm sure they have, but I'm not asking for a different vicar.'

'You can't be serious,' said Max. 'You didn't want a church wedding in the first place.'

'I know, but now I'm having one I want Shona to marry us –'

'That's ridiculous. I mean, what does it matter?'

'It matters to me, Max. She has been so helpful and so kind – and the service this morning was lovely. I'll ring your mum and talk to her.'

'You're being unreasonable, Jess.'

She stared at him in amazement. '*I'm* being unreasonable?'

And then he smiled again and shook his head. 'Look, let's not argue about this, why don't we think about it? We'll talk when I get over to yours. I'll see you in a little while –'

'What you mean is you're hoping I'll back down and change my mind, just like I've done over everything else,' Jess snapped furiously.

He shook his head and took hold of her hands. 'Don't be silly. I don't mind who marries us, it's just that if it's a woman I don't think my parents will want to come. Is that what you want?'

It was such a preposterous thing to say that it took her breath away. Jess glanced back over her shoulder; Molly and Nick were at the top of the path staring at them.

'No, it isn't what I want,' hissed Jess, trying hard to keep her voice down. 'And I don't want us to argue about this at all. I want it to be easy.' She paused. 'This is crazy – I'm so fed up.'

He swung round.

'I don't want us to fight, Max. I've been looking forward to seeing you all week. I've missed you,' she said.

'Missed me?'

'You've been away –'

'Yes, but only for a couple of days.'

'Well, it feels like longer,' she said, catching hold of his arm. 'A lot longer.'

He looked uncomfortable. 'I'd better be going,' he said. 'I'm blocking people in.'

263

Jess reached towards him. 'Aren't you at least going to kiss me?'

He hesitated long enough for Jess to feel horribly embarrassed. It felt as if she was offering him full sex there on the grass verge in front of the scouts. Finally Max leaned in a little closer and kissed her on top of the head. 'There,' he said. 'I have to say I'm not awfully struck on PDAs.'

'What?' said Jess.

'It always seems a little tacky.'

Her brain was working overtime. PDAs? It took a second or two to work it out: public displays of affection.

'Right,' said Jess, slipping her arm out of his. 'In that case I'll see you at mine for lunch.'

'It doesn't mean I love you less, Jess, it just means that I don't want to stick my tongue halfway down your throat in public.'

'Don't, then,' Jess snapped and headed back up the hill towards her mum and Nick. They were holding hands. Jess didn't look back at Max because she didn't want to catch his eye in case she cried – or worse.

An hour or so later Molly and Jess were sitting in the big bay window at Jess's dining table in Heaven's Gate drinking coffee and looking over the wedding to-do list, while waiting for lunch to cook. From the kitchen came the warm, mouth-watering smells of chicken roasting in garlic and lemon. Nick had taken the dogs out for a walk.

'Photos, invitations, cake, flowers, order of service – cars. The cars occurred to me in church.' Molly's attention moved down the list. 'Sounds like you've more or less got it covered. What about hair? Make-up?'

Jess pulled a face. 'I can sort all that out.'

'Are you all right? You look a bit peaky.'

'I'm fine, just a bit tired after yesterday,' said Jess without quite meeting her eye.

'You should have come to ours for lunch,' said Molly, reaching into her handbag. 'I've brought my mother of the bride book over if you want to have a check through to see if you've missed anything.'

Jess's expression didn't improve. 'Kind, but no thanks.'

'I meant to ask you yesterday. Have you spoken to Marnie since going down to Hampshire?'

Jess groaned. 'No, but she emailed me to see how things were coming along, and to ask if I needed Noo's help with anything. So I thought I'd get Noo to sort out the cars, the coach, and hotel arrangements for the guests. God knows what Dad's paying her, she might as well do something for it. Halley Hall has got its own florist so we just need to sort out the church. Shona said that we can't have flowers because it's Advent but we can have greenery and candles, so I was thinking we could maybe have holly and ivy and ribbon – I'm going to ask Krista if she'd be happy to do it. She did offer.'

'That sounds lovely, really tasteful,' Molly said. 'It'll look stunning. I'd forgotten what a pretty church St Mary's is.'

Jess smiled ruefully. 'And I'm hoping a whole lot cheaper than flowers. I feel really bad about all the money we're spending. It's not what I wanted at all. I'd have been happy with a registry office do and having a party here.' She glanced out of the window. 'It all seems such a waste of money.'

Molly hesitated and then said, 'Well, your dad doesn't seem to think so. He wants the day to be perfect for you.'

Jess raised her eyebrows. 'You mean Marnie wants it to be perfect for her. Anyway, can you think of anything else?'

Molly glanced at her; Jess sounded flat and tired and looked exhausted.

'There's bound to be things we've missed but we'll get them sorted. Now is there anything you want me to help you with for lunch?'

Jess shook her head and then started to flick through the Halley Hall brochure that was open alongside her list. 'I was thinking about having the tables like this –' she turned the brochure so that Molly could see it '– with cream and gold balloons and posies and little bottles of bubbles. Once we've got the dress fabric we can match up everything else.'

Molly nodded, while Jess started working her way through the diary by the list. 'Oh, and we're in the radio station tomorrow for our interview.'

'Tomorrow?' Molly stared at her. How could that have slipped her mind?

'Come on, Mother, keep up,' Jess joked. 'You're the one who told me. Twelve fifteen, tomorrow lunchtime? I've got it down here. Interview on air, photos for website.' She tapped the entry in her diary and turned the book around so Molly could see. 'You're as bad as Max.'

Molly doubted it but smiled and nodded. 'Sorry – yes, of course.' She realised with a jolt that she'd been so busy planning the wedding that she had almost forgotten the conversation she wanted to have with Jess about Max. The scene in the church this morning had just about finished her off. And where was he now? Molly and Nick had gone home to change and they had still arrived at the cottage ahead of him. 'It'll be great.'

'Right,' said Jess, all business. 'Remind me to remind Max again. What do you think I ought to wear for the photos? Are we talking suit and posh dress or jeans?'

Molly made an effort to gather her thoughts together. 'Just wear something you like.'

'What about that blue dress with a little cardigan?' Jess mimed the front. 'The one with little pearl buttons?'

Molly nodded. 'That would be perfect. So, tomorrow –'

'We'll be there at quarter past twelve,' said Jess. 'Oh, and before I forget –' She scribbled something on a pad and handed it to Molly. 'My new phone number here.'

'That was quick.'

Jess nodded. 'So do you think Max should wear a suit?'

'Only if he wants to. I think the powers that be have lashed out on champagne. Well, cava.'

'Talking of Max, he ought to be here by now.' Jess glanced at the clock on the mantelpiece. Even though Jess had been in the cottage less than twenty-four hours, Heaven's Gate already felt like home.

Molly decided not to comment. 'Helen got off okay this morning?'

'Yes. It's been so brilliant having her here. I don't know what I would have done without her. I don't think she wanted to go really.' Jess grinned. 'And she's so excited about being a bridesmaid. I'm going down to stay with her for a weekend at the end of the month so I can have a fitting for the dress and we can buy some odds and ends, shoes and stuff. Maybe you should come too? There is this fantastic theatrical place she uses. Helen was showing me the website. And we've settled on the design.' Jess slid a folder across the table and opened it up to a double page. 'What do you think?'

What did she think? Molly stared down at the sketches that Helen had drawn for Jess and instantly felt her eyes filling with tears. 'This one,' said Jess unnecessarily.

The girl looking back from the pages of the sketchbook was pure Jess. The design Helen had created for her was as close to perfect as you could get. In one of the sketches, which Molly guessed was probably taken from a photo, Helen

267

had drawn Jess throwing back her head and laughing, showing off the dress's distinctive beaded neckline. Stapled to one corner off the page were swatches and combinations of fabric.

'Oh, my God, Jess, it's absolutely beautiful,' murmured Molly. 'And so you.'

Jess reddened and then grinned self-consciously. 'It is lovely, isn't it? I knew you'd like it. I showed her my wedding book.' She very carefully pressed the pages flat with her fingers.

'I can see,' said Molly, voice tight with emotion. 'Oh, baby, it's stunning.'

'You don't think it's too much, do you? With the boning and all that?'

Molly shook her head. 'No, not at all. It's so you. And I love the cloak.'

Jess beamed and then added, 'You won't say anything to Max about the dress, will you? I want it to be a surprise and it's not really his sort of thing, but I think it will be just perfect.'

'Me too,' said Molly.

'And you're going to be the one to interview us tomorrow, aren't you?'

Molly hesitated. 'Yes, of course.'

Jess pulled a face. 'What?'

It was Molly who raised her eyebrows. 'Well, I wasn't sure how you felt about being live on air. And obviously Max –'

'What about Max?' Jess sounded defensive.

'Well, I wondered if he might prefer to record it. He seemed a bit off this morning.'

'He's just tired, that's all, and it was Max's idea to do this, remember?' Jess said briskly. 'So he won't mind. He's not as jaded with the media as I am.'

Molly laughed. 'I work for local radio, not Hollywood.'

'You know what I mean. You wouldn't believe how many times when I was at school someone would come up to me and say, "Your mum was talking about you on the radio again . . ."'

Molly held up her hands. 'I did try and stop it once you pointed it out to me.'

'No one was ever fooled by you saying, "This little girl I know did something horribly embarrassing but *incredibly* funny yesterday –"'

They looked at each other and all of a sudden Jess started to giggle and, without expecting to, Molly joined in.

'I was so embarrassed,' giggled Jess.

'I did the same to Jack,' protested Molly.

'He had a thicker skin and he used to think it was so cool. I hated it.'

'I wanted the world to know what a clever, funny, talented person you are.'

Jess mimed vomiting. 'Oh, Mum, please.'

'No, it's true,' said Molly, coming over all sentimental. 'And I still do.' Which was why Molly knew she had to say something now because she didn't want her talented, lovely, beautiful daughter to end up marrying the wrong man. There was no time like the present. What was left of the giggle faded and a big silence opened up between them. It had been the first time they had really been alone in days and Molly felt as if it was now or never.

'Jess –' she began hesitantly.

'I know what you're going to say, Mum,' said Jess.

'You do?' said Molly, caught midway between relief and apprehension.

'Helen is sending me some bigger pieces of the fabric to take a look at just to be sure before we make the final decision. I was thinking the gold – this one?' She fingered one of the little squares, neatly clipped and pinned alongside the dress design. 'What do you think?'

'It's lovely,' said Molly, taking a deep breath. 'But actually, Jess, it wasn't the dress I wanted to talk to you about.'

'What then?' said Jess, getting up to check on the chicken.

Molly so wanted Jess to be sitting down so that she could see her face but was afraid that if she didn't say something soon she would lose her chance and her courage. 'This is really hard for me to say because I don't want to upset you.'

Although Molly suspected that was exactly what she *was* going to do – and if you didn't want to upset someone it wasn't a great way to start a sentence. Although at least Molly now had Jess's full and undivided attention.

'What?' Jess said.

'I have to ask you about this, Jess, and there's no easy way for me to say it. Are you sure you're doing the right thing?'

'The right thing?' repeated Jess. 'What right thing?'

'Marrying Max,' said Molly quietly.

Jess's colour drained and she swallowed hard. 'What the hell is that supposed to mean? Of course I am doing the right thing,' she snapped. 'What a weird thing to say, Mum. I wouldn't be doing it otherwise.'

'Only you don't seem –'

'What?' Jess said, with a distinct edge to her voice. 'What *don't* I seem?'

'I know you, Jess, and you don't seem happy or at ease with Max. It just doesn't feel right – I'm not trying to upset you, I want to talk about this because I love you.'

'Oh well, *obviously*,' snorted Jess. 'This is ridiculous. Of course I'm happy with Max, why wouldn't I be? I mean he's – he's . . .'

Molly, her heart beating furiously, waited while Jess hunted down the right words and then finally, when Jess appeared to be struggling, said very gently, 'He's what, Jess? Late?'

Jess glared at her. 'Don't patronise me, Mum. I'm an adult. Max is completely different when he's with me on my own. Okay, I have to agree that he's a bit of a geek and he's not always great in social situations with other people, and I know he can come across as being a bit odd at times, but who isn't? I mean, look at Dad. He's not exactly Mr Affable, is he? And you two were married for donkey's years.'

'Yes, that's true, and if I had my time over again I'd still marry him because back then I loved him – and I knew I loved him. But I was comfortable with your dad and we got on well –'

'Well, I love Max,' Jess insisted petulantly. 'And we get on well. Very well.'

'And I knew your dad loved me.'

'Well, good for you,' Jess snapped, staring at Molly, eyes bright. 'You really don't like Max, do you? You're not even prepared to give him a chance.'

'Jess, that's not true.'

'Why don't you just come right out and say it.'

'This isn't about me liking him, Jess, it's about you and what's right for *you*, not me. I just want you to be sure that you're doing the right thing. It's such a big thing to do. You have to go into it believing you want to spend the rest of your life with someone.' Molly glanced at her. 'Wake up every morning with him – look, please, don't be angry, I had to say something.'

Jess sniffed. 'I'm not angry. I don't know what I am. I thought you were pleased for me.'

'I am, but only if you're marrying the right man for the right reasons, Jess. Marriage is hard enough if Max is the right one, it's impossible if he isn't.'

Jess backhanded a tear away. 'But I love him.'

'I'm glad but don't feel that you have to marry him if you don't want to. Nothing is undoable.'

Jess stopped crying and stared at her. 'What? What the hell is that supposed to mean?'

'You don't have to marry Max if you don't want to.'

'I know that, Mum,' said Jess, incredulous. 'But I've just told you I love him and I want to marry him – what else do you want me to say? Or are you suggesting that I should cancel the whole thing and *not* marry Max just because you don't like him? Is that what you're saying?'

Molly stared at her. 'No, of course not – but I had to say something to you because I've been worried sick about you. You're losing weight, you look exhausted and you don't look happy. And look at the way he behaved at the church this morning. It feels to me as if you're being swept along in a mad rush – and I wanted to say that if you've got any doubts about marrying Max then my advice would be don't do it. Or at least don't do it just yet. I'm sure he would understand, and we could put everything on hold for the time being. I'm not saying don't marry him, just give it a bit more time – surely there's no real rush.'

As Jess opened her mouth to reply Max's car pulled up in front of the cottage.

'Jess –' Molly began.

'I can hardly talk about this now, can I?' snapped Jess, as she glanced in the mirror, making an attempt to repair the damage to her make-up with a tissue, before running her fingers through her already tousled hair and heading outside, leaving Molly feeling about as bad as she had ever felt about anything.

She had chosen the wrong moment. Now they hadn't got time to talk or argue or cry or sort it out and make up.

Outside as Max climbed out of the car Jess made a great show of hugging him and cuddling up to him, all of which made Max look deeply uncomfortable.

Molly turned away in case Jess thought she was spying on them, at which point Nick came in through the back door with the dogs, who were delighted to see her.

'Nice walk?' she asked in a slightly uneven voice.

'Great. What's the matter?'

Molly pulled a face. 'I talked to Jess about Max but I'm not sure it's done any good. And it was definitely not the right time to start talking about whether marrying him is a good idea. Nick, I think I've totally screwed things up.'

'Ah –' said Nick, in a sage-like tone, which Molly always suspected he used when he didn't know what else to say. 'Well, there was never going to be a good time, was there?'

'I had to say something.'

'I know you did.' He hugged her. 'And you did the right thing.'

'I should have found a better time.'

'Maybe, but it's done now.' His voice was gentle and sympathetic.

Seconds later Max came in through the front door. Jess had her arm through his and had him tightly pulled up against her. It looked for all the world, thought Molly, as if she was worried he might make a break for it.

He nodded curtly towards Nick and Molly.

'Hi, Max,' said Molly, painting on her professional presenter's smile. 'Lovely to see you. You find the cottage all right?'

'Of course you did, didn't you, Max?' said Jess before he could open his mouth. 'He's not stupid.'

Max looked confused. 'Actually, it is a bit off the beaten

273

track, isn't it?' he said. 'A bit isolated. And I'm not naturally drawn to the country.' He managed to make living in the country sound like some peculiar marginal religious practice.

'Wasn't it a lovely service?' said Molly, struggling to find a conversation to fill the growing silence.

Max stared at her.

'This morning, earlier,' she persisted. 'At the church?'

'Right,' said Jess cheerily. 'Well, maybe I should give you the grand tour, Max. Or would you like a glass of wine, or something?' As she spoke Jess walked briskly over to the table and closed the sketchbook that still lay open on the table.

'Actually I'm fine,' said Max, looking horribly awkward and stiff standing there in the hallway.

'Jack's coming over too,' said Jess, now busy pouring herself a large glass of red. 'He shouldn't be long. Would anyone else like wine?'

'I didn't realise you'd be here,' Max said to Molly. 'I mean, not that I mind or anything, I'm just a bit surprised to see you. You were all here yesterday – not that that's a bad thing – obviously.'

'Actually, it was a very good thing,' said Molly, as evenly as she could manage. 'Otherwise Jess would have had to move house on her own.'

Jess shot her a killer look.

'I just came in through the cemetery,' Nick said, leaping into the breach to try and lighten the mood. 'Had a lovely walk with the dogs.'

Molly looked up, only half-listening as Nick continued. 'It was terribly sad and rather sweet though. There is this huge bouquet of flowers out there on one of the graves, and chocolates and a bottle of champagne. I was thinking it must be an anniversary or something. How poignant is that?'

To everyone's surprise Max glared at him and snapped, 'I suppose you think that's funny, do you?'

Nick stared at him, totally at a loss, 'I'm sorry?' he began. It really was the most extraordinary thing to say.

'Think it's a great joke, don't you?' said Max. 'The flowers and the champagne.'

'I don't know what you mean!' spluttered Nick, glancing at Molly who was equally flummoxed by Max's reaction.

'Out there in the graveyard.'

At which point Molly made a big decision; their visit was unlikely to get any better and so, smiling, she said, 'Okay, Jess, I think we'll be heading off home now. It's been super to see you all settled in.' And then, still smiling, said to Max, 'I'll see you tomorrow for the interview.'

Max frowned but Molly had no intention of enlightening him. Jess meanwhile looked first at one and then the other. 'There's no need to go,' she began and then perhaps realising it was a lost cause continued, 'I'll show you out,' in a smaller voice.

Molly snapped the lead on Milo and, still smiling, headed back out to the car. 'You don't have to go,' said Jess, voice brittle with tears and frustration and God alone knew what else.

'I think we do. You and Max need time alone and he obviously wasn't expecting us to be here, so we'll be off.' Molly paused, uncomfortable at leaving Jess without making things better between them. 'What I said earlier –'

Jess stiffened.

'I just wanted to say that I love you with all my heart,' said Molly, hugging her. 'Nick too. Whatever you need, whatever you decide, and I do mean whatever, we are here for you.'

For an instant Molly thought Jess was going to snap at

her but instead Jess smiled and nodded; they seldom argued and over the years when they did have disagreements they had never lasted for long, but compared to this all those things seemed very trivial. Molly's heart ached as Jess turned back towards the house.

'I love you,' she said.

'I know,' Jess said in a whisper, now wrapping her arms around herself. 'I'm going to go back inside, talk to Max. I'll maybe call you later – and if not we'll see you tomorrow.'

Molly nodded. 'We'll nip in and tell Jack that lunch is off.'

Jess managed a thin, uneasy smile. 'Thank you.'

Max was waiting inside for Jess. If he had heard the exchange with Molly and Nick his face gave away nothing. Jess stared at him, wondering what to say next, but as she was about to speak he smiled, produced a tiny little package from his jacket pocket and held it out in front of him like a charm.

'I'm sorry,' he said. 'I didn't mean to upset them or you. I was just a bit stunned to see them here, I was really hoping we could spend some time together. *Alone.*'

Jess looked at the tiny, carefully wrapped present. Max's gaze followed hers.

'It's why I was late this morning,' Max explained. 'I didn't have time to get you anything from New York – so – so I got you this.' He held it out more pointedly and Jess felt obligated to take it.

'What is it?'

'Why don't you open it?' he said brightly. Jess looked up at him; she didn't want a present. She didn't want him to think she could be bought with some little trinket and she was hurt and confused by the way he had behaved at the church, and by the way he had snapped at Nick. Eventually she set the box down on the table unopened.

'What was all that with Nick?' she asked.

Max shrugged. 'Nothing.'

'It didn't sound like nothing.'

He stared at her. 'I said it was nothing. What's the matter?'

'I don't know if I can do this, Max,' she said. 'I always imagined getting married to someone would be the most wonderful thing. I mean, I'm a realist, I didn't expect it would be all plain sailing and happy ever after but this is such hard work. You're hard work, you're just not there for me –'

He looked stricken. 'What is that supposed to mean? If it's about the move, I'm really –' he began but Jess held up a hand to quieten him.

'It isn't about the move. I understand that some times work comes first but my mum asked me this morning if I was happy –'

'*Oh, right, so it's your mother.*'

'No, it's not her – it's me. She said that I didn't seem happy and you know what? She's absolutely right – I'm not. I feel like I'm getting ready for my execution, not my wedding. You and I want such different things, Max. And before you say anything – we do. I wanted something low-key with friends and family, you want a church wedding with some great big grand reception. You want us to be on the radio and make a big splash – well, the girl who wants all those things isn't me.'

Max stared at her.

Jess slipped the engagement ring off her finger and slid it across the table. 'I have to work so hard for everything you give me emotionally. I don't need it. I want someone who just loves me for what I am as I am.'

He said nothing.

'I want you to have this back,' said Jess. 'The wedding's off.'

Max stood stock-still, white as a ghost. 'Jess,' he said. 'Please don't do this.'

'I don't know what else to do, Max.'

'Let's talk about it. This is too drastic. You're tired and I've been so busy with work lately and I know I've been neglecting you. I need to make some time for you, I know that.'

'That's just the point, Max. We shouldn't *have* to make time for each other, we should do that without thinking – it should be a given. You shouldn't have to timetable me in.'

Max stared at her. Had he said then that he missed her Jess might have melted, if he had said that he loved her and couldn't live without her, she might have changed her mind. But instead he said, 'But I bought you a present,' in a whining, miserable, man-boy voice.

'Go,' she ordered.

For a moment he hesitated as if trying to weigh up whether or not she was serious. And then he turned and went.

For a few seconds Jess just stood there, rooted to the spot. She felt sick and shaky. The ring and the little box were still on the table where Max had left them. Jess waited until she heard Max's car pull away and then she began to cry with of mixture of sadness and hurt, tempered with a huge sense of relief.

She pulled a tissue out of her bag, feeling totally lost. The phone rang and without thinking she picked it up.

'Hello, Jess?' said a familiar voice. 'How are you?'

'Marnie?' spluttered Jess, backhanding the tears away.

'Are you all right?'

'Yes, yes I'm fine,' she lied, not yet ready for the truth. 'Onions. I'm busy peeling onions. For Sunday lunch.'

'Right, in that case I won't keep you long,' said Marnie

278

briskly. 'I was just ringing to see how the move went and also to say that Mimi is here staying with her husband – you remember Freddie. I was thinking. Your mother did say that you had already made your mind up about your bridesmaid but I know Mimi would be delighted to be your matron of honour. You've always got on well. I mean, just for symmetry's sake if nothing else.'

Jess took a deep breath, wondering what the hell to say, but Marnie was ahead of her.

'Obviously you're busy at the moment but just have a little think about it. We'd sort out Mimi's dress – Morwenna said you all enjoyed your trip to Gownena's last week. Presumably you'll be making up your mind about the dress fairly soon? She is very good but I think they have a bit of a wait for delivery so probably the sooner the better with your order. Anyway, I'll let you get on. If you could let me know about the dress for Mimi – we'll need to sort out a fitting for her.' And with that Marnie was gone and Jess was left with the phone dead in her hand.

On top of the stove in the kitchen were all the makings of lunch for five, a little pan simmering away with gravy stock, potatoes ready to boil, carrots all scraped. Jess wiped her face and slid the pans off the rings – there was no way she could face eating lunch – and as she did there was a huge bang which made Jess shriek and jump back in shock.

Somehow she had fused something and now the main switch was tripped and there was no power at all. Sniffling, Jess went on a hunt for the fuse box but there was no sign of it anywhere. So she picked up the phone to ring Nick; after all he and Molly couldn't have got far. Then she thought better of it. She really wasn't ready to face them yet. So Jess ran her finger down a list of numbers that was glued to the wall alongside the handset. Jack didn't answer and so Jess dialled the next number she came to.

'Hello,' said a deep, dark brown voice after a couple of rings.

'Hi, Oliver,' said Jess. 'I've got a bit of an emergency here.'

'Stay where you are. I'll be right over,' he said.

Meanwhile Nick had taken Molly and Jack to the Dog and Ducket – a handsome old pub in the nearest village to the estate – after Jack complained about missing Sunday lunch.

'Max is just a bit, well, you know,' said Jack, shuffling along the line with his tray at the carvery counter.

'A bit what?' said Molly. 'I get on with most people.'

'I know, but he's not most people, is he? Max is the person who is going to steal your little girl, isn't he? Make off with your precious baby.' As he spoke, Jack was smiling at the girl who was dishing out roast potatoes and by the time they moved on he had a huge pile on his plate.

Molly stared at him incredulously. 'You don't really believe I think like that, do you? I'm just worried about Jess. She's not herself when she's with him. She's not happy.'

'She seemed all right yesterday.'

'When Max wasn't there,' said Molly.

'Okay, well, maybe she's not happy, but maybe she's worried about the wedding plans. I would be. And maybe you've got Max wrong. You remember Wesley Harrison in my year – never made eye contact, great with computers? Used to chew the sleeves of his sweatshirt?'

'Jack, he had Asperger's.'

'My point exactly. I think maybe Max is just one of those people who gets on better with machines than anything with a pulse. He's probably a good bloke under that completely

280

up-himself exterior. Jess is no fool, Mum. Really. I mean, Wesley was really cool once you got to know him.'

'The only reason you liked him was because he hacked into the school computer and fiddled your exam grades.'

'And your point is what exactly?'

'That I'd always imagined Jess with someone warm and funny and kind and –'

'And not Max,' said Jack over his shoulder as he headed for a large empty table by the door.

Nick was bringing up the rear, picking up cutlery, condiments and persuading the girl on the servery to give him extra pork crackling.

'I think,' he said, as they all settled down at the table, 'that everything will turn out fine. Jess isn't an idiot. Max may or may not be the man for her but you should trust her judgement.'

'She is easily led,' said Molly.

'No, she's not,' Jack laughed. 'That's me – and anyway, Mum, we're talking about marriage here, not shoplifting gobstoppers.'

'Exactly,' said Nick, spooning apple sauce onto his plate. 'Give the girl some credit. I'm sure she'll sort it out in her own way.'

'There we are,' said Oliver, snapping the switch on the circuit board back to on. 'I've got no idea why anyone thought putting the fuse box in the shed was a good idea. Anyway, that's that sorted. I'll get someone to come out and look at the cooker tomorrow for you,' he continued, heading back inside the cottage. 'It smells lovely. Where is everybody, I thought they were all coming over for lunch today?'

'They were.' Jess stopped. 'They did. They went.'

He looked down at her as Jess struggled hard with a great wave of emotion that threatened to drown her.

'Your cooking's not that bad, surely?' he said with a grin.

Jess laughed in spite of herself. 'No, although actually under the circumstances it's probably a good job they did go. I wouldn't have been able to feed anyone without a cooker.'

'How long before the chicken's ready?'

'About an hour.'

'Okay, how about we take it all over to my place and finish it off there – presumably they're not coming back?'

'No, I don't think so, but won't Krista mind me constantly dropping in asking favours? You were away helping me move all day yesterday.'

He peered at her and then laughed. 'Krista? She's not my girlfriend, she doesn't live with me. She and her boyfriend live in Chiswick, I think. When she's working on the estate she stays with Bertie's housekeeper, Doris, she only comes over to mine because Doris won't let her loose in the kitchen. No, it'll be fine.'

'I don't want to put you to any trouble.'

'You won't be.' He looked around the kitchen at the various saucepans and dishes. 'Have you got a couple of boxes we can put all this stuff in?'

'I just moved in, remember?'

He grinned. 'How could I ever forget. Right, you fetch the boxes and I'll get the chicken out of the oven and make sure it's all switched off and safe. You'll have to take your car though, I came over on my bike.'

'Okay,' said Jess.

'Have we got any wine?'

Jess looked at him. 'We?'

Oliver's smile didn't falter. 'By the expression on your face when I got here I thought it might turn out to be a long lunch.'

Jess was about to come back with something sharp and funny but eventually settled for the truth and sighed. 'You could be right.'

Outside it started to rain.

'Come on,' said Oliver. 'We'll go over to my place and light the fire.' And then to Bassa, who was wagging his tail and looking expectant, Oliver said, 'Come on, old chap, as if we'd leave you behind.'

A few miles away in Wells-next-the-Sea, Max was parked up on the seafront, staring at the tide as it came swirling in around the salt marshes and the boats moored alongside the quay. It was raining.

He wasn't sure how he had got there. To say that Max was devastated was to devalue the intensity of what he felt. What he felt was that someone had reached into his chest and ripped his still-beating heart out from between his ribs, taking his lungs along with it, and then stamped on him just for the sheer hell of it.

He hurt so much he could barely breathe, barely think. After leaving Jess's cottage – a drive Max now couldn't remember making – he had headed blindly towards the coast. There had been no deliberate choice in where he had ended up, just a kind of instinctive force that had propelled him away from what had hurt him. So here he was, on the quay, in the rain.

There was a tap at the window which jolted Max from his thoughts. A man in a peaked cap and yellow slicker leered in at him. Max lowered the window.

'Are y'stopping, mate, only you'll need a ticket to park here.' The man, who was short on teeth, pointed to the sign at the edge of the quay. Max nodded. He felt as if he had forgotten how to speak. He pulled a note from his wallet.

Max sat for a while, letting the wind blow in and the rain. He could smell the sea and doughnuts and fish frying and now he was here he was hungry but didn't know if he could face the queue for chips and the press of humanity inside, all hot and wet and huddling out of the rain.

He couldn't quite believe what had happened with Jess. As well as being hurt he was also furious with her. What the hell had Molly said to her? And how dare Jess behave so badly when he'd brought her a present and everything. This certainly wasn't how he had imagined the day shaping up. He had expected a quick tour of the new cottage and the garden, a decent lunch, maybe a short walk around the estate with the dog and then a long, lazy afternoon together in bed. Not this – nothing could have prepared him for this and try as he might Max couldn't quite work out exactly what had happened. At what point had it all gone so horribly wrong?

Was it something he'd done, something he'd said? Max had re-run the morning's events over and over in his head. He had gone to church, just like Jess had wanted. So he was a few minutes late, but he had a perfectly reasonable explanation for that. He'd smiled at people and sung, worn a decent jacket, cleaned his shoes. So what the hell had happened?

It occurred to Max, as the smell of the chips made his stomach rumble loudly, that he hadn't picked up the engagement ring from the table or the matching earrings that he had picked out from Lucy's shop.

He had planned to give them to Jess a few days before the wedding, so she could wear them on their wedding day, but after the fiasco with the champagne, flowers and chocolates the night before he had felt guilty and in need of making a gesture. Maybe he had over-reacted to Nick finding his peace offering in the graveyard. Maybe he should have explained. And now it was all over. Just like that.

He had never expected that Jess would let him down like this. He had trusted her – but, despite a lot of convoluted thinking, Max still couldn't quite put his finger on what the problem was. What *exactly* had he done? Maybe she was hormonal, maybe she was having problems at work. Maybe the move had unsettled her.

One thing was for certain, he had trusted her to love him and look what had happened. And was this it? Were they *totally* finished or just in a holding pattern until things got sorted out between them – and could they sort out whatever the problem was? Which brought Max back full circle. What exactly *was* the problem?

He had wondered on the drive over to Wells if perhaps Jess was just toying with him, and this was some sort of a test. And if so how the hell did he pass it? Should he go back? Or maybe ring her? Send her flowers? Beg? God, and what if she really had finished with him? This was going to make him look like such a fool when it got out. What would his parents say? And then there was Lucy. Max groaned and dropped his head into his hands. He couldn't cope with her pity.

And did he want Jess back? Was she just getting stressed about the wedding? Or did this mean that she had fallen out of love with him – or worse still, had she never loved him? When she said *I can't do this* did it just mean the wedding, did it mean that their relationship was *completely* over or was it more that she couldn't face getting married to him?

Totally bewildered, Max found his thoughts went around and around, re-running conversations and possibilities until his head ached and none of it took him any closer to under-standing what was going on. His stomach rumbled again. Maybe if he ate something he would feel better.

A small boy wandered past carrying pie and chips in a tray. The smell made Max's mouth water so he opened the door and said, 'Excuse me, could I buy those off you?'

The boy, who was maybe eight or ten, had a crew cut and was wearing an England shirt under an open red puffa jacket, squinted at him. 'Do what?' he said.

Max got out of the car. 'Your pie and chips, I was wondering could I buy them off you? Or maybe you could go and get some for me?' Even as he was saying it Max knew it was a mistake. The boy eyed him suspiciously. 'Obviously I'll pay for them,' Max said, pulling out a ten-pound note.

The small boy reached out for the money, just as his father rounded the end of the whelk stall that stood behind Max's car.

'Oi, what the hell d'ya think you're up to, giving money to my lad?' shouted the man through a mouthful of chips. No amount of chips could disguise the threat.

'I was just asking if I could buy his chips.'

'Do what?' growled the man.

'Sorry,' Max said. 'I was only –'

But it was too late, in a millisecond the man had pushed the boy to one side, set his chips down on the bonnet of the van next door, gathered Max up by the lapels of his nice jacket and slammed him up against the car.

'If you don't fuck off out of it I'm going to punch your lights out, you bloody pervert –'

'But I wasn't – I never –' Max began, but the man was having none of it. He drew back his fist and hit Max so hard in the stomach that it felt as if it had gone straight through him and come out the other side. As Max buckled, the man brought his knee sharply into his face. Max, dropping to his knees in a puddle, dry-heaved, gasping for breath, while alongside him the man calmly picked up his fish and chips and walked on. The boy leaned over Max and prised the tenner from between his clenched fingers.

In Oliver's cottage lunch was back in the oven, the fire was lit and Oliver busy topping up Jess's wine glass. Outside the rain was lashing down, making it feel as if they were cut off from the rest of the world. Oliver's Jack Russells and Bassa were curled up together on the hearthrug and Jess was curled up on Oliver's battered old chesterfield with her shoes off.

'You look tired,' he observed.

Jess nodded. 'I am absolutely knackered – moving was exhausting, not just actually moving yesterday, but the packing and the clearing up. Also, I'm really busy at work at the moment.'

Oliver sat down in one of the big armchairs that flanked the fireplace. 'Then there's the wedding of course.'

And even though Jess felt fine about what she'd done and knew she had made the right decision, she felt her bottom lip begin to tremble and her eyes begin to fill with tears.

'Ah,' said Oliver. 'Sorry, are you that stressed out about it?'

'I don't think there's going to be a wedding,' she said, and although she didn't exactly mean to, Jess told him all about it. She told him about this morning at the church and her parents, but that it was much bigger than that, and before she knew it Jess was confessing things to him she hadn't even admitted to herself.

She told him about her sense of being rushed, about how weird it felt that Max didn't want her to move in and how different she and Max were. She told him about Marnie's booking Halley Hall, and the whole church wedding thing. While in some ways Jess felt as if she was betraying Max, in other ways it felt really, really good to say those things aloud.

They talked while he sorted out lunch and she helped dish it up, they talked while they ate and when they washed up. They talked while they walked around the grounds with the dogs and checked the greenhouses, Jess in the Barbour jacket Oliver loaned her along with a pair of Krista's wellies, they talked until it was done and then they talked some more.

Down on the quay Max crawled back into the car and locked the doors. His nose was bleeding and the adrenaline was pumping through his poor broken heart so fast that he thought it would probably kill him. He glanced up into the rear-view mirror; his nose was a complete mess and there was a good chance by the look of it that he was going to end up with two black eyes. Rootling around in the glove compartment he found an old teeshirt he used to wipe the windows, which he pressed to his nose to staunch the blood flow.

And despite everything he was still hungry. Across the quay the man and his son had climbed into a shiny black four-by-four with a lot of chrome on it. Max suspected they were watching him and he didn't like the way that felt. With the teeshirt still pressed hard up against his face Max turned the key in the ignition and drove slowly out of the car park.

The man in the four-by-four yelled something at him out of his open window. Max had no idea what he said but didn't hang around long enough to ask him to repeat it.

A few miles down the road he pulled into a fast-food restaurant, washed his face and ordered a giant cheeseburger and fries with the biggest ice-filled drink they had and then sat in the corner booth with the cup pressed to his nose. For the most part people gave him a wide berth.

'You need anything?' asked a middle-aged woman, dressed in burger livery and a hair net.

Max stared at her; it took a moment or two for him to realise that she was talking to him. 'No, I'm fine,' he lied. 'Hunky dory.'

'You don't look fine, you look awful. You need a doctor?'

He shook his head and instantly regretted it. 'No, I'm fine,' he insisted. 'Really. Absolutely. Thanks.'

The woman smiled and Max realised that she wasn't as old as he had first thought. 'What happened?'

'A man punched me.'

She nodded sagely as she sprayed and then wiped his table. 'Any particular reason or was he just having a bad day?'

'It's me who's having a bad day.'

'So I see.'

'My girlfriend just dumped me and told me the wedding is off.'

She nodded. 'It really isn't your day, is it?' she purred. She glanced back towards the counter where two spotty teenagers were cleaning down the servery between flicking each other with tea towels.

'I'm off duty in about fifteen minutes. How about you let me take a look at those cuts? I used to be a nurse.'

She was maybe late thirties with dyed blonde hair and she smoked, he could tell by her teeth and her skin. But she was quite attractive in a hard way and it came back to him as she winked at him that he had never had a problem with meaningless sex; in fact he was quite keen on it, it had kept him sane after Lucy had left him. After all, he had been dumped and they were both consenting adults. It would serve Jess right if he slept with her.

Chapter Twenty-Four

'It can happen to anyone,' said Viv, lighting up a Marlboro and handing it over to Max. 'I shouldn't let it worry you, it's probably the stress. You've had a bad day. Do you want a cup of tea? Only my boy'll be back from his dad's in half an hour.'

Max lay on his back, looking at the stain on the bedroom ceiling, blowing out a boil of cigarette smoke. 'I think I probably need to go and talk to Jess,' he said, head spinning as the nicotine raced through his bloodstream.

'Uh-huh,' Viv nodded. 'She your fiancée?'

He nodded.

'Good idea, she's probably worried sick about you. You want me to put some Savlon on that eye before you go?'

'I have had the nicest afternoon,' said Jess, as Oliver reached around her to unlock the door to Heaven's Gate. 'I can't thank you enough.'

He smiled. 'All part of the service. Now you're going to be all right?'

She nodded. 'Uh-huh. Thanks for listening to me. I'm sorry I've gone on – and on – so much.'

'Not at all. Let me get some lights on for you.'

He was so close that she could see the stubble on his chin

and smell his soft, masculine scent, a mixture of outdoors and new pencils and woodsmoke. It made her mouth water.

As Oliver spoke a car swung into the driveway, picking them out in the headlights. Jess was momentarily blinded, finding it impossible to pick out who it was. And then she heard Max's voice. 'Jess? Are you okay?'

'Max, I'm fine. The fuses went and Oliver came to rescue me. He's head gardener here. Oliver, this is my fiancé, Max Peters.'

Oliver extended a hand. 'Pleased to meet you. I've heard a lot about you.'

Max smiled grimly. 'All of it bad, no doubt.'

Oliver shook his head. 'No, not all of it. What happened to your face? You okay?'

'It's nothing,' said Max, waving it away. 'Just a little scratch.'

Jess stepped closer. 'Oh, my God, Max, what have you done – come inside and let me look at you. What happened?' She screwed up her nose as she got closer. 'Have you been smoking?'

Oliver, backing away, lifted a hand in farewell. 'If you need me,' he said.

Jess nodded. 'Thank you.'

'Seems like a nice guy,' said Max, as Jess sat him down at the table, turned on the lamp and came back with cotton wool and antiseptic.

'What on earth did you do?' she said, looking at the cut on his nose and the one above his eyebrow.

'Nothing much.'

He looked up at her, almost cross-eyed as she was so close. 'Did you mean it, about not being able to carry on?'

Jess dabbed the antiseptic into the deepest of the cuts, making Max wince.

'I don't know what I think, Max, but I do know we can't

just carry on like we have been without talking about it. You were really rude to my mum and Nick today.'

'I was preoccupied.'

She dabbed him again. 'That's no excuse. You're always preoccupied as far as I can see. I feel like I'm having this relationship on my own most of the time. You're just absent –'

What the hell was that supposed to mean? 'I love you,' he said.

'That's not a get-out-of-jail-free card, you know. Sometimes love and sorry aren't enough. I need you to take an interest in what's happening in my life, in our lives, in what's going on. I can't do it all on my own.'

Max was lost but he nodded anyway.

'And all this stuff with the wedding. I asked you what you wanted. I wanted you to help me plan it – not let me do it and then say that it isn't what you want. It's not fair.'

'But I trust your judgement.'

She fixed him with a stare. 'No, you don't, Max, that's just it. You've got very strong ideas about what you want and what you don't want and you let me make a decision and then you tell me it's wrong.'

'I don't think that's fair –'

'A church wedding? Halley Hall? That's what you wanted.'

'But not what you wanted?'

She shook her head. 'The thing with Shona was the last straw.'

'But my parents –'

'You should have said something before we asked her to marry us. You knew how they felt, for goodness' sake – take responsibility for it. Ring them, talk to them about it.'

'But –'

'But nothing,' said Jess, pulling the deeper of the two cuts

293

together with butterfly plasters. 'And if they don't like the idea then you need to sort out a solution, not me. And don't ever do that thing you did.'

'What thing?' He pulled a face.

'Emotional blackmail.'

Ah, that thing, but how else was he going to get her to do what he wanted?

Jess stood back to admire her handiwork. 'There, how does that feel?'

He made an *okay, it feels fine* face and then waited to see if it was over. Lucy used to do this, get really cross with him, shout, throw things, cry and stamp and then when it was over they would go to bed and have hot, angry, wonderful sex and then it would all be better. And so he waited.

'Can I stay?' he said, when it was obvious Jess had no intention of saying anything else.

'It depends.' She tidied the cotton wool and bits and bobs into the bin.

He sensed she was relenting. He picked up the ring where she had left it on the table. 'I need you to marry me, Jess,' he said. 'I really do.'

She looked at him. Max didn't add that if they didn't get married he would look a fool in front of Lucy, nor that he was worried what his parents would think; instead he kept it brief.

'Will you promise to help and tell me what you want rather than just tell me what you don't want when I've already made a decision?'

He nodded. To be honest Max would have agreed to almost anything.

She held out her hand and he slipped the ring back on. There was a moment when they both looked at it and then Max smiled.

'I'm so sorry I upset you,' he said and, putting his arms around her, pulled her tight up against him. 'Do you mind if I go and have a shower?'

Jess didn't say anything.

Chapter Twenty-Five

'We've got something really special coming up for you today on EAA. For those of you who were listening back in August you'll know that my daughter Jess announced her engagement live on air. We had lots of calls asking us what happened next. Well, for the next few weeks we'll be finding out as we follow Jess and her fiancé Max all the way up the aisle. We'll be going along with them as they choose their venue, the cake, the menus, the flowers and that all-important dress. We'll have lots of advice for brides-to-be, lots of tips and hints on air and on our website, and we've got a special podcast, so whether you're a bride on a budget or someone with money to burn we've got something for you.

To kick-start our wedding-day countdown, with under ten weeks to go, Jess and Max are here in the studio with us today. So, Jess, Max, how does it feel to have your wedding plans go public?'

Molly paused, expecting Jess would answer, but to her surprise Max, all smiles, leaned into the microphone and said, 'Actually it's all really exciting – I mean everybody's wedding is special but for us having it recorded is really the icing on the cake.' He grinned. 'The wedding cake, obviously.' And then he laughed. It was the most amazing performance.

'To be honest I'm not very good at this kind of thing but

Jess has been absolutely brilliant at getting everything organised. She is the most amazing, beautiful, talented lady and I'm really so lucky to have her in my life.'

Molly was so stunned she was almost speechless – not great for a radio presenter. As he spoke Max lifted Jess's hand up to his lips and kissed it in a real Kodak moment, and he spoke with so much warmth and affection that Molly found herself almost believing him.

She could see that Phil and Stan in the outer office were totally sold. Stan gave Molly a big sweet-as-a-nut A-okay, with his thumb and forefinger. Molly raised her eyebrows. So much could be said without words.

'I'm a very lucky man,' Max purred into the mike, gazing lovingly into Jess's eyes.

'Line two,' said Stan in Molly's headphones, 'Phyllis from Stalham wants to know if Max has got an older brother.'

And the calls kept coming in, while they all drank cava and Max was charming and funny and Jess was nice and sweet. As people rang in with their wedding stories, in the studio they talked about wedding traditions, black cats and chimney sweeps, and something old, something new, something borrowed and something blue and the phone lines kept on buzzing and before you knew it, it was coming up to one o'clock and time for the news.

'That's about it for today,' said Molly into her mike. 'Next week we'll be back with our first wedding update on Jess and Max and some tips on picking the perfect spot for that perfect wedding. Thanks for joining us here on EAA and I'll see you tomorrow when we've got some wonderful guests lined up for you. Have a great day.' And with that Molly slipped off her headphones and faded up the jingles.

'That was tremendous, well done you,' she said, smiling at the two of them.

For the first time since she had met him, Molly had finally caught a glimpse of what it was that Max brought to the party. On air he had been charming and warm, self-deprecating and great company. Convincing enough to warm the chilliest heart.

Jess grimaced and, pulling off her headphones, yawned. 'Back to work then.'

Molly gave her a hug. 'You're okay about coming in and doing a couple more?'

'And give up my lunch break?' said Jess, raising her eyebrows. 'I'm wasting away here.'

'We could maybe lay on some sandwiches next time.'

'What do you think?' Jess turned to Max, who was busy picking up his jacket and briefcase.

'Sorry?' he said.

'Mum wants to book us in for a couple more programmes before the big day.'

'Fine,' said Max. 'Why not? Can we have some copies of the photos they took before we went on air?'

'I'm sure you can, let's talk to Phil on the way out, he's got the diary.'

'So when will the podcast be up on the website?' Max asked as they headed out into the little reception and production area between the station's two studios.

'Great show,' said Phil. 'Stan's still taking calls.'

'Today, tomorrow?' Max said, ignoring Phil.

'As soon it's edited,' said Molly. 'We got a good response on the phone-in so I'd imagine they'll have it up as soon as they can, along with the photos.' She smiled at Phil and took the diary from him. 'Thanks. So,' she continued, turning her attention back to Max and Jess, 'let's have a look – when do we think? How about four weeks' time, that'll be the week beginning 26th October?'

'Did you mention the invitations?' asked Max, ignoring Molly completely.

Jess sighed. 'No, not yet.' She pulled an invitation out of her bag and handed it to Molly. 'What do you think? We're going to put a sheet of directions and stuff in there as well.'

It was very simple: the palest heavy cream card with elegant black text, and in one corner raised and embossed inter-twined hearts. 'It's beautiful,' said Molly, eyes misting over as she worked her way down over the words.

Jonathon Foster and Molly Foster
request the pleasure
of the company of

. . . .

at the marriage of their only daughter,
Jessica Alice Foster,
to Max Peters
at St Mary's Church, Crowbridge, on Saturday
6th December at 2.30 p.m.
and afterwards at the reception in the Anderton Suite,
Halley Hall, Halburton.

RSVP
Castle Lane House
Mill Row

'This is your dad's address,' said Molly in surprise before she had got to the bottom.

'You don't mind, do you?' said Jess, flustered. 'Actually it was Max who suggested it. I meant to ask you but it totally slipped my mind. I spoke to Dad about it and he thought it was a good idea.' She paused. 'You know. Keep them sweet.

Oil on troubled waters. Max will put it all on a spreadsheet and all I've asked is that Marnie just updates it and forwards it to us.'

Molly raised her eyebrows. 'So how is Marnie?'

'Dad says okay, but she rang me yesterday after you and Nick left and I'm thinking much the same as usual. She can't understand why I was upset with her and is totally narked that I haven't asked Mimi to be matron of honour.'

'Look, if you two are going to gossip,' said Max, 'I really need to be going. Can we sort these dates out later?'

Molly stared at him.

'Some of us have got work to do,' he said.

'Actually, we all have,' Molly purred effortlessly; *bloody arrogant man*. 'Jess and I will take a look at dates. Thanks for coming along.' She extended her hand. Her tone was cool and professional although if Max noticed, it didn't show. He barely touched her fingertips.

'Talk to you later,' he said to Jess and then he was gone.

'All she has to do is tick people off unless –' Jess stopped mid-sentence as Molly watched Max's progress. 'What is it?'

'Is he always that rude?'

Jess reddened. 'I'm so sorry. No, he's just busy, that's all. And he was great during the show, wasn't he? That's what he's like when we're alone.' She paused. Molly said nothing.

'Okay,' said Jess. 'So maybe some of the time. Most of the time. I suppose I'm used to it now – and we're all a bit stressed at the moment. Sorry. And I'm really sorry about yesterday. I have got no idea what was the matter was but –'

Molly took a deep breath. The last thing she wanted was for Jess to take the blame and to apologise for Max, but her daughter was ahead of her. 'Please, not a word, Mum. You were right to say something about the way it was going but Max and I had a long, long chat yesterday and we cleared a lot of things up and yes, you're right, I haven't been happy, but we've both been working too hard and there were a lot of things that needed sorting out and saying to clear the air, which we hadn't been doing – but we've done it now. And yes, he can be moody and rude but you heard him on the show. He's happy as Larry we're getting married and he's a good man, Mum – really he is, I know he is.'

'Okay,' Molly said slowly, forcing herself to smile, and then she glanced up at Phil, who was still standing there like a lemon. In the other studio across the way Bob Green had just kicked off the afternoon programme and made a point of waving at them and mouthing, 'Well done. Great show,' over the track that was playing.

Molly nodded her thanks and then said to Jess, 'How about we take the diary through to the office and grab a cup of tea? Have you got time for one before you go back?'

Jess nodded.

'Fabulous show,' said Nina in passing as they made their way back through the office to Molly's desk. 'The front desk is still getting calls. They'll be well chuffed upstairs.'

'Thanks,' said Molly, and then turned to Jess, looking for neutral ground. 'So how's it going in the cottage?' To her delight Jess's face lit up.

'It's absolutely fabulous. Max had to drive in to work early before it was light, so he didn't see the deer. There were deer in the churchyard first thing this morning. I was watching them while I was in the bath. Bassa loves it – he's straight out of the door into the countryside, chasing rabbits, bouncing about. Oh, and Oliver said he'd come over and let him out at lunchtime with his two Jack Russells, and Krista rang me to say she'd drop by later with some ideas for flowers – well, greenery – for the church. It's just a shame I can't stay longer there. It's fabulous. The drive in to work this morning was okay. I was talking to Oliver about it and he said that Bertie has got a couple of bigger cottages on the estate that he rents out. One is empty at the moment, right on the edge of the wood.'

'Have you mentioned it to Max?'

'In passing, but he's not keen on being so far out of town.'

'Is most of his work in the city?'

'He likes the convenience of being central.'

By now they were sitting at Molly's desk. 'Right, so, dates,' said Molly, pulling the diary closer, at which point Phil arrived bearing a tray of tea, followed close behind by Stan.

'That went down an absolute blinder,' said Stan, pulling out a chair. 'I was thinking of ways we could maybe go for a bigger tie-in with the radio station. Maybe involve more of the crew. You're not looking for a couple of pageboys by any chance, are you, Jess? I reckon me and Phil'd look the dog's bollocks in tartan.'

Chapter Twenty-Six

'She's asked Marnie to check off the guest list as the RSVPs come in.'

'Makes sense,' said Nick, as he flipped the steaks he was grilling, and rubbed them down with a split garlic clove before sliding the grill pan back under the heat.

Molly stared at him. 'Really? You're serious?'

'Are you saying you want the job?'

Molly was making the salad. 'I'm the mother of the bride.' She paused. It sounded petulant. 'No, not really, I suppose, but it was on my list.'

Nick grinned. 'Well, now it's not. My feeling is it's purely a political move to curry favour with Marnie and keep Jonathon sweet. Besides, how much harm can she do ticking names off a list? And she's got bugger all else to do. This will give you more time to focus on the important things.'

'Which are what exactly?' said Molly.

'There's buying a really good hat,' suggested Nick.

Molly hadn't flicked anyone with a towel since swimming lessons at junior school – funny how it came back when you needed it.

The following Friday evening, just after seven, the Reverend Shona Edwards was busy pouring tea in the sitting room of

St Mary's rectory. As she handed round the cups she pointed to the plate of shortbread at the centre of the occasional table and said, 'Please, do help yourselves. I'm absolutely delighted that you could both make it this evening. I do realise it's not easy for you. There are a few things we need to get through; we need to talk about when we're going to read the banns, and book a date for a rehearsal at the church. I know it may seem a good way off yet but it'll come around soon enough. And also –' she reached round to take a small pile of things off the desk beside her armchair '– I've got a couple of booklets here for you to take away that I thought might help with exploring what modern marriage and relationships mean. We won't follow them slavishly, I prefer to use them as a guide, but they give us a nice framework for the pre-marriage course. Obviously I do appreciate that people aren't as naïve or as unprepared for the realities of marriage as they used to be. Even so, within the church we believe that we should still enter into a marriage knowing that we are taking on a commitment and partnership for life. Talking about marriage and giving advice might seem a little unnecessary in an age when people live together and –' Shona stopped talking and glanced across the table at Max.

Jess's gaze followed hers. As they watched, Max's head tipped back and then fell sharply forwards. As Jess reached across to poke him, he began to snore.

Chapter Twenty-Seven

Molly and Jess stood on the platform of Norwich railway station waiting for the train to London. It was Friday evening a couple of weeks after the wedding lesson and Jess was holding their itinerary – an email from Helen printed off in purple – which seemed to extend to several pages.

'So taxi to her flat, I've got the address here, and then supper followed by a DVD. It says Patrick Swayze, Johnny Depp, Ralph Fiennes, Colin Firth, Leonardo DiCaprio, please delete as applicable.'

Molly raised an eyebrow in enquiry.

Jess shrugged. 'Who could possibly choose? I said get them all and we'd do a lucky dip. Then tomorrow we're off to . . .' Jess pulled another sheet of paper out from the pile in a folder and scanned it.

'Jess, why don't we do this on the train?'

Jess hesitated. 'Because there is so much to talk about. I'm afraid that we won't get it all in.'

Molly laughed. It was a real joy to see Jess so very obviously happy. 'So how are things going?'

'Brilliantly. We're having this Hallowe'en party on the estate; it's going to be so much fun, and Bertie has organised a ghost walk for all the staff and tenants. He is so sweet. He came over with a box of vegetables from the walled garden as a welcome present. I was going to ask you and Nick if you'd like to come over for Hallowe'en, and maybe ask Helen down too. They're got a barbecue and –'

'I meant with the wedding,' said Molly.

'Oh, that,' said Jess, doing an oh-shucks gesture with her hand. 'Fine. If I'm not careful it just grows to fill every spare hour. That reminds me, I want a quick whiz through the seating list with you. Maybe we should do that on the train? Max is making much more of an effort. Anyway, tomorrow afternoon we're going to some big costumier's where Helen did her work experience, to look at tiaras and maybe get some shoes and other stuff. Oh, and the boys are coming down.'

'The boys?'

'Oliver and Jack, you know I asked them to be ushers? As it's morning suits, rather than hire them from somewhere local Helen said they had got some amazing ones at this place where we're going tomorrow. She's going to sort out cummerbunds and bow ties in my dress fabric.'

'So is Helen seeing Oliver?'

Jess shrugged. 'Seeing? Who knows? I know she keeps on about him, every time I ring up it's *"Oh, so what did Oliver say, oh, so then, what did Oliver do?"* At the very least I think we're talking a grade-A crush. Not that you can blame her. He's gorgeous and really kind. She'd be mad *not* to have a crush on him. Is that our train now coming in?'

They were both leaving from work and if she was honest the only thing Molly wanted was to curl up on her own sofa with Nick, eat junk and watch 'Gardeners' World', but she could hardly say no to Jess's invitation to London to see her wedding dress.

'So have you bought your outfit yet?' Jess asked.

'No, but I've been looking. I was thinking about –'

'Good, because Helen said we could maybe find you something there too. At the costume place. You know, hire it.'

'I'm not sure that that's –' Molly began but Jess was on a roll.

'They do stuff for films and TV and Helen was saying you won't believe the things they've got there. All sorts of designer stuff – it isn't just pantomime dame, fancy dress.'

The train rolled into the station. Molly followed Jess, still talking, down the platform. She was stuffing things back into her bag as she walked, oblivious, cheery, full of life and fun, the Jess that Molly knew best.

'And how is Max?' Molly asked as they climbed aboard and found a couple of seats with a table between them.

Jess rolled her eyes. 'Working. I mean he truly is making more of an effort although last week I had to go to marriage classes on my own. It's not what you want really, is it? Shona is lovely though, very understanding. The good news is that he's getting the house cleared and next week we're going to sort out what colours we want the rooms upstairs painted. Oh, and Saturday night apparently we've got some sort of treat.' Jess's mind and conversation butterflied back and forth, as they settled down for the journey.

'You and Max?'

'No,' Jess laughed. 'Not me and Max, you, me and Helen, only she won't tell me what exactly.'

Helen's flat was on Lillie Road, with Olympia at one end and Hammersmith at the other. It was on the first floor of a large terraced house that had been divided up into apartments.

Helen was delighted to see them, practically running down into the road to meet them as they piled out of the taxi.

'You both look great,' she said, looking from face to face. 'Come on up. God, I'm so glad you're here. I feel as if I've been waiting for hours. Gray's cooking.'

'Gray?' mouthed Molly, as she followed Helen and Jess upstairs.

'Gay neighbour,' Jess whispered.

The flat was small by Norfolk standards, but nicely done in neutral colours with stripped wood floors, lots of trendy lighting and sparse but comfortable furniture. Opposite the bathroom was a tiny box room, which Helen informed them was off limits as it had Jess's dress in it.

In the kitchen a good-looking guy with great highlights and a neatly clipped goatee was busy stirring something on the stove that smelt divine. He was dressed in a black v-neck teeshirt which accentuated his broad shoulders and six-pack, tight black jeans, and pointy black leather slip-on shoes – all of which made him look like an escapee from a Britpop band. He raised his head as they came in and, grinning, sang, 'Here come the girls,' over one nicely muscled shoulder.

'Hi,' said Molly. Gray winked; she liked him straight away.

'Don't mind me, I'm just the hired help,' he continued, still stirring.

'Ignore him, he's sulking because I wouldn't let him put red-hot chilli paste in the sauce. There's a bed-settee in here,' said Helen to Molly, pointing to the sitting room. 'It's really comfortable. And Jess, you're sharing with me.'

Jess groaned. 'Pillows down the middle and no snoring.'

'Oh, and you can talk,' said Helen. 'Now the plan is we eat and then Gray is going to take a long, hard look at your hair.'

Jess stared at her. 'He is?'

'I most certainly am,' said Gray, from the kitchen. 'That dress, you need great hair.'

'And he says he'll come down and do it for the wedding.'

'Really?' said Jess, swinging round to look at him, unable to keep the surprise out of her voice.

'I'm an absolute sucker for weddings,' said Gray, coming in carrying a tray of nibbles. 'And besides I've got a couple of friends down that way that I'm planning to look up. If you'll cover my train fare –'

'Of course we will. Would you like to come to the wedding as well?' asked Jess.

'God no, I'd only cry and it plays hell with my contacts. So thanks but no thanks. Anyway.' He handed over the platter with a grand flourish. 'Nibbles, and then I've done this Tex-Mex thing we found in Delia, chilli chicken and –'

'And it smells like it's burning,' said Helen.

'Oh, bugger,' said Gray and scurried back into the kitchen.

In Norwich Max tucked the phone under his chin and waited for someone to answer.

'Hello,' said a tight, cultured female voice.

'Marnie?'

'Yes.'

'It's Max. How are you?'

'I'm fine, how very nice to hear from you. How's JJ?'

'Really well, actually she's in London this weekend with Molly. They're having a dress fitting.'

'That's nice,' said Marnie, not quite able to keep the barb out of her voice. 'I really hope this girl doesn't let JJ down. Jessica could have had any dress she wanted, you know that. Her father and I told her. Anyway, I'm sure it will be fine.

311

Jonathon and I are so looking forward to the wedding. I've been out looking at hats –'

'I was ringing about the guest list,' said Max, cutting to the chase.

'Oh yes, of course. Actually I'm upstairs in the office now. We've had quite a lot of replies already. Do you want me to read them to you?'

Max turned towards his computer and clicked open the spreadsheet for the guest list. 'No, no, it's fine. I've just got a couple of people for you to update.'

'Oh, right, I'll just get my glasses.'

There was a pause and the sound of rustling paper. 'I only need them for reading,' she said. As if Max cared.

'Right, fire away,' Marnie said.

'Stephen Shepherd plus one,' he said, idly making a doodle from the names on his notepad.

'They're coming?' asked Marnie.

'Yes.'

'Oh yes, here we are. Shepherd plus one. I've ticked the box now.'

'Wonderful. We asked them before Jess and I had sent out the official invitations and before we'd agreed on where to send the RSVPs. I got a text today to say they'd be coming.' Max glanced down at his phone. It said, 'We would be happy to come to the wedding. Anything you particularly want as a present, let me know, unless of course you have some ghastly wedding list in which case feel free to let me have that. See you soon. L x'

Not L and S he noticed, just L.

'Right-oh, and who is the plus one?' said Marnie, her voice cutting through his thoughts like a chain saw.

'Lucy,' he said, softly savouring the way her name felt in his mouth. 'We've known each other for years. Lucy –'

'And is that Shepherd? Not that it matters, although we will probably need a name for the seating plan.'

He thought for a split second. 'To be honest I'm not sure what she calls herself these days.'

'Shall I just put Shepherd down then?'

'Good idea,' said Max.

Chapter Twenty-Eight

After Helen and Gray had cleared away supper and the wine and everything that might spill or smear or make any kind of mark, Helen took Jess off to the bedroom. No one was allowed to look.

Molly waited expectantly and to her surprise found that she had butterflies, which multiplied as she heard little squeals of delight coming from the bedroom. Gray was in charge of clearing a space and putting a low wooden box covered in heavy white cotton in the centre of the sitting-room floor.

'You want me to dim the lights?' he called over one shoulder. 'Maybe a drum roll and some bunting?'

'No, just get the mirrors,' shouted Helen, with what sounded like a mouth full of pins.

Gray rolled his eyes.

'You want me to help?' offered Molly, who was sitting on the sofa.

'No, you're fine. They're not heavy,' he said. 'And if you catch sight of the gown before madam's ready that'll be my balls in a bucket.' With that he vanished away into the hall, coming back a few seconds later wheeling a mirror on a stand and pulling its twin; they were probably two feet wide and around five feet tall and on castors. 'We've got four of these – we found them in a skip,' he said by way of an answer to any questions Molly might have. 'Seemed such a shame to throw them away when Helen could use them – I mean, she does a lot of work for people.' He paused, checking his appearance. 'Vain people.'

He brought in the second pair, making a horseshoe shape around the wooden block.

'All ready,' called Gray.

'Well, we're not,' yelled Helen. 'Two more minutes.'

And so they waited. And then they waited some more and then finally Helen opened the sitting-room door. As Jess walked in Molly looked up and her eyes instantly filled with tears.

'Oh, Jess,' Molly whispered on an outward breath. 'Oh . . .'

Jess smiled nervously, eyes bright with tears. 'Is that all you can say?' If truth be told, it was.

The dress Helen had created was like something out of a fairy tale. Cut off the shoulder, with a corset top, the soft white silk fitted Jess like a glove and accentuated her slim waist. The neckline was picked out with embroidered gold leaves set with tiny crystal highlights, which descended in a flurry of embroidery and more crystals down over the back of the bodice and into the skirt, which trailed in a rich semicircle over the floor. The finishing touch was a hooded cloak in heavy gold silk brocade, the embossed pattern in the cloak's fabric echoing the dress's rich embroidery, and the effect was absolutely breathtaking. The soft, warm colour picked up on the tones in Jess's hair and made her skin glow.

'You look stunning,' Molly murmured.

'Doesn't she just?' said Gray, through a flutter of tears. 'Oh, look at me, have you got a tissue?'

Jess did a slow turn, admiring the effect in the mirrors. The dress whispered as it moved, soft and sensual and totally, totally magical.

'Now let me show you what we've been working on,' said Gray, hurrying out into the hallway, dabbing his eyes. He reappeared seconds later with a little tiara, made of leaves in twisted gold wire that were almost identical in shape to the ones on the cloak, along with various loose leaves and combs. He stepped up behind Jess and very gently lifted up her hair.

'I thought hair back off your face, really soft, would make the most of that long neck and those shoulders, with these on combs in the sides, just to round it all off. What do you think?' he asked, hands working magic. The transformation complete, Jess smiled at them; she looked like a fairytale princess.

'So what do you think?' Jess said nervously. 'Will I do?'

'Oh, yes,' sighed Molly. 'I think you look beautiful – stunning. Actually I don't know what to say.' Her voice was full of emotion. 'The dress is amazing. Helen, you are so clever. It's so flattering and Jess, darling, I don't think I've ever seen you look so lovely.'

Jess beamed. 'So you like it?'

'Oh, yes – it's breathtaking.'

'I was worried it might be a bit too much.'

Helen rolled her eyes heavenwards. 'It's your wedding, for God's sake, it's supposed to be a bit too much, that's what weddings are about. Now let's get you out of it before someone bursts into tears all over it.'

'Helen,' said Molly, 'it is amazing. You've done the most wonderful job.'

Helen laughed. 'Just wait till you see mine.'

Wedding dresses are a hard act to follow but Johnny Depp just about managed it in the boxed set of DVDs that Gray had brought upstairs with him. Once the dress was safely packed

317

away Helen broke out the wine, Gray contributed a bottle of Baileys and two of pink cava, and by the time they all went to bed Molly had giggled so much that her sides ached.

Max had finally cleared the bedrooms of the last of the computers. It looked like he had been burgled and to a certain extent it felt like it. Possum the cat stalked him as he moved between the upstairs rooms, contemplating the wide-open spaces. The man he had had in to give him a quote had suggested that they paint all the walls white as a base coat on which to apply the new colours, and that they lift the tired old carpets and sand the boards.

The ghosts of workstations and tables, desks and filing cabinets still clung to the dusty walls. Max poured another glass of wine and settled himself down on the floor of what had once been his office, back against the wall, to wait for Jess's phone call.

She rang just before midnight. She sounded drunk and happy, and he was envious.

'I've been thinking about who to ask to be my best man,' he said, running his fingers over the indented footprints of a desk he had moved.

Jess laughed. 'Good, and not before time.'

'How would you feel if I asked Jack?'

'Jack?' Jess said, surprised. 'But I thought you'd want one of your friends to be best man. You know, an old friend –'

Max laughed. 'Well, that's possible but a lot of friends I have are really just work colleagues and the others are from way back and I don't see them that often. No, I wanted it to be someone closer than that. And at least if I ask Jack then I know you won't run off with him.'

There was a pause and then Jess said, 'I'd forgotten about that.'

'It's all right. It's a long time ago now. But I thought it would be rather nice for Jack.'

'It's a big responsibility.'

'I'm sure he'll be fine. I just wanted to run it by you before I asked him.'

'Means we'll be an usher short,' said Jess.

'Do you think Nick would do it?'

'I'll ask Mum.'

'Okay.'

There was silence. 'So, how did the dress fitting go?'

And he heard the delight in her voice as she said, 'It is *amazing* – I can't believe it's mine. The sketches were great, but putting it on – it's magical, Max. I really hope you like it. Helen is a genius. It blew me away.'

'I'm glad. I can't wait to see it.'

She giggled. 'Not yet. It's bad luck for the groom to see the bride's dress before the big day.'

'Well, we can't have that, can we?'

'I wish you were here,' Jess murmured, sounding drowsy with drink and desire.

'Soon I'm going to be there every night. Look, I've got to go, sweetie. I haven't eaten yet.'

'You should eat.'

'Night, night,' Max said, as the cat arched up to be stroked.

He heard Jess blowing kisses as he hung up.

'Oh, my God – you look just like Daniel Craig and a young Pierce Brosnan,' said Gray, clapping his hands with delight as Oliver and Jack sauntered out of the changing rooms at the costumier's. Molly couldn't have put it better herself. The two of them were dressed in formal grey morning suits, complete with top hat and gloves.

Helen laughed at Gray. 'Wipe the drool off your chin.'

319

'So what do you think?' said Jack, doing a twirl.

The assistant who had kitted them out glanced across at Helen and Jess, who nodded appreciatively. 'If I wasn't taken –' Jess said with a grin, as she did a circle around the pair of them. 'You look fab.'

Then Helen went over to Jack and opened up his jacket. 'We're going to have waistcoats made up in the gold brocade I've used for Jess's cloak, and matching cravats.'

Molly nodded. 'I wish I'd brought Nick along now.'

'It's not too late,' said Helen. 'We can always get another one, can't we, Carl?' She glanced at the guy who had been helping them out. He nodded. 'We just need his measurements and then they can courier one down to him. They're all Italian wool – just feel the quality. Now.' Helen turned towards Molly. 'How about you?'

'Me?'

Jess nodded. 'Helen's picked out some things for you.'

'You're serious?'

This time Helen nodded and a female assistant indicated that Molly should follow her.

'What about you lot?' asked Molly, as she went into the changing area.

'Oh, we'll be fine,' said Helen, waving a hand. 'We're off to grab a coffee.'

'You can't leave me here.'

'Oh, we can. Jeanna will take care of you, won't you, Jeanna?'

The girl, who had the softest of French accents, nodded. 'Of course. I have the brief – something stunning and comfortable which will make you feel and look like a million dollars.'

Who could possibly argue with that?

Gray nodded, as Jack and Oliver went off to change. 'And don't worry about your hair, darling, we can sort all that out.'

*   *   *

320

'So where's this amazing dress, then?' asked Nick as he slid Molly's case into the back of the car. It was Sunday afternoon and Nick had just picked her up from the station in Downham Market, while Jess had taken the Liverpool Street line back to Norwich.

'It needed a little bit of alteration.' She grinned. 'God, I'm so tired. I'm way too old to stay up half the night. I tried on this dress Helen Mirren wore – oh, and this amazing suit Anjelica Huston had made for the publicity shots for something or other.'

'Is Jess going to be able to get home okay? I would have taken her, you know.'

'She'll be fine. Max is going to pick her up at Norwich station.'

'So what was her dress like?'

'Oh, Nick, I can't tell you how stunning it is – she looks amazing in it. Then last night, you know the surprise? Gray had got us tickets to see "Chicago". We have just had the best time.'

'And?' said Nick. 'You were going to say something else.'

'Was I?'

'You were.'

'Well, I had kind of assumed that Helen fancied Oliver; she's always talking about him. Then last night when we got to the theatre we were sorting out seats. This gay guy Gray I was telling you about had kind of adopted me and so we sat together and the others sat in front. And . . .'

Molly could see it now. Helen sat next to Jack – and as the curtain had gone up Helen had caught hold of his hand and he had grinned and leaned in closer and whispered something. Then Molly had glanced across at Jess and seen Oliver looking at her. The expression on his face and on hers had made Molly gasp. Jess had pulled away. And then the curtain had gone up but Molly was in no doubt what she'd seen. No doubt at all.

'And what?' said Nick as they pulled into traffic.

'Helen was saying that if you haven't sorted out your morning suit yet that she can arrange to hire you one.'

'So where's this amazing dress, then?' said Max as he slid Jess's case into the back of the car.

'It's not quite ready yet, it needed a little bit of alteration.' She grinned. 'God, I'm so tired. Mum kept us up half the night. God knows how she does it at her age.'

'Is your mum going to be able to get home okay? I would have taken her.'

'She'll be fine. Nick is going to pick her up.'

'So what was it your dress like?'

'Amazing – I can't tell you how stunning it is. Then last night, you know the surprise Helen promised us? Gray had got us tickets to see "Chicago". We had the best time.'

'And?' said Max. 'You were going to say something else.'

'Was I?'

'You were.'

'Well, last night when we got to the theatre we were sorting out seats. This gay guy Gray I was telling you about had kind of adopted mum and so they sat together and then the rest of us others sat in front. And . . .'

Jess could see it now. She had glanced across at Oliver, and the way he was looking at her made her heart do this funny kind of back flip and for a moment she thought he was going kiss her and so she'd pulled away. And then the curtain had gone up, but Jess was in no doubt what she'd seen or what she'd felt. No doubt at all.

'And what?' said Max as they pulled into traffic.

'Helen was saying that if you haven't sorted out your

morning suit yet that she can arrange to hire you one.'

'Right. Actually I've already ordered mine from a shop in Cambridge.'

'Seems a bit of a trek.'

Max shrugged. 'Not really, and they do a lot of hire for the college events, so they had a selection to choose from. I was thinking I could buy the thank-you presents for Helen and Nick, Jack and Oliver from the jewellers' while I was there. The place I got the ring from. Cufflinks and a chain and locket –'

Jess nodded, still thinking about the look on Oliver's face. 'Fine,' she said without really listening. 'Sounds like a great idea.'

Chapter Twenty-Nine

'So can you tell us what's happening now?' Molly tipped the mike towards the huge mixing bowl into which the master baker was busy pouring the ingredients of a fruit cake, destined to be a three-tiered, heart-shaped wedding cake.

'Well, this is the fruit we're using today, all specially chosen by my dad – the ratio of the fruit is a well kept family secret – and then it's all soaked in brandy . . .'

There was a laugh from behind them. Another baker, dressed all in white, hair tucked up under a paper snood, was busy sliding something into a large industrial oven. 'Fruit's not the only thing soaked in brandy around here,' he said.

The woman who had agreed to show Molly around slapped him with the back of her hand and then carried on. 'The fruit is very rich, very moist, they're all first-class ingredients, but the combination of fruit and the recipe for the rich fruit cake is a trade secret, passed down from generation to generation. Not everyone likes fruit cake these days, so we also offer sponges in all sorts of flavours as well as individual cupcakes. People really seem to have taken to them.'

Molly followed the process from mixing the ingredients through baking to a cooler side room where a large woman with arms like hams and tiny hands was icing a cake. To one side was a collection of tiny sugar roses and swags, waiting to be applied to the bottom tier.

'Those look lovely. Would you like to tell us what you're doing?'

The woman, whose artistry was quite obvious, smiled to reveal a mouth with barely a tooth left. 'I ice all the cakes we make, and do all the decorations,' she said, sweeping a hand over the long stainless-steel table. 'We make most of the decorations from scratch. That way we can match all the colours – the flowers and leaves, ah, and the little animals. Sometimes people like to have a mouse or a little frog on a wedding cake, once we had to make piglets. I've been doing it for nearly thirty years. A lot of customers send me photos. I love to see them, you know. Sometimes they save me a piece and send it on. The cake we make here is superb, you can't really go wrong with a decent bit of fruit cake, but I don't have the heart to tell them that it's coals to Newcastle here.' And with that she popped a sugar rose into her waiting mouth, as Molly stopped the recording.

'Hello,' said Jess, timidly. Another ten minutes and she needed to be heading off for their marriage class. Jess glanced up at the clock. She had been dreading this phone call.

'It's Jess. How are you?'

There was a split second's pause and then Max's mother, Daphne Peters said, 'Jess, oh, how lovely to hear from you. How are you? And how are all the plans coming along? I've been marking the days off on the calendar. Not long now. I'd imagine you're getting quite excited.'

Daphne sounded warm and happy and genuinely pleased to hear from her.

'And nervous,' said Jess, letting out a sigh of relief. 'I just rang up to talk to you about the cake?'

'Of course. Now did you get a chance to look at Marjorie's website?'

'I did. There are some fabulous cakes on there.'

'I know, it's amazing what you can do, isn't it? Did you find anything you liked?'

'Well, I did, but Max wasn't very sure how you'd feel about it, so I thought I'd ring up and have a chat.'

'Best to just fire away then,' said Daphne encouragingly.

'I was wondering how you'd feel if we had cupcakes? I know it might seem like an odd choice but quite a lot of people have them now. They are stacked up on a special stand in tiers like a wedding cake.' Jess paused, trying to gauge how she was doing. 'They looked wonderful. And I've spoken to Marjorie –'

'And they're sponge?'

'Yes,' said Jess. 'With different flavour icing if you want. I was thinking we could maybe have orange and lemon, with white icing.'

There was a moment of hesitation and then Daphne laughed. 'What a lovely idea. To be perfectly honest I've never been terribly keen on fruit cake. And I hate marzipan. Now, you say you've spoken to Marjorie?'

'Yes, we spoke earlier, she was very nice. She said that as it's a winter wedding we could have icing snow flakes or frosted berries on top.'

'That sounds absolutely lovely. Now can you sort it all out by phone or would you prefer to come down and see her? You'd be very welcome to come and stay with us if you wanted to. It would be lovely to see you.'

'Thank you.' Jess hesitated. 'I'll talk to Max about it.'

'Wonderful.'

And then a big silence opened up and Jess felt obligated to say something. 'There is something else I wanted to talk to you about. Max was concerned, and me, obviously. I asked him to ring but in the end I thought it would be better if I did it.' There was nothing left but the truth. 'The vicar who's agreed to marry us is a woman.'

'Shona Edwards,' said Daphne.

'You know her?' said Jess with surprise.

'Not personally but Lawrence Harris, our rector, does. Charming woman, he said, holds her in very high esteem.'

'So you don't mind?' asked Jess.

'Gosh no, not at all, why on earth should we? We're both absolutely delighted you've decided to get married in church. Given that Max was divorced, even though he was the innocent party – well, you know . . .' Daphne stopped, breaking off from wherever that thought was leading her. 'No, I'm really pleased and Harry too.'

'That's wonderful. Max was worried about her being a woman.'

Daphne laughed. 'I'm not sure what century he thinks we come from. We're really looking forward to meeting her. Now can I leave it to you to talk to Marjorie direct?'

'Yes, of course –'

'Only I don't want to cut you short but we're off to play bridge. If you want to come down, please do. And don't feel that you have to drag Max along. If you have to wait for him you'll never get here. I know what he's like, always working, tucked away in his office on those computers of his. I don't know how you put up with him. Is he there now?'

'No,' Jess laughed. 'Actually I'm at home, but I'll see him later. We're off to see the vicar this evening.'

Daphne sighed. 'I'm going to have to have a word with Max about neglecting you. You'd think he would have learned his lesson. Anyway, do let me know about coming to stay.'

And she was gone.

Jess hung up, feeling relieved and wondering what all the fuss was about.

At the under-gardener's cottage in Vanguard Hall the phone was ringing.

'Hello?' said Jack, rolling over to reach it.

'Hi, Jack, it's Max here.'

'Hi, Max, how are you,' Jack said, with a little giggle in his voice.

'Are you busy?'

Jack tucked the pillow up under his head. 'Well yes, actually I am.'

'Ah, do you want me to ring back?'

'No, no you're fine. I've just been sorting something out. How can I help?'

'The line's not great.'

'Sorry, it's some sort of interference. I am a bit busy at the moment –'

'Okay, straight to the point. I was wondering if you would be my best man.'

'Really?' said Jack, quite unable to keep the surprise out of his voice. 'Seriously?'

'Of course. A lot of my friends are really work colleagues and there are other people – you know – old friends, but we're not so close as we were years ago. You know how people can be friends and still drift apart. So – how about it?'

'I don't know what to say really,' said Jack. 'I'd be honoured.'

'So, that's a yes then, is it?' said Max.

'Absolutely.'

'Great, well, perhaps we could get together over the next couple of weeks, chat about the speech and –'

Jack grinned. 'And aren't I supposed to organise your stag night?'

'Well yes, but I wasn't thinking about that so much as –'

'Oh, come off it, Max, you can't have a wedding without a stag night.'

'Well, no.' Max sounded uncomfortable. 'But obviously I'm more concerned with making sure everything runs smoothly on the day.'

'Obviously,' echoed Jack.

'How about we get together some time next week? Wednesday or Thursday? I've got some notes.'

'Fine,' said Jack. 'I'm home most evenings although it's always an idea to ring first.'

'Right, so you don't get into Norwich, then? Only I'm a bit under pressure timewise at the moment. You know, what with work, and the wedding.'

'How about stopping by my place when you're over seeing Jess?'

'Right,' said Max, sounding slightly crestfallen. 'Let me get back to you about that. And thanks for saying yes.'

'Thanks for asking me,' said Jack. 'Be great to have you as part of the family.'

'Thanks. I'll let you get back to whatever you're doing.'

After Max hung up Jack rolled back into bed and slipped his arm around Helen. 'Now where were we?'

Helen giggled. 'I don't know. How about if we start over?'

Molly and Stan sat either side of her computer listening to the latest edited package for the wedding special. Stan glanced at the list they had printed out. 'So that's flowers, cars, cakes – that's got to be about it, hasn't it?'

Molly peeled off her headphones.

'We're nearly there. I want to do an interview – some sort of wedding countdown. The rehearsal and their reaction to it and then the big day.' Molly paused. 'Have we got the recording sorted out for that? Because obviously I'm not going to be asking any questions or doing a voice-over while they're getting married.'

Stan nodded. 'Me, Phil and Nina.'

'Brilliant, at least I know we can trust you lot – oh, and I've had an email from the vicar today confirming she's very happy for us to record the service, so it looks like it's all go.'

Stan nodded. 'So –'

'So what?' said Molly.

Stan seemed prepared to wait for an answer but eventually said, 'So, you look like shit.'

'Thanks for that,' Molly sighed. 'Too much to do, too little time. I'm okay.'

Stan raised his eyebrows. 'And when was it ever any different? You don't look it – are you and Nick sorted out?'

'Right as ninepence. I'm wearing an outfit they made for Dame Judi Dench and Nick's got a morning suit that makes him look like an extra for "My Fair Lady".'

'So – Jack?'

'Seems interested in Helen –'

'Jess's friend?' Stan said. 'Is that a good thing?'

'From the look on his face I should say so. He's been on his own since he split up from Pippa – but she's lovely.'

'Helen?'

Molly nodded.

'And remind me again who Pippa was.'

'The stalker, late-night phone calls, showing up everywhere he went, stealing the password for his computer? Threatening to kill herself if he didn't go back with her?'

'Oh, *that* Pippa – presumably she's not coming to the wedding?'

Molly hit him with her programme notes.

Jess was in her sitting room, working her way through the wedding to-do list. Most of the things were ticked off now or under control – except the way she felt.

Outside it was dark and the moon was slowly rising up over the trees, picking them out against the starry night-black sky. Somewhere close by a fox was calling. Jess stared out, reluctant to pull the curtains and close off the view. The grass was grey in the moonlight, twinkling here and there with patches of early frost.

Inside Heaven's Gate it was warm and cosy, the wood-burning stove was lit and Bassa was snoring contentedly in his basket. Jess stretched and yawned, feeling totally relaxed for the first time in days.

Just as she was thinking about banking the fire down for the night a vehicle swung into the yard, headlights cutting through the night like beacons. Jess tried to work out who it might be this late. Max? He had said he might be over if he finished work at a reasonable time. Jess glanced up at the clock. It was after ten. Did that count as a reasonable time?

A few seconds later there was a knock on the door. 'Anyone home?' called a familiar voice.

'Oliver? Is that you?' Jess said, getting to her feet to open the cottage door.

He stepped inside, letting in a blast of cold air. 'Still up?' he said, smiling.

She laughed. 'It's not that late.'

'You might want to get a curtain up there, keeps the heat in,' he said, pointing to the door. 'I was just going to lock the gates up and saw your lights on. I wondered if you were

332

all right as the curtains weren't closed. And then when I saw you, I thought maybe you'd like some company.'

'I'm fine, I was just thinking,' Jess said. 'Come on in – I've just poured myself a Baileys. Would you like one?'

He shifted his weight. 'I'm not really a Baileys man –'

'How about some wine, then? Or I think I've got some brandy somewhere. Or tea?'

'Tea would be great. I've still got to sort the gates out.' Oliver eased off his boots. 'You're nice and warm in here,' he said, glancing at the stove. 'You okay for logs?'

'Well, I've got some,' she said.

'I could drop you some off if you like. We've been clearing the bottom copse this week. There's loads of really well seasoned wood down there – just what you need.'

Jess nodded. 'Sounds great.' And then there was a funny, uncomfortable little pause when they both stood there, looking at each other, Jess with her hands in the pockets of her jeans, Oliver with his boots in his hand, and to break the moment Jess said, 'So, how have you been? I haven't seen much of you since the London trip. I thought maybe you were avoiding me?'

'No,' he said, all bluff and businesslike. 'No, not at all. We've been really busy, getting everywhere sorted out and tidied up for the winter.'

'Right,' said Jess. 'Well, why don't you come in and sit by the fire – I'll put the kettle on.' She waved a hand towards the table. 'I'm just sorting out the last few things for the wedding.'

'How's that going?'

'I'm more or less done now.'

'I thought Max might be here. Friday night and all that.'

'He said he might be over if he got finished early but it's a bit late for him now. We've been going to classes at the rectory – marriage classes, once a fortnight. On a Friday.' *And why the hell was she telling him all this again?* Jess filled the kettle, all fingers and thumbs.

'And that's going okay?' asked Oliver.

'It's hard to tell really,' Jess said flatly. 'The first one Max fell asleep, the second one I had to go on my own and then this one Max cancelled because he was working.'

Oliver laughed. 'Hardly a great track record.'

'That's what the vicar said.'

'So how many more have you got?'

'In theory just one, but Shona the vicar would really like Max to do this week's bit, so that's two more. Would you like a biscuit?' Jess got a tin down off the shelf.

'If you're certain it doesn't matter really though, does it?' Oliver was saying. 'I mean, if you know someone's right for you, you don't need lessons, do you?'

'I suppose not.' She paused. 'Actually it's been quite interesting – not at all how I imagined. There's a lot about communication and how to discuss problems before they get too big too handle, and loads of practical advice about money, sorting out who does what and how to make sure you don't end up misunderstanding each other. Plus Shona's great.' Jess smiled. 'Sorry, I'm talking too much, aren't I?'

'No, you're not,' said Oliver.

'And then there's church on Sunday –'

Oliver raised his eyebrows. 'Really? I didn't know you were religious.'

'I'm not, but they like you to go if you're getting married there and it seems a bit rude not to, and also they like you there when the banns are read.' Jess glanced at the clock again. 'Max still might show up,' she said.

'Great,' said Oliver. 'Be nice to see him. Not that I'll be staying long. I meant if he turns up while I'm here.'

Jess looked at him. She felt self-conscious and uncomfortable and wondered if he felt the same. Part of her wanted Oliver to go because it didn't feel quite right that he was there, but another part of her wanted him to stay, and anyway she was making him tea, so he could hardly leave now.

Just as she was beginning to feel more at ease the phone rang. although it was ridiculous Jess jumped on seeing the number, feeling guilty – which was silly, after all, what had she done?

'Hi,' Jess said, sounding way too bright.

'Hello,' said Max.

'Hi there. How are you, how's your day been?'

'Fine. Are you all right?'

'Yes, of course, why wouldn't I be?'

'I don't know, you sound a bit odd.'

'Just tired,' she said. 'And busy.'

'Okay, I just rang to say I won't be coming over tonight – I'm still at work and I'm knackered, so I'm thinking straight to bed.'

'Okay, that's fine.' Except that it wasn't. Nothing she was saying sounded fine or natural or true.

'How did it go at the rectory?'

'Not great. I wish you'd called and told me you were going to cancel. How about we talk about it later when you're not at work? Oliver just called in to see if I was all right.'

'I thought you'd got someone there, you sounded strange. Bit late for callers, isn't it?'

'He was driving past and saw the light on,' she said, smiling and nodding in Oliver's direction. 'He's going up to lock the main gates – oh, and he asked if I wanted any logs.'

'Okay, well, don't get too many, you won't be there much longer, will you? How's he getting on with Helen?'

'Helen?'

335

'You thought she fancied him?'

'Oh yes,' Jess stammered. 'I don't know,' she said, lowering her voice, while watching Oliver stretch long legs out towards the fire. He was wearing woollen socks and was wriggling his toes and looked perfectly at home there in the armchair. Bassa leaned against him, eyes closed as Oliver idly stroked him behind the ear. 'I haven't really talked to him about it.'

'I've asked Jack to be my best man.'

'Great. What did he say?'

'He said yes, but he was more concerned about the stag night than the wedding.'

Jess laughed. 'Sounds like Jack.'

'That's what I thought. Anyway I'll see you soon.'

'Oh, by the way I rang your mum tonight,' she said. But Max had already gone.

When she looked up Oliver was standing beside her and she felt her heart pitter-patter. 'All right?' she asked breathlessly as he reached out towards her.

Fine,' he said, taking the teabag out of his cup. 'I thought I'd come and sort the tea out as you were on the phone. Any chance of another biscuit?'

Chapter Thirty

'So, not long to go now,' said Molly, pushing up the slider that opened Jess and Max's microphones. 'How're you both feeling?'

Jess opened her mouth and was about to speak but before she could, Max jumped in. 'Everything is finally starting to come together now. The invites have all gone out, people are replying, we've got the reception booked, the church sorted.' He laughed, sounding warm and jovial. 'And my best man is busy organising the stag do so I think we're almost there and Jess – well, like I said before, she's been brilliant. I've got no idea how we'd have got this far if she wasn't as efficient and clever as she is. Pulling it all together. Oh, and the dress is finished although I'm not allowed to see it. Jess's friend Helen has designed and made it and – according to all the people who've seen it, and there aren't many – it's spectacular, but I'm reserving judgement until the big day.' He laughed again.

'And how about you, Jess?' said Molly, stunned by how jovial and cheerful Max sounded. It was certainly a great performance; on air he seemed to turn into a completely different person. 'How are things going for you?'

'They're going well, aren't they?' said Max, as Jess took a breath to speak. 'We've both been really busy, which has made things difficult, and we've got the rehearsal in a couple

337

of weeks which I think we're both looking forward to, and Jess is going over to see the venue for the reception to check everything is okay there – next week, I think? Aren't you, darling? It's just a question of waiting now. And you know what they say; the waiting is the worst bit.'

Jess looked at him and said, 'Actually, there are still quite a few things to chase up –'

'Are there?' said Max, all smiles. 'Like what?'

Jess was reaching down into her bag for a spiral-bound notebook, which she flipped open to a marked page. 'Where would you like me to start?'

Molly glanced up at the clock. 'Before the happy couple start a fist fight we're off to Jim Harris for the sports roundup. Any boxing on the cards for today, Jim?'

Jim, who was broadcasting from a little sound booth halfway down the corridor, chuckled. ''Fraid not there, Molly, although let's be honest, weddings put a strain on everyone –' and then she faded him out as Jim went into his spiel.

'Will you stop talking over the top of me,' Jess hissed at Max. 'You're claiming all the glory for arranging everything and so far I've done it all.'

Max looked surprised and offended. 'How can you say that?'

Jess glared at him. 'Because it's true. And where have you been all weekend? Look, can we cut this short today, Mum? Only I've got a million and one things to do.'

'Yes, if that's what you want. You should have let me know, honey. We could have rescheduled.'

Max turned to Jess. 'You can't just go. We said we'd do this. It's only half an hour.'

'You said you'd be there for Shona's wedding classes and you weren't. *And* church on Sunday, so don't lecture me about turning up for things.'

Max said nothing.

'Well? You promised. I didn't know what to say to Shona.'

'I've said I'm sorry. It was a callout – the company had a real disaster on their hands. That's what I'm paid for. Surely anyone in this day and age understands that. Work at the moment is really important. I can't just walk away from it, Jess. It's just the way things are. It'll change –'

'I wish I believed you,' said Jess.

'So what do you want me to do?' said Max. 'Turn clients away? We need the money, especially with all the things you want to do to the house.'

'Oh, so it's all *my* fault, is it?' snapped Jess. 'I might have guessed.'

Max smiled at Molly. 'Lovers' tiff,' he said, and Jess pulled a face that Molly suspected was meant to be a smile although anyone could see she was absolutely furious.

Molly glanced up at the clock; Jim and the sports report had another thirty seconds to run. 'Here we go, folks,' she said, fading her mike up.

'Thanks for that, Jim, more updates from the EAA sports report after the news. So, Jess and Max. Weddings, discuss. It sounds like you're both feeling the stress.'

Jess looked at her mother and then Max and raised her eyebrows.

And this time Max laughed. 'All right, all right. Jess has just been giving me a hard time because I'm stealing her thunder and that I've left a lot for her to do. I have to 'fess up, she's absolutely right. I know my mum's listening on line so I wanted to build my part up. You know what men are like, the first mention of frocks and orange blossom and we just glaze over.'

'Talking of orange blossom we've got an interview with local florist, Anita Fielding, coming up any second now,' said Molly. 'She'll be telling us all about the history and mythology

339

of flowers, and we've got some great floral give-aways on the website. First ten people to register will be getting – what is it they'll be getting, Anita?'

As she did the intro Molly skilfully slipped into a promotional ad from Anita, killing the sound in the studio. 'Do you want to cut this short?' she asked, looking at Jess. 'We've got lots of recorded stuff we can use if you want to call it a day.'

Jess waved the words away. 'No, I'm fine. I'm just feeling neglected.' She turned to Max. 'I thought you said you'd be over this weekend? I've seen more of Oliver than I've seen of you –'

Max looked hurt. 'I did warn you that it was going to be busy.'

'I know and I said we could always wait until next year but no, you were determined we had to get married before Christmas. It seems to me the time I need you most you're somewhere else. Even your mum said –'

He rolled his eyes. 'Oh right, now it's *my mum* –'

'Yes, I told you I'd rung her about the cupcakes and Shona.'

'So you did, I just didn't realise the pair of you had been moaning about me.'

'We weren't moaning,' said Jess.

'We're live in thirty seconds,' said Molly, fingers on the controls, looking from face to face.

The pair of them looked up and Jess smiled. 'Okay.'

'Okay?' said Molly, with a far bigger question in her voice.

Jess nodded. 'I just said okay, what do you want, a sworn affidavit?'

At which point Max leaned forward and kissed Jess lightly on the lips.

Jess stared at him. 'Don't push your luck,' she said, as Molly went live.

* * *

340

It seemed like a long, long show and no one in the control room spoke as they all traipsed out of the studio.

Jess was still snapping at Max. 'I need you to book another date with Shona,' she said, poking him in the shoulder. 'You, Max, not me. That's two you've missed out of four so far.'

'I'll ring her. It's not like the end of the world. Just keep your voice down, people are looking.'

'I don't care, Max. You are the one who wanted a church wedding and this is what it takes to get one. Get over it.' She ripped a sheet of paper out of her notebook. 'Here, this is her number.'

'Okay. I'll ring her. Have you spoken to Marnie this week?'

'No, what about?'

'To see how the RSVPs are coming along.'

'Not yet – Halley Hall want the final figures next week. Maybe that's something else you can do?' growled Jess.

Molly glanced at Stan and then back at the happy couple. 'Do you want to come over to my desk or would you like to carry on with your row here?'

Jess reddened. 'Why should I ring her, after all didn't you just tell everyone that you're the one who's doing it all?'

'All right, all right,' said Max, holding his hands up in surrender. 'I'll do it.' And with that he waved goodbye to Stan and Phil, nodded towards Molly, then turned and left. Jess slumped down onto the little sofa that stood in front of the bank of computers and monitors.

'Jess,' Molly began. 'Do you want to talk about this?'

'No, no, I don't,' Jess said as she gathered her things together. 'I've got loads to do and I don't want a lecture from you.'

Molly stared at her. 'Jess,' she protested.

'No, I'm serious, Mum,' Jess said. 'I'm all wedding-ed out.'

Her shoulders slumped. 'Actually that's not true but I still don't want to talk about it. All right?'

Molly nodded. 'How about we go and get some lunch?'

Jess shook her head. 'Great idea but I'm up to my eyes. Oh, and Helen's bringing the dresses down this weekend, so if it's all right we'll bring them over to your place, as there's no room at the cottage?'

'Of course it's all right.' Molly hesitated. 'Are you sure you don't want something to eat?' she said after a second or two. 'We could grab a sandwich – you look really tired.'

'I am,' said Jess and then she smiled and, leaning closer, hugged her mother. 'Don't mind me.'

'But I do,' said Molly. 'This isn't like you at all. I'm really worried.'

'Don't be. It'll be all right once the wedding's over and we can settle down to married life. I'm miffed at not seeing Max and he's annoyed with . . .' She paused and then laughed wryly. 'Well, from where I'm standing, just about everything but then again he has just turned his whole house upside down so I can move my stuff in. He's out working every hour of the night and day and instead of feeling grateful I just feel neglected and miserable. Pathetic, isn't it? I'm nipping down to the house after work today to see how the painting's coming along and to see if he still wants to marry a grumpy old bag like me.'

Molly nodded and bit her lip. In her opinion Jess shouldn't be nipping down to Max's house, or apologising. She should be living there so that she and Max *did* see more of each other and Jess got a long, hard look at what she was letting herself in for. Molly couldn't help wondering if Max had behaved like this with his first wife. If he had it explained an awful lot, although she kept the thought to herself.

'Tea?' she suggested as they made their way back to her desk.

Jess shook her head. 'No, I can't, I've got a client coming in, in half an hour.'

'Trouble in paradise?' said Stan, handing Molly a mug of tea as they both watched Jess hurrying out.

'Who knows,' said Molly. 'Certainly looks like it from where I'm standing.'

Max rang Marnie on the drive from the radio station to the office where he was installing the new systems.

'Max, how lovely to hear from you.' She hesitated. 'All's well, is it?'

Max groaned inwardly. 'You heard the radio show?'

'Well yes, I have to say I'm afraid that I did. I'm sure an awful lot of it is nerves. The thing is JJ has always been terribly highly strung and – well, I don't like to say this, but she's been awfully spoilt. In my opinion Molly over-compensated when she and Jonathon split up, and to be honest I think we're all rather glad you're taking Jess on, an older man and all that. She really needs guidance and someone to take care of her.'

Max smiled. 'I'm sure you're right, Marnie. Anyway I rang to ask how the RSVPs are coming along.'

'Really well. We've only got about half a dozen more to come in and then I think that's everyone.'

'Wonderful. Did you hear I'd asked Jack to be my best man?'

'No, oh, that's charming.'

As Max was saying his goodbyes another call came in but before he could take it, it went to voicemail. He picked up the message as he pulled into a parking bay outside his new office.

'Hi there,' said a painfully familiar voice. 'Only me, I just rang up to ask what you and Jess would like as a wedding present? Maybe you could give me a ring some time, only it's getting on and we're just hitting our busiest time of the year – so if you could just give me a clue.' His ex-wife laughed. She sounded warm and happy and full of fun, the way he remembered her when they first met.

He pressed the recall button. She picked up after the first ring.

'Lucy?'

'Hi, Max. You're on the ball. I wasn't expecting you to call straight back.'

'I didn't want to leave it in case I forgot.' The lie tripped easily off his tongue. 'We've had a busy morning; Jess and I have just been on the radio.'

'Oh yes, the wedding show. How's that going?'

'Really well – we're nearly there now, just one more interview and a little bit more recording and then the big day.'

'Great. So – wedding presents?'

'Well actually, we've asked people for money. Jess has got great plans for doing up the house and between us we've already got all the basics.'

'Oh, Max darling, that is just *so* boring. I've seen these most gorgeous bowls in a gallery.'

He laughed. 'And you're looking for an excuse to buy them?'

'Something like that.'

'Then we'd be delighted if you'd like to give us bowls as a wedding present. I have to say, asking for cold, hard cash seems a bit crass, although it was very tastefully phrased.'

'I don't think that at all, in fact if you could tell me what you wrote, Stephen and I might plagiarise it. I was thinking of saying, "Send us your money and not your toasters." What do you think?' She laughed some more and then said earnestly, 'Max, I couldn't be more pleased for you. You know that. Now I have to go, duty calls. Great to talk.'

'Oh, wait,' said Max. 'Do you think you could pick out something for the bridesmaid and the best man, I was thinking necklace and cufflinks?'

'Sure –'

'Something simple, tasteful.'

'Not a problem.'

'I'll pick them up when I come over to collect the wedding rings.'

'And I suppose you'd like me to giftwrap them?' When he didn't reply Lucy laughed. 'Same old Max.'

'See you soon,' he said. And then she was gone and Max was left feeling as if he had been robbed.

Chapter Thirty-One

'Okay, okay,' said the Reverend Shona Edwards, clapping her hands together. She was standing on the chancel steps in St Mary's church. Outside it was cold and dark and damp, a classic late November evening. Inside the church wasn't exactly warm but low yellow lamps and the candlelight made it feel snug and intimate.

'If I can have your attention please,' she said, making a show of looking at her watch. 'I'm delighted that you could all make it this evening and I really do think we ought to make a start. Is there any sign of the groom yet?'

'He rang to say he was on his way,' said Jess, glancing around nervously. 'He shouldn't be long now.' Everything about Jess's demeanour said *here we go again*.

Shona smiled. 'Not a problem, while we're waiting we'll go over the basics of what's going to happen during the wedding ceremony. Everyone okay with that?'

She turned to Jess who nodded, and then Stan, Phil and Nina from EAA, who had come along for the rehearsal to follow the action so they knew where to set up the recording equipment for the ceremony. Stan nodded and scribbled a note on a writing pad. Molly suspected it was to make himself look important.

They were arranged in the front pews of the old church,

huddled together around a portable gas heater that popped
and hissed. They were all there except for Max – Jonathon
and Marnie, Marnie looking like something out of Dr
Zhivago, all wrapped up as if she was going on a bear hunt,
along with Helen, Oliver, Jack, Krista, Nick and Molly and
the EAA crew.

Molly glanced at her watch. Max was fifteen minutes late
and counting.

'Righty-oh. Well, first of all let me welcome you to St
Mary's and say how delighted I am to be conducting the
service for Jess –' she smiled again '– and hopefully Max.'

There was a ripple of slightly embarrassed laughter.

'I've got some notes here that I hope will be helpful for
everyone involved.' She handed out a little pile of booklets
to Jack, who took one and passed it on. 'Practical things for
the ushers like which side the bride's family sit.' She smiled
at Oliver and Nick, who had been seconded into ushering
when Jack had been promoted to best man. 'I suggest you
all have a read through and if there are any questions you can
ask me now or give me a ring. It's all pretty straightforward.
Now let's run through what Jess will be doing, until Max
arrives.' Shona waved Jess over. 'And if we can have your
bridesmaid as well, Helen, isn't it?'

Helen got up. 'I feel like I've just been picked on a game
show.'

Marnie pulled a face. 'Such a shame Mimi wasn't asked,'
she said sotto voce, pulling out a hand mirror to add a little
more lipstick.

'Right, so if Jonathon would like to come over here too,'
Shona said, beckoning him over, 'and we'll take a little trek
down to the back of the church. Everyone else will already
be seated and waiting for you and Jess to appear. Jonathon,
as the bride's father, you'll have travelled with Jess in the

car and you're going to be accompanying her down the aisle. Okay?

Molly, you'll have arrived with Helen, so if you'd like to come and sit down while Helen waits for Jess in the porch. Now Helen, as Jess and Jonathon arrive, you are responsible for helping her to arrange her dress and my advice would be to take your time, Jess. Just settle down out there – there's no need to rush, give yourself a minute or two, no one's going anywhere, and this is your big moment. Let those nerves steady themselves. Take a deep breath. Give yourself a few moments to get composed.'

She smiled, walking back towards the altar where everyone else was sitting. 'Right, as the best man, Jack, if you could sit on the right-hand side with – I'm sorry, I know you told me your name but –'

'Oliver,' said Oliver, stepping into the aisle.

'Right, if you'd like to stand in for Max until he gets here, that would be a real help. So if we take it from the back of the church. Jess, if you'd like to take your dad's right arm – lovely – and then your entrance music will start to play. Everyone in the congregation will take that as their cue to stand. Even then, Jess and Jonathon, don't hurry, take your time to savour it, have a look around. And now if you'd like to walk nice and slowly. That's great. Don't hurry. People will want to look at you and your dress. Helen, if you would like to follow on a few steps behind –'

Jess smiled as she and Jonathon made a stately progress down the aisle towards the chancel steps where Oliver and Jack were waiting for them.

'Now, Jonathon, if you would like to take a step back and you too, Jack, so you're a little behind Jess.' Shona paused. 'And Helen, if you'd like to step forward and take Jess's bouquet. That's lovely. At this point, I'll begin the ceremony with a welcome and then explain the significance of marriage.'

Molly looked across at Jess and for the briefest of instants saw her expression as she glanced up at Oliver. But just as their eyes met there was a commotion at the back of the church and everyone turned around to see who or what it was, as the door slammed shut.

'Hi, sorry I'm late, sorry, sorry, sorry,' said Max, smiling first at one face and then another. 'Traffic coming out of Norwich was absolutely horrendous.' Still apologising he hurried down the aisle, caught hold of Jess's hand and said to Shona, 'Hi, I didn't miss anything important, did I?'

Shona raised her eyebrows. 'We're just glad that you could get here,' she said, and then turning to everyone else said, 'Well, now that we've got a full house, let's make another start, shall we? Oliver, if you'd like to sit down; thank you for your help. Right, Jess, Max – as your guests arrive the ushers will direct the bride's family and friends to sit on the left and the groom's to the right. Max, if you'd like to come down here and stand with Jack. We've already gone through what Jess and Jonathon will be doing.'

'Oh,' said Max, looking slightly miffed. 'I thought you would have waited.'

Molly glanced at Nick who was busy looking up, apparently oblivious to anything going on in the church. 'What are you doing?' she whispered.

'Just admiring the roof trusses, why?' he said. 'What did I miss?'

Men, thought Molly.

Chapter Thirty-Two

Molly threw her coat onto the arm of the chair. 'I can't get over Max. What if he's late on their wedding day? He hasn't turned up for their classes – for God's sake, he was late for the rehearsal for his own wedding.'

'I didn't think you wanted him to marry Jess,' said Nick, plugging in the kettle and getting two mugs down off the rack.

Molly glared at Nick. 'This isn't funny. I can't believe he was late tonight of all nights and you know Jess won't talk to me about it.'

'Because she knows you'll be horrible about him.'

Molly was about to protest when she realised Nick was right. 'She is being so defensive –'

'Can you blame her? You don't like Max and Jess knows it,' Nick said calmly.

'But –'

'But nothing, Molly. I know it hurts and it's driving you nuts but whatever you think, she's made up her mind to marry him. We've had this conversation; you can't make her mistakes for her.' Nick opened the fridge. 'I thought it was nice of Marnie to organise drinks and sandwiches at the pub afterwards. Although I thought her dress was a bit – you know.'

'Low cut?'

He nodded. 'When she bent down I could see her shoes. Has the woman got no shame?'

'If she had we could have probably seen it in that dress. I bet it cost Jonathon a fortune.'

'When she first took her coat off I thought she'd got it on back to front,' said Nick.

Molly smiled at him, guessing he was valiantly trying to change the subject. Trouble was, the fact that Jess was making such a huge mistake was haunting her. The closer the wedding got, the worse Molly felt about it. They were scheduled to do one more live interview but she could barely bring herself to think about it. The days to W-day were ticking by far too fast.

'Shame we couldn't have had the reception there really,' Nick was saying.

'The Crowbridge Arms?'

'Well yes, it's so handy being close to the church.'

'It's quite small.'

'Probably not upmarket enough for Marnie.'

They both looked at each other. 'This is ridiculous,' said Molly. 'Jess is getting married in a way she doesn't want, having a reception in a place she hates, to a man who is a complete disaster and we can't do anything about it. How mad is that? Max is a mistake. I'm going to ring her.' She made a move towards the phone.

Nick raised an eyebrow. 'And say what? You already said your piece and it made no difference.'

'In that case I'll ring Jonathon.'

'And what do you think he's going to do? Ring Jess and say, *your mother is worried about you*? And then there's Marnie – who's got her sights on the wedding of the year.' Nick sighed. 'We can't stop Jess from marrying Max.'

'Why not? Why won't she take any notice of me, Nick? Would you have a word with her?'

Nick nodded. 'If you want me to, but my feeling is that it won't matter what we say to her. How would you have felt if your mum and dad had said you didn't ought to marry Jonathon?'

'That *is* what they said,' said Molly grimly.

'And how much notice did you take?'

'That was different,' said Molly. 'They were wrong about him.'

Nick dropped a teabag into each of the mugs. 'I rest my case, m'lud. We can't stop Jess from marrying Max.'

Molly growled with pure frustration. 'This is madness. Why can't we? God, it's so much easier when they're little and you can just tell them to go upstairs to their room.'

Nick handed her a mug of tea. 'I suppose you could always try that.'

'If you're late on our wedding day I think I'll die. I keep imagining myself waiting at the altar with everyone looking at me.'

'Don't be silly,' Max laughed. 'I did tell you that it was going to be busy. And I won't be late.'

'You keep saying that.'

'I promise,' Max said, miming crossing his heart and cutting his throat. 'I promise I'll be there on time, all primed and ready to go. Now, what do you think of the new carpets?'

The whole house smelt of new paint and varnish. All of the rooms downstairs except for the kitchen were now white with sanded wooden floors. Upstairs, the new master bedroom was painted a light butterscotch brown, which brought out the colour of the sanded and sealed boards. Although the furniture hadn't been delivered yet there were opaque white blinds at the windows and heavy floor-length linen curtains in almost the same shade as the walls with a wine-red pattern in them that picked up the colour of the bedspread and cushions Jess had ordered for the new bed.

'I love it,' she said, smiling. 'And how about you? Are you happy about it?'

'You were right. I should have sorted this place out years ago. The new bed should be here first thing tomorrow. I thought we'd put your dressing table here.' He pointed to a bare wall that had once been lined with monitors.

Jess nodded. 'And maybe the blanket box under that window, with cushions on it? Possum will love it.'

'If you say so,' said Max. 'Meanwhile I'm still camped out in the back room.'

Jess laughed. 'Oh, come off it, don't sound so hard done by. You're hardly camped out, Max, you've been sleeping in there ever since I've known you.'

'Whatever. I thought we could sort that room out once you've moved in. I was thinking maybe we should turn it into a combination office and studio for the two of us.'

Jess grinned. 'Seriously?'

'Unless you'd prefer the little back room to yourself? Your call.'

'No, that would be wonderful. You're prepared to give up your old room?' Jess pushed open the door and looked inside, trying to imagine what it might look like as a studio.

It was the one room in the whole house that Max hadn't touched so far. In fact if anything, it looked more cluttered as he had squirrelled away his treasures from the rest of the house, the last bastion of the bachelor life. Clothes that Max hadn't put away hung from the picture rail, his shoes, books, papers and magazines were scattered across the floor. She resisted the temptation to tidy; this wasn't her home – not yet.

354

Max nodded. 'I thought you could keep yourself amused up here while I'm working.'

Jess laughed. 'Are you being sarcastic?'

Max looked surprised. 'No, of course not. The thing is now I've moved the computers out I'm going to have to spend a lot more time in the office. Don't look at me like that, Jess. It's what you wanted . . .'

'Hello, is that the Crowbridge Arms? I'd like to book a room, a double. For Friday 5th December – and can I organise a late checkout?' Max smiled as the girl went through all the spiel and he gave her his credit card details.

'It's a stroke of luck you rang,' said the girl. 'Normally we're quite quiet that first weekend on the run-up to Christmas but we're really busy, that's the last room we've got available for the Friday night. A lot of people are booked in for a big wedding party. Are you going?'

Max laughed. 'I hope so, I'm the bridegroom.'

The girl giggled. 'Good job we could squeeze you in then.'

'My girlfriend is worried I won't get there on time.'

'Well, shouldn't be a problem here, we're just across the road from the church.'

'Maybe I should get you to book me a wake-up call,' he suggested and something about the way he said it made the girl giggle some more.

'Maybe you should,' she purred.

Chapter Thirty-Three

Molly glanced down at her desk diary and flicked through the entries for the next few days. Less than a week to the wedding. The only thing Molly seemed to have thought about for the last few weeks was the wedding, and Jess, and then Max, and what the hell she could do or say that wouldn't end up with Jess hating her for the rest of her life. Molly looked up at the clock. They had been on air around ten minutes, done the news and weather and traffic updates.

Molly flicked on her mike. 'And so today we're doing the last of our wedding countdown specials. We've got the bride, who'll be on her way up to the studio any minute now, along with the groom, and we're already taking your calls. If you'd like to ring in with a wedding story our number is . . .'

This was the last live interview before the wedding and there was a real buzz in the studio. The whole show was going to be dedicated to weddings in general – weird ones, wild ones, lots of snippets from the build-up, interviews and vox pop about other people's weddings. It had all seemed a good idea when they'd planned it. Molly's head ached. Just five more days and it would all be over.

The station boss had ordered in flowers for the bride and all around the studio and between each of the computers were table centres donated by local florists, a business card tucked into each.

There was champagne chilling in the fridge, boxes of confetti and streamers of silver and white decorating the corridors, and a local classic car-hire company had lent EAA a vintage wedding car complete with chauffeur and ribbons for a photo-shoot after they'd finished broadcasting. This was meant to be a programme full of joy and expectation. Besides the station photographer, the local press had all turned out, along with a TV camera, and outside a crowd of well-wishers had gathered, hoping to see the happy couple.

'And with love and romance as the theme for today let's have something from Lionel Ritchie, requested by Gwen from Attleborough who emailed us to say that this is the song that was playing when her husband Robert proposed.'

The music glided in seamlessly. Molly flicked through her notes. What she didn't want was to fall out with Jess, not at the moment, not ever. Helen had been down at the weekend to do the last fitting on the dress and had brought down the morning suits and Molly's dress. Molly had invited the two of them over but Jess had said she was too busy. She had sounded businesslike and distant on the phone, which had made Molly's heart ache. It wasn't often that she dreaded an interview but today was one of them.

'I'll bring your outfit over to the studio on Monday when I come in,' Jess had said briskly. 'We've got the dress to sort out and then I'm going over to Halley Hall with Helen to take some of the fabric for their florist and then we're having dinner there.'

'You and Helen —'

'And Jack and Oliver. Max is in Manchester all week. He's had to cancel his stag night.'

'He *is* going to be there for the wedding, isn't he?' Molly had said, the words out before she had time to think. Remembering it now made her wince. Since then Jess hadn't been in touch and Molly hadn't been able to get her on the phone.

'They're here,' said Phil, through her headphones. 'The girl on reception just rang. They're being mobbed by autograph hunters.'

'What?'

'I'm serious, security is down there now holding back the crowd.'

'Oh, for God's sake,' said Molly, getting to her feet.

Seconds later Jess and Max burst out of the lift and into studio reception, Max grinning, Jess looking thoroughly rattled. She straightened her coat and ran her hands over her hair as Molly waved them through into the studio.

'God, that was crazy,' Jess said, finally finding a smile. 'It's like a Hollywood premiere out there.'

'That's because you're a celebrity now.' Molly gave her a hug. 'So how are you?'

'Really well,' said Jess. 'And finally we've more or less got the house sorted out. Bed's in and we've booked a van to bring my stuff over. Instead of having a honeymoon Max suggested we have a week off work to get things sorted and then we'll go somewhere in the New Year when things aren't so hectic – I'm really looking forward to it.' She glanced at Max, who was wearing an odd expression. 'What?' she said.

'Jess, I said *you* could take the time off, I've still got the final part of this implementation to complete.'

Jess rolled her eyes. 'Take no notice of him, he's such a joker.'

Max looked as if he was about to protest when Jess grabbed

hold of his hand and pulled him closer. 'So – are we all ready?'

Molly nodded. 'We're live in around a minute. If you'd like to sit down, Phil will sort your mikes out.'

It felt like she was interviewing two complete strangers. Max was all smiles and Jess wasn't far behind, laughing at his jokes, hanging on his every word. If Molly didn't know better she would have thought they were made for each other.

Chapter Thirty-Four

'Don't tell her how you really feel,' murmured Molly, through gritted teeth, staring at her reflection in the bathroom mirror. It was the night before the wedding. 'Don't say you think she's making the biggest mistake of her adult life. Smile. Be nice . . .'

Downstairs Nick had cooked supper. Jess and Helen were due to show up any minute and were staying overnight so that Jess could leave from her old home to go to the church. It made sense. Or at least it had when they had arranged it.

'You okay up there?' called Nick from the landing.

'Fine,' Molly called back.

'Liar,' said Nick, as he opened the bathroom door. 'Come on, come down and have a drink. Something pink and fizzy.'

'God no, please don't let me have anything to drink. I'm going to have enough of a job keeping my mouth shut sober.'

Nick looked at her askance.

'I feel sick. And I wanted us to have a really nice night tonight, just like before – before Max.'

Nick nodded. 'Good, because they've arrived.'

'They're here? How come the dog didn't bark?'

Nick shrugged. 'Dunno, oh, and Helen has brought someone called Gray with them and wanted to know if he

361

could stay too – he's a hairdresser apparently. I've got him cutting up the carrots.'

It was hard getting to sleep. Jess was in her old room lying awake, staring at the ceiling. Helen was in the guest room and Gray was in Jack's old room. This time tomorrow it would be all over and done with and she would be married. She would be Mrs Jessica Peters. Jess said it aloud: *Mrs Jessica Peters*. Her mind was racing with all the details of the wedding. Had she remembered to tell the florist that the gold ribbon was for the table settings and not for the balloons? What if the cupcakes hadn't arrived? And why hadn't she rung to check? What if they had arrived but were the wrong colour or, worse, a box of expensive crumbs? What if they had put the wrong date on the invitations and no one showed up? What if they had accidentally put the wrong time on them? What if Marnie started acting up because Jess hadn't asked Mimi to be a bridesmaid?

Jess sat up. She felt sick.

Worse still, what if Max was late? He had promised he wouldn't be and Jack had sworn he would get him to the church on time. And she trusted Jack.

Close by Jess heard her phone ping as a text arrived. She smiled, feeling the tension ebbing away. It was probably a good-luck message from Max, an *I love you* text. A message to tell her he would be on time and not to worry and that he couldn't wait to make her Mrs Peters. It was nice to know that he was thinking of her.

Jess rolled over and glanced at the clock. It was almost half past one in the morning. Obviously he couldn't sleep either; he was probably just as excited and nervous as she was. Jess flicked on the bedside light and picked up her phone, holding it up to the light to read the screen. There was one message. She pressed the key to open it. It was from Oliver.

In the room across the hallway Molly was also wide awake, staring at the ceiling. This time tomorrow it would all be over and done with and her little girl would be married. *Married.* She said it aloud. Next to her Nick snored a reply. Molly's mind refused to switch off: had she remembered to tell the cars to come to the front door? What if the doves didn't arrive? What if they did but were the wrong colour or, worse, Bassa got to them first and they ended up with a box of expensive feathers? What if no one showed up? What if Marnie started acting up because she hadn't asked Mimi to be a bridesmaid?

Molly sat up. She felt sick. Worse still, what if Max was late? He had promised he wouldn't be and Jack had sworn he would get him to the church on time. And she trusted Jack.

The morning of the wedding, and everyone was up early although no one, with the exception of Nick, looked as if they had had a decent night's sleep. Molly, Jess and Helen were sitting around in their dressing gowns. Gray was pottering about wearing a silk robe that left very little to the imagination.

Apparently Gray had been freaked out by how quiet and dark the country was. Helen had been awake half the night worrying about the dresses and between them Molly and Jess had been worrying about everything else.

'So what time do you think we ought to start getting ready?' asked Jess, tearing a newly baked bread roll into smaller and smaller pieces.

Molly glanced up at the clock. 'If the wedding is at two

thirty then probably around twelve, twelve thirty? After we've had lunch.'

Jess pulled a face. 'I don't think I'm going to be able to eat anything.'

'So I see – would you like some marmalade with that or are you just going to shred it?'

Jess looked down and then shook her head. Molly suspected that Jess wasn't even aware she had been tearing the roll up.

'No later than eleven thirty to twelve,' said Gray, topping up his mug. 'It's going to take at least an hour and half for me to do everyone's hair. And then there's make-up and climbing into your frocks. And you're going to want to be decent if anyone comes in, and be ready to roll by two at the latest.'

Nick nodded. 'Okay, so now we've got that sorted out. It's nearly ten – anyone fancy eggs and bacon?'

They all looked at him as if he had just suggested sautéing one of the dogs.

'I was only asking,' he protested, lifting up his hands in surrender.

Jess got up. 'I think I'm going to go for a walk.'

'Are you sure?' asked Molly.

Jess laughed. ''Course I'm sure.'

'I mean, there's a lot to get done.'

'I *do* know, Mum,' said Jess. 'I just want to clear my head. I thought I might walk down to Crowbridge, have a quick look round the church – see how Krista's getting on.' She grinned. 'Maybe pop in to the hotel and have one last drink as a single woman.'

'Do you want company?' asked Helen.

Jess shook her head. 'No. Before anyone starts fretting *I'm fine*. I just want to have a walk – it's going to be crazy today. It'll be nice to have some time on my own. Do you mind if

I leave Bassa here, only I'm not sure if they let dogs in church?'

Molly nodded. 'Not at all. Just wrap up warm – you can have a bacon buttie when you get back.'

Jess grinned. 'Done.' And with that she got up from the table and hurried upstairs to get dressed.

'Okay,' said Molly. 'Well, if the bride is off on a walkabout how about the rest of us have breakfast, have a shower and get our hair done? That'll leave Jess with a clear run when she gets back.'

Her bright tone seemed to lift everyone. 'Good call,' said Gray. 'Is there any more tea in the pot?'

The early December day that had begun overcast and dull began to brighten almost as soon as Jess left the house. Molly watched her from the bedroom window, walking up the lane wrapped up against the chill in her Barbour jacket and jeans, hands stuffed deep in her pockets, wearing a stripy knitted hat that Jack had bought her for Christmas. She had a spring in her step, and as Molly watched Jess tipped her head up towards the pale winter sun.

'She looks happy,' said Nick, coming up behind her to slip his arm around her waist. 'She doesn't look like a woman making a terrible mistake, does she?'

Molly sighed. 'Maybe you're right, maybe I was wrong after all. And you are right about one thing, we can't stop her.'

'Anyway, I came up to ask how you want your eggs?'

Molly snuggled up against him. 'C'mon, I'll give you a hand.'

The Crowbridge Arms stood on the village green. Parts of it dated back to Tudor times and it was a warren of little rooms, alcoves, and passageways, all of them set with tables, comfortable armchairs and sofas. Jess took her drink and went in search of a quiet corner. Her pulse kept fluttering – and even though she knew it was a combination of nerves and something less definable, it was still hard to ignore. The walk had done her good though, it had cleared her head, and made her feel more awake and less tired.

She had already been across to St Mary's. The old church looked fabulous. There were rich cascades of seasonal greenery in every window with a single cream candle in the centre of each and swags of ivy along each of the pews. Krista, helped by Jack and Oliver, really had done the most amazing job. She'd just been finishing off the last few flourishes when Jess arrived.

Jess glanced at her watch. Another ten minutes and she would start walking back, which would give her plenty of time to have a bath and for Gray to do her hair. But first she planned to have a quiet drink and grab a few minutes' peace before the wedding machine started to roll.

She was just about to sit down on a small sofa tucked away in a quiet alcove when she heard a familiar voice: Max. She smiled to herself. So this was how Jack had ensured he turned up on time. It was certainly a shrewd move.

Even though everyone said it was bad luck for him to see her before the service there was nothing about her seeing him and there was a part of Jess that just *wanted* to see Max. Even if it was only a glimpse to reassure herself, to settle her nerves, and besides, she wasn't superstitious. When it came down to it, Jess had always believed she made her own luck.

He was probably having a drink with Jack. She wouldn't talk to him, just catch a glimpse of him, off guard. The idea made her smile widen. She was about to peer around the partition into the next alcove when she heard another voice. A female voice.

'Nice place,' said the woman.

'Yes, I decided to stay overnight. All on my lonesome,' said Max with a funny mock-sadness.

The woman laughed and Jess very carefully eased forward, afraid that she might be seen. She needn't have worried. Max was sitting with his back to her, all his attention fixed on the woman who was with him. Jess stared, unable to believe what she was seeing. Sitting no more than a couple of feet away from him across the table was Lucy Peters – the girl she had seen in the photo on Max's office wall. The girl who had broken his heart, Lucy Peters, Max's ex-wife. Lucy all dressed up and ready to go to a wedding. Jess and Max's wedding.

'Stephen's away skiing with the kids until Tuesday. You should have given me a ring,' Lucy said, teasingly.

'I did, once,' said Max.

'Oh, ouch, that was a bit barbed,' said Lucy.

'Sorry, I couldn't resist it,' said Max, as she lifted a glass to tap his.

'Well here we are, thank you for the invitation.' Lucy took a sip. There was a little tremor in her voice. And then she looked across at Max and reddened and looked away. 'I don't know what to say really. Up until now I've thought this was all wonderful. But now I'm not so sure.' She bit her lip and started searching around in her handbag.

Jess held her breath.

'Sorry, don't mind me. I've got the rings in here some-where,' Lucy said between sniffs and dabbing her nose with a tissue. 'I made what's-her-name's the same size as the engagement ring. If the size is wrong . . .' But she couldn't get the words out.

Hidden by the narrow wall Jess was rooted to the spot.

Max leaned forward and caught hold of her hands. 'Lucy, please don't cry. You know how I feel about you, how I've always felt.'

Lucy bit her lip harder. 'Oh Max, please don't. You have to stop talking like that.' She made a show of pulling herself together. 'I thought I was all right about all this . . .'

By *all this*, Jess realised with horror Lucy meant the wedding.

'But I'm not, and then I remind myself that when we were together you drove me crazy. You were never there. I didn't think you cared, Max.'

'Cared,' he said, voice thick with emotion. 'I loved you more than anything else. I thought I was going to die when you left me. I'm crap at relationships, I thought you understood that. I just didn't realise how lonely or how neglected you felt. And then . . .' His voice faltered.

'Please don't blame Stephen, it wasn't his fault. Really. It was mine.'

'And I was an idiot. I'm so sorry, Lucy, so very, very sorry.' Max paused, sounding close to tears. 'Lucy, I have always loved you,' he said, his voice quaking with emotion. 'And I always will.'

In all the time Jess had known Max, he had never shown anything like this emotion. She felt as if someone had reached into her chest, caught hold of her heart and was squeezing it tight.

'What about –'

'Jess?' prompted Max.

'Yes, what about Jess? Don't you love her?'

Jess thought she might die in the seconds between Lucy's question and Max's answer. The fact that he hesitated was almost more than she could bear.

Finally Max said, 'I thought it was time I settled down. She's a lovely girl.'

Lucy leaned forward. 'That's not what I asked you, Max. Do you really love her? Because if you do I'll get up and walk away now.'

'Of course I love her,' said Max without conviction. 'But not the way I love you. She's not you, Lucy – I'll never love anyone the way that I love you.'

Jess felt as if she was moving in slow motion, full of pain and anguish. She felt hot and faint and sick.

Molly decided to go down to the church to pick up a button-hole for Nick and the bouquets that Krista had done for the bride and bridesmaid. Nick had said he would do it but Molly was worried that time was getting on and Jess wasn't back. Maybe she would see her daughter on the way, give her a lift home.

'Oh, you just missed Jess,' said Krista, halfway up a step fixing the final swag of greenery to the screen behind the chancel steps.

'Did she say where she was going?'

Krista nodded. 'She said she was nipping over to the pub for a quick drink and then was going to walk home and start getting fluffed up.'

Molly smiled; that certainly sounded like Jess. 'It looks wonderful,' she said, glancing around the church.

Krista beamed. 'Doesn't it. I'm really pleased with the way it has turned out. It's the first all-green wedding I've done. I'll just get the bouquets for you. They are at the back.'

'Thanks. I'll pop them in the car and then go and catch up with Jess,' Molly said. 'Time's getting on.'

Krista glanced at her own watch. 'Oh gosh, yes – you're right. I've just got a couple more bits to do and then it's all finished.' She had scrambled down from the steps. 'The flowers are over here in these boxes. Have you got your keys? I'll help you carry them out.'

Krista had done them proud. The bride's bouquet was an exquisite waterfall of white lilies and roses and twists of green-and-gold ivy, picking out the design in Jess's cloak. Helen's bouquet was a smaller version of the same design.

Once Molly had put the bouquets in the car she headed over the road and across the green to the Crowbridge Arms. It was warm and noisy inside with the buzz of early lunchtime trade. The girl behind the bar told her that Jess had been in and gone through towards the little snug at the back. Molly followed her directions and there sure enough on a small table she noticed Jess's distinctive woolly hat and a drink. Molly looked right and left. She couldn't be far away – maybe she had gone to the loo. Then Molly caught a glimpse of Jess on the other side of the room practically running out of the pub.

Molly picked up the hat and was about to hurry after her, but as she stepped around the beamed partition wall she caught a glimpse of Max sitting at a table by the log fire – and sitting with him was Lucy Peters. They were holding hands and Lucy looked for all the world as if she had been crying. Seeing them stopped Molly mid-stride.

Molly hesitated for an instant and then hurried after Jess, and as she did Lucy looked up and smiled at her. Max's gaze followed hers.

There was a split second as their eyes met when Max looked absolutely horrified and then, getting to his feet, pulling Lucy with him, he said, 'Molly, how lovely to see you. How are you? May I introduce Lucy, an old friend of mine.'

Molly nodded briefly in Lucy's direction and then said, 'Did you see Jess?' as evenly as she could manage.

'No. Is Jess here?' said Max, his colour draining as it occurred to him that Jess must have seen him with Lucy. Molly nodded grimly. 'She *was* here.'

Max paled further. 'Really? Shame I didn't see her. I'd like Jess to have met Lucy. But they do say it's bad luck, don't they –'

Molly stepped close. 'So is finding your groom holding hands with his ex-wife.'

Max forced a laugh. 'There's a perfectly innocent explanation,' he said.

'I'm sure there is, let's just hope Jess believes it,' said Molly coldly.

'I brought the wedding rings over,' said Lucy, holding out a beautifully gift-wrapped package like a shield. 'I made them.'

Molly didn't take her eyes off Max. 'And how does Jess feel about her wedding ring being made by your ex-wife?'

'She is delighted, isn't she, Max?' said Lucy, on the periphery of Molly's hearing.

Molly's eyes didn't leave Max's. She could feel him squirming under her scrutiny, feel his discomfort at being caught out and relished every second of it.

'And she was absolutely adamant that she wanted me at the wedding, wasn't she, Max?'

But Max didn't appear to be listening. Instead he spoke to Molly. 'Actually, Jess doesn't know. The thing is, I wanted them to be really special and Lucy is a great designer. I didn't think she'd mind. Let's not make a big thing out of this, Molly. Jess is a sensible girl . . .'

'And you,' said Molly, leaning in close so that Max wouldn't miss a word of what she was about to say, 'are completely and utterly despicable. If you hurt my daughter again I will never forgive you.'

And with that Molly hurried after Jess.

When she got outside Jess was nowhere in sight. Molly walked across the car park, looking left and right, and as she did, to her relief, Jess appeared from the pub garden.

'Are you all right?' asked Molly anxiously.

Jess nodded and then smiled. 'Thanks, Mum,' she said. 'I'm okay.'

'Did you see Max?'

Jess nodded. 'With Lucy,' she said.

Molly handed Jess her hat. 'You left this.'

Jess sighed as if the tension was draining out of her. 'Thanks and before you say anything, I'm fine about it, Mum. Absolutely fine.'

'Really?'

Jess nodded. 'Absolutely.'

'So what are you going to do –' Molly began.

Jess smiled. 'Get back to the house. I've got a wedding to get ready for.'

Molly stared at her. 'Are you sure about this?'

'Never more so,' said Jess, putting an arm around Molly's shoulder. 'Seeing Max with Lucy helped me make up my mind about what I want and why. I know you don't like him but please trust me – I know what I feel. I know what's best for me.'

'And you're sure about this?' Molly repeated.

'I've never been more sure of anything in my life,' said Jess.

Molly opened her mouth to say something and then thought better of it. What else was there? After all, Jess's mind was quite obviously made up.

Jess sat at the dressing table in her old bedroom looking out across the lawn. Even though the sun was shining, twinkling diamonds of frost lingered in shaded corners.

Gray was tucking the last of the gold flowers into her hair. 'There we are,' he said, stepping back. 'What do you think?'

Jess leaned forward and looked into the mirror. 'I look like a princess,' she purred. 'Oh, that is lovely. Thank you. It's perfect.'

Gray beamed and then stood back to let Helen and Molly see the bride. Jess slowly stood up and turned around. She looked like something out of a fairy story. The colour of the dress brought out the creamy richness of her skin and the exquisite laced bodice gave her an hourglass figure to die for.

Molly sniffed. 'You look stunning.'

Jess grinned. 'Don't I just.' She did a slow twirl. 'I'm so nervous.'

'Well, don't be,' said Helen. 'It's going to be fine. Everyone who loves you is there – we'll all be rooting for you.'

Jess looked across at Molly, and said, 'I know.'

'Now,' said Helen. 'Something old: the antique lace for the dress; something new, the rest of the dress. Something borrowed?'

'I wondered if you'd like to borrow this,' said Molly, holding out a little jewellery box. 'One day it'll be yours. It was my mother's and I wore it on my wedding day. For luck.'

Jess took the box and opened it. Inside was a tiny diamond brooch in the shape of a four-leaf clover. She glanced up, eyes full of tears. 'Oh, it's gorgeous. I'd love to.'

'Uh-huh,' said Helen. 'So that's your something borrowed. And in the hem,' she gently lifted it up to show Molly, 'I've put a whole row of blue glass beads as weights to keep the skirt down.'

'Knock, knock,' said Nick, as he opened the door just a crack. 'How's it going in there?'

'You can come in,' called Jess.

'The cars should be here in about –' Nick stopped dead

when he saw Jess standing in the centre of the bedroom. 'Oh, my God, you look gorgeous.' Jess grinned and did another turn.

'Doesn't she just,' said Molly, not able to keep the emotion out of her voice.

He grinned. 'You too.' Molly had forgotten that he hadn't seen the wine suit and hat that Helen had picked out for her. 'Wow, lady, anyone taking you home tonight?' he purred.

'You, hopefully,' Molly said with a grin. 'Assuming you are sober enough to remember.' Everyone laughed.

'Look, I've got to go and give Oliver a hand,' said Nick. 'You all going to be okay here?'

Molly glanced up. How could she tell him? She had a stomach full of butterflies and was so anxious that she could barely breathe. She followed him out of the bedroom and caught hold of his hands.

'You'll be all right,' Nick said, a statement more than a question. He leaned closer and kissed her gently. 'You look fabulous and you know that I love you, don't you?'

Molly nodded. 'She's going to marry him,' she said in a tiny voice. 'Even after seeing him with Lucy. He lied to her. What sort of man has a quiet drink with his ex-wife before his wedding?'

'I don't know. But short of kidnapping her there is nothing we can do, baby. She's a big girl now, she knows what she's doing.'

'If only I believed that,' whispered Molly.

She looked up at him. This was supposed to be one of the happiest days of her life and instead it felt like hell. 'You'd better go back,' said Nick. 'See you at the church.'

Inside the bedroom Helen was fussing with her hair. Jess was adding a dab of perfume and putting on the pearl earrings Molly had given her for her twenty-first birthday present. She seemed so composed and cheerful that Molly had to keep biting her lip to stop herself from saying anything she might regret.

'Does anyone want any more champagne?' offered Gray, holding the bottle up to the light.

'I wouldn't mind a glass,' said Helen. 'How about you, Jess?'

Jess shook her head. 'What if I spill it?'

Helen laughed. 'I could always hold it for you.'

'Or we could get you a straw,' said Gray.

'Like that would help. I'd be rolling drunk by the time we got there.'

Molly watched and listened almost as if she was watching a film. How could this be happening? And now they had moved on and were talking about Helen and Jack, and how they'd booked a room and were planning to stay overnight at Halley Hall together after the reception.

'Bridesmaid and best man, I mean it's traditional,' Helen was saying.

Molly's brain took a moment or two to catch up. 'But I thought you fancied Oliver?'

'Well, it was a close-run thing but eventually Jack won on points,' said Helen, as she topped up her glass.

'So how long has this been going on?'

'Not long. A couple of weeks –'

'*A couple of months*,' Jess corrected her, finally accepting the glass Gray was offering. 'More or less from the time I moved house but they thought they'd keep it a secret.'

'Because?' gasped Molly incredulously.

Jess shrugged. 'Because they thought I might think it was dead dodgy.'

'Which you do,' said Helen.

'Because he's my brother. But I guessed more or less straight away.'

'And we didn't want to say anything in case it was just a flash in the pan,' said Helen.

Jess laughed. 'And I wondered why she kept wanting to come down. I thought she was worried about the dress.'

Helen grinned.

From downstairs came the sound of voices. 'Sounds like Dad,' said Jess.

Molly leaned in close and, putting her arms around Jess, kissed her gently on the cheek. 'Are you sure about this?'

Jess nodded. 'Absolutely certain, Mum.'

'I want you to know that I love you,' Molly said, her voice cracking. 'And that whatever choices you make in life, I will always be there for you. I promise.'

Jess held her tight. 'I'm banking on that,' she murmured.

Molly pulled away, full of tears, feeling totally helpless and bereft.

'Come on,' said Helen to Molly, catching hold of her arm. 'Our car's here too.'

Molly picked up her handbag and headed out onto the landing. Jonathon meanwhile was already halfway up the stairs. 'I hope you didn't mind. I let myself in.'

'No,' said Molly, struggling to find any words. 'Jess is in there and Gray, the hairdresser, is going to lock up after everyone's left.'

'Righty-oh.' Jonathon smiled. 'You look wonderful, that's a fabulous outfit.'

To her surprise Molly felt herself blushing. 'Thank you,' she said.

'No, I mean it, I don't think I've ever seen you look so lovely – Marnie will be absolutely livid,' said Jonathon with a twinkle. 'Now, where's my baby girl?' Molly glanced at him, wondering if there was anything she could say to to him, but came up empty. Instead she pushed open the door. Helen came out, blocking his view. 'Helen, you look amazing too,' said Jonathon, looking her up and down. Her dress was a simpler version of Jess's, made in claret silk with the same gold embroidery across the neckline and down the back.

'Just wait till you see Jess,' said Helen, picking up her bouquet from the chest by the stairs.

'We've got to be going,' said Molly. 'We're supposed to be there before the bride not after.'

'We'll leave that to the groom, shall we?' said Helen sotto voce, as they made their way downstairs.

Molly raised her eyebrows, but decided not to comment.

The drive from the cottage to the church was barely more than a few minutes but all the way there Molly's mind was racing. Maybe she was wrong, maybe she had misjudged Max. Maybe she was busy turning into the mother-in-law from hell and couldn't see it. Maybe Max and Lucy meeting up *was* totally innocent. Maybe she should relax.

Helen was talking but it took Molly a few seconds to register what she was actually saying. Molly swung round. 'What did you just say?' she asked.

Helen flinched as if Molly had hit her. 'I know now's not the moment and I can understand you being upset with me for saying this but I think Jess is making a huge mistake.'

Molly stared at her.

'I keep thinking I should say something,' said Helen. 'But every time I've started she's just blocked me. And when I see the two of them together, Jess and Max, he seems so cold and distant and she's not like the Jess I know when she's with him. I'm worried that we'll lose touch once they're married. I suppose it's too late now.'

Molly swallowed hard, not knowing what to say. They were just pulling up outside the church, and the last of the guests was heading inside. Molly could see their friends and family. In the porch she could see Daphne and Harry, Max's parents, slowly making their way inside. Molly felt sick.

She looked at Helen, stricken. 'I tried to talk to Jess earlier –'

'Me too,' said Helen.

'And?' demanded Molly.

'And she told me not to worry.'

'Me too,' said Molly.

'Oh well, that's just great, isn't it?' exclaimed Helen as they got out of the car. 'What the hell are we going to do?'

Ahead of them the photographer was waiting with his camera, and Molly spotted Stan from the radio station having a crafty last-minute cigarette further along the path. He gave her a wave and mouthed and mimed that he would be there in a minute.

'Right,' the photographer was saying to Molly and Helen. 'If you could just stand under the lych gate – that's lovely, lovely –'

Helen waved him aside. 'Just get out of the way, will you?' she snapped. 'I'm bloody frozen.' The man leapt aside as if she had bitten him. Molly was most impressed and hurried up the gravel path after her.

Inside the porch Helen turned to Molly. 'Do I look all right?'

'Stunning. And you made a wonderful job with the dresses and I'm really glad you and Jack are going out together.'

Helen beamed. 'Thank you – he's really lovely,' she said, blushing crimson.

And then they were both quiet and looked at each other, aware that something awful was soon going to take place, in stark contrast to the joy Molly felt at Helen and Jack's news.

From inside the church came the babble of voices and people settling down before the service. Molly picked out faces she recognised, family friends, cousins, aunts, sisters – Noo sitting behind Marnie in a large hat.

Helen bit her lip. 'Let's hope we're wrong,' she said.

Molly nodded. 'Let's hope you're right.'

Stan stepped inside to join them, all smiles. 'Just wanted to let you know everything's okay. Max has got his radio mike on all ready and Nina – oh, there she is,' he said, waving to a figure in one of the side aisles. 'She'll be down here to wire Jess up as soon as she gets here.'

Nina hurried over. 'Oh, isn't it lovely – and the sun's shining,' she said, eyes moist.

Molly tried to look happy.

'You look nervous, are you all right?' asked Nina.

Helen and Molly exchanged glances. 'Just first-night nerves,' said Molly with a smile.

'Well, don't worry,' said Nina. 'We've got the radio car round the back and we'll be broadcasting live as soon as the service starts. It's going to be a real killer of a show – the boss has already said we'll be putting the highlights out in a roundup on Monday. So, break a leg,' she said, hugging Molly tight.

And then Molly stepped inside, walking slowly down the aisle, barely noticing the faces as she took up her seat beside Nick, who was sharing the front pew with Marnie.

On the other side of the aisle Max was fiddling with his gloves and staring straight ahead. He looked pale and nervous and Molly found herself feeling glad he looked so uncomfortable. Alongside him Jack grinned and waved.

Molly nodded back. She didn't want to be the one to disabuse him of the notion that all was well.

'Wonderful turnout,' said Marnie, eyeing her up and down. If she was at all impressed by the suit nothing about her tight little face gave it away and Molly was so anxious she

379

barely registered what Marnie was wearing, other than it being blue.

Molly looked back over her shoulder and caught sight of Nina off to one side, wearing a set of headphones.

They waited. Molly felt more and more sick. Nick held her hand and squeezed it gently, trying to comfort her. The minutes ticked slowly past and people began to get a little restless and for one glorious moment Molly thought that perhaps Jess had decided to cut and run.

Just as she began to wonder what she would say and what would happen to the radio show, she heard a little ripple of anticipation shiver through the congregation and then the music Jess had chosen – 'Arrival of the Queen of Sheba' by Handel – began to play over the sound system Stan had rigged up. A second later and Molly heard the gasps of delight and joy as Jess made her way very slowly down the aisle. She looked exquisite.

The music faded away as Jess reached the chancel steps, leaving her standing alongside Max. Her expression was unreadable. Max smiled, eyes bright as he looked at her.

Shona Edwards, dressed in her robes, stepped forward and said, 'I'd like to welcome every one of you here today to witness the marriage between Jess and Max. Marriage is a very special occasion for everyone involved, and not everyone here may be familiar with the marriage service. Take a look at the sheets given out to you by the ushers as we'll be following the traditional order of service which begins with a prayer. So if you'd like to kneel or close your eyes or spend a moment or two in quiet contemplation. Let us pray –'

Molly decided it was worth a shot and closed her eyes as Shona said the opening prayers. After a moment or two's silence as they concluded, Shona said, 'And now if you'd like to stand we'll sing our first hymn, "Love divine, all loves excelling", which I'm told was a particular favourite of Jess when she was at school.'

Molly glanced across at Jess but couldn't catch her eye as her daughter stared straight ahead, eyes fixed somewhere in the middle distance. Molly could hear her pulse beating in her ears. This was torture.

The hymn ended and Shona, smiling, began to speak. You could have heard a pin drop in the church.

'In the presence of God, Father, Son and Holy Spirit, we have come together to witness the marriage of Jess and Max, to pray for God's blessing on them, to share their joy and to celebrate their love,' said Shona. Her voice seemed to roll effortlessly out to the congregation, calm and warm and dignified. She could have a great career in radio, thought Molly as she worked her way through the order of service.

'Marriage is a gift of God in creation through which husband and wife may know the grace of God. It is given that as man and woman grow together in love and trust, they shall be united with one another in heart, body and mind . . .'

Molly was lulled by the words as they went on but had a growing sense of sadness and dejection that these beautiful, special words were being spoken about Max.

'Jess and Max are now to enter this way of life,' said Shona as the introduction came to a close. 'They will each give their consent to the other and make solemn vows, and in token of this they will each give and receive a ring. We pray with them that the Holy Spirit will guide and strengthen them, that they may fulfil God's purposes for the whole of their earthly life together.'

There was a little pause and then Shona, smiling, turned the page and said, 'First, I am required to ask anyone present who knows a reason why these persons may not lawfully marry, to declare it now.'

There was a hushed silence as Shona looked briefly around the faces of the congregation. There was a moment when Jess turned towards Molly and their eyes met. Jess smiled and then said in a loud, clear, even voice, 'Actually, I have one.'

As she spoke the air in the church seemed to solidify and then gasps and little outbreaths of shock and surprise rippled around the congregation. Alongside Molly, Marnie choked with horror. Molly could barely breathe. All eyes were firmly fixed on Jess.

Very slowly Jess turned towards Max, whose face had frozen into a peculiar grimace. 'Max,' she said in low, even voice that seemed to carry around the church, 'I can't go through with this. We both know I'm not the woman you love. I know you're very fond of me but I don't want to be second-best. I saw the way you looked at Lucy in the pub today. And I heard what you said to her. You still love her.' She lifted a finger to his lips to silence the words that were forming there.

'And before you say anything, there is no point in denying it. You've always loved her. And I think she still loves you. I don't want you to look at me in the morning and your first thought be that I'm not Lucy. I spoke to my dad on the way here and he understands. I want to be someone's first choice, Max, not an also ran. I wish you well but I can't marry you. I know it's hard but I want to live happily ever after, not be waiting for you to decide I'm not what you wanted after all.' Then she smiled and turned towards the congregation.

'I'm sorry to have wasted your time and yours too, Shona. It was lovely to see you all here but I know I'm doing the right thing. And I'm sure that eventually Max will under-stand that too.' And then she looked at Molly, who before she knew what she was doing was on her feet and threw her arms around her beautiful, special, gorgeous daughter.

'Oh Jess, I've been so worried,' she said.

'I told you it would all right, didn't I?' said Jess.

Behind her Molly could sense that the congregation were about to break loose, when Jonathon lifted up his hands to ask for silence. 'Ladies and gentlemen, family and friends,' he said. 'Although this isn't the outcome any of us had anticipated this afternoon, I am very happy to respect my daughter's decision and I suggest we all go over to Halley Hall and enjoy the reception – after all, it's already paid for.'

And with that the church erupted.

'Well,' said Stan sidling up behind Molly with his earphones still on. 'That's a hell of a way to end an outside broadcast.'

Chapter Thirty-Five

The cupcakes were wonderful. Molly decided she wasn't going to box them up and send them to people who hadn't been able to get there. It didn't seem quite right.

Jess stayed in her wedding dress all afternoon and Molly couldn't help but notice how many times she danced with Oliver or how happy they looked.

The food was fabulous and strangely enough lots of people stayed on to help them celebrate Jess not getting married.

Despite her sense of delight about Jess, Molly wasn't totally heartless and was worried about Max, so she was relieved when a waitress came up and beckoned her over, saying, 'There is someone outside who would like to talk to you. She said her name is Daphne?'

Molly nodded and followed the girl out into the foyer, bright with Christmas lights, and a log fire and a tree that had to be twenty feet tall. Daphne was waiting by the door that led through into the rest of the hotel. She had changed out of her wedding outfit into a sensible navy-blue skirt and sweater. Molly wasn't quite sure what to expect.

'I'm so sorry,' she said as they got within speaking distance. 'I had no idea that this was going to happen.'

Daphne nodded. 'But you're relieved?'

Molly nodded.

'Me too,' said Daphne unexpectedly. 'When I heard that Lucy was getting married to Stephen I was worried how it would affect Max and then he turned up out of the blue barely a week later and said he was getting married too and – well, he seemed to be in this mad rush to beat Lucy to it.' She paused. 'I did try to ask him about it but Max can be very hard to talk to at times.'

There was a pause and then Molly asked, 'Is he all right?'

'No, but he will be and of course Jess was right – he and Lucy still do love each other. There's a lot of unfinished business there. I'm convinced she only started seeing Stephen as a way to make Max jealous and get him to pay her some attention and then it all backfired on them. I'm sure that's why they've stayed in touch all this time and why she showed up here – and there was all that nonsense over her making the engagement ring and the wedding rings.'

'So what do you think will happen now?'

Daphne shrugged. 'In all honesty I have no idea. Harry is with Max. Having a drink, all very manly and stiff upper lip.' She stopped, although it looked as if there was more she would like to say.

'And Lucy?'

Daphne sighed. 'Came running out of the church after him. I couldn't believe it – she grabbed hold of his arm. I thought for a moment she was going to drag him into a car and make off with him.'

'It might have been easier if she had done.'

Daphne smiled and then gently embraced Molly. 'It's been lovely to meet you. I know it sounds mad, doesn't it – but I'm sure we could have been friends. I don't suppose I'll see you again.' And then she was gone.

Nick came out a few seconds later. 'So there you are. I wondered where you'd got to. Do you want to come and have a dance?'

Molly nodded. 'Why not?'

Epilogue

A year later almost to the day and the old Tythe Barn at Vanguard Hall was decked out with holly and ivy and baubles. The guests were laughing and singing and all having a great time. The smell of the hog roast rolled in on the breeze and the sounds of the ceilidh band warming up filled the air.

The bride and groom sat at the top table with Milo on one side, wearing a tinsel collar, and Bassa on the other in a little party hat on a string. Everyone was saying cheese and waiting for the photographer to say they could move.

'Don't they make a lovely couple?' said Molly as she watched Oliver move closer to kiss Jess.

'They certainly do,' said Nick.

'It's so nice to see them happy.'

'And Helen and Jack.'

The photographer waved the two of them closer. 'Now if the groom would just like to kiss the bride.'

Nick smiled and kissed Molly gently on the lips.

'Perfect,' said the photographer.

Read on for an exclusive extract from
Kate Lawson's next novel,
to be published by Avon in 2011.

Chapter One

'If you could just take the balloons and the rest of your equipment round to the back, please. We don't want anything to give the game away,' Maggie said, pointing the way to a young man who was standing on the front lawn of her parents' house. He had a helium cylinder and a large cardboard box on a trolley and what little facial hair he'd grown was shaved into what looked like a strap under his chin.

'And then if you could just move your van?'

The boy was wearing spotless navy blue overalls and a baseball cap emblazoned with the legend, *Danny from Cheryl's Party Paradiso – we help you live your fantasy*. The van was topped with big fibreglass balloons and a trail of lurid pink stars.

If acne was your fantasy Danny had it in droves.

'It's meant to be a surprise – ' Maggie said. It had been a long day, and there was still lots to do, but there was not so much as a flicker of comprehension from Danny.

'*For my parents*? Lily and Jack – it's their ruby wedding anniversary – it's written on the balloon? We're having a party. Round the back?' she said in desperation.

Still nothing.

'You really can't miss it, there's a great big marquee in the garden.'

Finally, Danny smiled. Maggie couldn't help wondering if he'd been sniffing the gas in his spare time.

'Is that that woman off the telly?' he said, pointing towards the front door.

'Ah,' said Maggie, groaning inwardly. 'Yes it is.' Her little sister, Lizzie, was standing on the doorstep of their parents' house wearing something artfully casual and horribly expensive and was apparently just taking in the view. To the untrained observer it might look as if she was there by accident – but after a lifetime of having Lizzie as a little sister Maggie knew she was standing there waiting to be noticed.

Danny reddened as Lizzie beamed in their direction and did a little fingertip wave before sashaying over. 'Well, hello there,' she purred, taking in the logo as she extended her hand. 'Nice to see you. You must be Danny.'

The boy, all embarrassment and eagerness, looked as if he might explode. 'That's me,' he said as their fingers met.

'And how are you, Danny?'

'Oh right – I'm fine – yeah, great – thank you,' he spluttered.

'Good, now would you mind awfully taking all this lot round the back of the house and getting rid of the van – only this is supposed to be a surprise party.'

'I've already told him that,' Maggie began, not that the boy was listening.

'Right-o,' he said to Lizzie. 'Course, not a problem. I watch you all the time on *Starmaker*, you know.'

'Really?' Lizzie smiled. 'Well, thank you, and you're enjoying it?'

'Oh yeah, this last lot was the best one yet – and that Kenny – I mean who would have thought he'd-a won. I don't suppose I can have your autograph, can I?' Danny said, thrusting his clipboard out towards her. 'Only my girlfriend will never believe me when I tell her I've met you.'

Lizzie's smile warmed a few degrees. 'Of course you can, Danny.' She took the pen. 'What would you like me to write?'

'Oh I dunno. I can't think –' he said.

Now there was an understatement, thought Maggie grimly.

'How about – *To Danny, thank you for making my party so very special, love, Lizzie Bingham, kiss, kiss, kiss?*' Lizzie purred, barely breaking eye contact as she scribbled across what looked like it might be their delivery note. 'Would you like me to put, *You're the star, that's what you are?*'

It was the reality show's catchphrase but on Lizzie's lips it sounded positively erotic.

Danny giggled and blushed the colour of cherryade. 'Oh my God, right, yeah – that'd be lovely, thanks,' he blustered, waiting to take the clipboard back, and then making an effort to compose himself, said, 'So, are there going to be a lot of famous people here tonight then?'

All smiles, Lizzie tipped her head to one side, implying her lips were sealed, while managing to suggest that anything was possible. 'We're just glad you're here,' she said after a second or two. Maggie shook her head in disbelief; the woman was a masterclass in innuendo and manipulation. Danny was putty in Liz's perfectly manicured hands.

'Righty-oh,' said the boy, coming over all macho and protective. 'Well in that case best I get a move on then, hadn't I?'

'Thank you, that would be great, I'll see you later – ' Lizzie said, all teeth and legs and long, long eyelashes.

'Put him down,' said Maggie under her breath as Danny strode away like John Wayne, dragging his gas bottle behind him. 'Do you have to do that?'

'Oh come on,' said Lizzie, switching the glamour off like a light bulb. 'You're only jealous and besides, you weren't getting anywhere with him – you saw him, he loved it. You always have to remember the little people, darling. They're the ones who can make you or break you – although I have to say it pisses me off that after ten years of a serious career in journalism, it's two series of that bloody reality TV show that's finally put me on Joe Public's GPS.'

'Oh come off it, Lizzie, you said you hated roughing it – all that living out of a knapsack with no toilets and constant helmet hair, and being embedded with the troops played hell with your skin.'

Lizzie nodded. 'It does – just look at Kate Adie and that Irish woman – have they never heard of moisturiser?' Lizzie peered myopically at her watch. 'What time did you say Mum and Dad are due back?'

'Still not wearing your glasses?'

'Oh please. It's fine if you're Kate Silverton, all feline and serious, the thinking man's love bunny, but trust me, it really hasn't worked in light entertainment since Eric Morecombe.'

'Contacts –'

'Darling, I've got more contacts than you could wave a wet stick at,' Liz said with a wolfish grin.

Maggie laughed. 'You know what I meant, and don't come over all starry with me, kiddo. Remember, I've seen you in your jarmies interviewing the guinea pig and Flopsybunny.'

Liz laughed. 'I'd forgotten all about that.'

'Well, I haven't. Anyway Fleur says she'll try and keep

Mum and Dad out till six if she can.' Maggie checked her own watch. 'She's planning to give us a ring when they're on their way back. So just on two hours, I reckon, if we're lucky. We've got to get the tables and chairs sorted out, flowers, banners up, red carpet, balloons. Get the cake sorted, check on the glasses – oh and the fireworks – God, actually there is loads more to do.'

Lizzie pulled a face. 'Sounds like you've got it all covered. You won't really be needing me, will you? You know I'm useless at all that sort of thing.'

At which point Lawrie, Maggie's husband, appeared from around the corner carrying a pile of tablecloths. 'For God's sake, you haven't got time for a girlie chat,' he said, talking and walking and heading for the back garden. 'I'm rushed off my bloody feet here. It's total chaos round the back. Can you get round there and give me a hand?'

Maggie stared at him. Like she hadn't been working since the instant her mum and dad pulled out of the drive, not to mention all the planning and hiring and booking and worrying about whether it would all come together.

The last few months had been a mass of subterfuge, stealth and planning, culminating in today's big event for Jack and Lily's fortieth wedding anniversary – *forty years*. Glancing at Lawrie's frustrated grumpy expression Maggie was beginning to think that another forty minutes was beginning to look close to impossible.

The whole party thing had grown out of a chance conversation they'd had when Liz came to stay with them for a few days over Christmas, after some trip to the Caribbean had fallen through. They had been thumbing through the family photo albums in the sentimental way you do when everyone gets together, and along the way Maggie had realised it was their parents' fortieth anniversary. Somewhere between the

wine and breaking out the Baileys they had come up with
the idea of throwing a party – which had somehow become
a surprise party and gone from a small family get together
to a blow by blow re-creation of their mum and dad's
wedding reception.

'It'll be absolutely brilliant,' Liz had said, topping up
her glass. 'We'll just need to try and get the original
guest list.'

At which point Maggie had turned over a group photo
that her mum had given one of her girls for a family history
project and said, 'Actually, a lot of their names are on the
back here.'

Liz had grinned. 'Fantastic, that's a start and I'm sure
between us we can come up with the rest of them, maybe
you could email Aunt Fleur? She's bound to know. Hang on,
I'll go and grab my diary. Tell you what – we'll tell Mum
and Dad that we're taking everyone out to dinner at Rocco's
– my treat.'

'You're saying *we* can't afford to take everyone to Rocco's?'
said Maggie.

'No, no of course I'm not, but we want to make it somewhere special so that they don't come up with a better
idea.'

'Good idea,' said Lawrie.

'We could have their original wedding cake copied too – '
suggested Maggie, not wanting to be outdone. 'And we could
easily do the flowers – I mean looking at these – ' she handed
Liz a stray photo of the bride and groom outside the church
looking impossibly young and happy – 'red roses and
gypsophila – it's not exactly rocket science.'

Liz pulled a *whatever* face. 'If you say so. Flowers are your
thing, not mine.'

'Actually my *thing*, as you put it, is fruit and vegetables.'

398

'Well, you know what I mean,' said Liz waving the words away. 'You're the family grower.'

'And you're the family star?' said Maggie, raising her eyebrows.

'Play nicely you two,' said Lawrie. 'And tell me again why we didn't throw them a big party for their twenty-fifth?' Up until the party plan had emerged Lawrie had been sitting on the sidelines drinking Margaritas and watching *The Great Escape*.

'I'm not sure really – Mum and Dad have never made that much of wedding anniversaries, you know what they're like, no fuss, no frills – and for their twenty-fifth we were all too young to really organise anything –'

'Or care, come to that –' said Lizzie. 'I'd just gone to Uni and you two were all loved up and getting married.'

'For their thirtieth they went to Rome,' said Maggie, flicking back through the album. 'And our girls were little then and it was Mum's fiftieth – I think their anniversary just got forgotten in the rush. The only downside is that the church hall where they held their reception was pulled down years ago.'

'It's the spirit of it that counts. I was thinking maybe we could hire a marquee,' said Lizzie.

Maggie raised her eyebrows. 'Have you got any idea how much those things cost?'

'No idea, but it'll be my treat, instead of picking up the tab at Rocco's,' said Liz.

'Probably be about the same if you pair have a dessert,' Lawrie had said with a wry grin.

And so here they were, six months, a lot of phone calls, Googling and a logistical nightmare later. Maggie took another look at her watch. 'I've told the guests to be here by 5.45 pm at the very latest.'

'And they're all going to hide in the house?'

'I think the marquee would be better, keep everyone in one place and I've asked everyone to park down on the recreation ground.'

Liz nodded. 'Right, well it sounds to me like you've got everything sorted out. I'm just going to go upstairs and grab the bathroom before everyone else arrives. Grant said he'd be arriving around six – I know he's just dying to meet you all. I'm sure you'll love him. Anyway,' she giggled. 'I really need to go and get ready. I wouldn't want him to think I've let myself go just because we're out in the sticks.'

'Lizzie, wait –' Maggie began, but too late, her little sister was already halfway across the lawn. 'You've only been here a little while and most of that time you've been on the bloody phone –' she mumbled after her.

'Where the hell's she going now?' said Lawrie in exasperation as he rounded the corner on his way back from the marquee.

'Apparently she's just going to get ready,' said Maggie, as casually as she could manage. 'I'm sure she won't be long.'

Lawrie stared at her. 'Well that's bloody great, isn't it? Why did you let her go? There are loads of things still to do and we could really do with another pair of hands. And I can't find either of our dear daughters either,' he said, voice heavy with sarcasm. 'The band have rung up to say they can't find us, the caterers can't find anywhere to plug in their equipment without blowing all the fuses, the photographer just texted to say he's running late and I'm getting fed up of being the one who is supposed to know all the answers. We never said we'd do all this on our own, Maggie, and so far it looks to me like we've done the lion's share.'

400

'I know – and we have, but Lizzie paid for a lot of it,' said Maggie, caught in the badlands between agreeing with Lawrie – which she did – and defending Lizzie, which she felt some irrational instinctive urge to do.

'I know, but that still doesn't mean she can just swan off when we need her. And come on, Maggie – she was the one who offered to pay, nobody twisted her arm. Although I'm sure Lady Bountiful isn't going to let us forget that in a hurry – '

'She said she needed to get ready,' Suzie said lamely.

'Oh, come off it. She always looks like she's just stepped off the front page of a magazine,' said Lawrie. 'Never a hair out of place –'

He hadn't added, *unlike you,* although Maggie thought she could hear it in his voice. She glanced down at her own outfit; faded, world-weary jeans and a tee shirt worn with a pair of cowboy boots that had seen far better days. Maggie knew without looking in a mirror that her hair was a mess, and there hadn't been the time for putting on so much as a lick of make-up because the whole day had been manic since the moment she opened her eyes.

'To be honest I don't know how she does it,' Lawrie said, his gaze fixed on the front door through which Lizzie had so recently vanished.

Maggie stared at him, surely he was being funny? 'A professional stylist, twice-weekly trips to the beautician, the manicurist and the hairdresser, a personal trainer, Botox and a grooming budget that would make your eyes water – plus the fact that she hasn't got a husband, two children, two dogs, two cats, a rabbit and a business to run probably gives her a head start,' growled Maggie, snatching up the boxes she had been taking to the marquee before life got in the way.

'Oh meow,' Lawrie said with a grin as he headed off back towards the car. 'Jealous, are we?'

Maggie swung round to say something, but he was too quick for her and hurried back across the grass, still laughing.

Jealous? As if.

What's next?

Tell us the name of an author you love

| Kate Lawson | **Go** ▶ |

and we'll find your next great book.